Sparky and the Waarheid Camera

Set in the City of Highbridge, 1970

Written by Stephen P. DeLuca

Part I The Epiphany

Chapter 1: Sparky's Malaise

"Sparky Donnelly! Behave yourself!" Sparky straightened up like he'd been zapped by a hundred volts of electricity. In trouble again! How many times today had Mrs. Pinkerton admonished him for something? Sparky counted three times, though only one of the occurrences could be officially classified as 'getting in trouble.' This time, it was because he was tittering. He was tittering because, for a change, it was someone *else* who was being victimized by the hard-as-nails teacher.

Mrs. Pinkerton paced back and forth in front of the class. She was waiting for Diana Werschel to respond to a question. Sparky and the rest of the class followed Mrs. Pinkerton back and forth with their eyes as she paced. Sparky was yearning for the three o'clock bell. He didn't want to get in trouble again, and he was afraid that Mrs. Pinkerton was nearing the end of her patience with him.

The question that had been posed a full two or three minutes ago was: Who were the Americans fighting against in the War of 1812? Diana was studious and knew the answer to the question, but she hesitated when she became suspicious that it might somehow be a trick question. The answer seemed easy– maybe too easy. She knew that the Revolutionary War was fought against the British and she was wondering if we would be fighting the British again so soon or if the French or the Indians were involved– or was it the Russians or Hessians– or were they Prussians? Were there such people as 'Prussians'? Or was that a name she made up in the confusion? She couldn't recall why the British would be fighting America once we had won our independence, especially since they are one of our staunchest allies. On top of that, she was at least a *little* afraid of Mrs. Pinkerton. So, with her brain overloaded and jammed with conflicting thoughts, she froze solid.

Mrs. Pinkerton attempted to draw out the answer with some broad hints and another, more leading, question. Unfortunately, Diana was now totally lost within herself in a fog. Mrs. Pinkerton remained very patient. Sparky did not. He squirmed and shifted in his chair. He couldn't wait for three o'clock and this pause in the action seemed interminable to him. He'd been scolded right after lunch for something. It was nothing too serious, just his usual enthusiastically rambunctious interaction in the classroom, getting out of his seat to help his friend, Les. But, it was the latest in a growing list of incidents. The previous week, a letter was sent home to his parents, which prompted a Family Meeting and an admonishment from his mom. Now he dreaded a possible follow-up letter and the awful consequences that such a letter would bring-- another Family Meeting. School was becoming a minefield for him, and his classroom experience was fraught with trepidation. Sparky didn't like getting scolded. It embarrassed him. He wanted out and that three o'clock bell couldn't toll soon enough for him.

'I'm dead,' he thought to himself when Mrs. Pinkerton shushed him. He watched Mrs. Pinkerton's stiff, starched form oscillate in front of the blackboard. 'She's got it in for me,' he deduced. He had eight more months of what he characterized as Mrs. Pinkerton's communist regime to look forward to and he could not envision getting through them. Sparky longed for the halcyon days of Mrs. Gardener. He never got in trouble in her classroom. He felt like a hero in her class. And, besides, Mrs. Gardner was pretty. By contrast, Mrs. Pinkerton was an old biddy-- witch-like-- who had the uncanny ability to read him like a book, knowing when he would misbehave-- even *before* he misbehaved.

"Diana," Mrs. Pinkerton sighed, as she finally began to lose hope, deciding to take a different path to lead Diana to the answer. "Against whom did the Americans fight during the Revolutionary War?"

A second ago Diana knew the answer to *that* question. Now, she was so intimidated by Mrs. Pinkerton that she no longer could say with certainty who fought in *any* war. That's when the tittering started, with Sparky in the vanguard. Not normally a cruel boy, nevertheless, he was enjoying seeing someone else suffering under Mrs. Pinkerton, for a change. He felt he'd had more than his share of turns this year. The fact that Diana didn't do anything to deserve the suffering made it even funnier, because it seemed so unfair. Sparky laughed hardest and longest, a fact not lost on the vigilant teacher.

"Surely you know the answer to *that* question." Still nothing from the girl. "Try *this*, Diana: What did Paul Revere cry out to the town during his famous ride?"

Diana thought hard. The name seemed so familiar to her. The answer was right on the tip of her tongue, and then it drifted away like a ferry

5

leaving the dock, just out of reach and then impossible to catch. By this time, most of the class was fidgeting and some groaned. Diana's best friends started whispering the answer to her, covering their mouths with cupped hand to conceal their clandestine rescue attempts. Raspy cries of 'The British are coming!' soon filled the classroom. Diana was the only one who couldn't hear them.

"Who knows the answer to this question?" Mrs. Pinkerton called out to the whole class. The madly waving hands went up and the simian 'oooh-oooh' calls went out, and Mrs. Pinkerton thanked Diana and waved her down to her seat. Diana glared at Sparky as they sat stiffly across the room from each other.

The lesson continued uneventfully until the bell was about to ring. Mrs. Pinkerton handed out some rexographed math homework assignments for that night and got the kids prepared for dismissal, placing their chairs on top of the desks. The class lined up along the wall, wearing their jackets and waiting for the bell. Sparky just wanted to get out of there. Despite the brief respite he'd had while laughing at Diana, the afternoon had been a real drag.

The students all stood against the wall, lined up in alphabetical order in the classroom. Sparky was sixth, behind the kids whose last names started with A, B and C. This was not the way Mrs. Gardener had conducted her class. She allowed her students to line up in whatever order they managed to work out for themselves in a brief free-for-all. Sparky flourished in that environment and was always very successful in claiming a position at– or near– the very front of the line. The only time the system worked against Sparky was when Mrs. Gardener was out sick for a week and the class had a substitute– a thickly built, gray-haired woman named Mrs. Gallagher, whom the boys in the class promptly nicknamed 'Mrs. Galloper'. On the second day, this Mrs. G had them line up as they always did. But, after they had each won their positions, with Sparky at the second slot, she had them about-face and marched them out the door at the back of the classroom instead! He always hated that sub because of that.

By Sparky's estimation, fifth grade was turning out to be a real hassle. He breezed through kindergarten, and the first four grades. This year, however, it was one thing after another for the first two months. Feeling picked on, school had become a dreadful grind. He was excited enough when he moved up from the half-days of kindergarten, but even going to school for a full day was getting old nowadays. The class roster was basically the same as the year before. His chums were again grouped together in the smart class, while the dull kids populated the second ('slow') class with Miss Petty, and the learning problem kids ('retards' in the vernacular) had Mr. Thicke.

Everything seemed the same– all the time, year after year and day after day. It was the same building, the same auditorium, the same gym, the same lunchroom, and the same old hallways. Even the old two-tone institutional paint scheme was getting him down.

It was supposed to be an honor to be in Mrs. Pinkerton's class, but Sparky did not feel proud. He had run afoul of Mrs. Pinkerton too many times, committing a variety of offenses that brought her wrath down upon him. He couldn't get away with much of anything this year. Not that he was trying to get away with anything, of course. He was just being enthusiastic. He knew what Mrs. Pinkerton's classroom rules were, but he was just helping out. It wasn't fair.

Admittedly, Mrs. Pinkerton didn't yell at Sparky (she never raised her voice, just changed the tone), nor did she punish him too severely. Sparky still thought it was unfair.

At last, the bell rang and the class was led out the door of room 311, along the hallway past the rooms where the slower classes were situated, and down the stairs on the heels of one of those other classes. Always the same path and always instructed to not jostle each other and always to stay to the right on the stairs.

Mrs. Pinkerton stiffly led her students to the gates of freedom and the class scattered out the door. Monitors on the sidewalk on 82nd Street prevented them from running until they were off the school grounds.

Sparky met up with his buddies, Les and Giant, halfway down the block.

"Boy, oh boy, Mrs. Pinkerton has it in for me again. She's watching my every move."

"Come on, Sparky, she doesn't treat you any worse than anybody else. Look at poor Diana. And I got in trouble on Monday for leaning my chair back. And remember last week? She yelled at me for nothin'."

"That wasn't exactly 'nothin'', you dummy," Giant interjected as he jostled his shorter friend.

"It was an experiment I was conducting," Les protested.

"C'mon, Les, you can't hook up the terminals on a dry cell to each other. Everybody knows they explode if you do that! Maybe she saved your life. You coulda been blinded or scarred for life."

"Yeah, burned by battery acid! Like the Phantom of the Opera! Woulda burned those freckles off your silly face, for sure!"

Les brushed off the advice. "The Phantom wasn't burned by battery acid, stupid! He was burned up in a fire. Anyway, Sparky, you're acting like a baby. Keep acting that way and they'll send you back to fourth grade. You'll see."

"Then you can marry Mrs. Gardener like you always wanted to, Sparky! Oooh, Mrs. Gardener! I love you, Mrs. Gardener! Ha ha ha!" Giant rolled his eyes, batted his eyelashes and clasped his hands near his heart in mockery.

"Cut that out, you big dope!"

"You're the dope, you dummy! You wanna marry Mrs. Gardener! Ha ha! Kisss mee, daahling!" Giant drawled out as he put his arms around Sparky and pretended to smooch. "You loved it when she hugged you like this, didn' you?" Sparky just barely managed to squirt out of Giant's arms.

"You homo."

"*You're* the homo, homo. You're a *dummy* homo. Ha ha!"

"No he's not. He's a homo *dummy*! Ha ha ha!"

"That's not funny! Quit it!"

"Sparky is a homo dummy, Sparky is a homo dummy. Ouch! That hurt!" Sparky stopped the chanting with a wild punch, which landed with a thud high on Les's chest. This brought more laughter from Gi-

8

ant.

"Ha! Les let a homo dummy punch him!"

Les was embarrassed. "You don't know anything, you big Jolly Green Giant."

The trio continued fighting as they turned the corner. Suddenly, they were distracted from their skirmish by a copper-colored Avanti sports car parked on Eighth Avenue, in front of the Chinese laundry.

"Wow! Cool! I wanna get one of those when *I* buy a car."

"Hey Giant, when you get old enough to buy a car, you'll be so tall, you won't be able to fit in one of those."

"Go to hell, pipsqueak!"

"Ooh! He told you to go to hell! You're gonna take that from him?"

"What do you want me to do? Beat him up? I can't even reach his face to hit it!"

"How much do you think these things cost?"

"Thousands!"

"She is pretty, though."

"I like the long hood."

"Not the car, stupid! I mean Mrs. Gardener!" Sparky rolled his eyes.

"Hey, Sparky, if you buy one of those, you'd be able to win Mrs. Gardener's heart, for sure!" Giant winked at Les as he teased Sparky.

"You'll never be able to buy one of these if you end up in an institution. You better get in line with Mrs. Pinkerton. Mrs. Gardner's not gonna wait for you to get outta the slammer, you know."

"Yeah, Sparky, Mrs. Pinkerton is not Mrs. Gardener. Les is right. You're gonna have to behave from now on. You're gonna have to reform."

"Giant's right. If you didn't mess up so much, you wouldn't get in so much trouble. She punishes everybody when they mess up– even the girls. You saw Diana today. And she didn't take it easy on Carole for drawing on the desk. She's tough, but she's been fair."

"She's *not* fair!"

Just then, a man dressed in a very crisp pair of slacks, with shiny white shoes on his feet and sporting a jazzy Oxford cap, came dashing out of the laundry and got into the Avanti. Sparky noticed that the man had a lot of keys in his hand and they made a lot of noise. The man also had super-cool long sideburns. The boys silently watched him get in, rev up the engine, pull away from the curb and speed away down Eighth Avenue.

"Who do you think that guy was? Somebody important, maybe?"

"I don't know. Maybe he's a businessman."

"Or a private detective! They drive cool cars."

"Could be– like Mannix. Hey, maybe he's a bachelor!"

"Whatever he is, Sparky, you'll never be it if you don't graduate from school."

"I'm tired of it all, anyway. I wish we didn't have to keep going to school."

"We got a lot of years left, pal. You can't drop out in the fifth grade. You'll end up in real trouble. You'll be a J.D. and they'll send you to live in an institution. Then you'll be cleaning toilets the rest of your life."

"I'm not gonna drop out. I just wish we could have more fun. School is a lot of drudgery– especially with Pinkerton."

"He's got a point there, Giant. We *did* have more fun with Mrs. Gardener."

10

"Yeah, I know you spent most of your days trying to look up her dress. But you know my mom says that Mrs. Pinkerton is a really good teacher. She says that she's all business."

"And I say who cares? Who needs 'all business'? Pinkerton's just a dried-up old prune anyway!" Les chimed in cheerily.

"I'll meet you guys at the park entrance at 3:30."

"I'm gonna go to Les's house first 'cause I've gotta give him back the comics he lent me."

"Well, I'll be there at 3:30 anyway. I'll bring my new Spaldeen."

"Oh, cool! See ya later." They turned left on Baumen.

Sparky headed up to St. Charles Street to his house.

Chapter 2: The New Spaldeen

"Sweetie, is that you?"

"Yeah, Mom."

Sparky dragged himself to the kitchen for the obligatory kiss.

"How was school today? You didn't get into any more trouble, did you?"

Sparky shuffled around a bit and talked down toward the linoleum. "Nah."

"Come on, Sweetie, what did you do?"

"How do you know I did something?"

"I'm your mother. I can read you like an open book, Sweetie."

"I didn' do anything, really. It wasn't my fault, either. Les started it and I ended up getting in trouble for it. It's no big deal, anyway."

"I'm not going to get a note again, am I?" She had her hands on her hips now. Laura Donnelly wore a perpetually pleasant expression and now her expression was as close as she could get to what you might call 'stern'.

"Nooo! It's not that big a deal. Mrs. Pinkerton's just decided I'm always the one to blame even if I'm not involved."

"That's not really true now, is it, Sweetie? You remember what we talked about with your father."

"Yeah, I remember. But it's like a person's guilty until proven innocent with her."

She gently tousled his hair and put her hand on his shoulder. "You just keep your nose clean and you'll see. She's not picking on you and she'll reward good behavior– if that's what she gets from you."

Sparky was disappointed. He had hoped to get some sympathy from his mom despite knowing that she would do the right thing. "Seems like a lotta work just to get by in life. The men I see on TV don't have to watch their behavior. If they run up against a bad guy– POW! – right in the kisser!" Sparky punched his extended left hand for emphasis.

"You're no Elliot Ness, and Mrs. Pinkerton is not Public Enemy No. 1, and you're not going to punch anyone in the kisser. So, banish those thoughts, young man!"

"Ah, you're no fun, Mom. I gotta go. I'm meeting the guys at the park. Where's my new ball?"

"Probably where you left it. You don't think *I* used it? Sweetie, change your pants and shirt before you go back out. I won't have you tearing your good school clothes."

Sparky ran to his room and did a quick-change into his dungarees and sneakers. His ball was right on top of his bookshelf where he had left it. The ball was brand spanking new. The writing on it was still vivid and it had the rough texture, characteristic of a virgin ball. He bounced it once on the floor and it bounced high– even on the rug in his room– and he couldn't wait to use it outside. He stuffed it into his front pocket, where it left a huge lump sticking out, and ran to the front door.

"Don't stay out late, Sweetie! If your father gets home early enough, we'll be eating a little after six!"

"Bye, Mom!" and he was out the door and down the block.

The park was actually the playground behind and adjacent to the Giovanni Biaggi Junior High School, situated between Baumen Road and 88th Street. There were basketball courts, handball courts, a softball field, swings, slides, etc., all of it paved with asphalt. In its dim, dark past, the building was originally the Sparta District High School. It was constructed in 1914 and had– as did all the old Highbridge high schools– five imposing stories. The blank whitewashed brick wall that faced the playground provided excellent stickball courts and a great venue for off-the-wall. The wall was too high for all but the biggest kids to be able to roof a ball.

This was the park to which Sparky hurried to meet his friends. On the

13

way there, Sparky bounced his new Spalding with great satisfaction, marveling at how easily it bounced above his head. He was careful near the corners, lest the ball bounce out of control and roll into a sewer. A couple of times it did hit an uneven crack in the sidewalk and bounced into the gutter between parked cars, but it didn't touch any dog crap and Sparky was able to retrieve it without incident.

Sparky got to the park entrance early and, being the first to arrive, he started practicing his pitching against the wall, using one of the painted strike zones as his target. He practiced imitating a few of his favorite major league pitchers' motions. First, he was Bob Gibson. Then he was Luis Tiant, dropping his hands countless times in the wind-up. Next he was Juan Marichal with that big kick. Lastly, he was Diego Segui, twisting wildly before the delivery. He made believe he was facing batters in crucial, bottom of the ninth, tie-game situations. He'd run up the count on the power hitters he was trying to retire: Ball one. Ball two! Fastball– 2 and 1. Uh-oh, curveball missed– ball *three*!! 3 and 1. Ball four– he walked him!! Then with a man on first and no outs, he'd bounce the next one to the wall: Ball one...

Sparky had some time. As he pitched, he let his mind wander. He was suffering from some sort of malaise. He no longer felt like the star kid he used to feel he was. He didn't like his current teacher. He assumed she didn't like him. His baseball team did not make it to the World Series. His dad's job had him working late most nights and he saw very little of him before bedtime. His home was orderly and civilly run, but he and his parents never seemed to have much fun together. It seemed to Sparky that he could recall years past when the three of them would venture forth and have fun. He remembered days at the park and going to museums and Imaginland Amusement Park. They never seemed to do fun things anymore. Lately, his dad sits in the living room with his face buried in the newspaper. Giant and Les obviously had grown to like each other more than they liked him. He was unhappy at school; unhappy at home and not so thrilled at being the third wheel with his best friends.

He and Les used to be thick as thieves. They were both about the same height and the same weight and had about the same abilities in most things. Except for Les's freckles, they could be mistaken for each other physically. They got along like brothers, having been friends for years. Things changed sometime during the summer. Giant's family, the Bergers, moved into a two-family house on 83rd, between Neptune and

14

Fifth– just half a block from Les's apartment building. Giant and Les started playing together a lot and they walked to and from school together as well. After a while, Sparky noticed the two of them sharing little asides and inside jokes that referred back to some secret shared experience or conversation. Sparky tried to act like he was in on whatever it was that was going on, but he felt left out and foolish. Once, Giant and Les cut out on Sparky at the candy store, leaving him to pay for the Hostess pies they all bought.

Just a few months ago it was Sparky and Les who were sharing these private jokes on Giant and Niles and Slimy Simon and others. Now, with this realignment, Giant and Les were close, Niles and Slimy Simon were close, Dougie and Aaron, the Bones Brothers (so-named because of their skinny, bony physiques) were practically joined at the hipbone, and the Sparky felt just like the cheese, standing alone.

Sparky bounced another pitch "in the dirt" just as Niles came along.

"Hey Sparks. You the first here, man?"

"Yep. Les and Giant are supposed to be here already. I don't know what's keeping them. Who else is coming?"

"Lemme see the ball, man." Niles examined it and test-bounced it. "You just get it?"

"Sunday."

"Cool! I bet I can roof it, man. Wanna see?"

"You can't roof it. And if you *do*, you gotta buy me a new one!"

"Aw, man, I don't think I can roof it anyway, man."

"Slimy coming?"

"Nah, man, he's got to go to the dentist or orthopedist or something." Niles fired a fastball at the wall and marveled at the life in the ball's bounce. "Nice, man."

"Simon's always got something happening. What the hell is an orthopedist?"

15

"They straighten your teeth, man. Don't you know nothin'?"

Sparky saw Les and Giant coming up the block with Aaron and a couple of the kids from Miss Petty's class, Eric and Little Gene. "Here come the guys."

Niles was throwing the ball up high on the wall and catching it on a fly. "Hey, man, let's get up a game."

"Where's the other Bones Brother?"

"Dougie's watching his little sister. His mom's working at the lingerie store." Aaron pronounced it lin-ger-ee.

"You look naked without him, man." They all laughed.

"Damn, we don't have enough for punchball. Wanna play off-the-wall?"

"Yeah, man, let's play off-the-wall." It was no surprise Niles suggested it, since he was exceptional at off-the-wall. He had sharp elbows and wasn't reluctant to use them.

"Okay. If you catch it off the vents, it's 2 points and if you let it bounce after you touch it, it's 1 point per bounce penalty."

"No way! The guy that hits the vent should get 2 points!"

"Eric's right. It should be the guy that hits the vent gets the bonus points."

"I agree with Les. 2 points for the guy that throws it, but I think it's hard to catch it off the vents. So, I think he should get extra points, too."

"We all know how much Giant loves Les, but no way should both guys get the extra points. What, just because Les says so, it's gotta be that way?"

"You're full of it, Aaron."

"No, *you're* full of it, Les! You and your long-legged lover over here!"

"Oh, sweat, man! You hear what he said? Ha ha! Oh, man! He got *you*, man!"

"Don't get all upset, Les. He's just being a dumb ass."

"I'm no dumb ass. *You're* the dumb ass around here."

"Can we play ball, already? Why do we always have to argue about crap? Okay, come on, Niles. You throw first since you got the ball already."

"All right, Sparky. Here goes, man." Niles gave the ball a good heave up two-thirds the way up the wall between the vents and the jostling and jockeying for position commenced.

After several rounds of play, Niles and Giant were leading the rest. Niles had the knack of slipping around the others, ducking in between and making some room with a well-timed and well-placed elbow and stealing the ball at the last second. Giant was taller and had long arms and could reach a ball that one of the others was sure would be their uncontested catch. They both were sure-handed. Eric was aggressive, but he couldn't catch a cold in the middle of winter in Alaska, and he was overweight and slow, so he ended up at minus 17 after dropping a couple of chances. One of his tries scooted away from him and bounced so many times before he retrieved it that the others agreed to count only the first 12 bounces against him.

Sparky was mediocre at off-the-wall. He was athletic and of average height, but the game was a bit too chaotic for his taste. He played it without any conviction and got predictably mediocre results. He would have preferred punchball– even with only seven guys. He let his mind wander again during the game and he realized he wasn't having any fun. He thought of off-the-wall as pointless and repetitive. Intrinsically, it couldn't have been much of a game. There was no professional off-the-wall league, after all. The sport was essentially theft. The crucial skill was avarice.

Sparky was glad when, after almost an hour of off-the-wall (interspersed with many long minutes of arguing), a couple of the guys suggested that they all quit and move on to something else. Giant had what

17

seemed, at that point, an insurmountable lead, especially when Niles flubbed one he probably shouldn't have tried going after and it bounced off his hands, hit Aaron on the top of the head and bounced six times before Niles could grab it. Niles attempted to get the points counted against Aaron because it had hit his head, but no one agreed. Ruining Niles's score, it sealed Giant's advantage and doomed the others. Eric suggested punchball, but most of the guys had lost their momentum at that point and were not eager to start up a new game. It was going to get dark soon anyway. Aaron and Little Gene, after conferring, started heading out toward the street.

"Hey, man, where you guys goin'?"

"We're gonna stop at the candy store. I wanna get a pack of scratch 'n sniff cards and pumpkin seeds. We'll see you guys later."

"Aw, man! There goes a third of our team. Wanna play more off-the-wall, man?"

"Nah, Niles. I'm tired of that," Sparky asserted himself. "How 'bout Chinese handball?"

"Not me. I ain't no Chink. That game sucks."

"You mean you suck at that game, Giant. That's what you meant to say, right?"

"Whatever. I'm not going to play Chinese handball. Maybe I'll just go home and watch the rest of the 4:30 movie."

"I'm going to go, too. It's been grand, guys."

"Aw, c'mon, Les," Sparky pleaded. "We could play some handball or go on the monkey bars. The 4:30 move is some Gidget crap."

"Nah, I'm done. C'mon, Giant. See ya, fellas." Les and Giant ambled off down Baumen Road, leaving Niles, Eric, Sparky and the nearly new Spalding.

"Must be your B.O. scared 'em off."

"No way, man. You're the one with the B.O., man. You smell like a bum's ass!" Niles wound up and tried to roof the ball.

"If I'm a bum's ass, then you smell like a dead bum's fat, rotten corpse's ass. And if you roof my ball, you *will* be a dead rotten corpse's ass!"

"I tell you what, man, you smell– hey, wait, man! There goes Julie and Stacy at the corner!"

"So what?"

"Let's go meet up with them, man."

"What for? Come on, wait a minute!"

Niles was out of the gate and hurrying up to the corner to meet them. As soon as the girls spotted him, they laughed and took off running up Ninth toward Andrews Boulevard. "Yo, Julie! Wait up, man!" It did no good. In a few seconds they were out of sight. "Oh, *man*!"

"Whadya expect? They don't want to hang out with us guys. Gimme back my ball. They'd just want to tease us, anyway. Why do you want to hang out with them?"

"I don't know, man. I just do."

"I think you like them, Niles. You're nuts! You need a headshrinker. Those girls are nothing but trouble. Gimme back my ball."

Then Eric, who had been a silent partner all along piped up. "I don't know. I kinda like Julie. She's okay." He zipped up his green hooded jacket. "I'm gonna head on home. It's startin' to get dark."

"All right, man. I'm gonna see if I can catch up to them. I know where Stacy lives. Maybe I can catch 'em there."

"See ya, Niles."

"Yeah, man." Niles trotted up the block, crossing the street diagonally from between parked cars and paying no attention to anything.

"Niles! Gimme my ball!" Niles turned and fired the ball back down the block toward Sparky. It bounced off the hood of a Pontiac and back into the street, where Sparky caught it before it could disappear down any sewers. "What an idiot."

"See you, Sparky." Eric headed the other way across the playground toward Longmuir Avenue.

Sparky headed toward his house. The excitement he'd felt at the possibilities embodied in his new Spalding had been dissolved by the subsequent usual dumb, crappy game and the reinforcement of his feelings of being left out. He gazed around as he walked down the block. It was the same drab neighborhood he had grown up in and played in and never seemed to leave. Nothing much ever seemed to happen that was worth talking about. Everything was gray and brown and tan and humdrum. Everything was routine. He bounced his ball on the sidewalk and felt it in his hand. It didn't feel new anymore. The writing on it was scuffed. He wished he had a new ball.

Chapter 3: The Epiphany

Sparky sat cross-legged on the floor in front of the couch. He was staring in the direction of the TV, but he wasn't watching what was on it.
Sparky was about to call out to his mom who was doing her ironing in
the kitchen. There was a long pause while Sparky assembled the
thoughts.

On the TV screen, Mike Douglas was laughing it up with Burns &
Schrieber. Sparky did not see them. Something he had seen during a
commercial break had him thinking. It could have been any of six
commercials or two public service announcements during that break
that could have given him a glimpse into an unfamiliar world at large–
that peek through the knothole of life that got him wondering.

In fact, it happened to be a commercial he had *not* seen hundreds of
times already. In fact, it was a commercial that he had never seen before. It ran as follows:

> A snappily dressed man and a very elegant and exotic-looking
> woman are finishing dinner in a very fancy restaurant. Upbeat
> and jazzy music is playing. The man and woman, clearly satis-
> fied with their meal and service are obviously having a won-
> derful time. The man, wearing a huge smile on his face, pays
> the tab, which must have been huge. The waiter and maitre d'
> are overjoyed at the experience of having served these glam-
> orous and charismatic people as their customers.
> The man and woman exit the restaurant, their car instantly
> brought to them by another employee, a valet. The car is dis-
> tinctive. It is an Avanti. They get in and speed off through the
> night, without a care in the world, to their destination– a five-
> star hotel. The commercial wraps up with an aerial view of the
> Highbridge skyline, sparkling in the darkness. Superimposed
> over the panorama, the logo of Cord Savings Bank and the
> trademarked name of its Cord Advantage Savings Plan.

The commercial transfixed Sparky. It struck him like a thunderbolt. He
saw this man! Well, maybe not *this* man, but certainly one just *like*
him! He had always thought these people he saw on TV were just actors and that all of it was just make-believe. He suddenly realized that
these people really existed! They were out there, really living lives just

as they depicted on TV. Not everyone lived a humdrum, mundane existence– going to school or to a dull job every dull day. Real people live exciting and fun lives, served by nice waiters, hotel managers and parking attendants!

"Mom?"

"Yes, Sweetie, what is it?" she replied, not looking up from a sleeve she was carefully and gracefully positioning.

"There must be lots of really exciting and interesting and nice people out there."

"Out where, Sweetie?"

"Oh, out there," he waved his hand in the general direction of the front door, "in the world, I mean." She couldn't see the gesture from the kitchen.

Sparky's mom deftly flipped the sleeve over and picked up the hot iron. "We-e-e-l-l, yes," she drawled out, hesitatingly, without looking up, "I suppose there are." The iron danced and twirled on the sleeve and up over the shoulder. She had ironing down to a kind of swirling dance of arms, hands and an electric cord– like Peggy Fleming, but plugged into the wall socket.

Sparky mistook his Mom's tone as a cue to continue. "Hey, Mom, do you know people like that?"

He couldn't see his mom. She was around the bend from his view. He could see her shadow moving on the floor outside the kitchen door in the dining area. It continued to move as she continued to iron.

"People like what, Sweetie?"

"Interesting and exciting and nice!" Sparky was getting annoyed. He assumed his mom was not really listening to him, which wasn't true, or that she was playing dumb, which also wasn't true. "You're not stuck in school all day like me. You get to see plenty of people, I bet, that are fun and interesting and have stuff to say that everybody wants to be around and listen to when they talk!"

The phone rang before she could address his question.

"Hold on to that thought, Sweetie. Hello? Hi, Marge." Sparky waited for his mom to finish the call so he could ply her with more questions. He thought his mom wasted the telephone. Her conversations seemed obscure and dull and she didn't do much more than listen most of the time anyway. "No, I...Yeah. You've been very patient with them. I wouldn't have...uh, huh...lovely...uh, huh...Seven or eight...Ha, ha! You're so clever, Marge."

Sparky waited.

"Pork roast...frozen peas...uh, huh...seventy-nine cents...lovely...uh huh...oh, a spanking!...Oh, no, not really!...twelve?...uh huh...that sounds so nice...Okay, I'll let you go. Will do, bye-bye."

Before she had hung up the phone, Sparky was probing again. "Well, Mom? How 'bout it?"

"How about what, Sweetie?"

"The people I'm talking about!"

"I'm sorry, Sweetie. Exactly which people are you referring to?" She was always pleasant– even when irritated. Her face had soft features and her expression was calm and detached, which was an accurate depiction of her demeanor.

Sparky gave up talking to his mom's shadow and scrambled to his feet, appearing at the doorway with an urgency that might have surprised her had she looked up and seen it. He tried a slightly different approach. "Tell me about the exciting and interesting people you get to deal with, Mom."

"Well, now. If you stop to think about it, you know plenty of nice and interesting and exciting people yourself, Sweetie. I don't know that the people I deal with are really any different from those at your school." She picked up the shirt by its shoulders and examined it, front and back, then folded it.

"Oh come *on*, Mom! Who at my school is interesting enough to be on TV? Nobody in the whole school could ever be a guest on *Mike Doug-*

23

las! What would they talk about? Nobody'd wanna watch them!"

Sparky's mom conceded his point with a nod. "That may be. But you know, Sweetie, there are many, many people– interesting people– who will never be on the *Mike Douglas Show*. They…"

"That's what I mean, Mom! *Those* people! Who are they?"

"Who are they…? Who are they…?" Sparky's mom ran a quick slideshow in her mind: The ex-class clown, pathetic greengrocer; the vulgar and insinuating butcher with his gross sense of humor; the officious postman with his gray skin and grayer personality; the snide, milquetoast dry cleaner; the obsequious, dim-witted milkman; the smelly meter reader (who always managed to find some way of bumping into her regardless of how much space she gave him to pass); the gas man ('he was kind of cute, I wouldn't mind *him* bumping into me' she thought as her mind wandered for a moment).

"Well, Mom?"

"Sweetie, I'm maybe not the best person to ask that of." She turned back to her ironing. "Perhaps there aren't that many very interesting or exciting people in the world, after all."

"But, Mom, that can't be true!"

"You should ask your father when he gets home. He knows some very interesting people. He certainly spends a lot of time with them. They must be *quite* fascinating. Not like people that live here, in this neighborhood."

"Sure! I bet you're right! He'd know millions. He works for a living."

As she passed the iron over his shirt pocket, she wondered whether or not her husband's associates are *really* any more interesting than her. She did the best she could and maintained a peaceful domestic atmosphere. Then she remembered the gas man again.

In the living room, the *Mike Douglas Show* was wrapping up to raucous applause, but Sparky was not watching the credits roll. It was five to six and he was on his knees on the couch, gazing out the window, looking for his father to be coming up the street from the subway station to ask him all about the exciting and interesting people in his life.

Chapter 4: Dad's Not Forthcoming

"Dad! Hey, Dad!" Sparky ran eagerly out the front door to meet his dad halfway up St. Charles Street. He could spot the lanky figure of his father miles away. Sparky's dad had the peculiar habit of walking in a zigzag pattern as he made his way along the sidewalk.

"Well, what have we here?" Amused and maybe a little concerned by the abnormally huge greeting, Sparky's dad extended his free arm out to envelope his son as he ran up to him. "Anything wrong, Champ? What's all the excitement?"

"Dad, you gotta tell me. I hafta know about the exciting and interesting people you know. Mom won't tell me anything."

"What interesting people are these? And what do you need to know about them?"

"You know, Dad. The people you work with; the people you see– fun and exciting people. What are they like? What do they do?"

"Hey, Champ, do me a favor, will you?" He stopped and stooped over. "Do you see anything on my shirt or my collar or anything?"

Sparky thought his dad was just changing the subject, but complied and scrutinized the shirt, anyway. "I don't see anything. What am I supposed to see?"

"Oh, nothing. That's great, thanks," Sparky's dad breathed out with relief as he straightened up and continued with the last few steps to his home at No. 50. "What does your mother say, Champ?"

"About what, Dad?"

"About these exciting people I'm supposed to know. Did she say anything to you about them?"

"What was Mom supposed to say to me? Hey, what did you think was on your shirt, Dad?"

"Oh, I thought I might've gotten something on it. You know how hard your mother works to keep my shirts sparkling white. I don't want to make her job any harder, you know?" He chuckled.

"What?"

"What 'what'?"

"What did you get on it?"

It was obvious Sparky was not going to let it go. "I thought I, uh, I might've gotten my lunch splattered all over it." He picked up his pace and strode a little ahead of Sparky, hoping to put some distance between him and the conversation. "You know your mom and how careful she is with my shirts. Don't want to get spanked over it." He added that last sentence under his breath. They walked through the front door.

"She what, Dad?"

"Nothing, Champ. Honey! I'm home!" He dropped his briefcase next to the umbrella stand and headed for the kitchen, where he knew she'd be.

"Dad, you had a ham and cheese sandwich for lunch today."

"So?"

"You can't *splatter* a ham and cheese sandwich!"

"Just a figure of speech, Champ. Don't worry about it."

"Hi, Dear. Dinner'll be a few minutes yet. You're a little earlier than usual." She twisted around and bent backward a bit and they shared a quick kiss. She was very supple.

"I left on time and the local was waiting with its doors open when we pulled into Peace Boulevard. Smells great. I'll go change and wash up."

"Hey, Dad! What about what I asked you?"

"Follow me upstairs while I get out of these clothes."

"Dad, Mom didn't want to answer my question, but you have to. I gotta know more about these people you know."

"I'm not sure I know what you mean, exactly. I don't spend all day having fun, you know. Your dad's not exactly living the bon vie."

"What's the bone vee?"

"That's French for the good life."

Sparky was discouraged. He was starting to think they just did not want to tell him. "I go to school and I see the same people every day. I've seen the same people since I was in kindergarten. They're the same kids I play with and the same old teachers all the time. And we're in the same classroom with the same old junk on the walls. Mrs. Pinkerton's got the alphabet stapled around the blackboard and the pictures of the presidents on the bulletin board."

"What's wrong with that? She had those pictures up when I had her in fifth grade, Champ. You don't appreciate tradition? She's added Nixon, Eisenhower, Johnson and Kennedy, I hope?"

"What I mean is, when I watch TV, I see people out there that are living really interesting lives and doing exciting and interesting things. I'd rather go to work like you. It'd be a lot more exciting and interesting than school. If I didn't have to go to school, I wouldn't go!"

"And be a truant?" Sparky's dad perked up and almost shouted down to his son, "If I didn't have to go to work, *I* wouldn't go either!"

"No way, Dad! Mom says you like to go to work. She said you didn't like your job at first, but you like it okay now."

"Your mom knows a lot about my job, huh? Look, if I was rich like those actors on the television, I would not get up at six o'clock and put on a tie and head out the door every morning to take a crowded subway to a lousy job and then have to come home. And I wouldn't be living here!" Sparky's dad hung up his pants.

"Well, where *would* you live?"

"Did I say 'I'? I meant 'we'. *We* wouldn't be living here."

"Anyway, I'm not talking about actors. I'm talking about real people. I see them…"

"It doesn't matter. They're all rich. If they're on TV, they're rich. Rich people can do whatever they want, with whomever they want. You'd better wash your hands so we can eat." Sparky's dad strode out of the bedroom.

"Then why don't we get rich, dad?"

During dinner, not much was spoken of Sparky's sudden interest with all those exciting and interesting people out there in the world. For the most part, his mom and dad conducted the usual routine dinner table conversation, which consisted on one hand of a review of a series of interactions with people at the grocery store and drug store, including the audacity of a sullen shelf-stocker and the notable decline in the health of an ailing neighbor, and on the other hand of a critique of the questionable policies, instituted at the office by lame-brains who had been promoted above their levels of competency. Sparky's dad never talked about what he did at the office anymore. He only talked specifics when he was asked about his working late.

Sparky listened with keenness for a change. He was carefully measuring what he was hearing against what he was certain *must* be the norm in the world– the norm he had glimpsed on TV today. In fact, he realized, it wasn't just today. He had been seeing this norm for quite some time without even being consciously aware of it.

Sparky didn't watch a lot of TV, but he did watch enough to see that there are lives being lived in furious excitement– full of dazzling creativity and populated by wise and clever people from the most glamorous and important locales around the world. People who take chances and live outside the rules of the workaday world. And not just around the world, but out of it as well! There are people actually living in outer space! Well, at least visiting it, anyway.

Sparky did try to commandeer the conversation when he found an opportunity and steer it toward his current preoccupation, but he met with little encouragement and he made no progress toward a clearer understanding of what wonderful people there might be out there in his mom and dad's daily world. Sparky was being stonewalled.

"Hey, Dad. These lame-brains you work with, what do they do at the company?"

"Ha! They don't do anything, from what I can see."

"But, they've got to do something, Dad, or else why would they be working there?"

"They're buddy-buddy with the management is why they're working there. Could you pass down those peas, Champ?"

"Here, Dad. What do you guys talk about at work?"

"We talk about the game, or maybe– I don't know. What do we talk about? I don't know. We talk about whatever comes to mind. I suppose we gripe about the upper management a lot."

"What about, um, what about saving lives or important stuff? The arms race?"

"We don't save lives! I'm no fireman, Champ. What sort of thing would be so important that I'd need to talk about? I don't really have any friends at work. It's not a place to make friends."

"That's not quite true, dear, is it? You go out after work with people from work."

"That's not true. I mean, I *do* go out after work, but you know it's all business meetings and stuff. Do you think I have fun going out after work?"

"I don't know, Dad. I just figure that you guys are probably up to some pretty important stuff at work. What about crime or gross national products or starving out hunger?"

"You hear that, Honey? The kid thinks what we do is actually important. Ha! Now, don't look so sad, Champ. Your Old Man is up to some really big doings. Honest. We do some pretty important things. Consulting is very important. Without consultants, nobody'd know what they should do next. They'd be lost– babes in the woods. We look at all kinds of charts and we examine all sorts of figures..."

"I bet you do," Sparky's mom slipped in there, almost inaudibly.

"Huh? What'd you say, Honey?"

"Oh, nothing, Dear. Go on with your thought."

"...and we write up reports and submit them and then we have to re-write them and rewrite them and rewrite them until they bear no resemblance to reality." He paused for a beat and then started firing a second volley. "And *then* they expect..."

"Norm, please! Don't harangue the poor boy! It's not his fault what goes on in that office or outside of it."

He stopped and looked long and intensely at his wife, then took a breath. "One of these days my ship will come in and then we'll see." Sparky wondered for a moment if he was talking to himself, but then his dad snapped out of it. Hey, listen, Champ, one of these days I'll take you to work with me and I'll show you the building and the office machines– the whole layout. You'd get a big kick out of it."

"Sure, Dad. That sounds exciting!"

"Sweetie, are you finished with your food?"

"Yes, Mom."

Sparky's dad helped clear the stuff off the table and Sparky could hear him and his mom in the kitchen disagreeing about something, though they tried to hide it with hushed tones. Sparky drifted away from the table and ambled to his room.

Sparky had a little homework to do before he'd get dessert. The homework was simple enough– just a review of some spelling and multiplication problems– but he took longer than he should have. He was distracted and troubled and, after just a few math problems, he stopped and drifted into his own thoughts.

Sparky thought about the frustrating and fruitless conversations he'd had today with his mom and dad. He contrasted them to conversations he witnessed on the TV. The people he'd seen on TV broadcasts knew just the right things to say. They seemed to either always get the laugh they were after, or cause the change of heart necessary to diffuse a conflict or defeat the bad guys or save a man from eternal doom. Today, Sparky couldn't even elicit a response from his parents for what he was certain was a simple request for information about their lives. Sparky thought about that. He figured it was one of two things: They didn't want to answer or they couldn't answer the question.

He knew for a fact that they would frequently decline to answer his questions. They'd always give him one of their stock replies in those cases. "When you're a little older," or maybe, "That's not for little boys to worry about." Sometimes they'd drag out that tired old refrain about curiosity and the cat.

This time, oddly enough, they hadn't used any of those tactics. They just sort of avoided it. They didn't seem to agree with his premise in the first place and then eventually they got distracted or sidetracked. Was it possible they *couldn't* answer the question? He'd asked them innumerable questions in the past– tough questions about volcanoes, Indians, bugs, digestion. He'd asked them some pretty difficult questions to which they had been able to provide sensible answers or advise him where he could look to find the answer for himself. They didn't do that this time.

Sparky was absolutely certain that his parents must encounter fascinating and wonderful people in their daily sojourns. That being the case, what could be the reason for their withholding? Were they hiding some secret? Was there danger involved? Are these people criminals or government agents? Were his parents in some kind of trouble? These all seemed unlikely. Searching his memories of conversations he had overheard and impressions of people he had been introduced to, he could find absolutely nothing to support such wild possibilities. There had never been any talk of criminals or crimes nor had he met any friends or relatives of either his mom or dad who seemed to exhibit the typical characteristics or behavior of those who live outside the law.

No, it must be something else. He just didn't know what.

Sparky assessed his parents. They were a year or two younger than his friends' parents. They were both attractive people– his mother, pretty and nicely proportioned. They kept themselves fit and well-groomed. His dad had recently started taking more care in his looks, which Sparky assumed was at his mom's urging. She wore her dark hair long, which fit well with her graceful movements. She was about average height. She had that gentle and kind expression most of the time. He was taller than average (Sparky thought he must be over six feet tall). He had a full head of hair, which set him apart from some of his friends' dads. He used to play basketball and baseball and retained some of the athleticism of his youth. He was handsome and had long sideburns, which made him at least a little bit cool. They could conceivably live glamorous and exciting lives. Why weren't they? Or were they? Maybe they already did, though it didn't feel like it. All this speculating led nowhere.

Sparky did the last few math problems and packed up his books for the next day. He ambled back out of his room and went back to the kitchen where his mom was finishing up with the dishes. She was still dressed well. She never wore a housedress. She preferred attractive street clothes and if she wasn't wearing pants, she wore dresses, skirts or shorts that showed off her long legs. His dad wasn't there. He was in the living room, reading the newspaper.

"Hey, Mom, what's for dessert?"

"Did you finish your homework, Sweetie?"

"Yep."

"All of it?"

"Yep. Every problem."

"Good boy. I made an angel's food cake this afternoon. How does that sound?"

"Mmmm." Sparky licked his lips.

"Go call your dad to the table. Here, Sweetie, take these plates out to the table. Careful, don't drop them."

"Sure, Mom." Sparky gingerly took the plates and with care he walked out to the dining table and placed them down. He hurried the few additional steps to the living room to fetch his dad, who was on the couch, reading the sports pages.

"Hey, Dad! Are you having any cake?"

"Your mom make it?"

"I don't know. Can she make angel food cake? I thought only angels can make that stuff." Sparky hoped in vain for a chuckle from his dad.

"She's an angel, isn't she? That's what *she* thinks, anyway. I guess I'll have a piece. I don't have to ask you if you're having any, do I?"

"You bet I am! I'm taking the biggest piece!"

"Hey, Champ, what's all this talk about all these supposedly 'exciting' and 'interesting' people we're supposed to know? Where'd you get this notion, anyway? Has anybody been talking to you?"

"I don't know, Dad. I just sorta figured it out, I guess. I don't get why it's such a big deal."

"Your mom and I are not exactly jet-setters, you know. I mean, we've had our fun. You have fun, too, don't you, Champ?"

"I suppose so, Dad."

"You don't seem so certain. Well, for instance, we have fun when your Uncle Steve and Aunt Sarah visit, right? We play Careers and Risk. And when we went to Edgewood Park, or like the time we walked to the middle of the Blackstone Bridge and watched the boats passing underneath? We've gone to ball games. We have lots of fun, don't we?"

"Yeah, that stuff is plenty fun." Sparky calculated how many ball games they had gone to and recalled exactly when they had last gone to Press Park to see a major league ball game. They had gone to a grand total of three games– and none since August 30th, 1969.

"What kind of fun are you talking about, then?"

Sparky thought. He thought long and hard.

"It's not just fun, I guess. I know there's things going on out in the real world. I don't know what's going on, but it's gotta be pretty important." His dad listened patiently as he continued. "I see there's things going on and I see people going places in fancy cars or flying on air-planes. And I wonder 'what do these people do?' I bet those people are important! They sure *look* important to me. And I bet they do really interesting things! I see them on TV and they look different and they act different than the people we know. I bet they'd be fun to talk to. I bet they're doing things that nobody knows about."

Sparky's dad put the newspaper aside. "Where'd you get this idea about people doing secret things?"

"I don't know. I just kinda thought…"

"You might be surprised," His dad chuckled to himself. "The people you already know might be living more interesting lives than you think."

"How's that? Who?!" Sparky was excited to hear the surprise.

His dad stopped himself and took a new tack. "People are not really like what you see on the TV. Those people don't really exist. You fol-low me, Champ?"

"They exist! I've seen them! They're *real*! I saw one man just today that was like on TV!"

"Of course they're *real*, Champ. That's not what I mean. They're just not like that in *real* life– only when they're on the TV. When they're not on the TV, they are just like you and me. Things don't always go smoothly for them."

"No way! Why would they be on TV if they were just like you and me? And the guy I saw today was just like you'd see on TV. I bet things go smoothly for *him*."

"Boys! Cake is served!"

"Let's go have some of your mom's delicious cake, huh?"

They made their way to the table. As his dad patted his shoulder, Sparky was more perplexed than ever. He was getting conflicting mes-sages.

"Are you still worrying about these super-interesting and exciting people, Sweetie?"

Sparky nodded an affirmative. Pulling up a chair, he groaned out his perplexity. "I don't understand. These people have to– the people we see on the city subway and Regional Rail, or that fly or take limousines– where are they going? What do they do?"

His mom and dad exchanged a glance.

"Sweetie, all those people are going to work or going home. Or, maybe they're going to visit friends after work." She glanced at her husband. "They're not special in any way. They're just like your dad or me or you, for that matter. They're just going about their business. They're not Superman or Batman, Sweetie. They're just people. Right, Honey?"

"That's right, Champ. Your mother is telling you straight."

"I don't know. I'd like to believe it, Mom. I don't see how that could be. They live in a different neighborhood; they dress different; some of them speak a foreign language; they're going to different places, sometimes late at night."

"Look, Son," there was irritation in his dad's voice now as he sat forward, "just because somebody speaks French or Italian doesn't mean he's any more interesting than some good, old fashioned American."

"Oh, I don't know. Sometimes I think that some European men can be quite charming." Sparky's mom stopped the conversation cold with that assessment.

"This cake is really moist, Honey."

"Sure is, Mom! Hey, Dad, what's merde?"

"Sparky! Where did you hear that word?"

"On TV, Mom. This comedian said it and the audience laughed hysterically and Mike Douglas looked really squirmy."

"Well, Champ, it's a sort of moist brownie that French people eat." His mom and dad glanced at each other and suppressed a laugh.

"Maybe you could make *that* tomorrow night, Mom."

"I don't think you'd like it, Sweetie." Both adults laughed together. Sparky enjoyed the moment. It was a lighthearted moment in an otherwise increasingly heavy household.

Sparky's mom smiled with satisfaction as her two boys stuffed her cake into their mouths. She thought of Jean Paul Belmondo.

Chapter 5: Sparky Takes Stock

Sparky had gone to his room to retrieve his Matchbox cars. He wanted to play in the living room, where his parents were sitting and watching a TV show. He brought out his BP gas truck, Jaguar E-Type and beige Daimler double-decker bus. He left the Hoveringham (he pronounced it 'Hooveringham') dump truck, the Cadillac ambulance and a couple others in his room. Parking himself by the bookcase and the hi-fi, he imagined the patterns in the wood flooring to be the streets of the City of Highbridge. The darker slat nearest the bookcase served as bustling Hudson Street while the slat with the split in it was, to Sparky's mind, B Street, the commercial street in nearby Sparta, parallel to the one on which they lived. West Sweeny Avenue ran straight past the left leg of the hi-fi console and all the way to the baseboard.

Sparky had mapped out much of Highbridge on the living room floor despite the disparity between the shapes of the city and the room. He'd had to leave out the bay, and Belleville beyond it, because the living room wall created an impenetrable barrier just beyond Hudson Street, and he had never been to Belleville anyway, despite it being right across the bay from his neighborhood. Edgewood Park was the region directly underneath the coffee table. That put Downtown and Commerce around the green chair. Sometimes Sparky would run a car or truck all the way from Old Downtown to Hudson and then east on Hudson Street, passing Broken Hill and the great High Bridge (the TV stand), and on to the windows and the small table beneath, which marked Press Park. The couch to the right of the table was not only the airport, but also the entire East End and Maurice. The area to the right of the gold chair was Rosterdam and to the left, Boardwalk Beach.

Sparky had it all figured out. He was well schooled in the geography of Highbridge. He loved to study street maps and the subway map of the City. In fact, Sparky had never been to most of the City in which he lived. He had been to most of the "places of interest", such as the Museum of Science, City Hall and the Municipal Park, Press Park including Imaginland Amusement Park and the baseball stadium where he and his dad watched the Buccs play, the beach, and the zoo and world famous Monkey Paradise.

These sites were scattered throughout the city, but there were many square miles in between that he had never experienced. There were streets that he knew the names of that he had never seen. There were entire neighborhoods he knew existed that he had never walked the streets of. He couldn't be certain if he had ever seen inhabitants of those neighborhoods or not, though he assumed he must have seen someone from Ducommun on a subway train at some time or other. He was pretty sure he must have seen some inhabitants of Finklea or Apple Hill, which were located farther along the subway and bus lines from his stop, but had no idea who they might have been. He was pretty sure he had never seen anyone from Lingstrome Flats, though he couldn't state exactly why he thought so. He was absolutely certain that he'd never even talked to anyone who lived in Linden Farms– or even to anyone who knew someone from Linden Farms.

Sparky's Matchbox vehicles traveled the streets of these strange neighborhoods and he tried to imagine what these places were like, basing his conceptions mainly on the sound of the names and the patterns of the streets and not much else.

As for the inhabitants of these exotic locales, he was really in the dark. His own neighborhood he knew was mostly white and middle-class. He knew that many other kinds of people lived in Highbridge, including black people from the Deep South, Spanish-speaking people from places in South America such as Puerto Rico, Cuba and Spain, and many people from Greece, Italy, Germany, Poland, Turkey and China. He knew there was a Chinatown in Highbridge, not far from Downtown, but he'd never been there. They ate Chinese food occasionally at Mandarin Palace on Peace Boulevard, within walking distance of the house. Sparky naturally assumed the workers there lived in Chinatown.

Sparky's Aunt Sarah and Uncle Steve lived on Thirty-Sixth Avenue, just off the corner of Nostrand Drive. He'd visited them a couple of times and saw that their neighborhood, Brooklynville, looked something like his with a mix of small and larger apartment buildings except the buildings looked different somehow. There were fewer complicated shapes and ledges and sculptures on the buildings where his aunt and uncle lived. The people in that neighborhood were pretty much the same: white, not poor, nor rich. Sparky's own neighborhood of Hudson looked a little beat-up compared to theirs.

Sparky's other Aunt, Minny, lived near the airport. They'd never visited her there as far as Sparky could remember, though she came to their house every once in a while. Aunt Minny wouldn't take the bus or subway, preferring to drive a car, but her car was an old wreck. Sparky's dad called it alternately 'a road hazard', 'a jalopy', and 'a death trap'. Aunt Minny called it 'Copernicus' because it was a 2-door Comet.

One of Sparky's Matchbox cars was a red Ford Galaxie police car, which he sometimes pretended was his Aunt's 'death trap'. He'd mimic the sounds of a failing motor conking out, then the inevitable screeching tires, followed by the fatal crash and fiery explosion. He'd repeat the same grisly scenario numerous times, trying to embellish and perfect the sound effects and make the herky-jerky motion of the sputtering car even more herky-jerky, if possible, than the last. He'd repeat it numerous times and then repeat it some more. Finally, he could hear his dad moan out, "Jesus Christ! Somebody please take this kid's license away already! How many times are you going to blow up that car?!" Sparky would laugh. He always got a big kick out of that.

Sparky's mom would sometimes visit a friend who lived on E. 43rd Street near Ninth Avenue. If Sparky didn't have school that day, she would take him along. His dad never came with them when they'd go there. This woman, whom Sparky only knew by the name of Mrs. Dominguez, lived in a very nice neighborhood. The streets had tall trees that blocked the sun and made a high, shady tunnel. The houses were large and they had big yards in the front. Mrs. Dominguez was a little older and much shorter than Sparky's mom and she had a husband. He was never there when they visited. Sparky's mom said she and Mrs. Dominguez used to work together before Sparky was born. Mrs. Dominguez always wore a uniform, kind of like a nurse's uniform. Sparky wondered if her life was exciting and interesting. It didn't seem so, but he couldn't be sure.

All in all, Sparky had been around, here and there, but mostly in his own neighborhoods of Sparta and Hudson. Highbridge is a large city and Sparky could boast of seeing only a small percentage of it. Many neighborhoods remained a vague mystery and many more people remained an entirely unknown quantity.

As Sparky ran his toy vehicles around his miniature version of Highbridge, he let his mind drift into wondering about all the people, the variety of buildings, the possibly alien sounds and smells of the rest of

40

the city. He pushed his BP tanker truck along Neptune Avenue, making sure to stop at every gas station he imagined was along the way south from Peace Boulevard. He let his mind construct impressions of what Neptune Avenue might look like as the truck drove farther and farther down the street, leaving Peace Boulevard behind in the distance. Sparky stretched out on the floor a little more so he could get the BP tanker a little farther on the floor and a little farther south along a street he himself had yet to see. As he pushed the truck toward another gas station, he rested his head on his arm to get lower and to watch his truck from down at street level.

Sparky had had a long, tiring day. He had a day of school and he hung out and played ball for a couple of hours after school with "The Gang". Then he got all involved with this realization about other people and their fun and exciting lives. Then he struggled with his parents in an effort to extract more information about these people.

He wished he could take the time to go out exploring these exotic regions of the City. If only he could get his dad to take him around. But Sparky knew his dad had to go to work the next day. Maybe his mom could do it. Maybe she would take time away from her busy day to accompany him on this Great Journey. He could be like Stanley Livingstone, exploring the darkest recesses of the Dark Continent. He wished he owned an Avanti. He imagined driving down Neptune Avenue behind the BP tanker as it made its way down, down, down into areas he was afraid he'd never see in real life. And as he pushed the toy truck farther he remembered that the next day was a school day, and that his mom wouldn't let him go on any journey, anyway. Sparky closed his eyes and wished he didn't have to go to school tomorrow and his hand let go of the BP tanker.

Part II The Dream

Chapter 1: The Morning Routine Disrupted

Sparky woke up and got himself ready to go to school. His mother had not come in to wake him this morning. Sparky guessed that she must have known that he would wake up on time. He absently went through his morning routine and gathered his schoolbooks together. His room was very crowded and small– smaller than usual– and he was almost incapable of turning around without his shoulders hitting and knocking something over.

He also was struggling to get past his bed, which had somehow drifted away from the wall. He pushed back toward the wall, but the bed wouldn't budge– or rather, it did move a little, but moved right back to its original position plus a couple of inches more. Each time he tried shoving it, it moved back plus some. It felt as though something soft was jammed behind the bed, but he didn't have time to investigate it further. Thinking he was going to make it worse if he pursued it, Sparky let it go and just barely managed to squeeze himself out of his room.

The hallway was quite chilly by contrast to his room, though it was small and crowded, too. There were logs stacked up on one side of the hallway and in front of the bathroom door. Sparky was pretty sure they hadn't been there when he had used the bathroom the night before. Sparky made his way through the clutter and into the living room. On the floor, instead of a rug, was a street map of Highbridge, in color with the major arteries highlighted in dull yellow. It filled the entire center of the room and even ran under the couch and chairs. He thought for a second that he could see cars and trucks moving, but he wasn't sure and didn't look closely enough to confirm the impression.

"Sweetie, you're up! Very good. We've run out of cereal and eggs, so I'm afraid we're going to have to have last night's cake for breakfast this morning. Mommy's so sorry, Sweetie."

Sparky was not exactly distressed by the news, though he recalled that there had been plenty of cereal left in the box just yesterday morning. In fact, since the cabinet was ajar, he could plainly see all three shelves stuffed full of cereal boxes where normally only one had cereal on it.

He didn't want to think his mom was lying, so he assumed she must be saving it for some reason or perhaps she needed to get rid of the cake before it spoiled. Either way was fine with him.

"Uh, that's okay, Mom. I can get by with just cake I suppose. As long as it's just for one day, of course."

"If you miss your eggs a lot, Sweetie, we can have them for dessert tonight."

"No, that's okay. Mom. We should probably try to finish off the cake first."

Sparky sat down in front of his cake and stuck his fork into it. Something was wrong. It had turned kind of gooey overnight. "Hey, Mom! My cake's all funny. It looks like it's turned back into batter, or something!"

"Oh, Sweetie, don't eat that with a *fork*! You broke the rules. Now there's no more cake and your dad will spank me! He won't believe me when I tell him it was your fault. He likes to blame me, instead."

"What was my fault?" Sparky protested, "All I did was try to eat my cake!"

"All I said is that you could *have* it." Sparky's mom snatched the goo-covered plate away and, to Sparky's astonishment, stuck it back in the fridge. "He'll never think to look in here for it. Maybe he won't have the energy to spank me tonight. If he comes home very late tonight and if I forget to wear any panties, he might forget to spank me. That's it! That's what I'll do!"

"Mom, what in the world are you talking about?!" Sparky noticed at that moment that his mom's dress was extra short and frilly, like that of a little girl. "And, why are you dressed like that? You look like an overgrown Shirley Temple!"

"Mommy is a *big* little girl, Sweetie. Mommy eats candy and ice cream." Sparky didn't know what to think. "Are you still hungry? I could fix you a nice bowl of cereal, if you'd like?"

"I thought we didn't *have* any cereal in the house. That's what you

43

said."

"Of course. You're running late, Sweetie. Off to school you go!"

"What about my lunch, Mom?"

"You just finished breakfast and you're talking about lunch already? How could you be hungry? It's only just past eight A.M. P.M. A.M. B.M.– Ooh, Mommy said B.M, tee hee!"

Sparky felt embarrassed for her. "You're acting really weird, Mom. Don't you have anything for me to take for lunch– or even breakfast?"

"Mommy doesn't have the time today, Sweetie. Here, take this money and buy yourself something at the luncheonette around the corner." She pressed some money into his hand and started ushering him down a long ramp toward the front door.

"Hey, Mom, can we move those logs from in front of the bathroom? I want to pee one more time before I leave, but I can't get over them."

"Those logs are there to stay, Sweetie. You know that." They continued the long walk down the ramp.

"I do? What are they there for, anyway?"

"One day, Mommy will have a fireplace in each room of the house and we'll burn the logs and have a nice warm glow. You'd like that, wouldn't you, Sweetie?"

"I don't know. I don't see where we have room for any fireplaces in this house. As it is, I can't even turn around in my room without knockin' things off the shelves!" The ramp had leveled off and now was on an incline. Still they continued walking to the front door.

"You'll see. One day we'll have a huge house with hundreds and hun- dreds of fireplaces everywhere. Mommy's saving the logs until that fateful day."

"But, how are we going to afford to live in a huge house? Dad doesn't make that kind of money." They finally reached the front door, which had been left wide open and was letting in the brisk autumn air from

44

outside.

"No, Sweetie. I've been talking to the Principal of your school. Mommy's going to sell her panties and then we'll all be rich beyond our wildest dreams! You'll see!" With that she sent Sparky off to school without his books.

Chapter 2: Sparky Meets Some Real Characters

Sparky wasn't sure what he'd do without his books all day. At this point, it seemed stupid to go back in to get them. His mom was acting kind of funny and he wasn't sure what she'd do or say next, so he opted to go to school without them. If anyone asked, he could truthfully blame her for his being without. He was pretty certain someone would lend him paper and a pencil and he could share textbooks with Karen, whom he sat next to.

'What am I going to say to Pinkerton?' he thought. 'She's gonna write a letter again. Maybe she won't notice.' At that moment, a garbage truck passed by him on St. Charles, making its pickup.

"Hey, sonny! Where are yer books, sonny-boy? Ha ha!" It was the garbage man hanging off the back of the truck. He laughed as they sped by and he was waving in the air what seemed to be a pair of frilly panties. "We sure like yer momma's garbage a lot, sonny-boy! Ho ho! We'll pick up her cans, anytime!"

Sparky watched the truck disappear down the street, honking its horn all the way. 'How does he know what garbage is ours?' He realized something more immediately worrisome to him: 'If even the garbage man noticed that I don't have my books with me, I'm never gonna get away with it at school!'

Sparky started walking slower, not eager to get to school without his books in hand and thinking what he could do to escape the inevitable punishment. He passed the Chinese laundry, which he had thought was located on Eighth Avenue, but today it was on St. Charles. In fact, most of Eighth Avenue's businesses were on St. Charles Street today. Or maybe he was really on Eighth Avenue. He wasn't sure. He hadn't been paying much attention because he was so worried about not having his books. The workers at the laundry were outside today, washing white shirts in a tub with a washboard set in it. They were out by the curb next to several trashcans full of stinking garbage. There were dozens of flies buzzing around the garbage and he saw dead flies floating in the washtub. The dead flies were being smeared all over the white shirts as they rubbed them against the washboard. Sparky wondered why would anyone pay them to clean their clothes when they obviously do such a terrible job.

46

"Hey lady, how come you don't pick the flies out of the water? They're getting all over the shirts!"

Nobody responded until Sparky repeated his question. Finally, the youngest woman in the bunch spoke up. "What do you know about doing laundry, kid? You ever wash clothes? The Chinese have been doing laundry for thousands of years. Hell, we Chinese invented laundry! So, shove off before I call the cops on you."

"Why would you call the police? I'm not breaking the law."

"You're a truant. That's breaking the law. You should be in school."

"But, I *am* going to school."

"No you're not. You've got no books. No bookee, no schoolee, right ladies?" They all laughed and nodded at that. "Get lost, kid." She flicked a fly out of the dirty water right at him. They all laughed again as he jumped back.

"You don't *sound* Chinese."

"Oh? What's a Chinese person supposed to sound like?"

"I don't know. Maybe foreign or with some kind of an accent, or something?"

"I got an accent. I got a Highbridge accent. We all got a Highbridge accent. Sue and Lily and Florence and me, we all got a Highbridge accent. Hell, kid, we were born in Highbridge. What kind of accent you think we'd have?"

"I don't know, I just always thought all Chinese people talked kinda funny, that's all. When you see them on TV, they– "

"Oh, I see! Well, kid, you can't believe what you see on the TV."

"Why do you say that?"

"Because, kid, TV is just the opiate of the masses, that's why. And if there's anything us Chinese know something about, it's opiates. Am I right, ladies? Ha ha!" They all joined in, laughing.

Sparky noticed that one of the ladies was now sitting in the washtub, taking a bath. "Hey, how did you–? You shouldn't be taking a bath out here in the street!" Sparky could see a fin-like projection on her back and wondered if all Chinese people had one.

"Young man, if you're not going to wash my back, I can't answer your question."

"Hey, kid, seriously, we have an awful lot of washing to do and it's our private bath time. You'll have to excuse us and move on or Lily, here, will have to administer a good sound spanking."

Sparky took her advice and decided it was best to let them get back to what they were doing. Not to mention that he was not keen on getting a spanking. "Well, I gotta get to school, anyway."

At the corner of Eighth Avenue and Baumen Road, Sparky was startled by a garbage truck that roared by, splashing through a puddle of gutter water and almost hitting him. There was a Chinese garbage man hanging off the back of the truck. He was holding something white and frilly in one of his hands and chuckled as he looked back at Sparky. Sparky was amazed. He didn't know there were any Chinese garbage men.

"Who do you think picks up the garbage in China?"

The voice seemed familiar. Sparky turned to see who had spoken to him and it was one of the kids in the slowest class at school.

"You're in Mr. Thicke's class, right?"

"That's correct. My name is Logan Brogan. It's a pleasure to meet you…" He seemed quite wise now that he was outside of school.

"Sparky. Sparky Donnelly. I'm in Mrs. Pinkerton's class." They started across Baumen. "What kind of name is Blogan Bogan? Sounds Irish or something."

"Logan Brogan."

"Bogan Glogan?"

"No, Logan Brogan!"

Sparky was having a lot of trouble getting the name just right. "I'm sorry. It's Loban Logan, right?"

"Are you stupid? My name is L-O-G-A-N, Logan. B-R-O-G-A-N, Brogan!"

"Gogan Glogan." Sparky was getting frustrated at his own inability to get this kid's name right. It was embarrassing, too, because this kid is one of the dumbest in the school.

"You're hopeless, Sparky. How did you end up in the top class, anyway? Did your father bribe the Superintendent of Schools or something?"

Sparky wasn't really listening and couldn't answer. He was running the kid's name through his head, over and over, with no success. Inevitably, he started repeating the ones he had run through already. Logan Brogan was talking to him and looking at him, but Sparky was in a mental cave. 'Blogan Broglan. Roglan Blogran.'

"Is anyone in that head of yours?" Logan leaned over and tried looking into Sparky's eyes. He shook his head. "I give up." And Logan did give up and walked away.

Sparky was alone for a moment until his fixation was interrupted by the guy at Mel's Fish Market dumping a bucket of water on the sidewalk in front of him.

"Look out, boy! What's with you, huh? You look like you're on dope or something."

"No, I was just thinkin'."

"Thinkin' like that'll get you run over or somethin'. Hey boy, you like the smell of my fish?"

"No, it stinks."

"That ain't fair. You're judging my fish by schoolboy standards. Fish can't smell nothin' anyway. They swim in the ocean– the Atlantic Ocean." The man pronounced Atlantic Ocean as if he were talking to a two-year old. "They say that I am startin' to look more and more like a fish every day." He chuckled. "Is that what you think?"

Sparky was feeling uneasy about this conversation, but answered anyway. "I don't think you look much like a fish. You've got a mustache. Fish don't have mustaches. Fish don't have ears." It was then that he noticed the man had one deformed ear that was bulbous and magenta and had some stuff– not earwax– oozing out of it. Sparky was worried he had insulted the guy, but his unease was overshadowed by strong disgust and a sudden urge to vomit. Yet Sparky could not look away from the ear and he could see it very close up. He also thought he could smell it. He retched as the man continued talking to him.

"I betcha they don't teach you nothin' about fish in that school you go to, do they?" Sparky was sure he could smell the ear. It was a rotten smell. One that he'd smelled before– like rotten meat or maybe a bad infection. He retched again and looked away, but all he saw were bloody, slimy, smelly fish. "What's the matter, boy? You look like you never seen a man rotting before. My brain's rotting and coming outta my ear. You don't like that, do you? You look upset. Look at me, boy!"

Sparky couldn't take it anymore. He darted away from the man and ran as fast as his legs could take him down the block. The man continued to call after him as he ran. "Hey, boy, better run before you catch my disease! I might drip on you! 'Discharge' the doctors call it. You want some of my 'discharge', boy?"

Sparky couldn't get the smell out of his mind and he had the willies from it. He felt like he had run for a long time– for hours– but, he was just nearing the end of the block he was on. 'Jeez, this is one day from hell,' he thought to himself. 'I'd better cross over, just in case that guy tries coming after me.' He crossed over to the east side of Eighth Avenue and saw some of the kids from school standing outside the candy store. He was winded and could not seem to catch his breath.

"Hi, girls. Who're waiting for?" He was trying to hide how winded he was.

"Hi, Sparky. We're not waiting for anybody. Maybe we're waiting for you. Are you here for us? Or are we here for you?"

Sparky looked at Diana and Gwendolyn then back again to Diana– looking for a clue about how to answer such a question. "Well, I didn't come here to meet you, if that's what you mean. I just crossed over to get away from that guy at Mel's."

"What guy at Mel's, Sparky?" Gwendolyn asked in a suspicious manner.

"You know, that guy– he's like a monster. He's got that ear with the stuff oozing out." Sparky felt like retching again. "You know."

"No Sparky, we don't know." The two girls looked at each other. Gwendolyn spoke again. "You tell us, which 'guy'?" A crowd of school kids had gathered around– perhaps 30 or 40, from all the classes.

"I don't know. He's got a bad ear. You know, big and reddish-purple and stuff." Sparky wondered why there was so much interest in this conversation. The crowd seemed to have grown to at least twice its previous size– maybe a hundred in all. There was an almost palpable excitement and everyone was egging them on, like they were all hoping for a fight.

"My father works at Mel's," Gwendolyn said.

"So does mine, Sparky."

"How could both your fathers work there? Is that true?" Neither girl responded.

Sparky glanced around quickly and nervously, feeling as if an attack was imminent. He saw not only the kids, but also a few of the teachers, as well. He could see Mr. Fuller, who taught the 5th grade middle class. And Mr. Solti, who taught the slow 6th grade class and whom the students called 'Mister Salty' and made cracks about him being a crummy teacher– except that Mister Salty looked all skinny and sickly and weak here, which he normally wasn't, and his pants were so short Sparky could see his scrawny ankles all the way up to the calves and several dark purple scabs on his shins. Mr. Fuller turned to Mister Salty and remarked that Sparky didn't have his schoolbooks with him.

51

"What do you make of that, Mister Salty? That's not going to go over well with our darling Mrs. Pinkerton."

"No, sir. Him in heap big trouble." They both laughed.

"And how!" Fuller held up his hand in mock Indian fashion. This had the two teachers doubled over in hysterics. The crowd joined in the merriment.

"Him get heap big spanking," Mister Salty added, just barely able to get the words out before laughter overtook him.

As the others were laughing, Diana stepped toward Sparky and reached into a cigar box she held in her left hand. "If you can tell me what this thing is, we'll let you off the hook– this time."

"Off *what* hook?" Sparky felt like he was the only one who didn't know what was going on.

"The coat hook. The fish hook." Diana fished around for a second and grabbed something and looked up at Sparky.

Sparky held his breath. Diana pulled out a toy car.

"That's a toy Avanti," Sparky declared with great relief and confidence. It wasn't an Avanti. It was a Pontiac Catalina and Sparky knew it. He worried that someone might spot the lie.

"Why did you laugh at me yesterday in class, Sparky?"

Sparky was glad no one cared that he was wrong about the car. "I– just– I was glad someone besides me was getting some of Pinkerton's treatment, for a change."

"Diana liked you, Sparky." Sparky noted Gwendolyn's use of the past tense.

"You hurt my feelings. I never laugh when you're singled out, Sparky."

"I didn't know it would hurt your feelings."

"Sparky, Sparky, tsk, tsk," Gwendolyn shook her head slowly. She

52

never took her eyes off his and Sparky could swear he didn't see her blink the entire time, either. "You deserve a sound spanking, Sparky."

"Who's going to give it to him, Gwendolyn?"

Chapter 3: Breakfast at the Candy Store

The crowd was gone. Sparky assumed they had all dispersed and headed off to school. He couldn't believe so many kids would be so late to school. He was certain he was late this morning. It was seemingly taking him forever to get there today. He thought for a moment about going into the candy store and buying something. His mom had given him some money to buy food. Maybe he could buy a Hostess cherry pie out of the funds he had gotten? His mouth watered at the thought.

Sparky reached into his pocket and pulled out the money she had handed him as she rushed him out the door. It was a wad of bills such as Sparky had never seen before in his life– excepting on TV, of course. There were several twenties, some tens, fives and maybe thirty dollars in singles! "Holy cow!" Sparky figured there might be three hundred dollars in his hands. "She must be nuts! I could feed the entire school with this much money!" He suddenly felt very scared, as if he had done something criminal. Waves of panic overtook him for a moment and he couldn't think what was the right thing to do. He was hungry, though, and that blotted out all other concerns for the moment.

Sparky looked up from his bankroll and was about to walk into the candy store when he saw that the floor at the entrance, and the pavement just outside, were all broken up. There were holes and gaps and cracks, and what remained was so rough and flimsy that he was afraid to step on it or across it. The flooring looked a thousand years old and so thin that Sparky could hardly believe it ever supported the weight of a human being. The holes were so deep that he couldn't see their bottom and he was afraid that one false step would land him below the pavement or even below the basement! However, he was so hungry that he decided he'd chance it. So he lined himself up for a standing broad jump and coiled, ready to spring across.

No matter how hard he tried, though, he couldn't bring himself to jump. He remained coiled and ready to spring, but couldn't pull the trigger and jump the 25 inches he needed to clear. Other people were walking in and out of the store without any difficulty, as he remained rooted to the spot. Still, he couldn't do it. He had his books with him and the additional burden made him afraid he would get dragged down. 'Why do I have my schoolbooks with me?' He couldn't remember if he'd had them all along since leaving the house. 'Mr. Fuller and Mister Salty shouldn't have made fun of me when I really did have them.'

He was thinking of the consequences if he didn't make it across. He could fall through a gap and break a leg or get a really bad gash and the get the inevitable case of lockjaw. He could fall and crack his skull. Still, these other people seemed to have no trouble negotiating the hazard. Why would he? He thought he might get a cramp or get distracted just as he was about to jump. If anything like that occurred, he'd never make it. He'd land on the thin section of flooring and fall right through. While these others took no notice of the condition of the entrance, Sparky couldn't see anything *but* the cracks and holes.

He glanced around as he crouched and saw some of his buddies passing the candy store, on their way to school. Unable to make a move either way, Sparky went into a panic. He knew he was running very late, now. These endless moments at the threshold were a huge waste of time and were making him impossibly late. Every second he hesitated was a second closer to him walking into school dead last of all the students. Yet, he didn't want to go to school hungry. Time was ticking away. He needed something to eat. He couldn't jump over the entrance, but he couldn't leave, either.

Sparky saw a man in the candy store buying a gigantic pile of magazines and newspapers. The man was dressed in an old fashioned way, with a top hat and spats and he had one of those ridiculous mustaches and slicked hair like the guy on the Monopoly cards. He had two armfuls of magazines that were so high, he couldn't see over them. There seemed to be more magazines than what the store carried in its racks– perhaps 150 different publications. The odd man didn't seem to struggle at all under the burden and wielded them as easily as if he was carrying only a few magazines. It appeared to Sparky that the man was used to making such a purchase.

Sparky was standing next to him, inside the store now and in front of the cash register holding a Dutch Apple Hostess pie. The old German woman was ringing him out, taking payment and making change for each magazine– one magazine at a time! The woman and the man chatted away about the weather, the price of milk, how cheaply made things were these days, whether or not the teamsters were justified in striking. Sparky was horrified. He'd never get to school on time with this new delay. Sparky, not one to speak up under normal circumstances, nevertheless blurted out: "Hey, could you let me pay for my pie?" They both stopped and stared at Sparky. Immediately, he felt embarrassed and scared.

"Well! Hmpf! Madam Schnauzer, can you believe the insolence of such guttersnipes these days?"

"Tsk, tsk, Herr Abernatty. Ven I vuz younk, ve coodent talk zo! Ve must show ze rezpeket."

"Why, Madam Schnauzer, if I had had the pretension to have presented myself as anything but deferential to my elders and betters, I would have been reprimanded in the most aggressive manner." The woman nodded her agreement. "In fact, Madam Schnauzer, I believe– and, please, Madam Schnauzer, feel free to correct me if I am saying anything but what is most truthful and accurate– I would go so far to say, if memory serves me correctly, that a guttersnipe who felt that it was his right to outrage his elders and betters with such effrontery– and that's not to say it ever happened in my presence, such a rare occasion it was, though I certainly do not wish to give the possibly false impression that it *never* did, for certainly it *must* have– would be inviting for himself a caning and a lengthy stay in the state reformatory for delinquents. Am I telling the truth, Madam Schnauzer?"

"Ja, Herr Abernatty. Dat vill be zevendy sthree zendts."

"Certainly, Madam. Do you, by any chance, have change for a five-dollar bill?"

"Vell, Herr Abernatty, I vill go into ze beck oaf ze store undt zee. Vait vun minutes, danke." This tank of a woman waddled her way past stacks of papers and magazines and boxes of candies and cigarettes to the back of the cramped shop and disappeared behind the curtain into the back room.

Sparky waited. He shuffled around a bit and looked out the door to the street at the traffic. Delivery trucks, an A&P tractor-trailer and a bunch of school buses went by. The school buses reminded Sparky of how late he was. He turned away from the front of the store and went back toward the cash register. The German woman had not yet reappeared.

The pompous old gent stood with an exaggerated jauntiness, balanced on his right foot with his left crossed over, his right fist pressed against his hip and with his elbow thrust out. He looked down his big, red nose at Sparky and he sneered and pointedly sniffed.

Tired of waiting, with his mouth watering, Sparky ate his pie, savoring every bite. He bit through the thin sugar glaze and the soggy crust into the jelly filling. He bit off a chunk and tried not to drop any of the crust onto the floor. He chewed the sweet confection and felt the cherries crunch slightly between his teeth.

"Hmpf!" The old dandy was really steamed now. He was steamed as much because he had no sympathetic audience to share his insulted sensibilities with as he was with Sparky eating a pie he had not yet paid for. Twitching his chin and throwing his head back, he threw his balance to the other foot and reiterated, "Hmpf!" then added, "Ahem!"

Peeling back more of the waxy wrapping paper and folding the little white cardboard backing, Sparky took another bite. Once more he reveled in the sweet glaze, the salty crust and tart filling as he chewed. Sparky looked up at the man and could not suppress his laughter. The man was turning red in the face. He pulled a pocket watch from his striped vest, checked the time, then suddenly straightened his lapels and marched out without any of his magazines– even the ones he already paid for.

Sparky finished his last bite of pie and threw the wrapper away into a steel trashcan that was sitting in the middle of the store. He looked around for anyone who could take his payment, but the place was empty. Not a soul in there. So he steeled himself to venture behind the curtain to find the old German woman or anyone else who may be working there. He wouldn't normally be so forward, but he really did have to get to school. He was already late and was certainly going to be in a world of trouble as a result.

"Hello! Hello! Ma'am?" Sparky poked his head through the dingy olive-colored curtain. It was more of a blanket or a heavy drapery than a curtain. It had stains and cigarette burns and some crusty white stuff on it. "Ma'am?" 'Where is everybody?' The only sound was from the rattling old refrigeration unit right outside the doorway leading to the back room. Sparky couldn't even hear traffic outside the candy store, though the door was wide open. He wondered whether he should just leave and worry about paying for the pie another time. He didn't want to be accused of stealing however, so he passed through the doorway.

Sparky had never been in the back of any store before and had no idea what he might find there. What he did find surprised him.

It was a fairly small room, dirty, dingy and musty. It had a very high ceiling with the same stamped tin design as in the front part of the store, but it looked as if it hadn't been painted in many years– decades, perhaps. There was a small skylight way up at the center of the ceiling, but it was so dirty that it let in no light from outside, despite the bright sunshine of the day. Whereas the front of the store had fluorescent lighting, this room still had the old enameled light fixtures with cages over the bulbs, hanging from above. They threw little light and even less into the corners, where deep gloom obscured the details. The walls were painted in the same two-tone institutional scheme that P.S. 8 had. They were dirtier, though, with stains and splatters all over them. Sparky found stacks of newspapers and magazines and crates of soda bottles. He also found chopped meat and frankfurters arranged in piles, sitting on a large table. The meat was no longer pink and it smelled strong. There was a slick greasy mess on that same table, some of which had dripped from the table to the floor, where it mingled with other spills and stains. The walls had holes– dozens of them– and plaster flaked and fell from them onto the tables and floors. Leaning against the table with the meat on it was a dust-covered, old motorcycle. There was a large oil stain on the floor beneath its motor. In the far right corner of the room there was a phone booth with its phone torn out and filled with bags of Wise potato chips, Fritos and Cheese Doodles. Some of the bags had torn open and spilled their contents on the floor right outside the booth. Next to the phone booth there were dozens of shoeboxes stacked from floor to ceiling, filled with– from what Sparky could see– countless old newspaper clippings. Each box had some pencil writing on it. Most of the boxes were marked with years: 1931, 1937, etc. Some boxes had no year indicated, but had either a name or subject scrawled there instead. One box was labeled "Adolph Hitler"; another was labeled "Pontiac, Mich.". Sparky wondered what that could refer to. There was a 1956 Coca-Cola calendar on the wall behind– and partially obscured by– some of the boxes. The smiling cowgirl on the calendar had some of her teeth blacked-out with a black pen or marker and someone had also crudely drawn nipples in the appropriate places on her off-the-shoulder shirt. There was garbage on the filthy linoleum in the far left corner in a small open area. Scattered about in the piles of garbage were wads and shreds of what looked like used toilet tissue.

Sparky was disappointed at how dirty and disgusting the store was. He never liked the old woman who ran the business, but he always liked coming here. Now he wasn't too sure it was good idea even to have eaten that pie. He reassured himself that Hostess pies are packaged in sealed wrappers, however he could no longer recall if his pie was sealed or not when he picked it up, and didn't know if he had opened it. Sparky looked around again toward the front of the store and saw that no one had entered the store since that old dandy had left. It was then that Sparky noticed another door, to the left of the one he had entered through. This door had in it one large square pane of translucent wire glass. The glass was cracked in the upper left corner.

Sparky assumed the woman must've gone in there. He wondered for a second if it might have been a bathroom and he was reluctant to open it or knock, but Sparky tried the knob of the door anyway and cautiously opened it. It was dark in there, but there was light from the distance. The door opened up into a long hallway that looked abandoned. A bulb down the hall and around a bend provided the only illumination. The walls had tile up to around 4 or 5 feet, then there was shiny light blue paint above. Sparky made his way along the checked tile floor and followed the hallway around several turns and up and down a handful of stairwells until he started feeling like he was getting nowhere and perhaps was lost. Just as that feeling began to overtake him, he came up against an exit and pushed the handle, opening the door right onto the local platform of the A Street subway station.

At least it looked like the A Street station. Anyway, it *felt* like the A Street station, so Sparky figured that's what it must be. He was quite surprised that there was a door that led right into the station and didn't even force him through the turnstiles first. The platform was crowded and the Number 12 local trains were roaring in, swallowing waiting passengers by the dozens and speeding out again. The Number 13 expresses were blasting by at great speed on the middle tracks, either heading downtown with passengers jammed in together holding on for dear life to their straps and poles, or heading out to the Airport with a few, comfortably-seated passengers scattered throughout the ten cars.

Sparky was nervous that he hadn't paid for a token, but nobody seemed to have noticed him emerging from the door. Nobody noticed anything. They were all in their own worlds. He wanted to get on one of the trains and go somewhere, but he knew he was expected at school, so he reluctantly made his way down the platform toward the exit, dodging hurrying passengers along the way. Passing through the area near the token clerk's booth, Sparky avoided looking at the clock over the clerk's window. He was hit with another wave of panic about the time. He was sure it was way past nine and that he'd be incredibly late for school at this point, so he was afraid to see the actual time.

Sparky did glance at the token booth and at the clerk on duty inside it, and did a double-take. There behind the cage was the German woman who owns the candy store! He stared and hesitated. 'How can that be? How can you run a candy store and...?' Sparky suddenly remembered that not only hadn't he paid for a token to enter the station, but that he hadn't paid for that Hostess pie, either. And here was the very woman he didn't pay! He lowered his eyes and quickened his pace, heading toward the stairs and the sanctuary of the street. He felt everyone's eyes on him, certain they all knew that he didn't belong on the subway at this time. He was certain they all could clearly see that he was a truant, and he dreaded being nabbed for being out of school and wandering around free. He knew that parents of truants got in as much trouble as the truants themselves. He'd heard stories of how parents were hauled up before the judge and lost custody of their children due to truancy. The thought of his mom and dad standing before a judge, being humiliated in public like that, struck fear in his heart.

So Sparky ran past the token booth and scrambled up the stairs to the street. He ran like hell once he got to the street, leaving the A Street station far behind, and found himself running up 82nd Street to P.S. 8. He was straining hard and pushing as hard and fast as he could. After a minute, however, he realized he was running only about as fast as the people in the street were walking. Sparky pushed harder, trying to increase his speed. He strained himself and was digging and leaning and kicking as hard as possible. He still was able to run only about as fast as a comfortable walking pace. He thought that he should just stop running– that he could walk just as fast. But when he stopped running, he immediately fell behind the others, so he dug in and started trying to run once more. He was nearly exhausted and out of breath by the time he reached the corner.

Chapter 4: Francis and the Reconstruction

Sparky looked up the block and tried to see his school. The corner
looked different to him. It didn't exactly look *un*familiar, but definitely
not like 82nd Street. There was a car dealership where the Dutch Boy
paint store should have been, and the Wanderlust Travel Agency was
where The Coaster Bar and Lounge normally is. Sparky wondered for a
moment if he was on the wrong street, but a quick glance at the street
sign reassured him. He started again for P.S. 8 and it was then that he
could see that the school wasn't even there! In place of his school was a
huge construction site, with crews working steam shovels and erecting
the building's framework using a crane to hoist the huge I-beams.

Sparky was astounded. He stood with his mouth agape, trying to take it
all in. He just stood and stared for a time, his eyes scanning the entire
scene, wondering what to make of it and what he should do. It was after
a moment that he focused on the large painted sign that announced the
future new home of P.S. 8. The sign had a utopian depiction of the finished structure in 3/4 view, showing green trees and bushes and lawns.
It seemed to Sparky that what they were showing in that sign could not
possible exist in the tight space allotted to the school on 82nd Street,
nevertheless, there it was in full color and executed in great, painstak-
ing detail. Sparky noticed that the artist's conception of the building
itself looked just like the 21 year old structure that had existed there
already. He wondered why they would bother to build the same thing
all over again.

"Whadya doin' here, kid?"

Sparky turned toward the construction entrance, where a rotund, red-
cheeked man stood with a soggy, unlit cigar in the corner of his wet
mouth.

"I, uh, I'm supposed to be in school now."

"Then you better get goin', kid. Don't keep hangin' aroun' here no
more. This is no place for kids to be playin'," the man growled.

"But this is my school!"

"Ha ha ha! Then you're really in duh wrong place, kid! Or you're real early for class! Ha ha!" The man's shirt was untucked from his pants and the bottom of his big, hanging belly showed above his beltline. The belly bounced when he laughed. "Seriously, kid, you should get along to school before ya get inta any trouble."

"But, no kidding mister, this *is* my school. It was yesterday, anyway. How could you have done all this since yesterday? I don't see how..."

"Look, kid. You see that machine there? That thing eats buildins. It works all night while we sleep or watch the test pattern on the TV. The guy that runs that machine– Phil– he's sittin' over there by the shack– he trows the switch at 5 when we all clear outta here and– *PFHVTT*!– it starts eatin' the buildin'. And it's all automatic!"

"That doesn't explain how you could have put up the framework and laid those bricks over there and, well, not to mention the basement and stuff!"

"Kid, you gotta lot to learn about modern construction. This school is a kit. We bought it at Asburton's downtown store. They delivered it at 4:24 pm yesterday and all we had to do was to come in today and it was put together. Hardly break a sweat, these days. You don' know, kid. It ain't like it use ta be back in the Middle Ages. Nope."

Sparky listened and tried to absorb what it all meant. He always thought construction was a complex and skilled endeavor. He knew that architects went to college to learn the trade; that bricklayers and carpenters served apprenticeships and learned their crafts over years of backbreaking experience. Now he was being told that, these days, just about all you had to do was to show up and the building practically built itself! He could hardly believe it.

"Ha ha, you look dumbfounded, kid!"

"But what does it mean to the guys who lay the bricks or the carpenters or the guys that install windows or..."

"We still have our jobs. See there, the guys are workin'. Nothin's changed."

"But you said the building put itself together. Why do they need a construction crew?"

"The union guarantees our jobs, kid. Nothin' goes up without a full
crew on hand. An' we get time-and-a-half if we don't gotta do nothin'.
But I tell ya, it's backbreaking work and a thankless life. No one appre-
ciates what the reglar guy does, nowadays. I'd like to see a world without buildins. Winter's comin'. Everybody'd be freezin' their tits off
without a roof over their head! Oh! Sorry, kid, I shouldn'ta said 'tits'.
That's a bad word– tits."

"That's okay, mister. You can say that word. *I'm* not allowed to say it.
What are they building over there?" Sparky pointed through the fence
toward what looked like a subway tunnel without a roof covering it.

"That there's the new subway line. Runs right under the school and out
to the city dump. We put a stairway direct from the candy store to the
downtown platform. That way nobody's gotta get wet when it rains,
anymore. In three weeks, we'll be puttin' in a hallway between the
men's room an' the Municipal Buildin'. You could walk around the
whole city and never see anybody."

Sparky wanted to be impressed, but he was unsure how this would be
desirable or even practical. How could a hallway run from Hudson to
Downtown? Who would use it when there's a subway line that can
whisk you downtown in 15 minutes for the price of a quarter?

"Are they going to charge money to use the hallway?"

"Well, kid, everybody's already paid to use it."

"What do you mean? You mean like taxes?"

"Nah, not taxes! The guy went around." He stared at Sparky, looking
for a sign of recognition. "The guy!" Sparky cocked his head. "The
GUY! He went around. The guy– with the spats and the cane." Sparky
continued to stare blankly. "He's got the fancy clothes, the vest. He's
got a long waxed mustache. You musta seen him. Ya can't miss'm!"

"Oh, yeah! I saw him this morning! He was buying a big stack of
magazines at the candy store! But, then I saw him at the token booth in
the A Street station. No, wait– that was the German lady– I don't know
what I saw. This has been the craziest morning! I don't even know
what I'm saying anymore." Sparky held his hands to his temples, shook

63

his head and groaned.

The man looked at Sparky sympathetically and patted his shoulder. "You know what you need, kid, is a vacation. I know because that's what *I* need, is a vacation. You should go to Bermuda! That's the place to go to get away from it all. I went there with Adele, my girlfriend, last year. We was there fer three days and I never felt more relaxed. I came back to work an' everybody said 'Whoa, Francis, you look like a million bucks!' My wife even noticed the difference! Take my advice an' book a flight to Bermuda, kid."

"How can I fly to Bermuda? I'm only ten years old! I can't fly anywhere. I don't have permission and I don't have money!" Suddenly Sparky recalled the wad of bills his mom gave him on the way out the door.

"Look, kid, I don' know what to tell ya. All I know is that it did me a world o' good. It's nice to go to a place where they take care of everythin' for ya. Ya practically don' even hafta wipe yer ass. They do it for ya!" Sparky wondered how that would work. Would they have someone stationed in the bathroom, waiting for the guests to use the toilet? "Kid, the hotels they got there are outta this world." He kissed his fingertips and opened his hand like a flower. "I stayed at the Avanti Resorts and Hotel. Beautiful place! You wouln' believe how fancy it was."

Sparky perked up. "Did you say 'Avanti'?"

"Yeah. Why? You know the place, or somethin'?"

"That name is real familiar. I know it from somewhere."

"Yeah, well, you know what they got there? In the bathrooms, they got this thing they call a bidet. This thing– get this, kid– shoots water up yer ass when yer done takin' a dump. Can you believe it! Shoots water up yer ass, fer Chrissakes!"

Sparky pictured this man on the toilet and felt a little queasy. "Shoots water up your ass, eh?"

"Yep. Now, if that ain't fancy I don' know what is!"

64

Sparky was impressed. Not with how fancy the hotel was, but with how gross this man was. "Yeah, that's fancy, alright." Sparky was getting that odd sensation that he might be stuck talking to this guy for a while, and that he was already getting to know too much about him for comfort's sake. "Hey, mister, I better get going to school. I'm already late as it is and I don't want to be any later."

"Whaddya worried about, kid? There ain't no school to go to, anyways. You shoulda stayed in bed. But since ya didn't, here, lemme show ya somethin'." Francis reached into his back pocket and pulled out a big fat wallet. "I gotta coupla snapshots of the place. Here, look at this, kid."

Francis held out the photo so Sparky could see it. Sparky was expecting a clean and modern hotel, but what he saw perplexed him. In the photo was a smiling woman wearing sunglasses, standing in front of a ramshackle bungalow. The little building had badly weathered wood siding, its paint peeling, boards cracked and splitting. Sparky could clearly see broken window panes and, sprouting up in front of the bungalow, hip-high weeds. He pulled out another photo for Sparky to see and it was more of the same.

"Look at that gate, there. You see that? That's all 24karat gold leaf. And that's solid mahogany they used for those doors. You wouldn't believe it, kid."

"You're right, mister. I don't believe it." Sparky didn't know what to think. He really was uncomfortable now, thinking this guy was wacky. "Those are great pictures you've got there, but I've really got to get going."

"Wait, wait! Lemme show you the beach." Francis rummaged through his wallet for that particular shot as Sparky sidled off, waving his goodbye.

65

Chapter 5: The Lincoln-Mercury Dealership

Sparky wasn't sure what to do. P.S. 8 had been taken down and was being reconstructed. He looked around, but couldn't find any of his schoolmates. He wondered how they could tear a school down and not let the students know in advance what they should do or where they should report. He was convinced that all the other kids in the school had gotten to school and been rounded up and transported somewhere to spend the day. Sparky surmised that he had been left behind because he was so absurdly late that the teachers probably thought he was just plain absent. He had no choice, 'I'd better call my mom. Maybe she knows where they took everybody for the day. Maybe she can call the District Office to find out. On the other hand, she did seem kind of distracted this morning.' Sparky dug into his pockets for a dime, but he had no change. He still had the wad of bills, though, and started looking around for a place that could make change for him.

He thought about it for a second and walked back up the block to the businesses there. He wandered onto the car dealership lot and looked around for anyone who could help him. There were innumerable shiny new cars on the property. The large sign over the modern showroom said 'Dan Plotz Lincoln-Mercury', but the cars all seemed to be Pontiacs. He saw Grand Prixs, Firebirds, Bonnevilles and Catalinas, but no Continentals, Mark IIIs, Montereys or Cougars.

"Hello! Hello!" Sparky walked up to the door to the showroom, which was wide open. There was a man sitting at a gray metal desk. He was smoking a cigarette and pouring over some paperwork. "Hello, sir? Sir?"

"What is it, boy?" The man grumbled it without looking up from his papers. "How come you're not in school? Shouldn't you be in school?"

"They tore down my school. That's my problem. I need to call my mother."

"You can't do it here, boy. This is a Lincoln-Mercury dealership not a phone booth."

"Do you have a payphone here?"

"No." The man coughed a nice rumbling, wet, phlegmy cough; then took a long puff on his cigarette. He jogged the stack of bills on the desk and placed them in a two-hole punch. He finally looked up as he dropped the lever down on the stack of bills. "You still here, boy?"

Sparky got a good look at him. He was old– maybe fifty. His face was sunken and pitted and he had a neatly trimmed mustache. His ears were big, with long, saggy lobes and his eyes had big round bags under them. He had full head of a super healthy-looking, reddish brown hair, neatly combed. Funny thing, though, Sparky noticed he had dark brown and gray sideburns below that reddish hair.

"What happened to the paint store?"

"I don't know what you're talking about, sonny. We just opened. I don't know anything about a paint store."

"You didn't used to be a Lincoln-Mercury dealer."

The man looked confused. "What do you mean, 'used to be'? We've *always* been a Lincoln-Mercury dealership."

"Why does your sign say Lincoln-Mercury when you've got all Pontiacs?"

"You know what, boy, I don't have time for this tomfoolery. I've got these invoices to reconcile and you've got to get to school so you can grow up to be smart instead of a smart aleck." Smirking, the man turned back to his stack of papers and picked up his blue pencil.

"I'm not being a smart aleck! I just walked through the lot and there aren't any Lincolns or Mercurys out there!"

"Look here, sonny, if you don't clear out of here..." He stopped in mid-sentence to answer the phone. "Helllooo! Plotz Lincoln-Mercury, best deals in town. This is Gordon."

Sparky shuffled his feet and waited, looking out the showroom window, he spied a cat sitting on the roof of a Le Mans. He also noticed the reflection on the inside of the window of a man sitting with his arms folded at an empty desk in the showroom. The man was still– motionless, really. He was fat and colorless.

67

"No, I can't take delivery yet. No, I…Uh huh… That's right…By the 30th…This month…*This* month…Okay…Alright, bye-bye." He hung up. "Unbelievable. How do they expect me to sell cars when my lot is empty? What is the matter with those people?" Then, turning back to Sparky, "Are you still here?"

"I need to call my mom. They tore the school down last night."

"How come you didn't go with the rest of the kids on the buses? They had them lined up and down both sides of the street. You should have gotten on with them."

"I was late this morning and I guess I missed them. When I got here, they were already gone. Where did they take everybody?"

"Who the hell knows? You must've been pretty late, sonny. The last bus pulled out of here more than 20 minutes ago."

"I saw a whole bunch of school buses on Eighth Avenue a while ago. I didn't know. Listen, Mr. Gordon, can I use your phone to call my mom? I don't know what else to do. I don't know where to go."

Gordon sat back in the swivel chair and thought for a moment. "Alright, sonny, you can make one call. It's against Ford Motor Company rules, but I'm going to make an exception here since this is such an unusual situation, them tearing down the school and all."

"Thanks a lot, Mr. Gordon!" Sparky rushed to the phone, which was on Gordon's desk.

"I'll dial the number for you," Gordon insisted. "What's the number?"

"HU6-1088."

Gordon pressed a button on the phone and dialed while reciting the number out loud. Sparky waited. Gordon listened for a few seconds, then he dropped the handset back down.

"Busy. Sorry, sonny."

"Are you sure? Did you dial it right?"

"You saw me. Now clear out of here. I've got a lot of work to do."

"Can we try again in five minutes? Maybe she'll be off the phone by then."

Gordon rose from his chair and, with a hand on Sparky's back, walked him to the door. "Good luck, sonny." He turned back and returned to his desk. Sparky stood just outside the door wondering what he was going to do next. He turned back to look into the showroom. The quiet man was still sitting in his office chair. He hadn't moved. Gordon was back to shuffling the pile of papers on his desk.

Sparky looked across the lot, over the roofs of the cars and examined Wanderlust, next door. He'd never been in a travel agency and wasn't sure what kind of facilities they offer, but he was fairly sure they would have a phone and that he could have them call his mom. He knew the candy store had a payphone, but he couldn't go back there since walking out without paying for his pie. Wanderlust seemed like the best bet at the moment. Sparky made his way through the maze of Bonnevilles and Catalinas and back out onto the sidewalk. Sparky wondered momentarily about the preponderance of Pontiacs, but his thoughts returned to those of calling his mom. Sparky continued up the block toward the travel agency.

Chapter 6: Wanderlust

The entire office was plastered with full-color posters of every exotic destination you could imagine. There was a reclining Hawaiian girl, wearing a grass skirt and a lei, viewed from behind, in front of a stunning sunset over the Pacific and framed by palm trees. There was a demure Japanese girl, her hair done up in the traditional fashion, her lips painted tiny and red, wearing a kimono and holding some cherry blossoms, in front of a pagoda at the foot of a steep green mountain. There was a rapacious-looking black-haired senorita wearing an off-the-shoulder peasant blouse and colorful skirt, holding a red rose between her stark white teeth, a bullfight occurring in the background. There was a smiling, pink-cheeked blonde cowgirl, wearing cowboy boots and shorts, on a rearing bronco in front of cacti and buttes.

Etcetera.

Sparky marveled at these images and the ones of modern jet planes, pictured flying through the skies to drop off lucky tourists, their mouths– at least the men's– watering at the thoughts of the girls depicted in the other posters. TWA to Europe, Pan Am to Asia, Braniff to South America, BOAC, Alitalia, Swiss Air, Eastern, Northeast's Yellowbirds to Florida, and so forth. 'What a feast for the eyes!' Sparky thought.

The countertops and desks were festooned with pamphlets and brochures and fliers. There were stand-up displays showing cruise ships on the high seas and railroads on steep, mountain passes. There were gondolas and sampans and rickshaws and Vespa scooters.

"Hi there, young man! What brings you here? Looking to book a flight to Fiji?"

Sparky stepped forward, but kept gazing at all the travel posters everywhere on the walls and counters. "I came in to ask for help, ma'am."

"Are you in some sort of trouble?" The woman was very sharply attired and her blonde hair was cut, styled and sprayed so that it defied gravity.

"I have to call my mother and wondered if you could let me use your telephone." Sparky finally had his fill of the travel posters and focused

70

on the lady behind the desk.

"What's the matter? Are you lost?"

"No, but I don't know where to go! I got to school late this morning and they've torn it down and they bussed everybody to some other school. My mom got me out of the house so late this morning that I missed the buses. Now I don't know where I'm supposed to be."

"Well, young man, you *could* be anywhere." She gestured with a tilt of her head to the walls behind her. "You could go anywhere. You could see anything. You could do..." here she paused a second and leaned forward in her chair "...anything."

Sparky was impressed, but also a little scared. "I don't know what you mean exactly. What could I do?"

"What's your name, young man?"

"Sparky." Sparky waited, but the woman continued to stare at him, expecting more. "Donnelly. Sparky Donnelly."

"Well, Mr. Donnelly, it's a pleasure to meet you." She smiled slightly. "My name is Wanda Miles. I own this agency." She gestured at her desk nameplate and then laced her fingers together over her pelvis. "Tell me, Mr. Donnelly, did you *really* want to go to school today?"

Sparky didn't have to think about that question very long before coming up with the answer, but he was reluctant to go on record. He wondered if there was a 'right' answer. The woman waited.

"Today?"

"Yes. Did you want to go to school– today?"

Sparky smiled. "No, actually. I didn't."

"Does your mother know about the school's demolition? About the students being relocated?"

"I don't think so. She didn't say anything to me about it last night. This morning, she just sent me off like any day. Except..."

"She got you out of the house very late this morning, didn't she, Mr. Donnelly?" The woman rose from her chair and walked around her desk. Sparky was normally irked being addressed as 'Mr. Donnelly', because it was usually accompanied by a scolding. He didn't mind it from this woman, though, and he noticed that he didn't mind it.

"I left the house without breakfast, too! That never happens. Mom always feeds me before school."

"Have you eaten yet?"

"Yeah, that's the funny thing. She gave me money to buy breakfast and lunch with a lot of money! More than I'd need for one day!"

"Are you sure it's more than you'll need? Mr. Donnelly, did you consider that your mother might have wanted you to do more with the money than just buy lunch?"

Sparky thought for a moment. He thought he recalled his mom instructing him to buy something at the luncheonette, but he was no longer sure of anything. "She told me to buy something at the luncheonette." It was almost a question.

"How much would breakfast and lunch cost at the luncheonette?"

"A buck and a half? Maybe two bucks altogether."

"How much money did your mother press into your hand this morning?"

"Four hundred seventy one dollars." Sparky wasn't sure how he could know this amount. He hadn't counted the money, but somehow he knew it was $471.00. There was no question about it.

Wanda Miles stood near Sparky with her arms crossed under her breasts, but she was relaxed– not imposing. She spoke softly. "Mr. Donnelly, what do you think your mother wanted for you by giving you all that money?"

"I think she just made a mistake. I don't think she knew what she was doing. If she did, she wouldn't'a done it! We don't have a lot of money."

"Your mother doesn't normally make errors like that, does she?"

Sparky knew she already knew the answer.

"Does your mother love you?"

"Of course she does!"

"Does she take pains to make sure you are dressed properly?"

"Yes."

"Does she make sure you have what you need for school?"

"Yes. Except I left the house without my books this morning."

"Does she ensure that you have enough of the right foods to eat?"

"Yes."

"Mr. Donnelly, did your mother ever give you one hundred pencils to take with you to school? Did your mother ever put fifty pairs of socks on your feet?"

Sparky grinned. "Nah!"

"Did she ever pile four hundred seventy one hamburgers on your dinner plate?"

Sparky chuckled and shook his head.

"Has your mother ever fed you only one or two strands of macaroni? Or maybe only a couple grains of rice?"

"Of course not."

"Nor does she serve you twenty or thirty pounds of food for dinner. Correct?"

Sparky nodded.

"Doesn't your mother do things for you or give you something without your asking for it or your even knowing about it?"

"Yeah, I suppose."

"Doesn't your mother always seem to know what is best for you?"

"Yeah, she does."

Wanda Miles advanced half a step, placed her hand on Sparky's shoulder, and looked him straight in the eye. "Listen to me, young man. Your mother gave you that money this morning because she knew you would need it today."

Sparky wondered at that. "You mean she meant to? I don't know. She acted kinda funny. You mean she knew they tore the school down? But why four hundred seventy one dollars?"

"I don't know. I'm not your mother." She gestured toward her desk. "Why not try calling her?"

"Can I?"

Wanda Miles picked up the phone and turned it outward to face Sparky. She handed him the handset and stepped aside.

"You won't be able to reach her, though."

Sparky stopped in mid-dial. "How would you know that?"

The woman smiled slightly. "She's very busy."

Sparky continued to dial. The line was busy.

"How could she still be on the phone?" Sparky felt a little panicky. He also started to feel very much alone. He stood still, listening to the busy signal, wondering if his mom had gotten off the phone since he'd called before. 'What am I going to do? What if she *never* gets off the phone?' Sparky was close to crying. He knew his despair was overblown. After all, he lived only a couple of blocks away, but he couldn't help himself. It seemed so impossibly far at this moment.

"Listen to me, Mr. Donnelly. Your mother is busy. She knows you're safe. She knows you have enough money to get you through the day–whatever you may come up against. You have no schoolbooks to anchor you down."

"I thought I had them with me. I wonder what happened to them?"

"Do you know what I do here all day?"

"You book flights for people going on vacation?"

The woman walked back around her desk and sat down. She motioned for Sparky to take a seat, as well. "I help people in a special way. People like to be comfortable, Mr. Donnelly. People are also intrigued by adventure. People like to come home to the same house or apartment every evening, and to sit in the same couch or chair, next to the same companions and to watch the same man give the same news on the same television set, night after night. At the same time, they drool over commercials and advertisements calling them to visit exotic destinations and showing them how exciting and glamorous their lives can be." She gestured to the wall posters behind her. "Are you following me, so far? For people to live exciting and glamorous lives, Mr. Donnelly, they must give up being comfortable. That's where I come in. I provide people with the opportunity to be uncomfortable, and to sample an exciting and glamorous life for a while." She paused to light up a cigarette.

Sparky didn't know what to think. Being comfortable was a good thing, wasn't it? He always thought vacations and travel were supposed to be fun. This woman made it sound almost scary. He had a quick thought that he was glad that his parents never took him on a vacation anywhere. As she was lighting up her cigarette, though, Sparky had the chance to give it a second thought. He himself was one of those people intrigued by the possibility of a different or better life, full of excitement and adventure.

"Don't you have to have a lot of money to do that?"

"All the time, yes. Occasionally, no." She puffed and exhaled. "Occasionally is usually enough."

"But why would anybody want to go back to their normal life after the fun and exciting stuff?"

"Nobody wants to be uncomfortable all the time, and the shine of the fun and exciting wears off and gets dull if it's overused."

"Maybe I could get my parents to come here and get some fun and excitement." Sparky noticed the clock on the wall over Wanda Miles desk. School would have already started by now. "I better go home now. I'm worried about being out of school on a school day. I could get in trouble."

"It's been a pleasure, Mr. Donnelly."

Sparky turned and walked out of the agency.

Chapter 7: The Spartans

Sparky walked outside into the bright mid-morning sunshine and headed home. The street was very busy, filled with the noise of trucks and buses, delivering goods and people. It was a different crowd than Sparky was used to. Sparky saw the delivery trucks parked and double-parked along Eighth Avenue in front of the stores. Lift-gates were deployed, lowering stacks of cartons to waiting hand trucks. Side doors opened onto conveyors with hundreds of silver metal wheels. The conveyors bridged the sidewalk between the truck and the store's basement entrance and dozens of boxes rolled effortlessly from one to the other and into the waiting hands of stock boys.

Sparky was captivated by this bustling activity and since he was running so late and had no idea if he was even going to make it to school today, he decided to take the long way around to his house. He turned south on Eighth Avenue, detouring one block to B Street instead.

He didn't get down to B Street too often despite its proximity. B Street has fancier shops and boutiques– more for the adult shopper– and Sparky normally had no business there. For that reason alone the street held a fascination for him. His parents liked to say they lived in Sparta, but Sparky knew that was stretching things a bit. They really lived more in Hudson than Sparta. The more well-to-do kids in P.S. 8 lived in Sparta proper. This stretch of B Street, between Peace Boulevard and W. Sweeny Avenue, was lined with exclusive shops and upscale restaurants and ritzy co-op apartment buildings. The residents liked what they had and were diligent about preserving it. The streets were cleaned properly, the parking regulations were strictly enforced, there were no potholes, the police maintained a constant presence and no riff-raff was allowed. Sparta didn't want riff-raff passing through it– not even underground! When the City constructed the Number 12 and 13 subway lines, it was forced to divert them from the intended route under B Street because of the clout held by the neighborhood's Save Sparta Association. They were built in Hudson, under A Street, instead.

It was a fine day to stroll out of his way. The sky was blue, the cumulus clouds providing a pretty contrast. The air was dry and clean. Everything looked its best. The shops and boutiques along B Street were just opening their doors. The green grocer had his stands of fruits and vegetables out on the sidewalk. All the produce looked fresh and vivid in the sunshine. The old folks were going into and coming out of Robin's Diner, which was serving breakfast. The old guys were wearing hats, and the ladies were in dresses.

Two doors down, just past the law offices, was Atlantic Fish Market. In contrast to Mel's, this place didn't smell horrible. The sidewalk was dry and clean.

"You! Hey, young fella!"

Sparky turned to the voice. It was a policeman. Sparky hoped for a split second that the officer was talking to someone else, but he knew better. The officer approached him. He was a big man– maybe six-two– and he covered a lot of ground with each step as he twirled his nightstick by its thong. He wore his hat with the brim low over his eyes and he looked down on Sparky without tilting his head forward.

"Now, what have we here? You oughta be in school, young man, not roamin' the streets lookin' for trouble."

Sparky was quaking. "I was going home, officer."

The policeman took out his book and a pencil. "You were goin' home, eh? And where do you live?"

"Number Fifty St. Charles Street."

"Why are you goin' home? Feelin' sick or somethin'?"

"No, they tore my school down last night and I got in too late to be on the buses. They took everybody away on buses. I don't know where they went, so I'm going home to my mom."

"What school do you attend?" The policeman was jotting stuff down as he spoke.

"P.S. 8."

The officer stopped writing and glared at Sparky. "That's on 82nd and Ninth!"

The policeman's tone had changed drastically.

"What? Yeah, it is. What is it?" Sparky asked, suddenly alarmed.

"I *thought* you looked suspicious." The policeman closed his book and put it away. He reached for Sparky's wrist and quickly slapped on a pair of handcuffs. Sparky was aghast.

"What are you doing? What is it?"

"You're a little felon, aren't you? What were you up to before I stopped you?"

"I told the truth! They *did* tear down my school! I was late and I missed the buses! Honest!"

"That I believe, young man. You weren't going home, though, were you?"

"I *was* going home!"

The policeman chuckled. "You musta been takin' the scenic route, then, eh?"

Sparky began to understand. "As a matter of fact, I was! I figured I was so late, and my phone line was busy, so…" The policeman's loud laughter interrupted his explanation. "So, it was such a nice day…"

"'A nice day'!" The policeman repeated the words broadly. A small group of old people gathered to watch.

Sparky was getting frustrated.

"He's probably a shoplifter!," an old women called out from the crowd.

"Check his pockets, officer!" called another.

"I am not!" Sparky was really worried, now that he was being ganged-up on.

"I saw him steal a clock from Marsh's the other day!"

79

"He's the one who tried to break into Gus's Hi-Fi shop last Sunday!"

The policeman reassured the crowd and took control of the situation. "Now, now, everybody. Let's not let our imaginations run away with us. As far as I know, this lad is just a truant– probably a runaway– and he'll be taken downtown to be processed."

The policeman pressed his hand against Sparky's back and led him through the hostile crowd and toward a dark green panel truck. The lettering on the side read "POLICE DEPT CITY of HIGHBRIDGE JUVENILE DIVISION". There was heavy metal mesh over the windows of the back doors, and a large bolt locking mechanism to secure them.

The senior citizens they left behind commiserated with each other about the awful state of things and the lawless youth, running wild in the streets these days. They all agreed with each other and were satisfied that this young outlaw deserved to be getting what's coming to him.

"Why won't you believe me? I'm telling the truth."

"It's not my job to figure out who's lyin' and who's tellin' the truth? That's for the judge to decide." The policeman unbolted the back doors and helped Sparky up the step and inside.

"Can't we call my mom? *She'll* tell you I'm not a truant. She got me out of the house late this morning."

"Sorry, kid. You shoulda called her first thing instead a' wanderin' around where you don't belong, gettin' into mischief."

"I did try to call her, but the line was busy! Officer, can't you just drive me home? I live just a couple blocks away. She'll tell you."

The policeman stopped and thought for a moment. "I'll tell you what." He rubbed his jaw and glared down at Sparky. "You look like a beginner to me. I'm gonna cut you a break. I'm gonna drive by your house and if your momma's home and she backs up your story, I'll leave you with her and let her punish you." Sparky brightened. The policeman pulled Sparky back out of the wagon and slammed shut the doors. "Come ride up with me and point out your house." He stopped Sparky

80

before putting him in the front and glared down at him again. "I'm warnin' you, young man. If you try to pull any shenanigans, I'll make you regret it. You got me?"

Sparky simply nodded. He climbed into the passenger side door and sat while the policeman slid the door closed and locked it. Sparky was re- lieved that he was going home. He had been excited about exploring the neighborhood a little, but this day was shaping up so oddly that he concluded that he might be better off skipping it and rejoining his classmates– wherever they were.

The policeman climbed into the driver's seat and started up the engine. "St. Charles Street, eh?" He took off his patrolman's cap and placed it on the engine housing between the front seats. "Let's see if you're on the level, kid." He engaged the clutch and pulled out into traffic.

"Your momma get you off to school late a lot?"

"No, she never does. I've got great attendance," Sparky said with pride.

"Your dad at work, now?"

"Yeah, he works downtown."

"Got any other relatives at home?" The policeman pulled the wagon around a city bus and cut it off in the process of making his right turn. "Son of a bitch bus driver!" The bus stopped short and its driver honked long and hard. "So, *do* you?"

"No, just me and my parents."

"What's your mom look like? She got dark hair like you?"

"Yeah, she's got real dark hair."

"Is it long and wavy?"

"Kinda."

"Is she pretty?"

"I don't know. Why do you need to know that?"

"Well, I just want to make sure we don' miss her. I mean, she might be walkin' along the street, you know?"

"Oh, sure. Yeah, I guess she's pretty. I don't know."

"Does she have nice feet, kid?"

"What?!"

"Does she have long toes, a shapely arch? You know?"

"I don't know! They're my mom's feet! How's that going to help spot her in the street? She'd be wearing shoes!"

"Never mind. Never mind, kid. Just kiddin', anyway. Ha ha!"

They drove on in silence.

As they pulled around the corner and onto St. Charles, the policeman finally spoke up again.

"Where's– what did you say your house number is?"

"Fifty three. It's on the left side of the street, up a little more."

"I thought you said fifty, before. You tell me which house. I can't see the house numbers."

Sparky knew his house, but the buildings on the block looked different somehow. He couldn't recognize any of the houses. They looked familiar, but not quite. Sparky thought that maybe they were on the wrong block, but quickly remembered that he saw the policeman make the turn at St. Charles. He knew this was his block.

"Which house is it, kid? I can't see any addresses." The problem was that Sparky couldn't see them either. There either wasn't a number or there was a number, but they went by too fast to read it or there was something blocking the view of it. And none of the buildings looked quite right, anyway.

"Slow down a little. It's up here– no, wait– I think we passed it. We must've passed it. It's fifty– or is it fifty-three?"

"What are you tryin' to pull here? You sure you live on this street?"

"Yeah I live on this street! I've lived here my whole life! We passed it already. Can we go around the block again?"

The policeman made the requisite right turns and they swung around onto St. Charles Street again. "Go slower this time. I couldn't read the addresses before."

"I'm goin' eight miles an hour. That should be slow enough, kid." Try as they might, they could not spot any of the house numbers on St. Charles Street. None of the houses looked right to Sparky, and by the time they could read an address clearly, it read "111 St. Charles". The policeman lost his patience and Sparky was frantic. "That's it! We're goin' downtown, kid."

"Wait! Can't we go around the block again?"

"What for? You've been lyin' the whole time. You don't live here. There isn't even a Fifty-three St. Charles Street, for chrissakes!" The policeman shook his head in disgust. "I don't know why I thought you were worth a second chance."

"I *do* live on St. Charles!" Sparky was despondent. The policeman maneuvered the panel wagon through the mid-morning traffic, made his way east on Greene Street and turned left onto Neptune Avenue, pulling up right behind a BP tanker truck.

Chapter 8: Stopping at Munchies

"I don't get it. I couldn't see my house when we drove past it."

"Save it, kid. I've heard 'em all."

The policeman muscled the old panel wagon through the chaotic mid-morning traffic, around the double-parked cars and delivery trucks, past work crews patching the street or working in an open manhole, and blowing red lights when traffic permitted. Sparky would have thought it was cool if he wasn't so worried. He was a little concerned about being seen by someone he or his mother knew, but after the policeman got a few blocks south on Neptune Avenue, they were in foreign territory and *that* particular concern disappeared.

"I'm telling you the truth! I *do* live on that block. I don't get it. Maybe it looks different from a passing car. I don't get it."

"Kid, I like you an' all, but you're really a bad liar. I've had six year olds that have given me better stories. I had a second-grader once– pretty girl, too– who told me he– hold on, I'm gonna try to make this light– who told me she was running away from home because her father was molesting her ever since he was laid off from the Wonder Bread bakery." The panel wagon careened through the cross traffic while the policeman steered with his left hand and pressed down on the horn with his right.

"What happened?"

"Huh? What happened to what?"

"To the girl? The second-grader?"

"We brought her back home."

"What about her father?"

"He didn't hesitate a minute– pulled her panties down and spanked her."

"No, I mean she said he was molesting her. What about that?"

84

The policeman scrunched up his face. "He wasn't molesting anybody. He was okay. Poor guy got laid off 'cause the boss had it in for him. He was lookin' for a job when we rang the bell."

"Did you ask her mom if it was true?"

"About bein' laid off? We had no reason to doubt him."

"No, about her being molested and stuff."

"Boy, you're fixated on that! Aren'tcha? Ha ha!"

"But, what about it? Didn't you try to find out, just in case?"

"I can't remember why we didn't ask her mom." The policeman gazed off into the ether. "I don' think she was home. That's right, I remember now. She worked two jobs– first and swing shifts– so she wasn' gonna be home all day. I really felt bad for that guy. That girl's parents loved her very much. The dad was suffering a lot being home instead of working. Poor guy looked like hell: hair uncombed, unshaved, wearin' just a robe an' slippers; Mom out of the house all day, workin' to keep a nice safe place for their daughter. That girl jus' didn' appreciate how lucky she was! She was jus' tryin' to get attention, I say. She'd been talkin' a lot at school it turns out. She'd been bad-mouthing her dad for months to anybody'd who'd listen. Her friends an' her teacher. He was another nice old guy. Been teachin' thirty or forty years. A widower– no, not a widower– his wife's all crippled, or something. He didn't know what to do with her either. He'd keep her after school as a punishment."

"Did she stop then?"

"Nah, nothin' worked with her. After a week of stayin' an hour after all the others had gone home, she started accusing the *teacher* of the same thing! The Assistant Principal had a go at her also, but she didn't improve a bit. Just got worse. She started accusing him, too. That girl's nothin' but trouble I tell you. Pretty as a picture, with those sweet eyes of hers, but nothin' but trouble. I'd say she got off light with just a bare-bottom spanking! If she was my daughter, there's no tellin' what I'd do to her."

85

"They tell us in school not to let anybody touch us on our private parts. But they don't mention anything about your parents touching you."

"That's good they teach you that stuff. Anybody touches you, you make sure you tell somebody right away, kid!"

"Yeah."

"Listen, kid, I'm gonna take a little detour over to Munchie's Donuts. It's gettin' toward my break. You don't mind, eh?"

"I guess not."

The policeman swung the wagon around the corner at Vestor Road, cutting off a bus that was trying to pull out into traffic, and headed east to Third Avenue.

"You eat breakfast, kid?"

"Sure I did. I had blueberry pie for breakfast. Or was it cherry?"

"You sure you ate breakfast? You can tell me the truth. A lot of runaways don't eat regular. It's nothin' to be ashamed of."

"I told you, I'm not a runaway!"

The wagon clipped a grocery store delivery guy riding a bicycle.

"You know, I had a kid once– younger than you– what are you? Ten?"

"I think you hit that guy."

"I did not! I don't go around hitting kids!"

"No, the delivery guy on the bike! He fell off his bike back there."

"Who, the P.R. with the red cap?"

"Well, he doesn't have his cap anymore, but yeah, him."

"Anyhow, this kid told me that he was– get this– 'an emancipated minor'. 'Emancipated minor', for chrissakes! Ha ha! Said he worked for

one of the big financial firms downtown as 'an analyst'. He was eight
years old, for cryin' out loud! Ha ha! Now he was funny as hell. I liked
him a lot! He bent my ear all the way to processin' about the stock
market and the prime rate! Oh, boy! He turned out to be a wacko,
though. Told the judge his mother and father beat him and burned him.
Can you imagine? His own mother and father! Showed the judge all
these bruises and scars. The judge was a little concerned, but the parents explained how those things happened. As clever a liar as he was,
turns out he couldn't put one foot in front of the other without fallin'
down an' hurtin' himself. He was funny, though. Boy, oh boy. Told me
he had a degree in economics from Warfield School– or Warford or
whatever– in Philly."

"What happened to him?"

"Who knows? You like donuts, kid?"

Sparky nodded silently.

"This place has the best in the whole city. They make their own, right
in the back."

Sparky thought of the back of the candy store.

"It's across the street from the bus garage. That's why the bus drivers
are so damn fat! Ha ha! You know where that is, right?"

"I don't think so. I've never been in this neighborhood, except passing
through by subway, maybe."

"You've never seen the Third Avenue bus garage? Looks like a castle
with towers and those little portholes they shoot arrows out of.
Pzzsshheewww!!" He took both hands off the steering wheel and
mimed shooting arrows at the other vehicles. "Ha ha! Oops! Almost hit
that Buick. Ha ha!" The policeman grabbed the steering wheel with
both hands and steadied the wagon, pulling up to a red light at the corner of 60th and Vestor.

"Hey kid, you like the knights?"

"The team? Not much."

"No, the real knights. You know– knights and armor and stuff? Damsels and shields, spears. You know?"

"Sure, I guess so. Why?"

The policeman was somber for a change. "I always wanted to be one. You know, dressed in armor." The truck behind them honked.

"The light's green, officer."

The policeman leaned out the door and yelled an obscenity back at the truck, then he turned back to the road ahead and put the wagon in gear. "Can you believe this fu-u- this clown?! Anyway, as I was sayin' before I was interrupted," he flipped the truck the bird, "I always figured I'd end up a knight, all dressed up in chain mail and with the helmet and all."

"Why'd you wave at that guy?"

"I didn't wave." He glanced over at Sparky before he continued. "As it turns out, I am a sorta knight. I don' save damsels. Instead, I save kids in danger. See how life can turn out, kid?"

"Yeah, and instead of a visor pulled down over your eyes, you pull your cap down over your eyes!"

"Yeah, that's right. You got the idea, kid! And this here's my shield." He tapped his badge.

"And this is your horse!" Sparky said brightly, gesturing to the boxy interior of the beat-up panel wagon. 'What a nut!' Sparky thought.

"Here's Munchie's!" The policeman pulled in behind a Mercury Monterey standing in the bus stop and laid on his horn. "Get that thing outta there, pal or I'll have it towed! Son of a bitch." The driver started the car right up and pulled out into traffic without looking, narrowly missing a Chevy van. "These people can't drive worth a damn. All right, kid, here we are. Break time! You like jelly donuts?"

"Yep."

"I'll get you a jelly donut and a cup o' coffee. You take milk and sugar?"

"Officer, do they have a bathroom in there? I haven't gone since I left my house and my mom got me out before I could go one last time."

"I dunno…It's kinda against the rules, you know."

"You could stand outside while I go."

"Okay, kid, but if you try to pull a fast one, It'll weigh heavy against you when you get downtown. Come on."

Sparky stepped down from the wagon and looked around. The bus garage loomed across the street just as the policeman described it– like a massive castle. Sea green buses were lined up outside the gaping entranceways, each having finished their morning rush hour service. Bus drivers in gray uniforms milled about, chatting to each other, sharing stories from the morning runs and laughing together. Sparky wondered what the life of a bus driver would be like. They seemed to have a lot of fun together. He recalled bus drivers he had ridden with who had chatted jovially with passengers. He also recalled drivers who were dour and nasty and he wondered about them. Were they the exceptions? Were they the drivers who he saw enjoying life at this moment across Vestor Road?

Munchie's was a very busy place. The door was propped open and people and bus drivers alike were passing in and out of the establishment. It smelled really good. The aroma was a combination of fried dough, sugar and coffee.

"C'mon, kid." The policeman took Sparky by the arm and led him in.

"Hiya, Pyles! Who's the wayward tike today?"

"Oh, he's a kid I picked up lookin' for trouble on B Street."

"That's a tough neighborhood for a street urchin to be messing around in." He looked at Sparky while he said it, and he said it like a well-practiced lecture.

"Yeah, well, I think this kid is new to this game. Couldn' even give me a decent story. He claimed to live on St. Charles, but when I drove by the block, he couldn' even point out his own house." He glared down at Sparky from beneath the low brim of his cap, but the severity he had earlier was gone now.

"Tsk, tsk," the guy working behind the counter replied. "Whaddaya want today, chief? Jelly and joe?"

"Make it two– for me an' the kid. He's gotta use the head, do you mind?"

"Nah, go 'head. Milk and sugar for both?"

"Right." The policeman bent down and unlocked the cuffs around Sparky's wrists. "Over here, kid."

Sparky was grateful to have the cuffs off, even if only for a few moments. The door to the sole restroom in the place was unmarked and ajar. He opened the door and stepped inside. The door had regular hinges and stayed open, so Sparky pulled it closed behind him. The bathroom had no urinal– just a toilet and sink. The seat on the toilet was up and Sparky noticed the piss splattered on the rim of the bowl and on the floor around it. He opened his fly and aimed. He couldn't pee.

He wondered all sorts of things as he waited for the flow to start. He wondered if he was nervous, being in a strange bathroom in a strange neighborhood. He wondered if having someone waiting for him just outside the door was inhibiting him. He noticed all the hustle and bustle of the shop just on the other side of the door. He noticed and listened to the sound of the sink's leaky faucet. He saw the green stain below the faucet, caused by the water running all the time. He saw the writing on the tiles and on the walls above the tiles. One bit read: 'if you can still read this you aint been jerkin off enough.' Another bit read: 'nigger's suck my dick.' 'That's a pretty nasty thing to say,' he thought.

There was a knock on the door. "Must be a helluva piss! C'mon, kid! Morey's just about got our order ready!"

"Be right out!"

One bit of writing really caught his attention, though. It was a phone number– *his* phone number! 'What the hell?!' It was written in blue ink right next to a poem, written in a different hand and having something to do with "shits" and "tits" and "blow" and "grow." Sparky stared at his own phone number, certain he was misreading it, but it persisted in looking like his home phone number. 'Who would've written *that* here? Nobody knows me here.' Sparky thought momentarily about trying to wipe the number off the wall, but the dried snot that peppered the walls around it convinced him to leave it alone. He gave up trying to pee, since he no longer felt the need anyway. So he zipped up and opened the door behind him.

Sparky expected to see the policeman right there, but he was gone.

Chapter 9: A Trip to the Post Office

"There you are, young fella! Here's your order. That'll be a dollar-five, with tax."

"Where's the police officer?"

The guy behind the counter made a face and shrugged. "Who's 'the police officer'? A dollar-five, son."

Sparky looked around again just in case he had missed him the first time. He double-checked the people seated at the three small tables. They were bus drivers. The other patrons were bus drivers and a couple of gray-haired old ladies. "The policeman that brought me in here."

"I didn't notice him. A dollar-five. C'mon, son, we're busy this morning."

"You called him 'Officer Pyles'!"

"I don't care if I called him 'Officer Preparation H'! Speaking of which, you're getting to be a pain in my ass! I don't know who you're talking about. So, what's it gonna be? Dollar-five or out. You got it or not?"

Sparky gave up arguing and dug out a five dollar bill.

"There you go– three-ninety five is your change. Come again. Next! Ma'am? You're next"

Sparky took his bag and cup and wandered through the open doorway and back into the bright sunshine. The bus stop was empty. There was no police wagon, no double-parked car, not even a bus. Sparky did a 360-degree turn and scanned the intersection, the sidewalks and looked down Vestor Road and Third Avenue. There was a small triangular park where Third and Vestor and 60th crossed each other, so he made his way across the street to sit down on one of the benches and figure out what to do.

Highbridge is famous for its innumerable angled streets and avenues and the resulting triangular islands that, many of which, eighty years ago, served as watering stations for horses and have almost all since been converted to a modern function. Some of the smallest were appropriated by the Police Department and are used as permanent police booths for patrolmen or traffic control (much needed when several streets come together at odd angles). Some of the larger parcels were sold to real estate developers. The eight Great Wall Chinese Palace restaurants are all built on such triangular parcels. However, the vast majority of mid-sized plots were donated to the public in the 1930's in the form of small sitting parks. Each is outfitted with at least half a dozen shade trees, small patches of grass, park benches, and– most appropriately considering its original function– a drinking fountain. Almost all of them are nameless, except where neighborhood organizations have commemorated some local dignitary or war hero.

Sparky looked into the bag at the huge jelly donut with its granular sugar coating. The policeman was right about Munchie's. They made impressive-looking donuts. Sparky pulled the donut partly out of the bag, enough to start biting into it. It was still a bit warm from the oven. He pulled away the wax paper and bit into the part with the dark red jelly seeping out. He pondered his options while he chewed. He figured he should probably make his way back home, but he was enjoying sitting in this little oasis in the midst of the traffic and noise rushing around him. He could feel the periodic rumble of the Number 9 subway line below the street and he listened to the constant moaning and wailing of the passing of the herd of buses on Third Avenue. There was a lot going on here– much more than in his own enclave only a mile or two northeast.

'This *is* a good donut! Maybe Mom and Dad would come here some time.'

Aside from the bus garage, there was a lumber yard across the street. Men were loading an open-bed truck with long planks of wood. A forklift could be seen shuttling back and forth deeper within the yard. There was a U.S. Post Office a couple of doors from the corner. The building looked old– maybe built before World War II. The greenish metal letters read: UNITED STATES POST OFFICE BELMONT STATION. Across the way, on 60th Street, was Wilhelm's Used Cars. They had streamers all over the lot– the type that have hundreds of colored plastic triangular banners flapping in the breeze.

Sparky was enjoying his donut immensely, but he wasn't really hungry and could only manage to consume about half of it before he felt stuffed. They really were man-sized– maybe bus-sized– donuts. 'Geez, no wonder the bus drivers get so fat off these things,' he thought. There were a couple of other people in the park. There was a bus driver reading the newspaper and there was an old guy wearing an overcoat and listening to a transistor radio. Of course, there were pigeons. One of them was performing that mating dance where they puff up their neck feathers and spread their tail feathers and make themselves look unkempt in order to attract a mate. It seemed to not be working on his target pigeon. She kept scurrying away.

Sparky removed the lid from his cup of coffee and tried a sip. He'd had coffee at home with his parents a few times. He liked his coffee and tea with lots of sugar and milk. The donut shop coffee was pretty strong and did not have as much milk and sugar as he would have liked. It tasted bitter– especially after eating that sweet donut– but he took it like a man, figuring this is the way men like their coffee. He enjoyed sitting on the bench in this strange neighborhood, drinking coffee like a man. He wondered if the cause of much of his malaise might be that he's still stuck being a kid. Grown-ups seem to have more freedom. That policeman hadn't a care in the world. He came and went as he pleased and paid hardly any attention to the rules. Sparky laughed when he thought of the policeman knocking that guy off his bike. 'What a nut! He didn't care about that guy at all.'

"Excuse me, young man." A bony, white-haired old woman had walked up to him. "I wonder if you would like to help me with something."

"What sort of thing, ma'am?" Sparky gave her the once-over. She was at least sixty years old– maybe as old as eighty-five. She had very pale skin and round blue-gray eyes that bulged a bit out of their sunken sockets. The whites of her eyeballs were pinkish-yellow, typical of old people. Her mouth was almost lipless and she had deep diagonal creases dropping down from both corners. Sparky didn't like her. He was uncomfortable around old people, in general.

"Oh, so respectful! That's very rare these days." She was wearing a plaid wool coat and a beige head scarf. "Well, young man, I can plainly see that you are the right man for the job. I'm so pleased to have found you here."

"What do you need me to do?"

"You see, I am on the way to the Post Office, which is right there." She pointed a bony, blue-white finger up Third Avenue. "I have been sent some parcels through the post by a distant relative. You see, I have the slip of paper here..." She rummaged through her tiny pocketbook. "Ah, here it is. No, wait, this isn't it." She renewed her rummaging. "Ah, here we are. Yes. You see, this slip advises me to pick up the parcels at this Post Office." She unfolded it and showed it to Sparky, who was less than concerned about the notice.

"You need me to help you carry the packages?" He was willing to help, but he started to suspect that this might take a lot longer than necessary.

"Why, yes! Aren't you the cleverest young man! That's it exactly."

"Come on, ma'am. Let's go over and pick them up before they get crowded." He figured that would get her motivated to stop talking and start walking.

"Splendid. Let me just..." She painstakingly refolded the slip of paper and replaced it in her handbag, carefully shutting it, then refastening it. "There we are. Come along, young man." They crossed Vestor Road, which can be tricky and dangerous for the careless.

"What is your name, young man?"

"Sparky."

"That's a fine name, indeed! It suits you to a tee. Yes." There was a long pause. "My name is Mrs. Piper."

"Nice to meet you, ma'am."

"You have no idea what a great help this is to me, Sparky. I'm afraid I'm getting a little arthritic and it's very difficult for me to manage lugging packages back from the Post Office."

"What are you expecting?"

"Something very special. Something very fine, indeed! A thing so exquisite it almost defies description!"

95

"Sounds fancy. Who sent it to you?"

"My son."

"I thought you said it was a distant relative?"

"He is indeed quite distant. He lives in Seattle, Washington."

"What did he send you? Jewelry? A knick-knack or something?"

"He is a structural engineer. We shall see."

They walked into the Post Office as Sparky held the heavy bronze door for Mrs. Piper. The building was old, built before the Depression. It was mainly brick, with some limestone accents on the façade. The interior was less impressive. Except for the deep-colored wood and the clerks' cages, the interior was a completely utilitarian shell. The walls were painted in the usual two-tone institutional scheme: semi-gloss dark green up to about the five foot level, then a sickly-pale, flat green paint above. The high ceiling was gloomy above the hanging globes. There were few people in the lobby presently. Of those few, two were standing at cages and one was waiting on line. Two people were filling out forms at the counter under the towering windows. Everyone in there was old. The men wore overcoats and hats and the ladies all wore coats and scarves.

"Now, let's see...I do believe we should stand here...yes." The two people at the cages were finished and two tellers called 'Next!' at the same time. Mrs. Piper got excited and hurried over to the nearest open cage as quickly as her bony ankles could get her there. Sparky was thankful there wouldn't be a delay. He didn't know what he was going to do next, but he wanted to get started on it. Sparky hung back away from the cage and waited. The clerk took the slip of paper from Mrs. Piper once she had finished fishing it out of the pocketbook, and unfolded it. He wordlessly disappeared to the back of the vast building.

Sparky waited for a moment, then, having gotten restless, he wandered over to the wall displaying a collage of notices and charts. There were postage rate charts, reminders to 'Always use zip codes!' with Zippy, the Postman, hurrying along with his pouch, and there were the circulars with the Most Wanted criminals in the country. Sparky gravitated toward the Most Wanted posters.

There was George Horace Axelrod, wanted for murder. He had multiple aliases, such as John Harvey Axelrod and Horace Axell and a couple nicknames, including 'The Axe' and, inexplicably, 'Lulu.' 'I'd *hate* to be called Lulu! That's a homo name.'

Then there was Arnold Ames Worth, wanted for bank robbery and sodomy. Sparky wondered what sodomy was. He assumed it was some kind of conspiracy, having to do with the bank robbery or perhaps the subsequent getaway. This Arnold Ames Worth also had an alias, Francis Key, and nicknames, including "Aimless Arnold," "Arnold Worthless" and "Three-Legged Arnie". Sparky smiled, he liked the last one. It conjured up images.

At the far right on the wall of posters was one of a pale-faced old woman with bulging eyes and deep creases in the corners of her mouth. He turned and looked back toward Mrs. Piper. She was looking at him from in front of the clerk's cage and she was smiling slightly. Sparky looked back at the poster. 'Could it be her?' He wondered for a moment as he read the information on the poster. She was listed as Harriet Armstrong Pepper, 79 years old, white hair, 105 lbs., blue eyes. He scrutinized the photo closely. He glanced back to the cage. She was either looking at him again or still looking at him, and smiling slightly. Sparky read the description on the poster. Harriet Armstrong Pepper was wanted for kidnapping, attempted murder, bigamy and sodomy. Sparky refigured what he had thought sodomy was. Clearly there was no kind of bank robbery involved here. Perhaps it was a general term covering a multitude of different kinds of getaways. He couldn't be sure and didn't want to sound dumb, so he dismissed the possibility of asking someone. Sparky remembered comedians getting laughs talking about bigamy on TV, so he wondered why the FBI would want Harriet Pepper for it.

He looked back at the photo. It was a very clear photo, but he could not be certain it was the face of Mrs. Piper he was looking at. Her expression was different. The name was almost the same, but the aliases–Reppep, Pfeiffer, which Sparky pronounced in his head like 'feefer'–sounded nothing to him like Piper or Pepper. Her physical description was a match, but there are certainly many old, blue-eyed women staggering around the world. And how could a seemingly frail old lady like Mrs. Piper kidnap someone? A good kick in her bony, fragile shin would thwart any kidnapping attempt even if it *didn't* quite break the leg.

The information about her whereabouts seemed a contra-indication for Mrs. Piper. The last known address for the woman in the poster was St. Louis, Missouri. However, the attempted murder charge was for something that occurred in Tacoma, Washington. 'Didn't Mrs. Piper say that her son lived in Seattle, Washington?' Certainly that weighed against her and seemed suspicious.

Sparky was baffled. He wondered if he should be scared of her or not. She acted harmless enough, but he'd been taught to not trust strangers. If she was the woman on the poster, then why did she walk into the post office without a care? In the end, Sparky decided to do nothing and play it out. He figured he could always run away if he had to. There was no doubt that she could not follow him on foot.

Mrs. Piper was now finished at the clerk's cage. She walked up to Sparky and she handed him two absurdly miniscule parcels that weren't any larger than a pack of gum.

"Here you are, young man! Please be a dear and help me lug these packages home. It's such a frightfully long walk. I just know I could not manage."

Sparky looked at the two packages in his hand. They were so small that the postage stamp on each was actually wrapped around the corner of the box. He hefted one to assess its mass. It couldn't have weighed more than a few ounces.

"Are you sure you need help to carry these home, ma'am?"

"Oh, *my*, yes! There's no possible way I could manage such a burden!" Suddenly she looked alarmed. "You're not withdrawing your offer to assist me, are you? Why, I don't know what I would do at this juncture if you did."

"Oh, no, no, no! No, no. I just thought that– I figured– you know..." Sparky held the parcels up triumphantly. "See? Here, I got 'em, ma'am! Let's get these home before something happens to them." He cocked his head toward the doors.

"Yes! Excellent! We shall do so! Now, let me see..." Mrs. Piper methodically opened her pocketbook again and painstakingly removed her house keys and then replaced them, closing the snap. "Okay, very good. I have my keys. I just wanted to make certain that I did have them. Right! We're all set, then?"

"Yes, ma'am." Sparky was ready to crawl out of his skin, but he was taught to always be respectful to his elders.

"Come along, young man. We'll make haste so that you are not kept from your own business any longer than necessary."

Sparky opened and held the door for Mrs. Piper as she slowly made her way out of the Post Office and onto the sunny street. They walked to the corner along Third Avenue.

"Where do you live, anyway, ma'am?"

"I live on Eden Street, just off of the corner of Tillotson."

"Where's that?" Sparky had never heard of Eden Street and was worried that it might be far away.

"Why, it's in Linden Farms, young man. It's only twelve– no, thirteen– blocks from here."

"We're taking the bus, right?"

"Oh *my*, no! I couldn't possibly afford the bus fare! They've raised the fare again and you know that we old folks are on fixed incomes, young man. We must walk. Besides, the bus stops two blocks from my building. You shouldn't mind the walk, young man. You're young and strong and sound of limb."

Sparky calculated Mrs. Piper's velocity and multiplied it by the number of blocks and added the extra wait time at each corner (Mrs. Piper wouldn't cross on a blinking signal) and he blanched.

"Oh, I don't mind walking, ma'am. It's just– well, we could save some time– and my– I need to get to school. I'm late this morning and I might get in trouble."

"Oh, well. We can't have that, can we? We'll just hurry right along, then, so we don't make you late." Mrs. Piper took on the air of a hurrying person and the countenance of eager determination, but her pace stayed the same. Slow as hell.

"Ma'am, why don't we take the bus? I guarantee we'll save twenty minutes, at least. And they haven't raised the fare. See?" He pointed to a bus stop sign at the corner. "It's still twenty-five cents. And here comes another bus." Actually, the buses were passing in a continuous stampede of sea green and clouds of dark brown diesel exhaust.

"Now, don't you worry, young man, I doubt very much that we'll save any time at all by taking the bus. They invariably get stuck in terrible traffic jams and break down and suffer all manner of problems. You'll see, we will probably get to our destination faster than the bus would have transported us. Now, if we can only get across this intersection... Oh, my, we've missed the 'Walk' signal again. It has started blinking 'Don't Walk'. We'll just have to wait."

"We *can* make it. Come on!" Sparky was frantic.

"Oh, no, young man. I'm sorry, but I'm just not as young as I used to be." Mrs. Piper chuckled. "My legs just won't carry me as fast as they did when I was your age. Here, young man. Step back up on the curb. You mustn't put yourself in danger of being struck by an automobile. That just won't do."

Sparky could hardly hear Mrs. Piper's words over the roar of two consecutive Third Avenue buses accelerating through the changing light.

They waited.

"What if we take a bus and just get off if it gets stuck in traffic? Huh?" Mrs. Piper either did not hear the question or chose to ignore it.

"Oh, my! Look at that man! He just threw that wrapper right down onto the street! And look, there is a trash can right there on the corner!" She turned to the man. "Young man!"

Sparky looked at the guy she was now talking to. He was a slob. His hair was greasy and his shirt was dirty. He looked like he stank, though he was downwind, so that could not be verified.

100

"Young man, that sort of behavior is not acceptable. You will please pick up that wrapper and put it where it belongs."

The man glanced calmly at her, then ignored her.

"Young man, do you hear me? You will please pick up that wrapper and put it *where it belongs*."

"Lady, if I put it *where it belongs*, you won' like it one bit! I guarantee." He chuckled at his witty retort. "You pick it up. You probably need the exercise."

"Oh! You are an impudent scoundrel! You should feel ashamed to talk to someone in that fashion! Shame on you!" Sparky thought he could detect a little color in her face.

"Why don' you crawl back inta yer grave, old lady." He chuckled again, but not as light-heartedly as the first time.

"You are an undisciplined *beast*! Someone should administer a good, sound spanking! How can you speak in that fashion?!"

"I bet you'd like to give me a spankin'! Ha ha! Maybe I oughtta give your old ass a 'good, sound spankin'.' Bet you'd like me to, huh?"

Sparky was enjoying the scrap. He'd fantasized about talking to someone rudely, just as this guy was now talking to Mrs. Piper.

Mrs. Piper was flabbergasted. "Well! I *never*!"

"Well, you *oughtta*! Ha ha! At least once before you croak! Ha ha! Hey, you better take grandma home, sonny, before she takes a heart attack. Ha ha! Look at her. Her face is all red. She's gonna get a stroke! Ha ha!"

The man was still looking at Mrs. Piper as he stepped off the curb and was run down by a dark green Pontiac Catalina.

Chapter 10: The Bus to Freedom

The guy went down so fast that it seemed to Sparky as if he disappeared rather than fell. The double-thud of the car's impact and the man's contact with the asphalt was nauseating to Sparky and he wondered momentarily if he'd lose the donut and coffee. The Catalina hesitated almost imperceptibly for a split second before it continued on its way in an unhurried manner.

"Well, now, that takes care of that. The light is green, Sparky. We should hurry or we'll miss it."

"Wait a second! That guy's bleeding!" Mrs. Piper was already crossing the street. Sparky looked back to the curb as he followed her. "Are we gonna just leave him there? Maybe we should call the police or an ambulance!" The guy's body was slumped up against the curb in the filthy gutter, his face pressed down in the gray-olive muck.

Without turning back, she gave her reply. "I am not at all concerned about that man. He can *certainly* take care of himself. Perhaps he can spank the automobile that ran him over, do you think?"

"We shouldn't leave him in the gutter like that! He'll get run over again!"

"Young man, I have no intention of picking up other people's trash. It is the responsibility of the driver of that sedan to see to it that our former acquaintance is appropriately disposed of. Hurry along! The 'Don't Walk' sign is blinking already."

Sparky looked back one last time and could see an old Plymouth Valiant rush past the man, causing the wrapper he had discarded blow up and come to rest on his back pocket. Sparky also noticed a city street sweeper motoring through the intersection, taking advantage of the newly-green traffic light and wondered if the driver would see the body and avoid it, or if the sweeper would pull the guy into the steel brushes with all the rest of the debris. He didn't stay to watch.

The pair walked on down Third Avenue at the old woman's old woman pace. They didn't exchange a word for a couple of minutes. Sparky had an opportunity to really look around at the neighborhood. Technically, they were still in Vestor, but as they approached the great and vast Aqua Boulevard, they would be entering the neighborhoods known as Belmont and the adjacent Linden Farms. These areas used to be dotted with the "country" homes of the rich and powerful in nineteenth-century Highbridge. When the City grew up and burst out to north and east of its original confines, the rich and powerful moved on to vaster and more remote estates, leaving Highbridge to those who couldn't afford a better life and the businesses for whom those people worked.

The businesses here were different from what he saw close to home. The offices were more professional looking and the buildings that housed them were taller and more imposing in design. There were law offices and fancy-looking super markets and towering apartment houses. The sidewalks were wide and the people more splendidly attired. It was obvious to Sparky that there was more money here. The shoe stores looked exclusive, the Marseilles Hair Salon they just passed was certainly fancy.

"Young man, I hope you learned a valuable lesson from that whole unfortunate affair."

"What's that, ma'am?"

"Always look both ways before crossing a street. You do not want what happened to that ruffian to happen to you."

"No, ma'am." Sparky wasn't sure whether that was the quintessential lesson to be learned from what just transpired, but he declined to pursue it any further and he agreed with her assessment.

On the next block was the Continental movie palace. The gigantic marquee was unlit in the glare of the mid-morning sun, but Sparky could imagine its sequentially-blinking lights and the fluorescent glow behind the letters (currently displaying '2001: A Space Odyssey 9th Big Week!') and the red and gold neon letters above, spelling out 'CON-TINENTAL' in script. There was an old black guy sweeping the sidewalk out front.

Two kids were in front of the candy store next door to the Continental. Sparky thought he recognized them from one of the slow classes in his school, but he wasn't positive. The two were standing very close and looking at something between them, so Sparky couldn't get a clear view of either boy's face. He wondered why they wouldn't be in school and why they were here, in this neighborhood. He wished Mrs. Piper would walk a bit faster so he could hurry up and get a good look, but the woman continued at her pace. Just as they got close enough to the boys, they turned abruptly and darted into the candy store. Sparky peered into the dark store through the doorway as he passed, but couldn't see much and couldn't make out any faces.

"Somebody you know, young man?"

"Huh? Oh, I thought those kids go to my school, but I'm not sure."

"Speaking of which, why are you not in school today? I am not aware of any holidays today."

"No, it's not a holiday. It's kinda a long story. I left the house a little late this morning..." Sparky launched into an abridged account of his reasons for not being in school. "...and I was wondering if I should just go home when you came up to me and asked for my help."

"Who knows where you are, young man?"

"I guess nobody does. I couldn't get ahold of my mom. I suppose no-body does– except the policeman might be looking for me. I'm not even sure about that, though." Mrs. Piper smiled.

They walked the block between 69th Street and Aqua Boulevard, pass-ing the 69 Lounge and Aztec Lanes bowling alley. Sparky felt in his pocket for the tiny parcels and pulled them out to take a look at them again. He was startled at their size. He knew they were small, but they looked even smaller now, if that was possible. Sparky thought he re-membered the stamp as regular size and wrapped around the side of the parcel, but he saw now that there was a tiny little stamp in the corner above and to the right of the address. The address was written in the most microscopic script imaginable. Sparky's eyes were sharp, but even he had trouble making out the letters. He gained a new respect for the mailmen who had to deliver these kinds of things.

"Young man, how would you like to come live with me?"

The question startled Sparky and its import and the mysterious motives behind asking it gave him a sudden rush of adrenaline and made him flush with embarrassment. He became frightened. 'Why would she be asking me that?!'

"What do you mean?"

"I think it's a very plain question. I'm offering my home to you. You could stay with me. I have a bird at home in a lovely little cage. You could play together."

"But I have to go home. My mother…"

"Tut tut. You didn't really expect me to believe that simply ludicrous tale you just told, do you?"

"What tale?! About why I'm not at school?"

"Come, now, young man. Firewood stacked in front of the bathroom door? All that claptrap about your mother's panties and her getting spanked; Chinese people bathing in the streets; an abandoned candy store and a disappearing school? I wasn't born yesterday, young man."

"But it's true! It happened!"

Mrs. Piper stopped and turned toward Sparky and leaned forward a bit. "My dear, young man, there's really nothing to be ashamed of." She took his hands in hers and smiled a bit. "There are many street children in this great country of ours." Her gaze went distant and she looked through Sparky. "I have met many, many of them and befriended many," she paused, "many of them." Sparky tried pulling his hands from hers, but her grip was surprisingly strong.

"But I'm *not*! I *have* a home and parents! They *did* tear down the school last night!" Sparky tried again to tear away from her grasp, but he felt stupidly weak and puny and he could hardly even move his arms. "Let me go!" Sparky was alarmed and frustrated and he looked around for help, but not one of the passersby paid any interest in his struggle. He looked back up at Mrs. Piper's face and she was still wearing that smile.

"I know! We'll continue on our walk to my house and we'll stop at Birnbaum's and I'll buy us a nice container of orange sherbet. How would you like that, young man? I'll fix us some liverwurst sandwiches

on rye bread for lunch, and then we'll enjoy the orange sherbet while
we listen to the radio. How would you like that?"

Sparky had stopped struggling, figuring it made no difference anyway.
He sized up his situation and started to really worry that this frail, old
woman was going to be able to force him to live with her. He couldn't
imagine where she got her strength. He only knew that she grew
stronger as he resisted her. He felt such helplessness that he was on the
verge of tears, but he played it as cool as he could manage. "Sure, that
sounds delicious! What a good idea." The thought of liverwurst nause-
ated him. He pictured her apartment– an old woman's apartment– full
of old doilies and faded, old furniture and an old, worn rug and dingy
walls covered in ornately-framed faded, old paintings and a bird cage
standing next to an old vacuum tube radio and the putrid smell of gamy
liverwurst. He panicked in that moment, but his panic took the form of
another adrenaline rush, accompanied this time by clear thinking.
"Yeah, we oughtta do that! I should eat some real food for a change.
All I've had is pie and a jelly donut so far today. I haven't had the
chance to rifle through any dumpsters yet. A nice liverwurst sandwich
would hit the spot, all right."

Mrs. Piper predictably relaxed her iron grip and straightened up. "My
bird's name is Aloysius. He's such a happy little fellow. He sings
lovely songs and jumps from his little perch to his food bowl. He's a
happy little fellow in his little cage. I feed him meat, you know."

Sparky waited for the punch line. Mrs. Piper just smiled. "Meat? Hmm,
that's interesting. He likes meat? What kinda bird is he?"

"Why, he's just a lovely little bird, little Aloysius. Oh, yes indeed. He
positively loves meat. He likes liverwurst, too. Isn't that just darling?"

"Yeah, that's really something. I can't wait to make pals with him."

"Oh, I can't wait for you two to meet. I know you'll take a shine to
each other, right off! You both have so much in common."

"Well, maybe we should hurry up so you can give him some meat. He's
probably hungry by now, right? You've been gone a long, long time."

"I suppose he is. Yes, I suppose so. My, what a considerate little fellow
you are! Most of the little fellows I've had have been quite disrespect-

ful and *so* contrary! We most definitely should hurry along and get
home so that little Aloysius can enjoy his plate of meat."

They were right at the corner of Third Avenue and vast Aqua Boulevard and the signal was green and had not yet started to blink 'Don't
Walk'.

Aqua Boulevard, one of the three widest streets in Highbridge, is an
eight-lane roadway that starts one block from the waterfront and slices
westward across the city to the foot of Sunset Hill, near the airport.
Two lanes are set aside for parking; three lanes travel east and three
travel west. For much of its length, between the eastbound and west-
bound lanes, is a wide island plaza, which contains shrubs and benches.
For slow pokes, the 'Walk' sign stays green long enough to allow
crossing half way.

"You know, Mrs. Piper, I was thinking of poor little Aloysius and how
starved he must be right about now. I'm kinda thinking that maybe we
should take the bus after all. We'll never get home in time for him to
eat otherwise. What do you think?"

"Oh, well, let's see. Why, young man, you just may be correct about
that. I have been gone for quite a long time. Do you really think my
little Aloysius will suffer greatly if we walk the entire distance?"

"I think so. My friend Aaron had a tortoise and he used to get awfully
hungry if he wasn't fed on time. I think that's why he died. He got
hungry too many times. That's what Aaron's dad said, anyway."

"That is such an awful thought. I'd hate to be the cause of yet another
death."

"We don't know that guy died. Maybe he's all right. He might've just
been knocked unconscious or something."

"Oh, no. I wasn't thinking of that horrid man! No, I don't mind if *he*
was killed. And I certainly don't feel one jot of responsibility for his
welfare, young man. Not one jot!"

"Oh, well, okay then." Just then a Third Avenue bus blew by them and
across the intersection. "Ma'am, the light's about to change. Why don't
I run across and hold that bus so we can hurry home and take care of

little Aloysius?" The light had started blinking 'Don't Walk'. Mrs. Piper seemed befuddled for a second, then let go of Sparky's hand.

"Yes, yes, that is a good plan. Oh, dear! I won't make this light, I'm afraid."

"Don't worry! I'll hold the bus for you!" Sparky dashed across the intersection as fast as he could and was at the bus as it was still letting passengers off. He looked back toward Mrs. Piper, but the stream of exiting passengers blocked his view. He dug into his pocket and pulled out a quarter as he stepped aboard. He was the last boarding passenger. Before he could take a seat, the doors had closed and the bus was accelerating toward Forcer Street and leaving Mrs. Piper well behind, blocked by the rushing torrent of traffic on Aqua Boulevard.

Chapter 11: The Long Arm of the Law

Sparky stumbled to the forward-facing seats in the rear of the lurching bus. The few times he had ridden in buses, he had liked to face forward and look out the window. As he scurried past the rear exit door, he peered out the wide rear window for Mrs. Piper, but didn't see her running after the bus, as he had feared he might. In fact, he could not make her out at all. He moved past an assortment of anonymous characters, each of which was absorbed in their own world or gazing absently out the window at the assortment of anonymous characters passing by. There was a choice seat in the back row, next to the window on the sidewalk side of the bus. Sparky grabbed it, propping his right foot up on a projection from the bottom of the wall of the bus.

The driver called out the stops as he muscled the bus through the maze of traffic along Third Avenue. '57th Street!' 'Bronx Avenue-55th Street for the 1st Avenue subway lines!' '55th Street!' 'Hicks Street!' Traffic was dense and the bus couldn't get up any significant speed. This gave Sparky the chance to really see the people and buildings of Midtown.

Most of the businesses were intrinsically no different from the ones he had seen in his own neighborhood or in Sparta and Belmont. There were supermarkets, shoe repair shops, banks, toy stores, hardware stores, restaurants and bars– just like home. There was a big difference, however. That difference was that the buildings were bigger and taller and the little neighborhood stores were not here. There were no houses, no stoops, and no empty lots. It was wall-to-wall businesses and the apartments were above the businesses.

The people were all business. The old ladies and old men were few and far between. Instead, the people bustling about were like Sparky's parents or maybe a little older. The men wore business suits and many carried briefcases just like the teachers at P.S. 8. The women were dressed much like Sparky's teachers, too. Everyone looked sharp. Everyone seemed focused and determined. No one seemed to be wandering or resting. Even the guys standing on the sidewalk next to the loading dock of an office building and smoking cigarettes seemed to be very purposefully waiting, like soldiers in a foxhole, for the action to resume.

'Felter and Bradley!'

Sparky and the Waarheid Camera

Sparky wondered if he should get off here. He didn't really have any intention of taking the bus all the way downtown. He didn't really have any intention at all, but hopping on board the bus seemed the best thing to do when he did it. The side sign on the bus read "43 to U.S. PLAZA". Sparky thought about taking the bus all the way and he felt a bubble of fear (or was it excitement?). 'Isn't U.S. Plaza right next to some of the oldest and seediest streets in Highbridge?' Sparky decided to stay on the bus a while longer.

Looking at the people who got on and off the bus, Sparky wondered what they did all day. If these people were movers and shakers, then moving and shaking must be a grim task, after all. Everyone seemed to be traveling alone and no one was talking. There was no joking and no interaction. A couple of the passengers had said 'good morning' to the driver to which the driver responded likewise. At one point, the driver was talking on a black phone, which was hanging next to the fare box. He talked for a moment or two to someone on the other end. Sparky would have liked to know what he was saying or maybe who he was talking to, but could hear nothing from the back of the noisy bus. A man stumbling toward the rear exit door bumped another and mumbled an apology, to which there was no response. It was only as the bus was nearing Turtle Street and Lingstrome Avenue that anyone really spoke to anyone else. A young woman suddenly turned and started pummel-ing a sharply-dressed older businessman who was making his way past her toward the rear exit. She called him a 'son of a bitch' and a 'per-vert'. He was expressionless and didn't respond to her name-calling. Sparky figured the man must get that kind of treatment frequently since he showed no surprise. The woman had not seemed nasty before she struck out at the man, but Sparky was learning that people can be quite unpredictable at times.

Sparky turned his attention back to the outside world and could see down Turtle Street toward Highbridge Avenue. Over the tops of the smaller buildings he could see the lofty spire of the 919 Turtle Street Building and some others, which he could not identify. Crossing Ling-strome Avenue meant leaving Tillotson Flats and entering the district of Lester. Sparky knew next to nothing about Lester except that most of the City's subway lines passed through here and much of the City's banking and corporate headquarters were located here. There wasn't a lot going on here that would concern a boy of ten. The streets started to take on a sort of uniformity that made the trip less exciting for Sparky.

110

He wondered if the rest of the trip would be as repetitive as these blocks were. Seeing some of Highbridge's greatest skyscrapers would be exciting, though.

'Highbridge Avenue!'

The bus pulled into the stop after crossing the giant thoroughfare, but the driver didn't release the rear exit door. The six or seven passengers wanting to exit were puzzled and frustrated for a moment and a couple of them called out to the driver, 'getting off!', but he still didn't release the back door. After a bout of grumbling, they started filing forward squeezing past the boarding passengers to get off. Sparky wondered if this was standard procedure at Highbridge Avenue– maybe because of the volume of passengers or something. But, when all the passengers had either exited or entered the bus, the driver emerged from his cock- pit and stood at the top of the steps, talking to someone standing just outside the bus. Sparky could not make out who he was talking to. At first, he thought it must be a dispatcher, but the driver kept looking back toward Sparky and nodding and gesturing as if it had something to do with him.

Suddenly, the driver looked right at Sparky, pointed and crooked his finger twice. Sparky's stomach twisted into a knot. "C'mon, kid!" the driver called out. Sparky sidled out of his seat and walked hesitatingly up the aisle.

"What is it?"

"C'mon," was all that the driver said. He wasn't mad or nasty– just grim. The other passengers may or may not have been paying attention to what was transpiring, but Sparky felt like he was being stared at, anyway. The driver stepped back a bit to let Sparky pass him.

"It's you! I wondered what happened to you!"

Sparky was amazed. It was Officer Pyles, the policeman who had nabbed him on B Street.

"Thought you could give me the slip, eh?"

"Give *you* the slip? I came out of the bathroom and you were gone!"

"Well, anyway, there's no sense arguin' about it now. Actually, I'm glad we met up again before you got yourself into any more trouble."

Sparky stepped off the bus as the policeman thanked the bus driver.

"You did the right thing, chief. This kid's up to no good an' he woulda' gotten into real trouble if you hadn't called it in. I was tryin' to find out if he's homeless or not when he gave me the slip."

"How'd he manage that?"

"I don' know exactly. He sneaked out of the bathroom at Munchie's, somehow."

"I did not! I came out of the bathroom and you were gone!"

"He is a feisty one, alright."

"See what I'm tellin' you? He's tricky. Makes out like he's dumb, tellin' the stupidest lies, then just when you think he's okay…" the policeman snapped his fingers "…disappears!"

"You sure got your hands full. Good luck!" The bus driver re-boarded his bus, shut the doors and pulled away.

"Now listen here, kid. Why don' you make it easier on yourself? I was pretty reasonable. I took the handcuffs off you and I was gonna buy you some food, wasn't I?" Sparky nodded. "All I'm asking is that you play ball, eh? No funny stuff. Look, I'm a pretty reasonable guy when it comes right down to it, but I won't put up with any more shenanigans. Understand?"

"Yes."

"Good. Now, I gotta take you down to be processed, but I missed out on my donut and coffee and it's almost lunchtime now," he checked his watch, "so, why don't we see what we can grab?" The policeman looked around and rubbed his chin. "There's a place near here. Come on, kid, I'm parked around the corner."

The policeman guided Sparky around the corner onto 44th Street and there, parked in front of a hydrant, was the old police wagon.

Chapter 12: Doing the Dirty Work

"Say, kid, how *did* you get outta Munchie's without me seein' you?"

"I'm telling you, when I came out of the bathroom, you were gone!"

"I was gone, huh? And where did I go? Into thin air?"

"I guess. All I know is that, when I came out of the bathroom, you were gone."

"Forget it. Just get in."

"Where are we going?"

"Like I say, I gotta take you downtown, but there's a pub on the corner of Brothers and J Street. I'm in the mood for one of their Reuben sandwiches. It's almost noon, anyway."

"How did you know where I was?"

"I didn' know. The bus driver called in that he had a probable truant on board. I was on Highbridge and 49th, so I met the bus."

"Oh, I see. I saw the driver make that call. I wondered who he was talking to."

"Ya see, kid, you can't escape the long arm of the law. We'll getcha sooner or later. Sooner or later we get 'em all. It's like I'm on a quest, see?" He pulled the wagon out into traffic and made a left onto Highbridge Avenue. "I see myself as a knight on a quest."

"I remember you said."

"It's like my nightstick is my spear."

"Lance."

"Yeah, right. My lance. Anyway, you kids are like the Golden Fleece and I…"

"That's not knights, that's Jason and the Argonauts!"

"Who?"

"The ancient Greeks. Haven't you ever seen the movie?"

"What movie?"

"Jason and the Argonauts!"

"I guess not. I don't go in for those kinds of things."

"What kinds of things? I saw it on the 4:30 movie. Jason fights these skeletons and bird-women. He goes after the Golden Fleece. It's the best!"

"Well, I don't get to watch much TV."

"You have to work late? My dad works late."

"No, I'm on first shift. I just don't stay home much, I guess."

"What do you mean, you go to your friends' houses when you get home?"

"No, I don't really have any friends, exactly."

"Hey! I think something's dragging. I can hear it."

"I think you're right." The policeman pulled the wagon over to the curb and cut the motor. He walked around to the passenger side and peered at the rear wheel. "Yep, there it is." He stood with his hands on his hips.

Sparky got out and looked. "It's a shopping cart!"

"Sure is. I wonder how that got there? Here, kid, gimme a hand and let's see if we can get it loose." The policeman got down on all fours and examined the twisted metal, giving it a tug or two in an exploratory effort to dislodge it. "It's pretty stuck, but if you help I think it'll come out. Are you game, kid?"

"Sure I am! What do you want me to do?"

"If you can get under the van and pull on this bar here while I move the van backwards, I think it'll come out. Think you can do that, kid?"

"You're not going to run me over, are you? Seems kinda dangerous."

"Nah, it's nothin', kid. Look, just get yourself under this part here an' stay low an' you'll be fine. You're small enough so it shouldn' be a problem." Sparky hesitated. "C'mon, kid! It's the only way. We can't drive it like this– draggin' a shopping cart through the streets! C'mon, I'm gettin' hungry. I missed my break 'cause of you!"

"That's not right! *You* disappeared– not me!"

"Well, anyway, let's not argue about it. Let's just get this goddamn cart outta there, huh?"

"All right, I'll crawl under. But don't run me over!"

"I won't run you over, I won't run you over, already! Whaddya think I am, anyway?"

"Well, you're not the best driver I ever saw. That's for sure."

"Oh, come on! I'm a fine driver! Why, because of this? Somebody probably pushed it under the van as a joke. Pranksters are always doin' stuff like that. They egg me all the time."

"There's groceries still in this cart! I don't think it was pranksters. Hey, there's a purse stuck in here, too!"

"Some crazy old lady. Are you ready, yet, kid?"

"Yeah, I guess so."

"Okay, I'll start it up and you just pull down, okay?"

"Yeah. Hurry up, I'm starting to get the heebie-jeebies down here."

The policeman climbed back into the van. Sparky could see his feet disappear as he stepped up. The vehicle rocked and the springs creaked

115

as the policeman took his seat.

"Here we go, kid!" the policeman called out as he started up the engine. Sparky grabbed the tubular metal of the shopping cart and shifted his weight so that he could roll quickly out of the way of the wheels– just in case. The policeman gunned the engine loudly and Sparky could see a linkage move as the vehicle went into reverse, grinding and clanking as it did so. Sparky's heart started racing and he coiled himself to roll out if anything went wrong.

The policeman yelled something out, which Sparky could not hear except for the words 'pull' and 'kid', then, the vehicle started moving backward. Sparky pulled down as instructed and the cart got caught under the back tires and popped right out of the wheel-well. The contents of the bags inside the twisted wreckage got a second, and more thorough, squashing and various and sundry fruits and vegetables squirted out onto the asphalt. Sparky was fortunate enough to not get hit with the worst of it, but he did take some tomato juice and seeds on the shoulder of his jacket. He was trying to ascertain the damage when the van lurched suddenly. Sparky reacted by scooting toward the curb, just managing to avoid the front wheels as they rolled past. There was a crunching sound as the van came to a sudden stop.

Sparky jumped up and faced into the open door on the passenger side. "Are you nuts or something? I almost got run over!"

"Sorry, kid. The clutch pedal slipped. But, you're all right. That's the important thing. Looks like your jacket got some stuff on it."

"I know. My mother's going to kill me!"

"You still stickin' to that line? Look, kid, you can level with me. I'm not your enemy, ya know. Hey, did the shopping wagon come loose?"

"Yeah, it got caught under the back wheel and pulled right out."

"Ha ha! All *right*! I knew you could do it, kid! Come on, kid, let's get goin'"

"Wait! What about the station wagon you crashed into?"

"Whaddya talkin' about? What station wagon?"

116

"The Vista Cruiser right behind you! Didn't you hear that crunching sound? You crunched the guy's grill and headlights!"

The policeman craned his neck to look back through the rear view mirror at the unfortunate Oldsmobile. "Nah, I think that car was like that when we pulled up. I didn' do that. C'mon already, kid. We don' have all day!"

Sparky held his tongue and stepped into the van.

"You're a mess, kid. You better get cleaned up when we get to the pub. Ya' can't go around lookin' like a bum, even if you *are* homeless. And don' call me nuts. That's not a nice thing to say to one of Highbridge's Finest, ya' know."

"I'm sorry, but I was scared. You almost ran me over."

"Oh, come on, kid! Don't go makin' a federal case out of it."

"You've got to cut me some slack. It's been a rough day for me, so far."

The policeman pulled out into traffic and the pair was on the road once again.

Chapter 13: Old Meat

"Any chance we can try to call my mother again? Maybe when we stop for lunch?"

"Sure, kid. We'll call your mom. Think she still remembers you? When did you leave home?"

"About eight or so."

"You know what I'm talkin' about, kid. Stop playin' dumb. When did you run away?"

"I *didn't* run away! How many times do I have to tell you?"

"All right, all right. Calm down, already."

"I *am* calm."

"When did you get kicked outta the house?"

Sparky placed his hands on his temples and shook his head back and forth and moaned.

"Don' wanna talk about it, eh? Listen kid, we all got stories. Everybody's got somethin' in their past. If I told you I was kicked outta my house an' thrown out into the street, would you believe it?" The policeman looked at Sparky for a reaction. "It's true, ya' know. My ol' man left my mom an' me for some redheaded slut he met at a bar. She was a worthless tramp and she only wanted my ol' man for his money."

"Was he rich?"

"No, he wasn't rich. He cleaned toilets for a living."

"Was he a juvenile delinquent?"

"What? No! Why'd you say that?"

"No reason."

118

"Anyway, how much can you make doin' *that* twelve hours a day? That's why my mom started doin' what she did. It was bad enough that the kids in the neighborhood already were teasin' me 'cause my ol' man's name was Ted."

"Why'd they tease you about that?"

"They'd say his name wasn' Ted– it was 'Turd'! 'Turd' Pyles, they called him! They made me cry. Can you imagine havin' a father named 'Turd'? I was the laughing stock of the neighborhood. Then, as if that wasn' bad enough, my mom started up her business."

"That must've been tough. My grandfather had his own business. He ran a bunch of newsstands. It's hard to own your own business. Well, at least your dad had a steady job, right? And somebody's got to clean toilets, right?"

"Steady job? Hah! We didn' have two pennies to rub together when I was growin' up. We were the poorest family in the entire neighborhood. That's what drove my mom to start entertainin' men."

"She was an entertainer? Was she ever on TV? I watch the *Mike Douglas Show* in the afternoon! Was she ever on that?"

"No, not that kind of entertainer, kid. She had men come to the house while my ol' man was at work, cleanin' toilets. She locked me in my room and they'd drink and carry on. I'd cry and cry. That's when my mom started calling my ol' man 'Turd' behind his back. She and her customers would laugh at that 'til their sides were splittin'. I'd bury my face in my pillow an' cry some more. It was unbearable!"

"She got *paid* to drink with these guys?"

"They did more than jus' drink, kid, if you catch my drift. Anyway, after nine years of this kind of thing, my old man finally had enough and he went to the corner bar to have a drink."

"Why didn't he have a drink at home with your mom?"

"He was too mad at her to drink with her."

"Why didn't he have a drink sooner?"

"Sooner?"

"Yeah, nine years is a long time to put up with stuff, isn't it? Did he try talking to her? We have family meetings sometimes. I don't like them, but I suppose they help some."

"I don' know why. Maybe he didn' realize he was unhappy. I don' know. Maybe he didn' have time."

"For nine years?!"

"I don' know! What can I tell you? So, anyway, he goes out an' buys a drink and this– this broad– this floozy comes up to him in the bar an' he buys her a drink an' the rest, as they say, is history."

"What do you mean 'the rest is history'? What happened next?"

"You sure you really wanna hear this, kid? It's not a pretty story, ya' know."

"Sure, I 'm sure! What happened next?"

"Well, my old man comes staggerin' home, drunk as a skunk– no, wait– he wasn't drunk. He never got drunk. He was mad as hell, though– nah, that's not right either. Wait a minute, that was the other time, when he got fired."

"What other time? He got fired?"

"Did I say he got fired? He didn' get fired– he *quit*. He couldn' take it anymore. The bastards he worked with took his brushes and rags away from him an' made him clean toilets with his own damn shirt! And they all stood around and laughed at him when he left at the end of the day. He'd go home soaking wet, smellin' like crap, wet toilet paper blobs in his cuffs and pockets. They laughed and they called him 'Turd'. The guys he worked with even got him a work shirt with the name 'Turd' monogrammed over the pocket." The policeman gripped the steering wheel so tightly that his knuckles turned white as he related the tragic tale.

"Why'd he put up with that? That's terrible! I'd beat them up if they

120

did that to me!"

"Did what?"

"Make me clean the toilets with my shirt!"

"What the hell are you talking about?"

"What you just said– about them making your dad clean toilets with his shirt."

"Is that some kind of joke? 'Cause if it is, it's not funny, ya' know. That's sick!"

"But, it's what you said. I'm not making a joke, you just told me– never mind." Sparky went quiet.

"So, as I was sayin', my old man comes home drunk an' he tells mom he's leavin' for good an' he packs up his clothes in a paper bag an' he marches out the door. He didn' even close it behind him. I ran to the window to look out an' there's this redhead, wearin' a fur-lined jacket, behind the wheel of a '56 Imperial, waitin' for him."

"Wow! A '56 Imperial!"

"She was sittin' there, an' she's calmly puffing away on a cigarette through one of those long holders, an' she's got the radio blastin' a Doris Day tune. To this day I can't stand to hear her Que Sera Sera, an' all that crap! How Much is that Doggy in the Window– blecch!"

"That's Patti Page! She was on *Mike Douglas*, too!"

"Whatever. So, she's sittin' there, cool as a cucumber, an' all the neighborhood kids are watching what's goin' on. They were laughing an' callin' her 'Turd Lover' an' sayin' that the Imperial was the fanci- est toilet bowl they'd ever seen. An' they were lookin' at our apartment window an' pointin' an' laughing an' callin' out at us. An' all this time Doris Day is singin' 'Love Me or Leave Me.' It was horrible! The worst day of my life."

There was a long silence as the policeman pulled to the curb in front of the hydrant at the corner of Brothers and J Streets. He misjudged the curb and parked with the front tire up on the sidewalk. The sign over the establishment there read: Dehoolie's Pub and Grill– Fine Food and Drink.

"I'll never forget that day, as long as I live. June 12th, 1957. Not June 12th. June– no, July 8th. I remember it was after the Fourth of July, because I had my hand in a bandage."

"Why was your hand bandaged?"

"'Cause I'd burned it holdin' a bottle rocket. But, then that musta' been 1956, 'cause I was in fourth grade. I tell ya', I'll never forget it. Well, here we are, kid!"

"Am I allowed in there? It's a bar, isn't it?"

"Don' worry, kid! You're with me, remember?" They disembarked from the van. "Yep, 1959 was one terrible year for me."

"What happened in 1959?"

"Weren't you listenin' to what I was just tellin' you?!"

"You said it was 1956."

"That wasn' '56. All that took place in the summer of 1954. I remember it as if it just happened."

"It couldn't have been the summer of 1954, because you said that the redhead was driving a '56 Imperial. That would be impossible."

"You mean the blonde? She was in a Buick, I think– not an Imperial."

"What blonde? The redhead! The one playing Doris Day on the radio!"

"What the hell are you sayin', kid? You weren't there! What do *you* know about it? My wife would only drive Imperials. Anything else wasn' good enough for *her*!" The policeman said it more to himself than to Sparky. "How can a man on a cop's salary afford to keep his wife in fancy cars an' fur-lined jackets, huh?"

"I thought it was your father's girlfriend who was wearing the fur coat?

122

I'm getting confused. Who's the redhead, then?"

"Well, my wife dyed her hair red. The slut left me a day before our ninth anniversary for a guy named Ted. I'd picked out a nice anniversary present for her. It cost me a bundle, too– a jeweled cigarette holder. She liked those things. I thought they were stupid, but she wanted to look elegant, ya' know? She came from the lowest of the low, but diamonds and pearls for her! Nothin' but the fanciest restaurants and nightclubs for Doris! $50 shoes; $100 cigarette case." He was talking to himself again.

"Then, if your wife is the redhead, who's the blonde? Your mom?"

"Did I tell you my mom was blonde? Well, she *wasn't*! Who told you that?"

"I thought you did! Who drove a Buick, then?"

"My sister drove a dark green Buick. Slide that door closed, will ya' kid. I don' like this neighborhood an' I got my duffel bag in there. Yeah, my sister drove a '56 Buick. She was somethin' else. The apple doesn' fall far from the tree, I tell ya'. She was a slut, too. Yeah, dyed her hair blonde so she could look like Doris Day. The slut."

"I always thought Doris Day was kinda nice. My mom's got dark brown hair."

"Yeah, I know, kid. That's the best kind. Nice, dark, shiny hair. Cute nose. Nice legs, too."

"How d'you know? You didn't even believe I have a mother!"

"We all have a mother, kid. Even if she is a slut."

Sparky was aghast. "She's *not* a slut! Why'd you say that?!"

"Forget it, kid. I don' know why I said it. I only know *my* mother was a slut. That's why I ran away from home."

"But I thought you said your mother left you and your dad. You said..."

"You gotta learn to listen better, kid. You got things so jumbled up, you're even confusin' me! Let's forget all that stuff. It's all buried deep in the past. Let's go inside and eat. Aren't you hungry?" Sparky, with his belly still full of jelly donut, mumbled 'no' under his breath, but it went unheard.

Dehoolie's was a shabby-looking corner bar. The exterior had a layer of blue-gray stucco, carved to look like stones. The windows were dirty and greasy, as was the glass on the door. There was a pair of filthy green dumpsters next to the entrance. They reeked of old beer and rotting food. There was a black, furry tail sticking out of one of the dumpsters. The two windows housed neon signs, advertising Ballantine and Pabst Blue Ribbon beer. The door scraped against its own threshold when it swung open and an awful shriek announced Sparky and the policeman's entrance.

"Julio! Que pasa, Julio."

The bartender looked up from his task of stocking the bar and flashed an almost toothless smile. His greasy hair hung limply over his eyes like oily black pasta and helped to hide the angry, overripe pimples it helped to create on his gray forehead. "Teddy! Waz hapnin', my man." The two slapped five over the bar and Julio cackled, "Heh, heh!"

The place was nearly empty despite the hour and the few poor souls who did occupy space did so in a slumped, doughy, dark sort of way. More like human dumplings than vital people. No one looked up from their spot, and only one man was doing anything at all besides staring down. He was doing the Hide-a-Word in the Highbridge Herald.

The lights were off except for the neon signs in the windows and the lighted clock over the door to the restroom. The only other illumination there was came from whatever photons could squeeze themselves through the grimy glass of the door. Other than the few cubic feet around that door, Dehoolie's was all gloom.

"Duh man in blue. Wuz new, eh? Who's duh new syekick? Wuz your name, Shorty? Cato? Huh? You name Cato? Show me you stuff, Shorty." Julio did some kind of karate move that, to Sparky, looked surprisingly expert and lightning fast, then he cackled again, "Heh, heh!"

The policeman smiled at Sparky, who just stood there unsure of what he should do or say. "I'm takin' him down to be processed. Found him messin' aroun' up on B Street."

"Oh, man! Heh, heh! You dunno what you doon, man! Messin' roun' B Stree', man! Shorty got ball, man! Yo, you gotta amid ih, man! Dat take cojones."

"Yeah, he's a slick one, alright. Gave me the slip outta Munchie's while I was buyin' us a couple of donuts this mornin', too. Can you believe that?"

"Oh, shi', man. Heh, heh! You gay my man duh slip? Oh, man! Heh, heh! Nobod' gi' my man duh slip! Shorty all righ', man. You all righ'. Gimme fie." Julio put his hand out, palm up to slap five with Sparky. Sparky was more scared not to do it, so he forced himself to drop his palm down on Julio's. Julio's palm felt rough and damp at the same time, and it had no perceptible temperature. Sparky felt like he just slapped five with a monitor lizard.

"Yeah, but I caught up with him on the Number 43 about a half hour ago."

"Heh, heh! Yo, Shorty gi' my man duh slip! Yo, Shorty, you wanna drin', man? You bedduh ha' sump'n, 'cause you in fo' a lon' day, man. Heh, heh! When dey geh you in dat cour'room, you gonna nee' sump'n. Righ' Off'cer Teddy?"

"You're corrupting the morals of a minor, Julio! He's just a kid! He's too young to drink. Give me a beer and give him a Coke."

Sparky whispered to Officer Pyles, "do you understand what this guy's saying?"

"Some of it. The trick is to look into his eyes when he talks."

Julio drew a glass of beer for the policeman and placed it on a coaster. Then, while the policeman emptied it, Julio filled another glass most of the way with Coke, and, winking at Sparky, fiddled with it under the bar. He placed the full glass on a coaster in front of Sparky.

"Hit me again, Julio."

"You gon' jus' drin' yo lun', man? Or you wan' sump'n eat?"

"I've been in the mood for a Reuben. You like Reuben sandwiches, kid?"

"What is it?" Sparky sipped his drink, which tasted odd to him. He chalked that up to the fact that it wasn't right out of a bottle and this wasn't your traditional soda fountain.

"Corned beef, sauerkraut, Swiss cheese on rye."

"We don' gonno rye, man. It on whi' breh."

"What did he say?"

"White bread. Whatcha think, kid?"

Sparky thought for a moment, pondering the sandwich. "Sure."

"Ih' no corn bee, man. Ih's anoth' kina mea', man."

"Well then, whatever you got is fine. It doesn' have to be corned beef."

"You goddi', man. Heh heh."

Julio disappeared into the back and Sparky turned around on his barstool, sipping more of his Coke. He looked over the clientele individually. The guy doing the Hide-a-Word had fallen asleep *in situ* and his pencil had dragged across a third of the page and rested on an ad for mattresses. The man sitting under the neon Ballantine sign was rolling bits of a napkin into little balls and lining them up in rows like little soldiers. A man had shuffled out of the restroom and ambled back to his barstool at the far end of the bar. His cigarette jiggled between his lips as he coughed volcanically. There was one woman in the place, sitting in the darkest corner of the room, to the right of the door to the restroom.

Sparky sipped on his Coke and tried to make out some details in the woman. He couldn't tell much through the darkness, but he could see that she was white and dressed in very fancy clothes– almost like a costume. The clothes looked old-fashioned to Sparky, the sort of feath-

126

ered, satin and lace style that the old women along B Street might still
be wearing– fifteen years beyond their time. She smoked a cigarette
through one of those long, fancy holders like the one the policeman
mentioned in his story. The woman seemed as disengaged as her fellow
patrons until she suddenly spoke up without looking up from her cocktail glass.

"Well, look at *him*, will ya'." Her voice was deep and husky with the
smoke of thousands of cigarettes.

"Don' pay her any attention, kid. She's nuts." The policeman patted
Sparky on his knee in a gesture of reassurance.

Sparky sipped at his Coke. He started getting used to the odd flavor.

"Lousy son of a bitch."

"You should know," the policeman called back to her across the room.

There was a long thick silence for many seconds. The guy working the
Hide-a-Word woke up, sniffed loudly and renewed his interest in the
puzzle. Sparky looked around at the awful place and its awful inhabitants and smiled. He could see more clearly now than he could when
they'd first walked in. The guy under the Ballantine sign could now be
seen for who he really was. Sparky could see that he was not completely preoccupied with making spitballs that would never be
launched, but that he had been using that as a diversion from his true
purpose. The man was obviously paying very close attention to everything that had been said and done since the policeman and his captive
had walked in. The man was strategizing; looking for anything he could
use to profit from what was happening or about to happen. Sparky dis-
cerned this, having drunk more than half his beverage.

"Highbridge's intrepid man in blue, saving the world from the evil
clutches of school kids. Ha!"

"Somebody's gotta look out for the youngsters. Lord knows, you ain't
interested in the welfare of a child. You're just a wasted old slut. You
were *always* a slut. You didn' care how awful it was for me, as long as
you could get some."

Sparky was fascinated by this exchange. The woman never looked up

127

from her drink– not once since they came in, yet here she was arguing with the policeman, out loud and across the bar, about something seemingly important and private.

"You two know each other or something?"

"Go on, dog catcher. Tell your young pup about us."

"No, kid. I don' know this hag. Don' pay any attention to her. She's just an old drunk. Julio! Bring me another beer!"

"Cumn righ' up, man!" Julio emerged from the kitchen and drew another beer for the policeman.

"Sure, 'she's just an old drunk,' he says. I was stone cold sober when I got married, I'll have you know. It was *you*! You were the drunk that day. Most days after that, too," she added under her breath.

"Were you?"

"Was I what, kid?"

"Drunk? Seems to me she knows what she's talking about."

"I wouldn' believe a word she says, kid. She's a liar. Always has been." The policeman upended his glass.

The woman chimed in again. "Hey, young pup, is he still a terrible driver? He was always a terrible driver with me. He was in too much of a hurry and didn't care about anything but his own needs."

"Maybe if I had a better vehicle, I'd be a better driver. You ever think of *that*? Huh?"

"Yeah, he *sure* was a bad driver. He went too fast and he had lots of accidents. I needed someone who took their time and was considerate. But, that wasn't him. No sir. He was in such a rush all the time that he almost always arrived too soon."

"Well, he did get us here in a hurry, I guess."

"Hey, young pup, ask Sir Galahad here where *his* son is. Go ahead, ask him." She took a sip of her cocktail to punctuate her dare.

"He ran away from your whorehouse!"

"You got a son? Hmmm. That's kinda interesting." Sparky finished his Coke. He could see quite clearly now.

"You got all the answers, eh? You never came up with an answer to the question of marriage, did you? And he never came up with the answer to the question of where his own son disappeared to. Well? Did you?" Sparky could hardly tell who she was talking to.

The policeman uttered almost inaudibly: "No."

"Young pup, ask him why he drives around in that beat-up paddy wagon all day, looking for children in the streets. Ask him who he's looking for. Go on. Ask him."

"Viper! Let the kid alone, will ya'? Don't poison him with your evil. He's a good kid. He's just a little lost, is all. Right, kid?"

"No, not really. I…"

"He'ou go, Teddy. Two Reuben, hod-doh' duh grill. Mmm, goo', man." Julio dropped the plates in front of Sparky and the policeman. The bread of the sandwiches looked translucent with grease, and the meat, poking out from between the slices, was an unhealthy pinkish-gray hue.

"Are you positill these are A-Okay, chief? Ha ha, I said positill!" Sparky started laughing.

"Now the *kid's* losin' his mind. What's the matter with you? Geez, is the whole world nuts, or what?"

The woman piped up again. "Now the whole world's nuts but him. Ha! If you ask me, the young pup is the only one in here that makes any sense at all."

"No one *did* ask you. Why don' you just shut your damn mouth before somebody shuts it for you!" The policeman talked through a huge bite of sandwich as he wolfed down a couple mouthfuls.

129

"Such a big, tough guy. Listen to how he talks to a woman." It was the man rolling spitballs chiming in this time. "Not to mention, he talks with his mouth full."

"Question is: Full o' what?" It was the guy at the end of the bar.

The policeman was about to react to the man's comment, but he was distracted by Sparky.

"Are you sure about your sandwich? No, really, this sandwich looks funny to me." He picked up his plate and held it out to the policeman. "Here, smell my meat." Sparky giggled. "Smell my meat! Ha ha!" The policeman stared disgustedly as Sparky put down his plate and held his belly, doubling over with convulsive laughter, tears streaming from his eyes.

"Maybe you oughtta go outside and get some air, kid. This cigarette smoke mus' be gettin' to you." The policeman took another huge bite of his Reuben, then tapped his beer glass to signal Julio for a refill. "This Reuben is tastier than usual. You outdid yourself, Julio."

"Ha ha! Smell my…Ha ha!" Sparky couldn't get the words out as he started sliding off his stool.

Julio smiled. "Is nah duh cigreh smo', Off'cer Teddy."

"Huh?" The policeman thought for a second. "You spiked his drink! You son of a bitch!" The policeman was appalled. "Gimme another beer."

Sparky managed to compose himself and get back onto his barstool while the policeman finished the last bites of his sandwich.

"You haven' touched your Reuben, kid. You're gonna get hungry."

"I'll take my chances. I don't think this meat is quite right. Looks like dog meat or something." At that, Sparky burst into peals of laughter again.

"Jesus Christ! I gotta take this kid downtown. I can't show up with him like *this*."

"You could tell the judge you found him drunk." The guy working the Hide-a-Word chimed in.

"Yeah! No, that won' do it. When the bus driver's statement gets filed, I could get in trouble. He wasn' drunk on the bus."

"You've done it now, you jackass– bringing a young pup into this hell-hole saloon."

"It wasn' me! It was Julio's fault!"

"Heh, heh!"

"Shuddup, you dope! That was really a dumb thing to do. Whatcha give him, anyway?"

"Cheebas Rego, man. Jus 'nuff to tay duh edge off'. Heh, heh."

The policeman laughed momentarily at the thought of Sparky drinking Chivas Regal. "Oh, boy. What the hell. I don' feel all that great, myself. Maybe I drank those beers too fast."

"Don't worry about me, officer. I feel super-duper. You don't look too good, Offer Plyles. You look kinda green to me." Sparky hesitated. "I said Plyles. Ha ha!"

"I feel kinda green. Shit. I feel sick to my stomach." The policeman had indeed turned a ghastly green-gray and had broken out in a cold sweat. "I gotta run to the toilet. Don' go nowhere!"

"Yo, Shorty, you no wan' yo Reuben?"

"Blahg! No way. It's dog meat. Ha ha!" Sparky held his belly as he laughed again.

"Ih' no dog– es carne del cat. You no wan' ea' cat?"

"It's cat meat? Hey, now *I* can understand you, too!"

"Heh, heh. Ih' no corn beef– ih' corn *cat*, man. Heh heh!"

131

Sparky could hear sounds of violent regurgitating emanating from behind the bathroom door.

"Well, young pup, now that the dog catcher is indisposed, what are you going to do?"

"I guess I'll go. I don't like this place. It's really depressing. Ha ha!"

"The boy is right. Dontcha think, Douglas? You just sit there under your neon sign, like a fly or something. If that ain't depressing..."

"I'd be depressed if I couldn't finish one of those stupid word-search puzzles. Any moron could finish one of those things. Even a fly could find more words than you do."

"You guys all know each other? How come you don't sit together?"

"Because, young pup, we don't get along." The woman removed the burned out butt from her elegant holder and lit up another cigarette.

"You sure *sound* like you get along. Are you guys all friends? Or related to each other?"

"We're former customers. Doris is– or was– our vendor, so to speak. We're business associates."

"Oh, okay. Why are you just sitting around in a bar? Is business bad these days or something?"

"You could say that, young pup. It's the law of supply and demand. They ever teach that in your school? Supply and demand?"

"Yeah, in social studies! They showed us a filmstrip of big manufaction– manufactories and the trucking business. I know all about it. I'm just having trouble saying it."

"Then you know that when the supply of goodies gets old and spoils, the demand drops along with the goodies. And when that happens, the supplier has to drop her prices. It hardly seems worth the price of a room after a while. Understand me, young pup?"

"Absolutely! That's what happened in The Depression. People were outta work!"

"Ya see, kid? The Depression was no fun. Now ya' know why De-hoolie's is such a depressing joint. The unemployment rate is high here these days."

"I see!"

"You're a clever young pup. You should trot along, now. I'm sure you have better things to do than to spend your time here."

"But, what about Officer..." Sparky gestured toward the bathroom, from which could be heard the atrociously rude sounds of violent torrents of diarrhea.

"He's in no condition to come out any time soon, kid. You'd better go."

"I was going to wash this off my jacket. See? I got some stuff on it."

"There's a dry cleaner on the corner of Robinson and 46th."

"No it's not. It's on Unice and 46th. Alvarado's. They can do that for you while you wait."

"Okay, well– let him know I'm gone, will ya'?"

"We sure will, kiddo."

"Heh heh, Shorty gonna gibm hell! Buh' you gonna pay foh' duh Reuben, firs', Shorty."

"He's right, young pup. A man has to pay for his meat. Didn't your father ever teach you that?"

"I don't know. He never mentioned anything specific about any meat, as far as I can remember. Should he have talked to me about meat? My mom usually does the shopping. She talks about meat sometimes."

"What does she say about meat, boy?" Sparky could no longer tell precisely who was speaking to him. All of the bar's patrons had reverted back to their passive, introverted manner. It could have been the Hide-a-Word player or maybe the spitball roller. He wasn't sure. No one was

133

looking at him anymore.

"Well, she's mentioned color a lot."

"And what did she say about color? Can you remember?" Sparky was sure it was the guy at the end of the bar, but when he turned to respond, the man looked inert.

"My mom says that meat oughtta be red and not green."

"What about wrinkles? Or sagging? Or brown spots? Have you ever really looked at meat?"

"She never told me– Wrinkles! Ha ha! Why would meat have wrinkles! I wouldn't buy any meat that had wrinkles! Yuck."

"You're not alone, young pup. Nobody wants to pay for meat that has wrinkles. After a while, they don't even want it for free."

"That's the way it is, isn't it? When the meat gets old, you don't want it anymore, right? I mean, it makes you sick just to look at it sometimes."

"You should pay your check and go."

"I still don't think it's fair that I gotta pay it." There was silence all around. "All right, how much is it?"

"Nihteen-fitty sis, Shorty, my man."

"Here's twenty dollars."

"Don't you forget Julio's tip, kiddo."

"How much is that?"

"Leave him three bucks."

"Geez! Three bucks?" Sparky handed over the bills. "I can't believe you're makin' me pay for a cat meat sandwich that I didn't even eat! Not to mention all those beers the officer had. I can't believe you guys are taking his side!"

"You want Julio to call the cops on you?"

Sparky conceded the point with a shake of his head and made his way to the door. He could still make out the vile sounds of distress from the bathroom as he left the bar. Sparky opened the screeching door and walked back out into the blinding sunshine and breathed a lungful of relatively clean Highbridge air. The police wagon's door was ajar. Sparky wondered if someone had swiped the policeman's duffel bag.

Chapter 14: The Waarheid Camera

Sparky walked south on Brothers Street toward 46th. On Brothers, between J and 47th Street, he noticed a shabby bum dancing in the middle
of the street, doing a twirling imitation of a waltz and waving a duffel
bag in his left hand and singing, 'la di da di da.' The bum made himself
dizzy with all his twirling and spinning and he plopped down on his
backside in the middle of the northbound lane. Laughing, he flung the
bag about fifty feet into the southbound lane where it was run over by a
semi.

Sparky wondered if it was the policeman's bag. He might have retrieved it and returned to Dehoolie's to give it back to him. But now it
was squashed and its contents probably rendered useless, and he didn't
really want to go back there, so Sparky kept walking. Sparky caught the
aroma of fried food wafting through the air and he realized that he was
getting hungry, after all. The 10:30 donut had finally worn off and the
distance he had put between the cat meat Reuben sandwich and himself
had rekindled his appetite.

Sparky spied the source of the fried food smell across the street. It was
a typical burgers, fries, hot dogs and shakes kind of joint, but Brothers
Street was so seedy that Sparky chose to wait to eat. He had to get the
tomato stain off his jacket before it dried completely. He only had a
couple blocks to go to reach Alvarado's, so he marched on past the old,
grimy brown and black storefronts and service entrances. The street
was quieter than the busier ones he had been on all day. There was only
commercial traffic here on Brothers Street and the street was flanked on
both sides by the rears of skyscrapers fronting on neighboring Unice
Street and Highbridge Avenue. The canyon formed by these buildings
kept Brothers Street away from much of the noise of the rest of the city
and allowed the banging and scraping and creaking sounds of the laborers and the roaring of the commercial garbage trucks to echo up and
down the sidewalks.

Sparky crossed Brothers and turned up 46th Street, looking for Alvarado's. The moment he turned up 46th, the condition and quality of
the businesses improved immensely. There was a nifty-looking camera
shop, displaying dozens of examples of cameras from Instamatics to
very imposing professional models and every grade in between. The
window display also contained various movie cameras, from Super 8 to

massive behemoths festooned with levers and dials and multiple lenses. Sparky pressed his face to the glass and looked inside through the window display and saw an entire wall of shelves stocked from floor to ceiling with different types of film. Another wall held shelves behind glass doors, stocked with countless lenses and filters.

"Hey, punk! Get away from the window!" Sparky jumped as the man barked his order. It was one of the men who work in the camera shop, poking his head out of the doorway. He was holding a sandwich in his right hand that was a big bloody slab of raw meat hanging out from between two slices of untoasted white bread, which were soaked through with blood. "Move it! Get goin' before I call the cops!"

"I was just looking through the window."

"You have no business here. You should be in school at this time." He gnawed some meat off his sandwich. Blood splattered on his chin and white shirtfront. "Did you hear me?" He spoke with his mouth full of meat.

"I wanna buy a camera."

"You want a camera? You have money?"

"Of course I do."

The man tossed his meat into the gutter and wiped his mouth on his sleeve and his hands on his dark blue slacks. "Come right inside, young fella. We'll fix you up with a nice camera, a flash, whatever you need to get you started taking fabulous pictures right out of the gate." He cradled Sparky in the crook of his arm and pulled him along through the doorway. The store smelled of chemicals and light machine lubricant and it was brightly-lit with fluorescent fixtures from above and from within the counter displays. There was a fat, sweaty bearded man at one of the counters, looking carefully at some kind of precision device and breathing loudly through his nose. An attendant in white shirt and tie clicked his retractable pen repeatedly as he waited behind the counter for the man to finish his examination.

The salesman led Sparky past an obstacle course of tripods and freestanding spotlights and silver umbrellas with floodlights installed in them. It was all quite fascinating to Sparky, though he had no clue how one would use such equipment. They didn't stop until the salesman had gotten them to the counters that held the still cameras.

"I assume, sir, that you are in the market for a *still* camera. Is that correct?"

"For pictures? Sure!"

"Well, sir, are you looking for something to use for portraiture? Or photojournalism? Or commercial photography, perhaps? If you give me some guidance, I'm sure I could recommend the ideal device." He rubbed his hands together, eager to please.

"I didn't give it much thought– I mean I haven't decided yet."

"Are you a photography student, sir? Perhaps still trying to find your way?"

"Yeah, I'm a student. Honestly, I don't know where I'm going."

"Excellent, sir. In that case, let me show you something here." He slid the back door of the case open and reached in for a camera. This item here is a wonderful model. It is a Nikon– Japanese, you know. Here, sir, let me show you." The salesman proceeded to pull out the Nikon and many other cameras of Japanese, German and American origin. He pointed out the advantages and disadvantages of the different film formats, body types and quirks, specific to the numerous manufacturers. He took the time to point out and demonstrate the myriad settings and controls of the cameras to Sparky, who took it all in yet understood only a little.

"So if I point this at something, this gauge here tells me if I have enough light to get a picture?"

"Simply put, sir, but essentially you are correct. For instance, you may find that you actually want to capture an image with too little light. If that be the case, then you would use the gauge merely as a point of reference rather than as a commanding voice. Do you see?"

Sparky pondered the question. "What would happen if I took a picture with too little light, though?"

138

"Well sir, the image that would result would be murky and indistinct."

"You wouldn't be able to see anything clearly?"

"Correct, sir."

"That wouldn't be any good. It seems to me that you'd want to see everything as clearly as possible. You'd want to see *everything*. If you could, you'd want to be able to look at a picture and know everything there is to know about the thing you shot. You wouldn't want there to be any question or doubt about it. Otherwise, why take the picture?"

The salesman stared at Sparky for a moment, then returned the various cameras to their positions in the display case, sliding the door closed. Sparky wasn't sure what he had said to shut down the conversation and end the demonstration, and he was afraid the next thing he'd be shown would be the door. But the salesman, instead of giving up and kicking Sparky out, leaned forward in a conspiratorial manner, glancing furtively around them. Finally, with Sparky leaning in to listen, he spoke in hushed tones. "Do you mean what you said– about knowing everything about the subject of which you are taking the picture?"

"Sure, I do!" Sparky replied in equally secretive fashion. "What's the point of taking a picture if it doesn't show you something– you know– real?"

"I believe, sir, that you have come to us just at the most opportune moment. Did you notice our sign?"

"What about your sign?"

"It states proudly that we have been in business for seventy three years."

"So?"

"It's not true."

"It's not?"

"No, it's not."

"How long have you been in business, then?"

"Three weeks."

"Why are you telling me this?"

"How would you know how long we've been in business? You come along, you see the sign, if you didn't remember seeing the store last month, you might assume that you just hadn't noticed us before or that we might have just moved here from another location. Right, sir?"

Sparky shrugged and nodded.

"What if you took a picture of the store?"

"You'd see the store?"

"That's right. But, what if..." He looked around again. "...What if you could take a picture not of the store, but of the *truth* of the store?"

"The *truth* of the store?"

"That big fellow at the other counter, speaking to Adam right there. Don't stare! If you take any of these cameras I've just demonstrated for you and snapped a photograph using any of the films we stock on that wall over there, what would you end up with?"

"A photo of that guy, right?"

"Yes, yes! But, what if you could take a picture of the *truth* of that fellow? You'd really have something, then, wouldn't you? Why, you'd know everything there was to know about him, wouldn't you? I mean, everything that's worth knowing, anyway. That would be really important, wouldn't it?"

"Well, it sure sounds important, but I don't understand how you can do that."

"Look here, sir." The salesman reached down below the display case and pulled out a black box with gold embossed lettering on it. "Let me show you this machine. We ordered three of these from the manufacturer in Belgium. They're expensive, but– for the right person, anyway– I think they are worth every red cent. I think you may be the right person, sir."

"Me? Why me?"

"I could tell from what you just said, sir. You are a person who is dedicated to getting to the truth, who is determined to see things for what they are– not merely what they appear to be. You're looking for something, aren't you? And you don't know what it is you're looking for, do you? At least you haven't seen it yet, have you?"

"How'd you know that?"

"It's my trade, sir. I don't believe you'd be satisfied with any of these– these ordinary cameras. They just take ordinary snapshots of the world as it appears to the naked eye. You've seen the world already. Am I right?"

"Well, I haven't seen all that much of the world, I guess."

"But what you've seen so far hasn't satisfied you, has it? There's more to be known beyond what's been seen and heard so far, isn't there?"

"Yeah, I get that feeling, sometimes. But, I don't understand how a camera..."

"It's *amazing*, sir. Let me show you how to operate the camera." He pulled the top of the box off and placed it aside. Sparky read the gold lettering on the lid. 'Waarheid Systeem Camera - Leuven Belgie'. It was all Greek to him, but he was intrigued and eager to see what it could offer.

"It doesn't use film, sir."

"Then, how can it take a picture?"

"I'm not sure. I only know that it *does*. It uses these little pads, here. They fit into this slot in the back compartment like this."

Sparky examined one of the pads. It was one of those tablets used as score pads in board games– the kind that you write on, then lift the plastic film to erase. Sparky's heart sank.

"This is just a score pad from a game! You can't take a picture with this! You can get these things in a Cracker Jack's box!"

"That is exactly what they are, sir, but don't judge too quickly. These Belgians have figured out a way of capturing and impressing the essential truth of things on these cheap score pads. I'm sure you'll agree, once you see the results, that you really don't need anything fancier or more permanent to capture truthful essences." He looked at the unit, turning it in his hands. "It's really so simple. It's marvelous."

Sparky stared at the unit, noticing the sleek design and the apparent quality of the workmanship. One thing that was obvious right off was that the camera had no real lens to speak of. It had a little pinhole in the center of the front of the body, surrounded by a large flat silver-plated faceplate with a brushed finish. There was a viewfinder at the top, where you'd expect one to be. On either side of the faceplate was a jutting metal nipple made of a yellow-colored metal. The nipple on the right stuck out a little further than the other. There was no way to advance film, since it used only those score pads to record an image. There was no exposure counter either. The sides and back of the unit were covered with black leatherette, embossed with an alligator pattern. The neck strap was made of black leather. It was very heavy and everything about it was quality– except for those score pads.

"Does it have a focus knob? I don't see how to focus. These other cameras you showed me had focus knobs."

"That's because it doesn't need to focus. It's not concerned with light and the properties of photons. With this unit, you are concerned with the true essence of things and that's something more consistent than some object's distance from the camera or how much light is reflecting off it. You'll notice, sir, that the only control is the trigger– I won't refer to it as a 'shutter release'– and the latch on the back to load or remove the pad."

"It's really heavy! *Much* heavier than any of the other cameras you showed me."

"I have heard that they use one of the heavy elements in its workings. It's not uranium or anything like that. I won't disassemble it to find out either. That would void the warranty."

142

"Can I try it?"

"Be my guest, sir." The salesman loaded one of the pads into the camera and shut the cover, handing it to Sparky. "Go ahead."

"Just point it at something and press this?"

"That's all."

Sparky raised the camera to his eye and peered through the viewfinder. He scoped the store and paused when a browsing customer at another counter came into view. He pressed the trigger.

Nothing.

"Nothing happened! Do I have to do anything else? It didn't click or anything."

The salesman smiled as he took the camera back from Sparky. He deftly opened the back cover and removed the pad. He glanced at it for a second, then handed it to Sparky, who looked at it immediately.

"Oh, my god! Neat-o! I don't believe this! This *is* amazing!" He looked at the salesman with eyes wide as saucers. The salesman only smiled back and nodded.

"Well sir, was I telling the truth?"

"This is amazing! It's like this guy's life is written here on this stupid little score pad. It's impossible. It didn't even make a noise– nothing! But here it is. Wow!"

He looked again at the information on the score pad. Sparky wondered how this pad enabled him to see this truth, though he didn't really "see" it, since it wasn't an image in the strict definition of the word. More than anything, Sparky "got" it rather than "saw" it. He got the man for what he truly was and he felt a mixture of feelings ranging from revulsion to sympathy all at the same time. He could see why he was the way he was and truly *what* he was.

"But, what does it mean?"

"What does what mean, sir?"

"What I'm looking at here– what does it mean to see the truth?"

"Well, sir, I'm not really qualified to say. I suppose it could mean something different to different users. All photography is the same. A photograph can be a very different experience depending on who you are and what you bring to the viewing experience. Even your mood at any given moment can affect your experience of an image."

"It's very complicated, isn't it?"

"Yes, sir. Are you interested in purchasing the camera?" Sparky hesitated, looking at the unit. "We do have a liberal return policy, sir. If you would like to try it out for a week and see if it satisfies."

"Okay, I will! How much is it?"

"It's a fine machine, sir. I can offer you the camera and a box of twenty pads for two hundred-ninety nine dollars and ninety-five cents plus tax. I assure you, it's a *very* good offer."

"Whew, that's a lot of money. What do I do with these pad things? I can't frame 'em. Do you sell a lot of these things? I mean, what do people do with them?"

"No, sir, I haven't sold many Waarheids. I must say that there seems to be very little demand for such a device. I showed this item to you because you seemed to be a person who would be interested. I sold one to a fellow who brought it back after two days. He said that it made his life too complicated and exchanged it for a fixed-focus, point-and-shoot Instamatic. My associate, Adam, sold one to a customer who came back and ordered twenty-five boxes of pads. He said he was a playwright, working on a new comedy and needed them to catalogue his cast of characters. The police department and the courts have expressed interest, but..."

"I bet *they'd* want the truth. That'd make their jobs a cinch!"

"I heard that, in fact, the camera made their jobs *more* difficult. They dropped the program and decided to not adopt the technology. I guess the truth somehow complicated their jobs. I don't know."

Sparky was perplexed, but still convinced he could benefit from the information such a device would offer, he dug out the wad of cash his mother gave him that morning. "I'll buy it."

Chapter 15: Lunch with Werner

Sparky was excited as hell. He had never spent such a huge sum of money before. Truth be told, it's likely he had not yet spent three hundred dollars during the entire span of his life. He trembled with awe at the possibilities of this investment. He had spent the entire previous afternoon and evening lamenting that he was living a life devoid of fun and excitement. Yet, here he was, as excited as a boy could possibly be, poised on the edge of figuring it all out, with the help of this European invention. He couldn't get a straight answer from his parents, though he persisted all evening, but he'd get answers now.

He couldn't stand still as the salesman wrote up the sales receipt. "This is gonna be great! I've been trying to get some questions answered and I've gotten nowhere. This is gonna fix *everything*!"

"Yes, I believe you'll be very satisfied with your Waarheid. Though, I caution you that this is merely an instrument. As with any instrument, it only plays as well as its owner and no better. Take your time and learn how to use it and you should be very happy with the results, I should think. Here you are– two ninety-nine twenty-five for the camera and twenty pads, plus five percent sales tax, which comes to seventeen ninety-nine. That's a grand total of three hundred seventeen ninety-two. Here, you see I've marked it 'paid in full'. Here's your copy and your change. Save that sales slip if you should decide to return it. And here you are, sir. You're all set, now."

Sparky was beaming and so absorbed in the possibilities of his new Waarheid that he failed to respond verbally to the salesman. Making his way past the tripods and lights, he came up to the huge man, still mulling over some light meters and lenses. He pulled the camera out of the box, loaded a score pad, and snapped an image of the man. He pulled it out with great anticipation and examined the results. It was plain as day. "You're wasting your time with this stuff, mister."

The man glared at Sparky, his nostrils flaring as he hissed through them. "And what do you know about it, kid? You some kind of expert?"

"Nope. It's just that you think you need better equipment and you don't. Your pictures are good enough. It's that you take yourself too serious."

"What? What do you know about my book?"

Adam spoke up. "Please, young man, we cannot have our clientele being harassed in this manner!"

"No, wait, Adam. You know, he's got a point there. I've been sort of stuck for a while now on this book project. Maybe it does need a lighter touch."

"Oh, you are a writer, sir? I took you for a photojournalist."

"Yeah, a historian. I've been working this particular book project for six and a half years, now. It's pretty much finished, but I haven't been able to sell it to any of the publishers here or in New York. I thought it was because my accompanying photos were lacking something, but now I'm not so sure. Maybe the youngster's right about this."

"Well, sir, what is it about, if I may ask?"

"It's the *History of Flatulence in Central and North America– 5,000 BC to the Present.*"

"Well, that sounds like a splendid book. Written in a breezy style, I assume?"

"I would say it's not. I hate to put on airs, but it is a scholarly work– twelve hundred and eighty pages, with two hundred and twelve pages of endnotes. It has eighty eight illustrations, including sixty nine of my photographs."

"A monumental tome, indeed, sir! I would think that once publishers got wind of it, they'd be clamoring for the rights to it."

"Not so far, Adam. You know, young man, I'm going to take your suggestion to heart and revisit the text. What's your name?"

"Sparky Donnelly."

"If this book gets published, I'm going to dedicate it to you, Sparky. Thank you." He extended his hand and they shook.

"Glad I could help. Well, see ya'." Sparky jauntily marched out the door. Once outside, he turned left and continued his search for the cleaners to get the tomato splotch out of his jacket. Up the block and near the corner of Unice Street was Alvarado's. Sparky was about to walk in, but hesitated a moment and whisked his new camera out of the bag. Loading a pad into the back just as he had seen the salesman do, he pointed the camera at Alvarado's and snapped an impression.

Sparky pulled it out and studied the truth about Alvarado's. It had been in business a long time, but was run by a Chinese family, now– no longer Armando Alvarado. They did quick work, but were sloppy and often lost garments. They charged more than their nearby competitors because Armando Alvarado had built a solidly good reputation and they felt they could get away with it. Sparky decided to try another place instead.

Sparky thought of his mom as he turned south on Unice Street, looking for another cleaner to take care of his jacket. His mom was always talking about how to be a smart shopper, looking for the best prices and the best quality. Sparky was planning ahead to using the camera to determine what really were the best deals. His mom and dad would hail him as a hero!

Suddenly, Sparky remembered that he hadn't attempted to call home in several hours. It was now about three o'clock and all his school chums would be getting out of school and heading home. If Giant or Les or any of his other friends would call his house or stop by, looking for him, he'd be in real trouble. Sparky decided to find out the time and attempt a call home before he was missed. He continued down Unice toward the 42nd Street station of the Number 7, Listen-Unice subway line, figuring there might be more stores and another cleaner near a station entrance. Sparky also came to the realization that he was very hungry, so he determined to keep his eyes open for a place to buy a frank or a burger and a shake.

"Young man! Young man!"

Sparky turned and saw the author from the camera shop huffing and puffing up the street trying to catch up to him. Sparky was afraid he had done something wrong back in camera shop, but because it was a customer and not a salesman running after him, he calmed down a bit.

148

"I wanted to catch up to you," he was breathing laboriously and sweating. "Sorry, I'm not used to this kind of workout. Lemme catch my breath."

"Did I do something wrong?"

"No, not at all! I was just really impressed by what you told me back there. I thought more about it and I'm convinced you're absolutely right about it." He continued huffing and puffing and sweating between phrases. "I think you saved my hide with what you told me. I'd like to pay you back somehow– more than just a lousy dedication. What can I give you?"

"Oh, that's okay. I wasn't lookin' for anything. I'm just glad I could help."

"Where'ya headed?"

"I need to get my jacket cleaned, but I was looking for someplace to get something to eat. I had a jelly donut at 10:30 and I'm kinda' hungry."

"Let me buy you lunch. It would be an honor."

"Well…"

"Come on, I'm feeling hungry myself. The diner up the street here is pretty good. What'ya say? Come on."

Sparky thought about the twenty-three dollars he paid for the policeman's lunch. "Okay!"

They walked down Unice Street until they came to the Bon Voyage Diner between 42nd and 43rd Streets, on the ground floor of the 55-story Clark Tower. On the way, they talked about the camera shop and how well organized the store is and how friendly and helpful the salesmen are. The man introduced himself as Werner Weaner.

"I've been teaching at St. Charles College for twelve years. I'm in the history department."

"I live on St. Charles *Street*."

149

"That's a coincidence. Anyway, *The History of Flatulence* is my third book– well, my fourth, but one of them I haven't tried to get published. That was *A History of Fallen Arches, 1730-1950*."

"Why didn't you try to get that one published?"

"My editor said it was too similar to another book that had come out the previous year. I still have the manuscript. Maybe I'll revisit it in a few years, I don't know. So, I was saying, my first book was *Forgetfulness Through the Ages*. Academic Horizons published that one in '63."

"What was that one about?"

"Just what the title says. I don't get cute with my titles. There's nothing I despise more than some catchy title that has little to do with the book itself. I studied the causes and effects of forgetfulness in everyday society, going back to the Mesopotamians."

"Wow. That's something, huh?"

"I taught a course on that at St. Charles. Did you know, Sparky, that forgetfulness cost the British Empire more than six hundred million Pounds during the reigns of Queen Victoria and King Edward?"

"I didn't know that. Why'd it cost them so much money? I mean if I forget to bring a book back to the library, they charge me a late fee. Is that the kinda thing you're talking about?"

"Not exactly. It's more complicated than that. I devised a graph that takes into consideration 117 factors– I call it the 117 Point Formula– and multiplies them by various cost factors to arrive at a dollar figure that represents real loss."

"So, how do they get that money back?"

"They don't. That's why forgetfulness is such a problem."

"How can you stop it? Is there some kind of a cure or something?"

"Not that I know of, but I thought government and economists should know what their up against."

"Sounds handy."

"My second book took me four grueling years to research. When I finally finished it, I really thought I might never venture to write another."

"What was so hard about it?"

"It required me to live the life of a swimmer– to train, to eat, to move, to even think like a swimmer."

"A swimmer?"

"Yeah, I wanted to get into the mind, the psyche of a person who swims, so that I could understand it and be able to express it."

"What was it about? The life of Buster Crabbe, or something?"

"I'm not a biographer. No, it was *Swimming in the Dark Ages: Monks and Mermaids in Medieval Europe*. Here's the restaurant, Sparky."

The restaurant was very upscale by Sparky's standards. There was lots of dark brown Formica and a dark red carpet everywhere. The jukeboxes were brand new and shiny. A woman in a very snug, short, white dress showed them to their table. Sparky noticed that she smelled nice– a nice change from Werner Weaner, who exuded stale sweat odor.

"I can't sit at a booth." Werner patted his large midsection. "Can we have a table?"

"Certainly, Mr. Weaner. What about right here?"

"Great, thanks." The woman left the menus and withdrew.

"She knew your name!"

"They all know me, Sparky." He picked up his menu and opened it. "I like the chef's salad. The chicken-in-a-basket is good here, too."

"I like chicken salad. If they have a chicken salad sandwich, that's what

I'm gonna get."

"Get whatever you want. It's on me."

A waitress showed up and plunked down two glasses of water and some sesame-covered breadsticks. "Hi, Werner. What can I get you to two gentlemen to drink?"

"I'm ready to order. Are you?"

"Sure! I'll get a chicken salad sandwich and a Coke."

"What kinda bread, hon?" Sparky looked blank. "You want that on white toast?"

"Sure. Hey, you don't put anything in the Coke, do you?"

"Not sure what you mean, hon. Like ice or cherry syrup?"

"No, I mean stuff to make you woozy. Never mind. Forget it."

"Sure, hon. An' what about you, Werner?"

"Give me the chef's salad with bleu cheese dressing, large fries– what's the soup of the day?"

"Potato bisque."

"It's not spicy, is it?" The waitress shook her head. "Gimme a bowl of potato bisque. And a large Tab." The waitress wrote frantically. "You're gonna bring some bread, right?"

"Sure will, hon." She snatched the menus and retreated to the kitchen. Sparky noticed that her uniform was so short in the back that he could see her panties through her pantyhose under the hemline.

"Did you miss lunch, too, Werner?"

"No, why?"

"No, I– just askin'. You ordered a lot of food. Aren't you afraid it'll spoil your dinner?"

"No."

Sparky grabbed a breadstick and tapped it on the table. "So, are you famous?"

"Me? I don't know. I suppose you could say…"

"Have you been on TV shows?"

"Well, no, not really."

"You've never been interviewed by Mike Douglas? Or Johnny Carson?"

"Nope."

"Dick Cavett?"

"No."

"How 'bout that guy with the eyes– William F. Buckwheat?"

"Buckley. No. I don't know if you've noticed this about TV, but you really don't see a lot of historians on TV these days. Hey, how'd you get out of school early? It's just now three o'clock."

"It's a long story, but I basically missed the bus this morning and I couldn't get back home, so I wandered into the camera shop."

"You're not a runaway, are you?"

"Why does everybody think I'm a runaway?"

"Well, you're running around downtown, alone, on a school day and your clothes are a mess. It's a natural assumption, I think." Werner crunched down on a breadstick and initiated an avalanche of crumbs on his shirtfront. "These things are stale as hell."

"So how famous are you?"

"I don't know. I suppose I'm well-respected in academia."

"Where's that?"

"The world of education– you know, among historians. Nobody is more highly regarded than I am in the areas of medieval swimming, foot pain during the age of enlightenment or the mores of puking in the Dutch colonies, for that matter. I guess I'm a kind of minor celebrity, you could say."

The waitress brought their drinks and withdrew again without comment. She was no longer wearing the pantyhose.

"Does this taste like Tab to you?"

"I can't tell. I think mine is sweeter. I'm not sure."

"I don't understand why I can't get a Tab in a restaurant to taste the same twice in a row."

"Maybe you could write a history of fountain sodas, next."

"Don't get smart. Something's been on my mind. How did you know what direction I should take with my book? I mean, how could you know I was on the wrong track with the camera equipment? You were all the way across the camera shop from me. You couldn't have heard what I was saying to Adam."

"It's this." Sparky pulled the Waarheid from the bag and placed it on the table. "I took a shot of you and read the score pad. It told me."

Werner picked up the camera and examined it, turning it and looking at every angle.

"It doesn't take a picture of what you see, it captures the essence of things instead," Sparky stated proudly.

Werner pointed the camera across the restaurant, getting the feel of it. "It's a heavy piece– well made. I can see *that*, at least." He looked at the bottom. "Belgian, eh? I didn't know they made anything except chocolate and new Belgians. How'd you hear about this thing?"

"The guy at the camera shop showed it to me. He showed me a bunch of cameras, but nothing was the right thing until he showed me this."

"I don't understand how it captures the– how did you put it?– the essence of things. Where does the film go?"

"It doesn't take film. It uses these score pads." Sparky pulled out the box of pads.

"I don't believe it."

"What do you mean?"

"Are you *serious*?"

The waitress brought Werner's bisque. Werner added a lot of salt and a little pepper before tasting it. Sparky watched the waitress's rear end as she walked away. Her cheeks were a bright red.

"Come on, Sparky. There's no way you can capture someone's essence on one of these score pads." Werner added several packs of crackers to the soup. "That's just some plastic and waxy cardboard. We used to keep score on these things when we played Careers. Sorry, kid, but I think you got rooked." Werner swallowed mouthfuls of hot soup between phrases. "How much did they take you for, for that thing? Two hundred? Two-fifty?"

"Three hundred-sixteen dollars."

"You should take it back– get your money back." He signaled the waitress for more crackers by holding up the last pack.

"But, the thing works! Just like it's supposed to! I captured your essence, didn't I?"

"That's ridiculous. Lemme see the image you got." The waitress brought Werner a whole plate full of crackers, which he promptly opened up and dumped into the remaining soup.

"Here. Don't get crumbs on it."

Werner glanced briefly at the image on the pad. "That's not my essence. That's not me." He tossed the pad on the table.

"You just barely looked at it!"

"Don't you think I could recognize myself? Take it back. I'm telling you, it's worthless– just some kind of trick novelty thing."

"You don't know what you're talking about! It's not a trick!"

The waitress brought out the rest of the food. "Here you go, gentlemen. You wanna move your camera, hon? There's your tuna salad on whole wheat and here's your chef salad. Your fries are coming out in a minute. Is there anything else you need?"

"Ma'am, I ordered chicken salad not tuna salad."

"Hon, you ordered tuna salad on whole wheat. I got it written down right here." She waved her pad without looking at it.

"I did not! Why would I order tuna salad? I *never* eat tuna. I don't like fish."

"You tryin' to tell me my job or somethin'?"

"I'm not trying to tell you your job, but I didn't order tuna salad. I didn't even pick the bread– *you* did. White toast, you said. Look at your pad. It's right there."

"Look, hon, I don't gotta look at my pad. I know what I wrote and I know what you ordered. You've been too busy lookin' at my ass to know what the hell you ordered."

"She's right, Sparky. And you *did* order the chicken salad on white toast."

"Yeah, that's what I said, but she said I ordered the tuna! I said I ordered the chicken salad. And who said I was lookin' at her ass?!"

"Well, that's what you got, so what's the problem?"

"I'll get you your fries while you sort this out." The waitress withdrew to the kitchen again.

"I don't get it. She said she brought me tuna salad on whole wheat. She said that's what I ordered. You heard her, didn't you?"

"Yeah, I heard her. She got your order right, didn't she? Why don't you forget about it and enjoy your meal. We came here to celebrate, didn't we?" Werner poured the salad dressing over the chef salad. "I'm gonna need more of this bleu cheese dressing. If you see the waitress, try to get her attention, will ya'?"

Sparky calmed down and looked at the sandwich. The bread looked odd to him. It was brown. There was a generous helping of salad on the bread, plus slices of tomato and lettuce. Sparky picked up half the sandwich and bit into it.

"This *is* tuna salad! She lied!"

"What do you mean she lied? She told you she brought tuna salad on whole wheat. What's the problem?"

"I didn't order this! I ordered chicken salad. Where *is* she? And this bread has seeds in it. I can't eat this."

"Didn't you order chicken salad on whole wheat?"

"I'm not gonna answer you. You're just trying to confuse me. Where is she?"

"Look, Sparky, you're making a scene. Why don't you just eat what you ordered and not fuss. It's not fair to the waitress. She has a hard enough job as it is without you changing your mind on her. She's gotta put up with customers looking up her dress all day long, trying to see her ass."

"Maybe she should wear a longer uniform. I'm not gonna eat this bird-food bread. Look at this– it has seeds!"

"What do you expect? If you order rye bread, you get seeds."

"Where did she go?"

"Why don't you just scrape the chicken salad off the bread and eat it that way?"

"Because it's not chicken salad. It's tuna salad."

"You should've gotten the chef's salad. It's really good."

"Maybe if I'd ordered the chef's salad, she woulda' brought me chicken salad."

"That doesn't make any sense. You know I thought about writing a history of the chefs in the French monarchy during the 18th and 19th centuries. In the end, I decided against it."

"Why's that?"

"I didn't think there'd be much interest. I ended up collaborating on a history of rowdyism during the Hellenistic age. These fries are good. They taste like potato not like grease."

"How'd you get your fries!?"

"What do you mean? The waitress brought them."

"I've been looking for the waitress the whole time. I didn't see her come back!"

"Well, she did. And I asked her for more bleu cheese dressing and she came back and brought that cup of it right there. Then she dropped off these." Werner held up a pair of frilly panties. "What's your problem? You should pay more attention to what's going on."

Sparky just stared, open-mouthed and looked around, incredulous. "This is really weird." Werner started to interrupt Sparky, but Sparky cut him off. "No, really. This is weird. I've been looking for her to get me my chicken salad sandwich and I didn't see her."

"You want another?" Werner pounded the back of the ketchup bottle on the last few French fries.

"Another sandwich? I never got one in the first place. It was tuna. On bird bread."

"You got chicken salad on toast. You told her you didn't want it and she took it away."

"That's ridiculous. You're pullin' my leg."

"Oh, yeah? If it's so ridiculous, then where's your sandwich? Answer me that."

The sandwich *was* gone– just as Werner said.

"C'mon, Sparky. Let's get dessert. They have good cakes and pies here. Hey, miss!" Werner waved her over. "We're going to get dessert. What'll you have, kid?" Sparky didn't know what to ask for. What he really wanted was lunch, but he surmised that he wasn't going to get any, here. "How 'bout an éclair, Sparky? Do you like those?"

"Sure– an éclair."

"Bring him an éclair and I'll have blueberry pie and a chocolate malted. And bring me another Tab. Thanks."

"Comin' right up, hon." Sparky wanted to look at her and catch a glance of what he was sure was her pantyless rear end, but for some reason he couldn't turn his head in her direction until it was too late. She had already passed through the doors to the kitchen.

"You want to be a photographer or something? I mean, what possessed you to buy such an expensive camera?"

"I don't know. I suppose it's just the thing for me. I don't know why I decided to buy the thing. I didn't plan to. I didn't even know there was a camera shop there. I was walking past when I stopped to look in the window."

"I wanted to be a photographer. I wanted to be a professional and take pictures of women, you know? I bought my first camera when I was thirteen and I took shots of all kinds of things. I photographed my family when we went on picnics or to the zoo. I photographed my classmates in school and in the playground. I went to the airport and took shots of the planes coming in for landings. I photographed the Blackstone Bridge from the Jackson Avenue Bridge. I took several rolls of film in the formal gardens in Edgewood Park. I photographed the demolition of the old Bingham Hotel down on Cord Street. You're too young to remember the old Bingham. Yeah, it was fun while it lasted," Werner sighed.

"Whaddya mean 'while it lasted'?"

"I only had the camera for six months."

"What happened? Did it break?"

"No, my dad took my camera away from me."

"Why'd he do that?"

"He got angry at me. I was selling pictures of my kid sister, Scarlet."

"Wow! You were selling your photos when you were only *thirteen*?"

"Yeah, I made enough money to pay for my film and a nifty tripod and have some pretty good pocket money, too. My father put the kibosh on that. He didn't approve."

"But, you wanted to be a professional. Professionals sell their work. That's what makes them professionals. They work for magazines who pay them big bucks for their photos."

"That's what I told my father. Didn't make any difference. He sold my camera and equipment."

"Did he keep the money?"

"He said he used it. He claimed he had to pay for therapy for Scarlet, or some bullshit."

"That's not fair– using your money to pay for her therapy. They should have paid for therapy for *you* instead."

"What the hell do you mean by *that*?"

"Well, you're the one that lost the camera."

"Oh! Right. You're right. You finished with your éclair? I'll meet you up front at the cash register. I gotta hit the restroom first." Werner sucked down the rest of his Tab and headed to the restrooms in the back. Sparky left a bite or two of éclair on his plate. It was too rich for him to finish on an empty stomach. Sparky gathered his new camera, the bag and his school books, which seemed to have come back into his possession after a long absence, and headed to the front of the restaurant. On his way up front, the waitress accosted him with the check.

"Don' wanna forget this, hon," she said glibly as she tore it out of her book and handed it to Sparky. "Don't see your eatin' partner, so you're the lucky fella. Have a great afternoon, hon." She withdrew to serve the other patrons in her station.

Sparky hung around the cash register, pacing slightly back and forth and kicking his heels on the dark carpet, waiting for Werner to reappear from the bathroom.

Chapter 16: Looking for the Hotel Cat

"You going to pay that check? Or are you waiting for Mommy and Daddy to pay it?"

Sparky looked up from the carpet and addressed the question posed by the cashier– the same girl that seated them when they came in, except she didn't look the same. She'd put on some weight and gotten considerably older. "I'm waiting for my friend to come out. He said he was going to pay."

"You've been waiting a while. Is he in the restroom? I can have someone check on him for you, if you'd like." She summoned one of the busboys and sent him to the back to check the men's room. Sparky resumed staring at the carpet and pacing in circles. The busboy returned and reported quietly back to the cashier, who sighed loudly and spoke again to Sparky. "This friend of yours– he's not in the restroom."

"He said he was gonna use the bathroom and that he'd meet me up here."

"Felipe checked both restrooms and no sign of your friend."

"That can't be right! That's the second time!" Sparky didn't know what to say.

"Looks like he stuck you with the bill, young man."

"He must still be here. How could he get out?"

"I know one possibility." She caught the eye of the busboy again. "Hey Felipe, ask them in the kitchen if anybody walked through there." Felipe trundled off to the kitchen and soon reported back that the kitchen staff had seen a big, laughing man go out through there.

"Werner is a big guy. That musta' been him! But, he said he was treating me."

"Sorry, little fella, but looks like you got stuck with the bill. You should've been more careful. Werner pulls that trick all the time."

"You *know* about him? He's done this before?"

"Oh, yeah! A dozen times at least."

"Why'd you let him do it again?"

"We don't care. As long as the check gets paid, everything is cool as far as we're concerned."

"That's not fair! He ate ten times as much as me!"

"Is it fair that a waitress and busboy worked hard to provide a fine dining experience without getting compensated? You two occupied a table that we could have filled with paying customers. Is that fair to the restaurant?"

"The place is almost empty."

"You think it's okay to stiff an empty restaurant, but not a full one?"

"No, I guess not. I don't know. I *do* know that I didn't even get the right sandwich. I ordered a chicken salad on toast. She brought me tuna salad. I couldn't even eat it."

"You should've complained."

"I did, but she said it *was* what I ordered."

"The waitress said you ordered tuna salad?"

"Yeah, she said I ordered tuna salad, then she said I got chicken salad. I don't know what she was saying. Then Werner said I didn't eat the sandwich because I wasn't hungry, but I was starving! I ended up eating an éclair while he stuffed his face with soup and a gigantic salad and fries and pie!"

A man in a suit walked up at that moment. "Please, young man. Let's keep our voices down, here. We don't want to disturb our diners, do we? What seems to be the difficulty, Abigail?"

"Werner again."

"Ah. Well, I *am* sorry, young man, but you will have to pay the check or we will be forced to summon the police. It's your choice, of course."

Sparky thought of the consequences. "I'll pay. What's the total?"

"Thirteen-eighty." Sparky presented a twenty to Abigail. "Felipe, do you know if Werner left a tip?"

"No tip, Abby."

"How much should I leave as a tip?"

"Two dollars would suffice."

Abigail gave Sparky his change and bade him farewell and good luck. "Come again!" she added, cheerfully.

Sparky muttered "what a rip-off," under his breath and walked out onto Unice Street. The shadows were getting longer and the traffic was picking up. Sparky wondered exactly what time it was. In fact, he was getting really concerned that his mother might be worried, not knowing his whereabouts. From the look of things, Sparky thought it was probably about four o'clock, maybe a quarter after four, and he figured he ought to warn her his mom that he was not going to get home until dinner time. He started downtown again, in the hopes of finding a payphone and figuring that, afterward, he could keep walking to U.S. Plaza and grab the Number 13 express at Miller Avenue and M Street.

He spied a payphone right away at the corner of Unice and Lester Place. When he stepped into the booth and prepared to slip a dime into the slot, he saw that someone had stuffed chewing gum in it. He picked up the receiver, but didn't get a dial tone, so he hung it up and continued downtown.

At 35th Street, he spied another phone booth. There was a man already in the booth, talking quietly to someone. Sparky decided to wait to use the phone and since he had to wait, he pulled out his camera and snapped a shot of the man and the phone booth.

He excitedly pulled the pad out and took a look at it. Even in the gray afternoon shadows, the impression was clear. The man was nuts. He was talking, but to himself. The phone was not connected to anyone else. Sparky looked again at the man to see if there was some kind of error, but could not discern anything by just looking from outside the booth. The guy looked normal enough and the conversation had the usual pauses and interjections in it– just like his mom's conversations. He knocked on the door of the booth to get the man's attention.

"Hey, mister, can I use the phone?" The man glanced over his hunched shoulder, but made no response. Sparky walked around to the right side of the phone booth to put himself right in the man's line of sight, then knocked on the glass. "Can I use the phone, please, mister?"

The man looked blankly at Sparky, then pulled the receiver away from the phone with all his might, groaning with the strain, until the cord separated. He opened the door to the booth and stepped out, addressing Sparky with no rancor and no teeth. "No, I'm shorry, you can'tch ushe the phone. Unfortchunatchely, itch's oud of order. The resheiver haj jush come off in my hanj. Can you believe itch?" He started walking away as he spoke over his shoulder, "Good tching I warned you, kidj, or you woulda' washted your tchen shentchs, huh?"

Sparky looked at the wrecked phone for a few seconds, then back at the figure of the man receding up the street, then continued his march downtown in search of another payphone.

At the entrance to the Unice Street subway station on M Street, Sparky came upon a bank of four phone booths. The first one was blackened by fire and the phone was partially melted. Someone was in the second booth, not on the phone, but hunched over and doing something secretive. Sparky couldn't see what. There was a lady in the third one, rifling through the yellow pages and meticulously tearing out just the ads she needed, very considerately leaving the rest of the book intact. The fourth booth was empty. Sparky stepped in with a dime at the ready and deposited it in the slot. He listened for the dial tone. Nothing. He reached up and jiggled the coin return lever a couple of times. Nothing. He pounded his fist on the area at the top where the coin slot is. Nothing. He flipped down the coin return hopper and checked for his dime. Nothing. 'This is unbelievable! Is there one stupid payphone that works in this entire city?!' He tried hanging up the receiver, listening for his coin to be released. 'Now it ate my dime!' Picking up his bags, he exited the booth, deciding to wait for one of the occupied booths to open up.

Sparky waited and waited. Not having a watch, he couldn't tell exactly how long he had waited, but estimated four or five minutes at least. Finally the man that was in booth number two finished his covert ministrations and exited. Sparky stepped forward and produced another dime, which he slipped into the slot. The coin passed through and dropped into the coin return hopper. He tried again, this time forcing the dime in with some added velocity, but the coin passed right through the phone once more. He jiggled the coin return lever just in case it was stuck in the return position and tried a third time with no luck. Taking his dime, he stepped out and looked at the other booths, all of which were occupied– including the one with the melted phone, wherein a man was carrying on a conversation with someone at the other end of the line. 'I wonder if that guy's nuts, too.' Sparky waited a minute or so before his frustration got the better of him and he gave up and scoped out the surroundings for other payphones. He saw no other phone booths, but he spotted someone who he thought could help him. Sparky hurried over to a frankfurter vendor operating a cart at the corner.

"Whaddya have, kid?"

"These phones here are no good. Do you know where I can find another payphone?"

"You can use the Hotel Cat."

"What?" Sparky stared at him, thinking this guy's nuts, too.

"Did you hear me, kid?"

"I'm serious. I need a payphone. I've gotta call my mother and let her know I'm gonna be late."

"Look for the Hotel Cat. Up the street there." He gestured toward M Street, west to the waterfront. "That's your best bet."

"How am I gonna find a hotel cat? What's it gonna be just sitting there, or something?"

"Whaddya think? It's gonna just walk away?" He snapped his fingers.

"What would stop it?"

166

"It's not gonna just go somewheres. It's been there a long time."

"How long has it been there? Do you know?"

"A long time. It's very old. It wasn't always the Hotel Cat."

"What was it before it was the hotel cat?"

"I can't remember." The man sucked his teeth.

"What does the hotel cat look like?"

"I don' know, kid. Brown, I think. Yeah, it's brown. It's big. You can't miss it." The man picked his back teeth and ate whatever his finger had dislodged. Then he turned to serve a businessman, who had come up and ordered a frank with onions and sauerkraut.

The businessman chimed in. "What's he looking for?"

"The Hotel Cat."

"Yeah, son, you can't miss it. It's a few blocks down."

"Do you know what side of the street it's on?" Sparky had to wait for the completion of the businessman's transaction for his answer.

"It's on the right side. You'll know it when you see it."

Sparky assessed his options and decided to go along with the preposterous suggestion. He didn't want to wait again for one of these payphones to open up, and he was heartened by the fact that the businessman corroborated the existence of this cat. "Thanks for your help, mister."

The frankfurter vendor scratched the side of his greasy head then ran his finger through the channels of his left ear. "Yeah, good luck, kid."

Sparky turned to cross Unice Street again and wondered to himself if he was losing his marbles, too. 'Everything *looks* normal and sane enough here, but if my best hope of finding a working phone booth is to consult a cat, I wonder.'

The sidewalks were getting more and more crowded as the government employees along M Street started getting out of work and Sparky wondered how he was ever going to spot a cat outside with all the foot traffic milling about. He kept his eyes down and peeled, however, and he also looked in doorways and alleyways and any niche large enough to hold a cat. He wasn't sure how far down M Street this cat may be lurking and he wasn't really prepared to walk all the way to Waterfront Drive, but he got the impression from the street vendor that this thing must be fairly close by.

As he made his way slowly down the street he attracted the attention of the passersby.

"You lose something, son?" a woman asked him.

"No, ma'am, I'm looking for a cat."

"Hey, miss, what's the matter with him?"

"He says he's looking for his cat."

"How'd he lose a cat around here?"

"I have no idea. Ask him."

"Hey sonny, how'd you lose your cat around here?"

"I didn't. It's not my cat. I guess it belongs to a hotel."

"Did it run away?"

"Mister, I have no idea why it would be out here, but that's what I was told. All I want to do is find a working payphone and make a call home, and for some reason, I can't seem to do that."

"Do you need to borrow a dime?"

"No, that's not the problem. I've got a dime. I can't get a working phone. The frankfurter guy thought my best chance was to find the hotel cat. It sounded stupid, but when the other man agreed with him, I thought maybe it was good advice."

"The hotel cat? Oh, the *Hotel Cat*! That guy meant the Hotel Catalina! The sign says 'The Hotel Cat', but that's 'cause it's busted. It's the old Catalina Hotel that guy meant. He had you actually looking for a *cat*? Ha ha!" The few people who had stopped to assist got a big laugh out of Sparky's naiveté.

"That's not nice, laughing at somebody like that!" Sparky started to get peeved.

"We're not laughing *at* ya', son. Ha ha! We're laughing *with* ya'. Ha ha!"

"But, I'm not laughing."

"Oh, I can't wait to tell my wife when I get home. That's a classic. The hotel *cat*! Ha ha!"

The small crowd dispersed and left Sparky standing there alone, at which point he shook his head in disgust and continued westward, now in search of a hotel called The Catalina.

Sparky picked up his pace as he hustled down M Street to his destination, coming upon the unique intersection, where Third Avenue meets Concord Avenue, M Street and Queens Avenue as they all pass over Miller Avenue. The city dug the trench for Miller Avenue during the Great Depression to help alleviate traffic congestion and provide employment for thousands of laborers. It cost many millions of dollars and spawned the adjacent U.S.Plaza project and its excellent park, but in the long term, it eased traffic woes not at all.

Sparky stopped on the overpass and leaned over the side, looking down at the traffic and pedestrians on Miller Avenue– those government and civil service workers scrambling to get on their buses or subway trains to get home. 'Hey! This is the perfect place!' Sparky loaded a score pad into the Waarheid camera and pointed it at the sidewalk below, toward the entrance of a large government office building, and pressed the release button. He opened the back and pulled out the pad, examining it carefully for clues to what all the hustle and bustle was about and what great things were happening here.

He had deduced from countless references in textbooks and filmstrips, and from several films shown during assembly, that the government

169

was one place where some of the most exciting and interesting things were taking place. As one film had worded it, 'The government was the vanguard of innovation, the nemesis of world hunger and disease, the greatest team of men and women ever assembled, working tirelessly for the common good of all mankind, guarding civilization from the plague of communism...' and so forth. Here, before his eyes, however, Sparky saw only tired, frantic people, desperate to return to the sanctuaries of their apartment or house, willing to endure commuting on overcrowded public conveyances for the privilege of a few hours in front of their TV sets and a few more in dreamy solitude.

Where was the fun and excitement? Where was the profound satisfaction of performing a role in transforming the suffering, hopeless Earth into the glorious democratic Utopia it inevitably will be by the year 2000? Sparky looked everywhere on the score pad, but failed to find any of it. He began to suspect that the Waarheid was not all it was cracked-up to be. 'This thing is crap. This isn't showing anything that I can't already see with my own eyes. What a rip-off! These people look just like my dad when he comes home. That can't be right!'

Sparky decided to use another pad and snap a new image. Perhaps he hadn't quite gotten the hang of the thing yet. Perhaps there was a certain technique he had yet to develop. He pointed the camera again, this time straight down on the throng below. He pulled out the pad and examined the results, only to be disappointed again by what he saw. 'This doesn't make sense,' he thought to himself as he dug into the bag, looking for the instruction booklet.

Sparky hoped to find out something about the use of the camera that he didn't already know; that could explain why he was not getting the results he had anticipated. Despite the booklet being printed in some foreign language, he could plainly see that there was nothing in there but the procedure for loading and unloading the score pad and some drawings that clearly warned against dropping the unit or exposing it to extreme heat. The little foldout booklet contained no tricks about how best to use the Waarheid. It just depicted it being used.

Sparky put the booklet back in the box and the box in the bag. He looked again at both pads and looked down at the countless commuters, streaming out of the buildings below and shook his head and sighed. He thought about the heroes of American history, the Founding Fathers, the great Presidents and statesmen, the risk-takers and humanitarians, working tirelessly, fighting disease, testing dangerous new technologies, thwarting imperialism and rocketing across vast oceans of space to set foot upon the moon.

'I guess I was wrong. This isn't the perfect place to take an image.' He didn't know what that place might be.

Chapter 17: What's in a Name?

The entrance to his subway line was down there and he thought momentarily of descending and hopping onto the express, which would make a mere three stops and get him home in twenty-five minutes. He saw a pair of phone booths next to the newsstand at the top of the stairs, but both booths were occupied and there were a couple of people waiting to use them next. After hesitating a moment, he decided he'd trust the frankfurter guy and walk the last block to the Hotel Catalina, let his mother know he was all right, then come back and catch the Number 13 and go home. It would delay him at most fifteen or twenty minutes more and maybe ameliorate the punishment he was bound to receive for being so late– not to mention missing school. Sparky still didn't know what would come of *that* little indiscretion.

By the time he got halfway down the long block between Miller and Railroad Avenues, he could see the huge neon sign of the Hotel Catalina, hanging off the corner of the building. The frankfurter guy was right. It said 'Hotel Cat', in letters aligned vertically, with the 'alina' missing entirely. Sparky was reassured a little bit by having one thing appear as it was supposed to. Though, truth be told, he started to wonder why he should have to trudge all the way to this particular hotel just to make a phone call.

He started to feel really foolish and contemplated turning around and grabbing that express train right away, but immediately changed his mind and thought that it might be cool to walk into an honest-to-goodness hotel lobby. Never having been in one before, he'd seen movies and TV shows that had fancy, ornate hotels with palatial lobbies. World leaders, movie stars, famous athletes, top business executives and international spies all stay in hotels. Maybe he'd bump into someone famous. He might see Charlton Heston or Barbara Feldon or Forest Tucker or David McCallum or Ivan Dixon. Who knows? He began to feel excited again and it put a little spring in his step.

Here in Robinsonville, the buildings west of Miller Avenue were clearly much older than the government buildings at U.S.Plaza. They were built to a scale that seemed strange to Sparky. They were shorter and narrower, yet the windows were very large in proportion. Everything was stone and iron. The sidewalk, which was paved with huge slabs of granite instead of concrete, was grossly uneven in many places

172

and noticeably wider than in other areas of Highbridge, which made the buildings seem even smaller than they were. There were glass circles embedded in the sidewalk, for what purpose Sparky couldn't tell. He hypothesized that they might light up at night, or perhaps that they somehow improved traction in wet or icy conditions. The street itself was mostly covered with asphalt, but asphalt had worn away, revealing cobblestones in many places. The lampposts looked ancient here, too. They were dark brown and rusty and had an elaborate shape, with the posts grooved like ancient columns, but made of iron instead of stone. Even the street signs were old here. They looked like they were made of iron, as well.

The stores and businesses were of a different character than what he had seen thus far in his sojourn. There were hardware stores and pawn-shops and plumbing and electrical supply places. There were a couple of places that sold used office furniture. Most of the businesses had their goods strewn outside on the sidewalk, much of it displayed in wooden bins and trays. There was a plastics supply store that had every imaginable size and shape of plastic tossed about in bins. Sparky was fascinated with all this stuff, wondering what kind of people would come to one of the businesses here and pick out a bagful of what-have-you. He supposed that the branch of humanity called handymen would really love this kind of place and would know exactly what to do with a bin full of switches or pipe joints or little metal plates with three holes in them. To Sparky, it looked like a huge, mysterious erector set.

Just at that moment, Sparky spied such a handyman coming out of a place called Jorgenson's & Sons Hardware and Plumbing Supply. He quickly drew out his camera and took a shot of the man as he carried a cardboard box full of stuff to a van parked at the curb. The man was dressed in dark blue pants and shirt. He had a tape measure clipped to his belt and his shirt sleeves were rolled up to reveal a long-sleeved thermal undershirt beneath. In his shirt pocket was a pocket protector, which contained a pen and a couple of pencils. The man had that look of rough and calloused masculinity that men get when they work with their hands, often outdoors and exposed to the elements. His skin was leathery and his hands had that gray-brown, perpetually dirty look. His hair was bushy and unkempt. He finished loading the box into the side door of his van and, with his cigarette dropping ash on his shirtfront, he walked around to the driver's side and pulled away, leaving a cloud of blue-white exhaust in his place.

Sparky pulled out the score pad and examined the results. At last, the Waarheid delivered some compelling results. The pad showed a man who was very satisfied with his work, who took great pride in fixing broken things and setting things right and that he was clever and creative with his hands. He'd been married for many years and had two grown children and was about to become a grandfather for the first time. He lived a modest life nearby. He was friendly and generous. It also showed that the man lived a fun and exciting life, though Sparky was a little perplexed by the form that the man's fun and excitement seemed to take.

It was not the man's profession that afforded him the joy that registered on the pad. The fun and excitement in this man's life came from fencing stolen goods and from all the plotting and lying that participating in such activities necessitates. Sparky was surprised. There was nothing in this man's outer demeanor that would indicate that he was involved in any criminal activity. He appeared to be just a regular sort of guy. Yet, here on the pad it was plain that he made nearly as much money from crime as he did from his Regency Plumbing business. The extra money he made from selling stolen merchandise went into financing visits to a girlfriend. His home life was supported by the plumbing concern.

Sparky was elated to have learned something about living a fun and exciting life, but he never would have guessed that one had to be an adulterer and a criminal to have that fun and excitement. This left Sparky disappointed. He was *not* disappointed, however, in the Waarheid. It was an eye-opener in this case, and Sparky started thinking that he had made an excellent purchase. He looked at the image on the score pad one last time, then put the camera away and continued on down the block to the hotel.

Railroad Avenue has been home to the right-of-way of the commuter rail lines in and out of the City of Highbridge for a century, now. For almost twenty years, the tracks ran on the surface of Railroad Avenue, until traffic became so congested that the tracks were moved to a tunnel beneath the street. The trains have terminated at 33rd Street since 1871 and the railroad maintained additional stations at Ducommun Street, M Street and First Avenue from that time until the 1930s. Along that two-mile stretch, countless hotels sprouted up, the first within a mere twelve days of the opening of the railroad.

In 1904, at the northwest corner of M Street and Railroad Avenue, a grand structure was built, rising nineteen stories from the sidewalk to its rooftop gardens. It was named the Ravenna Hotel and it offered first-class accommodations to those out-of-towners who preferred to stay near the shopping and theatre district of Robinsonville rather than in the downtown business district. It is no longer common knowledge that Robinsonville was the cultural heart of Highbridge from roughly 1880, when the railroad was built, until 1918, when theatre-goers and shoppers migrated to newer, more fashionable venues in Lester and Midtown, a mile or more northeast. Little of that gay period of Robinsonville remains in its original state today. Though most of the structures of that vivacious period still exist, nearly none of them still houses the type of business for which it was built. One of the few that does is the building that once housed the Ravenna, though it hasn't been called that since reopening in 1946 as the Hotel Catalina.

The Hotel Catalina never offered the exquisite or exotic services to its own guests that its predecessor did in its heyday, but it was a significant improvement over what the Ravenna had become during the period between the wars, during which it degenerated into a seedy den of immorality and crime. The Ravenna was a favorite of the bootleggers and organized crime during the Jazz Age, but when Prohibition ended and the fast money dried up, the hotel never picked up the high-class clientele again. By contrast, the Catalina catered to the business and government traveler from its opening and remains a solid, bargain-priced hotel to this day. The roof gardens and real silver service are long gone.

Sparky's heart raced as he pushed the heavy bronze revolving door and entered the lobby. He stepped tentatively into the vast space of the lobby and his head automatically tilted back as he looked up at the impossibly tall columns holding up the impossibly high ceilings. He'd been in large and impressive bank lobbies before, but nothing prepared him for this space.

"Cool!" was all he could manage to say. He knew nothing about the history of the place, but he could tell from the archaic design and the mammoth proportions that the place had a history. Looking up and across the lobby, Sparky could see a second and third floor, way up, yet still within the lobby space! The columns that held up the building were enormous and had ornate capitals with sculpted gold leaves sprouting at the top. There were paintings decorating the ceiling panels between the columns, though there was not much light up there and the images were

175

faded and dirty-looking, but Sparky could discern scenes similar to those he had seen in the Stroud Museum of Fine Art, with gods and cherubs flying around. When Sparky finally lowered his eyes and looked at the ground floor of the lobby, he saw that it was decorated with contemporary, modern furniture and the walls were painted with garish designs that were meant to evoke a tropical feeling. There were bright green palm trees and nearly fluorescent blue skies. Compared to the gloomy and mysterious recesses of the upper levels, the hyper-happy, cartoon-like ground level was a comedown.

Sparky looked around for phone booths, but didn't see any. There were a couple of hallways, and Sparky noticed a wide stairway leading to an even lower level, where a bronze sign read, 'To All Trains'. He figured the phones must be tucked away in one of those places, so he walked up to the front desk to ask for directions. He didn't have to wait more than a few seconds before a man in a Hotel Catalina jacket, festooned with palm trees, addressed him.

"And how may we help you, young man?"

"I need to find a payphone. I was told you have some, here."

"Are you a guest of the hotel, young man?"

"No, I live in Hudson, but I hafta call my mom. She's probably worried about me by now and if I don't call her, it's gonna be a calamity."

"Oh, I see!" The man had a name badge pinned to his lapel. It read, 'Mr. Plep, Ass't Manager'. Sparky was worried that he was in some kind of trouble for trespassing on the hotel grounds and he wondered if it would have been better to lie and claim to be a guest.

"Why didn't you just make the call from one of the payphones out-side?"

"They were all being used and the ones that weren't were out of order." Sparky waited for a reply as Mr. Plep stood and stared at him. "One of them was melted." Mr. Plep remained impassive. "Actually, it turned out that that one worked…" Sparky felt his face flush. "…but, I didn't know it– that is, until it was too late."

"Why was it too late?"

"Well, because someone else was using it. That's how I found out it worked." Mr. Plep continued listening. "I didn't know until then..." Sparky swallowed."...that it actually worked even though it was melted. See what I mean? Otherwise, I woulda' used it– if I knew it worked, that is." Sparky was certain he was in trouble for trespassing in the hotel.

"Where was this?"

"Where? Um, Unice Street, at the subway station."

Mr. Plep took a deep breath in through his nose. "And yet you came all the way to our hotel to find another payphone? Wouldn't it have been faster to wait for one of the phones on Unice to become available?"

"Maybe. You see, the frank guy told me you had payphones here." Sparky waited for a reply. None was forthcoming, so Sparky added, "Do you, Mr. Plep?"

"What do you mean by 'the frank guy'?"

"The guy that sells Sabrett franks from the cart. You know?"

"He advised you to come here just to make a phone call? There are probably six or eight phone booths between here and Unice. Why not any of those?"

"I don't know. I saw some at the U.S. Plaza subway station entrance, but they were all in use, too." Sparky wondered what kind of name 'Plep' was. To Sparky, it seemed more like an abbreviation or an acronym than a name. At the same time, it also sounded a lot like something gelatinous falling on a cold tile floor.

"It's quite a busy day for phone booths, it seems." Mr. Plep picked a speck of white lint from his motley jacket sleeve. How he spotted it in that cacophony of colors is anyone's guess. "Young man, why would your mother be worried about you? Doesn't she know where you are?"

Sparky knew he'd get this question eventually. Still, he dreaded having to answer it. "I doubt it. I haven't been able to call her all day."

"Weren't you at school all day?"

"No, I went to school, but it had been torn down and they were rebuilding it. Francis said it would be finished by tomorrow, but there was no school today. Not *there* anyway."

"What was torn down?"

"The whole school! The building was gone. I know it seems funny, but I went there and I got there late because my mother got me out of the house late and all the other kids had left on school buses and I don't know where they went. So, anyway, I was going to go home, but I took a little walk and got picked up by a truant officer."

"Didn't he try to take you home?"

"He didn't want to, at first, but then he did and, for some reason, I couldn't find my house. He drove past it twice and I think he maybe was going too fast, or something, so…"

"Did this truant officer try calling your home?"

"I don't know. I can't remember. That's funny. I can't remember."

"What's that stuff on your jacket? Up there, on the shoulder." He pointed to a spot.

"That's tomato, I think. I got splattered when I helped the officer get a shopping cart out from under his van. There was a bag of groceries still in the cart. A purse, too!"

"How did a shopping cart end up underneath his van?"

"He ran it over," Sparky said to the stone-faced Mr. Plep. "He's a bad driver. What can I say? He hit a delivery guy on a bike, too."

"Did this demolition derby cop bring you downtown?"

"No, not exactly. I took the Third Avenue bus when I was getting away from the crazy old lady."

"The 'crazy old lady', eh?"

"She was on the most-wanted poster in the– you think I'm lying, don't you?"

"Of course not."

"Why not? I haven't even told you the half of it and it sounds weird even to me."

"You don't understand, young man. I'm the Assistant Manager of the Catalina. *Nothing* sounds weird to me. We had a guest three years ago who choked to death on his own right arm."

"Wow! How'd he do that?!"

"He felt a tickle in his duodenum, so he reached in and tried to scratch it."

"Oh,of course."

"I think he had taken LSD. Otherwise he'd never have felt a tickle in his duodenum, right?"

Sparky hadn't a clue, but had heard horror stories about LSD. "That makes sense."

"Tell me, young man, what was this old lady wanted for?"

"I can't remember exactly. Sodomy, for one thing. The other was murder or kidnapping or murder *and* kidnapping." Sparky's mind wandered back to Mr. Plep's name again. He thought the name sounded alien. This notion led him to question whether or not this man really was from Earth.

"Sodomy!"

"Yeah. Why? What's that?"

"You could say it's a close interaction that should only be performed by consenting adults," Mr. Plep explained with delicacy.

"Like a contract or a duel, right?"

179

"Exactly right. That's very astute of you. Yes, and it can feel much the same in the end."

"Is a boxing match a type of sodomy, then?"

"No, because both of the contestants are covered by protective equipment. So, tell me how did you escape the clutches of this septuagenarian sodomite?"

"Huh?"

"The old lady."

"Oh, well, I cut out on her at Aqua Boulevard. I ran across and hopped on a Number 43 bus. Just like that." Sparky snapped his fingers for emphasis.

"And that brought you here. And now you need to call your mother to let her know you're all right. Is that it?"

"Well, aside from the cat meat sandwich and Werner Weaner, yeah, that's about the size of it." Sparky waited a beat or two, but Plep didn't offer any more information. "So, where can I find the payphones? I looked around, but..."

"You see, we used to have a bank of payphones along that wall over there." Plep gestured to the wall at the right of the entrance– the one that was decorated in garish murals of tropical island paradises. "But, as you can plainly see, we have removed them in favor of a more open look. There are plans in the works to remove the open space in favor of a juice bar by next spring."

"But, what about if somebody's gotta make a call? What do they do then?"

"Our guests have the freedom to use our house phone to place a local or collect call and there are telephones in each of the rooms that guests can use to place calls, if they wish."

"But, if you're not a guest? What do *those* people do?"

"I don't know. If we had a hot dog vendor here, we could ask his advice, couldn't we? Only kidding. Don't get uptight. All is not lost, young man. In fact, we have another bank of payphones."

"Where, Mr. Plep?" Sparky got excited with hope again.

"Downstairs."

Sparky looked toward that stairway he had spotted earlier. "You mean that one? The one that has the sign pointing to the trains?"

"That's the one. The trains haven't stopped here in many, many years, and nobody has any reason to go down there anymore, but there are indeed a dozen phone booths down there– all lined up and waiting for someone to use them."

"Am I allowed down there? I mean, is it okay?"

"Certainly. It's open to the public."

"*Nobody* goes down there, you said?"

"That's right. I can't remember anyone going– no, that's not right. I do remember a couple of people going downstairs, once. I just can't seem to recall them ever coming back up." Plep rubbed his chin, pensively. "Of course, it *was* a busy day and I probably just didn't notice."

"Are you trying to scare me, or something? Next, you'll be telling me there are blood-sucking ghouls down there." Sparky laughed.

"No, no, no. You'd never fall for a story like that. I will say this, however," Plep measured his words out slowly, "I have never, ever been down there in all the years I've worked at this hotel."

Sparky absorbed this tidbit for a moment. "Never?"

Plep shook his head. "Never." Plep turned toward the front desk. "Alexandra!"

A young woman at the desk looked up. "Yes, Mr. Plep?"

"Has any of us ever gone downstairs?"

"No, Mr. Plep. Not that I know of." Alexandra waited for further instructions.

"Thank you, Alexandra." Plep smiled and crossed his arms. "See?"

"See what? Are you telling me I shouldn't go down there?"

"Not at all. Why should I do that? If you need to use one of our pay-phones, you must go downstairs. There is a bank of twelve phone booths, just waiting for someone to use them. Why not you?"

"Would you go with me?"

"Downstairs?" Plep's eyes got big.

"Yeah, just to show me where the phones are, you know?"

"I'd love to. However," Plep checked his watch, "it's nearly five o'clock and my shift is over, so I will not be able to accompany you downstairs. I simply do not have the time. I'm certain that you'll have no difficulty in locating our twelve phone booths on your own. And, at this point, I will say good bye and that it has been a pleasure talking with you, Sparky."

"Can I ask you something before you go?"

"What might that be?"

"Your last name– Plep– is that Polish, or something?"

"Ha, ha! A lot of people ask me that question. Actually, just between you and me, it's a name that I took. My birth name was Mlem."

"What's wrong with Mlem? Why'd you change it?"

"I hated it. It was so common. Plep has so much more– I don't know– pomp? I changed my name legally seven years ago. It's made a world of difference in my life."

"What do you mean?"

182

"Socially and financially. I'm not the same person I was back in 1962. I changed jobs. I changed my apartment. I even bought a new car– a '63 Studebaker Avanti."

"An Avanti! We saw a guy driving an Avanti yesterday!"

"It wasn't me. I sold it a couple of years ago to a guy who lives in East End. I kept having trouble with the turbocharger."

"This guy we saw yesterday, he was coming out of a Chinese laundry on Eighth Avenue and he got into a copper-colored Avanti. He had these long sideburns and he wore a cap hat. He was carrying lots of keys, too."

"That's *my* car, I'll wager. Sounds like the same guy that bought it from me, too. His name was Tommy Cabot."

"He looked real cool."

"Yeah, you think he's cool? He wears that cap all the time because he's bald! And he's got all those keys because he's a just lousy janitor in the Addicott Building up on Hudson Street."

"I don't understand. I thought the Avanti was a cool car. How can a guy that works as a janitor afford one?"

"He couldn't have when the car was new. But, when the car is five years old and has more than sixty-six thousand miles on it and the tur- bocharger needs replacing, a janitor can afford one."

Sparky was a little confused and disappointed. "I wish I had my camera yesterday."

"I don't need to see a picture of him. I'm certain it's the same guy. There aren't too many Avantis in Highbridge, you know."

"No, it's not that. My camera is special. It takes pictures of the truth about things instead of just how things *look*."

"How can a camera do that?"

"I don't know." Sparky pulled it out of the bag. "It records an impression on this score pad."

"Oh, I get it. This is just a toy!"

"No! I just bought it at a camera shop on 46th Street. It's no gag. I paid over three hundred dollars for this thing and I've already used it a few times. It really works!"

"It is a heavy beast, isn't it? But, these score pads look the same as those things you get in a Cracker Jack box. I don't see how that could work."

"Here, look at this one I took of this plumber I saw coming out of a place earlier." Sparky presented the pad he had exposed earlier.

Plep looked at the impression for a few seconds, then, looked up at Sparky. "This came out of that camera?" Sparky nodded. "Alexandra! You've got to take a look at this!"

"Yes, Mr. Plep." Alexandra walked around the desk and sauntered lithely over to Plep, showing an astonishing display of shapely leg in the process. Plep and Alexandra looked at the pad and murmured to each other and broke out laughing. They repeated the murmuring and laughing a couple of times.

"Sparky, I have got to get one of these cameras. What's the name of the camera store?"

"I don't know. It was on 46th near Brothers."

"Did you keep your receipt? It ought to be printed on there."

Sparky rummaged through the bag and pulled out the sales slip. "Here it is, but it just says 'Camera Shop'. There's no name."

"Let me see that. There's no phone number– nothing. Hmm. 46th and Brothers, you said? Alexandra, see if information has any listing for them, please."

"Yes, Mr. Plep." She sauntered back, showing an equally pleasing display of the back of her legs.

"Hey, Mr. Plep, you called me Sparky!"

"That's your name."

"Yeah, but I never told you my name."

"Doesn't *everybody* know your name?"

"How could they?"

"You tell me. I can only speak for myself."

"I don't understand."

"There really isn't anything to understand. If you don't want people to know your name, change it."

"That old lady I escaped from– she changed her name. There's a kid in my school whose name is Logan Brogan. I think he's changed it. I bet that's why I have so much trouble saying it. I can never seem to remember it properly."

"You said it perfectly that time."

"I *did*, didn't I?"

"Mr. Plep, sir, I couldn't get a listing of any camera shops on 46th Street."

"Never mind, Alexandra. I'm not certain I'm ready for such a camera, anyway. Thank you, Alexandra, for checking, though." Plep was smiling as he stared at her.

"It was my pleasure, Mr. Plep."

They stared at each other long enough for Sparky to surreptitiously load a card and take an impression. When they looked away from each other, Sparky resumed his inquiry.

"I don't think it matters much."

"What doesn't matter much?"

"If you change your name, people will know your name anyway. They'll know your *new* name."

"That's true. Everybody knows Plep. It's always 'Where's Plep?' 'Is Plep here yet?' 'Give it to Plep.' I should change it again, I suppose."

"That's half the problem! You should never have changed it. It just drew attention to it. If you left it alone, I bet no one would have paid any attention to it."

"But, everyone knows *your* name, don't they?"

"That's the point. My name's not Sparky. That's my nickname. My name's Michael Donnelly. If I had left it Michael, I bet no one would know it."

"Donnelly's a pretty common name. We even have a man named Donnelly who's a frequent guest of the hotel. Never get any Pleps, though. What if I change my name back to Mlem? Then no one would know it, right?"

Sparky thought for a moment. "No, because you'd be changing it again, so you'd just draw more attention to yourself." There was a long silence, during which Sparky and Plep tried to find a way out of this problem. "Maybe you could get rid of your name completely."

"Go without one?"

"Why not? Do you really *need* one? Plep isn't really a very good one."

"What's the matter with Plep? I've done very well with it so far."

"I don't know. It sounds like the noise you hear when someone falls down on their fat, wet ass." Sparky laughed, but was suddenly worried that he might have offended Plep.

"That's what I *like* about it. The only problem I have is that people can't tell what it is over the phone. I'm not sure you could go without a name, though. How would anybody know who they were talking to on the phone?"

186

"Well, you have a title. You're the Assistant Manager."

"That's true. I could say 'This is the Assistant Manager.' But, how would I get paid? The checks are made out to me and I have to sign them with my name."

"You could sign it 'Assistant Manager'."

"But, then my name would actually become 'Assistant Manager', wouldn't it? That would draw attention." He turned back toward the front desk. "Wouldn't it, Alexandra?"

"Yes, it would, Mr. Plep."

Just then, a man who looked very much like Plep joined the small group.

"Still here, Plep? Who's the youngster? Causing trouble?"

"No, not at all. He's here to use one of our bank of twelve payphones, downstairs. We were just chatting about the concept of names and identity. Weren't we, Sparky?"

"Yep."

"Nice to meet you, Mr. Sparky. My name is Mr. Aioio. You need anything, you just ask for me." They shook hands. Sparky did all he could to refrain from laughing at this man's name.

"I sure will, mister. I guess I better go and make that call before my mom gets too worried."

"Well, it's been great talking to you, Sparky. I'm going to head home. If you have any problem, Aioio will fix it. He's a good man."

"I bet," Sparky replied cryptically, thinking to himself, 'with a name like Aioio, he'd better be good!' They all bid each other good-bye and Sparky headed for the stairway to the lower level.

187

Chapter 18: The Lurking Man

The stairway was wide and framed by brass handrails and railings in floral motifs. The steps themselves were a light gray marble and each had slight depressions where ascending and descending shoes had worn it down over the years. Whereas the lobby was fed by light from out-side and by powerful hanging fixtures, the downstairs was glowing with a yellow light that was so dim that it almost appeared brown. As Sparky reached the bottom of the stairs, he could feel cool, damp air wafting from up ahead somewhere. The floor of the lower level was covered with a dark red, oriental-style carpet.

Entering the downstairs was like entering a time capsule. Sparky felt that he had stepped into a color version of an old black and white movie. The lower level contained several shops that had closed their doors years– perhaps decades– ago. There was a barber shop, a news-paper and magazine shop, a tobacconist's shop, a luncheonette, a sa-loon, two clothing stores (one men's and one women's), a luggage store and a gift shop. All the stores looked like they had been very classy establishments back in their era. To Sparky, they just looked very old and very dingy, albeit fancy.

While perusing the shops, Sparky felt a gust of cool wind blowing in from the ramp at the end of the corridor. He wandered over to the ramp and looked down the incline toward the gloom in the distance, from which place came a rumbling, roaring noise. Sparky passed the bank of twelve old, wooden phone booths and an equal number of shoeshine stands on his way down the long, gradual ramp. There were signs say-ing 'To All Trains' in gold letters outlined in black, stenciled on the marble walls next to long, pointy arrows aimed down the ramp. Sparky wondered momentarily whether he ought to be here, but, since no one was around and the hotel personnel admitted that they didn't come down here, he figured he had little chance of getting in trouble.

The roaring got progressively louder and just as Sparky reached the bottom of the ramp, the blindingly bright light at the head of a com-muter passenger train came into view. The train slid through the sta-tion's gloom, its silvery bulk disturbing and displacing the station's air. There was no movement, but for the train and the air. There was no trash, no dust, and no people. In a few seconds, the train had passed into the pitch-dark tunnel again and the station became still and silent once more.

Sparky looked around and took in the architecture and design of the place. It was obvious to him that this was once a grand place. Lighting fixtures were elaborately carved, stone and mosaic tile were tastefully chosen and beautifully arranged, the high arched ceiling was imposing. Sparky was impressed. He was also a little spooked. Once the train had passed by, there was not a sound in the station. Worse than that, Sparky spotted a man down near the south end of the platform, just sitting on a bench, staring ahead, not moving. He had felt certain there would be no one down here and he was truly startled to see another person. Freezing in his tracks, Sparky stared at the lone figure slouching in his seat, but could not make out the man's features under his hat and he wondered whether or not the man was even *alive*. He decided to take an image of the man and then cut out as fast as his feet would take him.

Sparky reached back into the bag and pulled out the camera, careful not to make any unnecessary noise in the process. He wondered whether to pull out the pad he had exposed upstairs and reload using a new one, but elected to get this shot without delay by using the pad he had exposed of Plep and Alexandra, then get the hell out of there in case the guy got ticked off. He aimed and snapped the trigger. The man didn't move a muscle. Just then, Sparky's school bag, which he didn't realize he'd had with him, tipped over onto the camera shop bag, making a loud rustling noise. Still, the man did not move. Sparky started to think this guy might really be dead. He decided to try an experiment. Standing at the bottom of the ramp with both bags in his hand, Sparky whistled a couple of notes, just as you might summon a dog. Stillness. Sparky yelled, "HEY!" and flinched, ready to dart up the ramp if the man made a move toward him. But the man did not move. Unless the guy was deaf, there'd be no way he could have missed Sparky's echoing yell.

Resolving to go back up to the hotel lobby to get Mr. E-I-E-I-O (or whatever his name was) to look into it, Sparky slogged up the ramp, which was much steeper going up than it was going down, until he reached the twelve payphones. 'That guy can wait a little longer,' Sparky concluded. 'I'll call my mother, first.' Sparky picked one booth at random and slipped inside, closing the creaky old door behind him. The booth smelled musty like old wood. He dropped a dime in the slot and dialed his home number, but got a busy signal. He repeated the process several times and each time either got a busy signal or the phone rang and rang endlessly. 'This can't be right. There can't be a busy signal and the next minute nobody picks up.'

Suddenly, Sparky's heart pounded violently in his chest. The man in the overcoat and hat that had been sitting motionless in the station, was walking slowly– right past Sparky's booth, practically brushing his sleeve up against the glass on the door! Sparky caught sight of him out of the corner of his eye and practically jumped out of his skin. His heart was pounding so hard he could hear the blood in his ears and he felt a cold panic shoot through his limbs like a bolt of electricity. Sparky froze solid. He felt trapped in the booth, with no chance of escape. He was certain the man was going to see him in there and get him. He had no idea what the man would do to him, but Sparky was convinced he was as good as dead at that moment.

In a second or two, however, the man was gone. He kept trudging up the ramp and passed by without noticing Sparky or stopping at his booth. Sparky took a few seconds to breathe again and try to calm himself. His panic abated, but he no longer cared to stay there to attempt another fruitless phone call. Sparky longed to get back upstairs to the street and other people. Pressing his cheek against the door of the booth, Sparky peered to his right to make sure the man was gone. He could only see a few feet up the ramp without opening the door and he didn't want to do that just yet. So he waited what seemed like forever before inching it open just a crack. "Jeez," Sparky whispered to himself. He was really worried about getting back upstairs with that guy lurking about. He knew he didn't have much choice, though, and steeled himself for his unavoidable emergence.

Just then the phone in Sparky's booth rang.

Sparky's panic returned, full force. He was afraid the ringing would attract the attention of the lurking man. He thought about answering it to make it stop ringing. However, answering the phone would reveal his presence, too. He began wondering who would be calling this number? He thought that maybe his mom had somehow gotten the number from the operator after his calls had failed. He picked up the receiver.

"Hello? Mom, is that you?"

"Hello?" Sparky could hear a voice.

"It's me, Sparky. Can you hear me? Mom?"

"Hello?"

They couldn't hear him. Sparky banged the receiver on the heel of his left hand, trying to jar the microphone back to life. It was then that he noticed the cord connecting the handset to the phone was in terrible shape and the cloth insulation had frayed at the base.

"Hello? Mom!"

He could hear a little mumbling at the other end, then a click. "Damn! It's busted!" Sparky was frustrated and scared. He felt truly disconnected from the security of home. It reminded him of the time, a few years back, when he had gotten separated from his mother in the Sears on Peace Boulevard and couldn't find her. He began to panic now just as he had panicked then. He thought about trying another phone booth, but the doors to these booths were creaky and he would risk being detected by that man. He looked at the frayed cord and thought of trying to fix it– to patch it together, if possible. In the dim light of the phone booth, lacking any tools, he dismissed that idea immediately. Apparently, the lurking man either hadn't detected him in the booth or didn't care about him anyway. The problem for Sparky was that he didn't know which. If the man hadn't detected him, staying put might be the best course to take, but for how long?

Sparky suddenly felt the urge to pee. His right knee jiggled up and down as he sat in the booth, trying to decide what the best course of action would be. Resolving to get the hell out of that phone booth, he started slowly inching the folding door open, trying to make as little noise as possible in the process. Once the door was open a crack, he could hear the sound of a train approaching the station. 'Good,' he thought, 'I'm saved! If he can hear at all, he'll never hear me over the noise of the train.'

When the roar was just at its peak, Sparky grabbed his bags and poised to bolt out the door. He threw open the door and dashed out and to the right and up the ramp to the downstairs lobby. His adrenaline carried him quickly, fueling his heightened alertness as he ran past the shoeshine, gift shop, and tobacconist and up the stairs to the street level. He didn't see the man along the way.

Once he was back in the main lobby and felt safe again, he wondered if he should try going back downstairs for another attempt to call home, but he dismissed the idea. It frightened him too much. No wonder Plep and the rest of the staff had never gone down there! Instead, Sparky slipped back out to the street with the intent of going back to Miller Avenue and making his call from there.

Chapter 19: A Lesson in Justice

M Street was still buzzing with activity, people heading home from work, noisy traffic clogging the intersections, a couple of fire engines blasting their horns and sirens, trying to thread through the over-stuffed street. Sparky noticed that he was hungry again. The éclair he ate a few hours ago had worked through his stomach and now he could feel that stomach growling again, though he couldn't actually hear it over all the hubbub. Sparky was thirsty, too and started looking for a place to buy himself a soda or a grape drink before hopping on the train to go home. There was a sign for a hot dog stand on the south side of M Street, but traffic was so congested and jamming all the lanes to such an extent that Sparky couldn't even fit his legs between the bumpers of the cars, which were literally inches apart from each other. He looked up and down the street and didn't see any place that could accommodate a pedestrian crossing. Sparky noticed some Puerto Rican men tossing Puerto Rican girls over the cars to the other side of the street, just as if they were playfully tossing someone into a swimming pool– even counting 'uno, dos, tres' before letting go of their ankles and wrists! The girls didn't mind at all, though Sparky had difficulty imagining how they could survive the flight across M Street without some broken bones at the other end of the trip. He always did have the impression that Puerto Ricans were impulsive and reckless people. This just proved it to him.

The Puerto Ricans then turned their attention to the other pedestrians trying to get across M Street. They called out to the people who had been watching them toss the girls and offered to do the same for anyone willing to come across with a dollar. Some of the crowd declined the trip and walked on, but after one older man tried to cross between a bus and a cab and got his legs agonizingly pinned and probably broken, several of those still waiting opened their purses and wallets and let the two enterprising young men toss them over the cars and buses and trucks to the other side. The women were a little self-conscious about exposing their underwear, but squealed and shrieked as they flew twenty or thirty feet above the traffic in the street. The men tried to act nonchalant, but they, too, let out yells and howls of laughter as they left the grip of the Puerto Ricans and sailed through the air. Sparky watched until it came to his turn.

"C'mon, leetle main! I trow you, now!"

The two men grabbed Sparky.

He had just enough time to grab his bag (he had only the one bag again) before they hoisted him up and, to the cheers and encouragement of the remaining crowd, swung him three times back and forth, then sent him on his way, over the cars and trucks, toward the south side of the street. Sparky's feet were pointed west and he looked down between them. As he seemed to float momentarily above the middle of the street, he saw the buildings of M Street receding into the distance and, beyond them, the water and the fading light of the horizon. He looked up at the clouds overhead and noticed their pale blue and gray and pinky-peach high-lights.

He liked the feeling of being up in the air at the height of the second or even the third story offices, but he realized with a panic that he would soon be landing and he wasn't sure he knew how to land without break-ing every bone in his body. Sparky rolled his body over, in a movement akin to what someone would do by rolling over in bed, and landed un-harmed, on all fours, smack in the middle of the smooth stone side-walk. Puerto Ricans may be rash and carefree, Sparky thought, but they possess great tossing skills.

Sparky straightened himself out and brushed the sidewalk dirt off the heels of his hands. Looking around, he expected to see a pile of people who had been tossed ahead of him, but there was none. Everything seemed normal. He checked inside his bag to make certain that the camera was unharmed. He did not relish the thought that he might have spent all that money on a camera and then smashed it to bits– all in one day. He breathed a sigh of relief when he examined the box and the device, tucked it back in the bag and strolled over to where he saw the hot dog stand. He couldn't find it.

'What the hell? It was right next to this lamp store a minute ago!' Sparky looked left and right and the only things next to the lamp store was a branch of the Commerce Bank and Trust on one side and a liquor and wine store on the other.

A rotund woman, wearing a coat and scarf, noticed Sparky's perplexity and stopped to address him. "What's the problem, young man? Are you lost?"

194

"No, lady. I thought I saw a hot dog stand here and now I can't find it."

"There's a hot dog stand– a Nedick's stand– in the bank, behind the tellers' windows."

Sparky thought of going into a bank alone and the thought frightened him. "*In* the bank?"

"Yes, behind the tellers. I don't bank with Commerce, but some of my co-workers do and they sometimes get hot dogs and orange drinks from there." Sparky looked around, up and down the street. "Just go in and ask the guard. He'll show you where to go. Don't worry. I'm sure they get new customers all the time. It's all right. Honest."

"Thanks." The woman had started walking away. "Are you sure, ma'am?" She didn't hear him above the street noise and fire trucks and police sirens. Sparky looked at the imposing stone edifice and bronze doors of the old bank. His hunger and thirst won out over his trepidation and he stepped across the pavement and tried the door. It was locked. Sparky peered through the door and could see a guard inside, so he knocked and called to him.

The guard took notice and waddled up to the door as fast as his ancient and stiff legs could manage. "Whaddaya want, kid?"

"I need to get in!"

"We're closed! Come back tamarra!"

"I can't come back tomorrow. Can't you let me in?"

"I tolya, we're closed, kid! I ain't unlockin' the door!"

"Please? Come on! This isn't fair!"

"Whoever tolya life's fair, kid?"

"Come on, I'm really thirsty. Can't I get just one grape drink?"

"Ah! Why didnya say so in the firs' place? Hol' on a sec." The guard pulled his keys and started unlocking the door. "Sorry, I thought you was a *bank* customer, kid." He swung the door out and squeezed back against it to let Sparky pass.

"I can come in?"

"Yeah, yeah! Why not? The Nedick's is to the right, behin' that bank of twelve tellers' windas ova there. You go trough there, b'tween those desks."

"Through there?"

"Yeah. Right trough there."

"You sure it's all right?"

"Yeah, it's fine. Go on, kid." The guard nodded in that direction and waved his hand.

"Thanks, mister."

"No prollem, kid."

Sparky walked past the guard desk, past the islands, containing deposit slips and withdrawal slips, past the commercial loan desks and to the edge of the bank of twelve tellers' windows. "Over here?"

"That's it." The guard nodded again and waved.

Sparky walked behind the tellers' windows and past the stools and rolling carts the tellers use during the day. He also couldn't help but notice that several of the tellers' cash drawers were open and the trays were filled with cash. Sparky glanced back toward the guard at the front door, half-expecting him to be right behind him, ready to arrest Sparky. Instead, the guard was simply locking the front door again. Sparky looked back at the cash in the drawers as if they were filled with glowing radioactive isotopes– alluring, but dangerously untouchable– and walked past them toward the back.

Once Sparky had passed the tellers' windows, he could see the glow and noise coming from a recess near the huge vault. Around the corner there stood, as plain as day, a Nedick's stand, with its orange and grape drink machines circulating a continuous fountain of vividly-colored liquid in their clear plastic tanks. There were other patrons at the

196

counter. There was a middle-aged man in an overcoat and hat, stuffing a frank with sauerkraut and mustard into his mouth, a conical paper cup of orange drink in front of him, sitting in its plastic holder. Two kids were there, as well, both around Sparky's age or a year younger. One ate from a bag of potato chips, the other from a bag of Frito-Lay's. The man behind the counter wore a white shirt, white apron and a white cap that said 'Nedick's' in red letters on both sides.

"Whatya have, sonny?"

"I'm real thirsty. Can I get a grape drink?"

The man loaded a conical paper cup into one the bone-colored plastic holders and dispensed the cold grape drink for Sparky. "Fifteen cents."

While Sparky dug around in his pocket for a dollar, he watched the man to his right chewing the last enormous bite of his hot dog. "How much for a hot dog?" Sparky asked.

"Sixty-five cents."

"Lemme get one of those, please."

"Comin' right up. Want anything on it?"

"Sauerkraut and mustard."

"Mustard's in the dispenser right there." He gestured toward the big plastic jars.

Sparky plunked down the dollar as the man behind the counter gingerly placed the full-to-the-brim cup of grape drink next to it. They each took the other's offering. The man brought back the change and then worked on producing the hot dog.

"Oh, that hit the spot. No better frankfurter in the whole city." It was the man in the hat and coat. "Is this your supper, son?"

Sparky took a break from sipping his grape drink to answer. "Well, it's a long story. It's a kinda late lunch." The two kids to his left giggled quietly. Sparky looked at them, wondering why they were laughing.

"Ha! Late lunch, eh? You could say *that* again, right Stan?" The man behind the counter smiled and nodded in agreement. "It's nearly ten after six, son." He nodded toward the illuminated clock above the grill. "You and your folks must eat awfully late, eh?"

"No, actually, we eat around six or six-thirty every night. It's just that I won't get home in time for dinner." The two kids giggled again. Sparky looked at them and they were smiling, with mushy chips in their mouths and on their teeth. They quickly looked away from Sparky.

"You don't live around here, son?" The man wiped his mouth and hands with a paper napkin as he spoke.

"Hudson-Sparta. I'm gonna take the Number 13 at U.S. Plaza." The kids giggled again. Sparky turned and looked at them. "That's where I was heading, but I got thirsty."

"You're not taking the Number 13 anytime soon, son."

"What do you mean? Was that a question?"

"They're fighting a fire just north of the station in the tunnel. No trains are running. You're stuck, son." That statement brought guffaws from the two kids who, bent over in hysterics, were holding each other's shoulder for balance.

"What the hell is so funny!?"

"Take it easy. They don't mean anything by it, son."

When the two had calmed down enough to talk, the girl finally answered Sparky. "You– ha, ha– you look so s-s-s-tupid– ha, ha, ha!" They were off into hysterics once more, doubled over and clutching their bellies.

Sparky looked around at the men present and looked at his own reflection in the glass of the display on the counter. "What are they talking about? Do I have something on my face?" He checked for cowlicks, ducking low to see the top of his head in the glass.

"Nah, they don' mean nothin' by it, kid. Don't pay 'em any attention. They always act like that." Stan prepared Sparky's hot dog and placed

198

it atop the counter. "Sixty-five cents."

"I paid you already."

"No you didn't. You paid me for a grape drink."

"I *did* pay you! You gave me the change." Sparky pulled the two dimes out of his pocket and showed them to Stan. "See?"

"I didn' give you no dimes. Sixty-five cents, kid. Take it or leave it."

"That's not fair! You saw me pay him, didn't you?" He looked at the man in the hat and coat. "I put down a dollar bill and he gave me change. You saw, didn't you?"

"I wasn't watching, son. I'm sorry."

Sparky, hoping for corroboration, looked to his left at the two kids. He didn't even bother to ask them anything because as soon as he looked at them, he could see them straining, trying not to burst out laughing again. They were turning red. "This is ridiculous! Every time I've gotten something to eat today, there's been a problem! And every time *I* get stuck paying extra!" Sparky waited for some sort of reply from Stan. "I paid you already! I *did*!"

The last 'I did' brought the guffaws from the kids once more. The girl aped him between gasps, "I– ha, ha, I di– ha, ha, I did! Ha ha! Oh, man, I'm gonna die! Ha ha ha!" The boy farted loudly in mid-laugh, which sent them both farther into hysterics. The girl took advantage of the boy's bent-over posture to administer a vigorous swat to his rear end.

"Oww! Ha ha ha!"

Stan withheld the hot dog, waiting for Sparky to pay. Sparky waited for something to change. The kids kept laughing. One of them snorted, which brought forth even more laughter.

"Forget it. I'm not paying twice for a lousy frank."

"Your choice." Stan dismantled the sauerkraut, hot dog and bun, recycling all but the bun, which he tossed into the garbage.

"So, son, what are you going to do? How are you going to get home? You can't take the subway– not until they finish taking care of that track fire, anyway."

"I don't know. I guess I'll take the Third Avenue bus. That goes pretty near where I live. It'll take a lot longer than the subway, but at least I'll get home."

"That's a good idea, son. You can catch the bus over near the Plaza. I tell you what– I'll walk with you."

"You don't have to do that, mister. I think I know where it is."

"That's all right. I was heading that way, anyway." The man grabbed his copy of the Highbridge Evening Journal and tucked it under his arm. "Thanks, Stan. Delicious as always." He waved.

"My pleasure, Judge. Have a good night." Stan cleared away the refuse from the man's spot at the counter.

"We can get out through here, son. We don't have to bother the guard." The man led Sparky past the rest of the tellers' stations, reaching into one of the cash drawers and pocketing several wrapped packets of money as he shuffled by. "I like eating here in the bank. I honestly don't know why more people don't do it. There's nothing in the world that gives me a bigger appetite than being around a lot of money."

"I didn't even know there was a hot dog stand here. If it wasn't for the lady telling me about it, I'd never have found it. And I was right out- side the place! That guy, Stan, called you 'Judge.' Are you a real life Judge?"

"Sure am, son. I work downtown. I thought everybody knew about these hot dog stands. They've opened up a Nedick's in every one of Commerce Bank and Trust's branches. I think it's worked out nicely– very convenient. I read in yesterday's paper that Orange Julius is open- ing up franchises on the third floor of Cell Block D of the women's prison on Q Street and in the six Sanitation Department garages next April."

"How are people gonna get into the prison?"

"Same way you got in here, son. Tell the guard you're hungry and he opens the door for you."

"Will they let men in? Or is it only supposed to be for women?"

"Oh, I'm sure it will be for everyone. It's 1970, son. With the advent of civil rights and everything, you can't keep men out of an Orange Julius, regardless of its location. It's a violation of their First Amendment rights."

"Wow, you sure *talk* like a judge! Just like the judge on *Perry Mason*!"

"Thank you, son."

They reached the back door to the bank and the man pushed the bar to open it, setting off a wildly frenetic alarm in the process. They stepped outside and into an alley between two buildings.

"Oh, crap! We're in trouble, now!"

"How's that, son?" The man seemed unconcerned.

"The alarm. Shouldn't we run away or something? The police will think we robbed the bank!"

"We did. However, I'm not going to run."

"Aren't you worried you'll get arrested?"

"They're not interested in arresting me. I'm a judge. I'm one of them. You can run, if you like. Don't let me stop you. I never run."

"You've done this before?"

"A couple of times a week."

"Do you *always* set off the alarm when you leave?"

"A couple of times it failed to go off. I'm not sure why. That worried me a bit."

"You worried when the alarm *didn't* go off?"

"It's supposed to go off when that door is opened."

"So?"

"If it doesn't, that means there's something wrong. That's all."

"But I thought the alarm goes off when there *is* something wrong."

"Like what, for instance?"

"Well, like a bank robbery, for instance!"

"There's nothing really wrong with a bank robbery, son. They expect to be robbed. That's why they have the alarms. Just like the reason for gas stations."

"Huh?"

"You expect your automobile to run out of gas eventually, don't you? That's why they have gas stations. It doesn't mean there's something wrong with your automobile. If you buy yourself a car, thinking that it shouldn't run out of gas, you're a fool. If you build a bank, thinking it shouldn't be robbed, you're the same kind of fool. An automobile has a gas gauge. And, when the needle hits 'E', it's out of gas and it's time to pay attention. When the bank's alarm sounds, it's time to pay attention. You understand, son?"

"Yeah, but running out of gas is not a crime."

"Neither is robbing a bank."

"How can you say *that*?"

"Has anyone ever been convicted of something they've never been suspected of or arrested for?"

"I don't know. Have they?"

"Of course not. The crime is *not* robbing a bank, son. It's being *arrested* for robbing a bank."

"But what if they know you did something, only they haven't been able to catch you yet? You know, like those people on the wall of the Post Office?"

"Then they're fugitives from justice, but they're not criminals. You have to have been convicted of a crime before you can be called a criminal. And you can't be convicted of a crime if you have not been given the opportunity to defend yourself in a court of law. Understand, son?"

"You're the judge, not me. I don't know anything about it except what I see on TV."

"You can't believe what you see on the television. The way they twist everything around on these programs causes me much consternation."

"Why's that, judge?"

"Why the consternation? They have a very naïve and simplistic take on right and wrong. I find these misrepresentations very troubling. People come into my court expecting some sort of justice, because they saw some absurd program on television where the bad guy is arrested, tried and convicted for a crime that he actually committed. I don't know what world these people think they're living in. Then they get all upset. Things happen exactly as they should, and these people get upset. Strange."

"What's the matter with *that*? Isn't that how it's supposed to happen? The criminal gets convicted, right?"

"Heck, no!"

"What if they're innocent and they get convicted anyway?"

"Who do you know who is completely innocent, son? Everyone is guilty of *something*."

"My mom and dad are innocent! They've never..."

"Let's not talk about what your father has done. Ah, your mommy–sweet-faced, long-legged mommy, with her shiny, dark hair and that cute little wiggle. She's a perfect illustration of my point, son."

"You talk like you *know* my mother."

The judge reached into his overcoat pocket and slowly pulled out a wadded-up ball of some kind of silky, lacy material. Sparky could just make out a bit of elastic– perhaps from a waistband or leg band– before the judge slipped it back into his pocket.

"What's that? Wait! Lemme see that!" Sparky grabbed the judge's sleeve.

"Son, you'll have to take my word for it that we know your mother."

"What do you mean, 'we'? And why should I take *your* word for it? What did my mother do? Was she accused of a crime?"

"Now, son, calm yourself. There's no reason to get excited. Why, your sweet mother didn't do anything wrong. And, if I may say so, she did it better than any other I can think of, by god! Oh, yes, you should be *very* proud of her, son."

"Proud of what? What are you talking about? What are you accusing her of?"

The judge chuckled reassuringly. "No one's accusing your soft and lovely mother of anything, son." He patted Sparky on the shoulder and chuckled again. "She's the finest woman I've ever had, um, the pleasure of dealing with, I mean. Yes, indeed. Here's your bus stop, son. It's been a pleasure chatting with you. Bon voyage, as the Frenchies say." He tapped Sparky on the arm with his rolled-up newspaper and drifted off, hunched over, into the night.

Chapter 20: A Sympathetic Ear

Sparky looked up at the bus stop sign. Several lines stopped here and they were all listed on the sign. The Number 43 was not listed on the sign. Sparky looked at the people lined up, waiting for the next bus to arrive. He hoped to see a friendly face in the crowd, someone he could approach and ask if he was at the right stop. Everyone seemed completely absorbed in reading a newspaper or a book or making notes on a yellow pad. He decided to approach a young woman who was reading a copy of a book entitled *The Crystal Cave.*

"Miss, 'scuse me, but do you know if the Third Avenue bus stops here?"

"No, I don't. Sorry. I'm brand new here. It's all very unfamiliar to me."

"What bus are *you* waiting for?"

"I'm waiting for the Third Avenue bus."

"So, it does stop here?"

"I don't know if it does or not. It probably doesn't, but I'm taking a chance that it will– sooner or later. I've got to get home."

"Do you normally take the subway, too?"

"Why'd you ask?"

"Well, 'cause I would've taken the subway, but there's a track fire and the trains aren't running. So, I thought maybe you had the same problem." Sparky looked at the cover of the book she was reading. "What's 'The Crystal Cave' all about?"

"I don't know, really. It's all very confusing and mysterious, but I'm only halfway finished. I assume that by the last page I ought to be able to figure out what's been going on all along."

"You're halfway done and you don't know what's going on yet? It must be a terrible book. If I got halfway through a book and couldn't figure out what was going on, I'd give it up."

"No, it's not necessarily a bad book. I just finished reading "The God-father" and I couldn't make heads or tails of what was happening until the last few pages. That's when everything came together and finally made sense to me. It turned out to be a great book. You can't just give up on it because you can't yet understand what's happening and why it's happening. When you get to the end, it all becomes clear, some-how. At least that's how it happens to me, anyway."

"Maybe that'll happen to me today. I've had the queerest day ever. I never made it to school today and I got arrested by a truant officer– twice, as a matter of fact– and somehow I ended up down here and I'm hungry as hell. At least I bought this cool camera! Wanna see it?"

"I don't know. Sure, I guess. I don't know much about photography."

Sparky excitedly pulled the device from the bag. "It's made in Bel-gium, but it doesn't shoot a picture of what you see. It captures the true essence of things."

"That's amazing! I've never heard of such a thing." The young woman examined the camera. "If you wanted to know what this queer day of yours was all about, all you'd have to do is to take a picture and see the true essence?"

"Exactly! Except I don't know exactly what to snap an image of that will give me the true essence of my day."

"Well, I certainly don't know, either." She finished looking it over and handed it back to Sparky. "I guess if you knew that, you wouldn't need the camera."

"Of course you would! Just 'cause you know where something is doesn't mean that you can see it. With this, you can *see* it. Do you know what I mean?"

"I guess you're right. Like if you're in a dark room and you know there's a chair or a bed, but you need a light to see it."

"That's where this thing comes in." Sparky hefted it in his hand.

"You're so *smart*! Would you take a picture of me?"

"Sure, lemme load a new pad." While Sparky changed score pads, the young woman fussed a bit with her hair and neatened her collar. "Don't bother with all that, miss. This machine will capture your true essence no matter how messy you are."

"Oh, okay. I'm ready, now." She lengthened her neck and set her features and posed for the snapshot. Sparky snapped once and lowered the camera. "Isn't it working?"

"Sure it is." He pulled out the pad and handed it to her.

"But, I didn't see a flash or anything."

"Doesn't need it. You can't hide the truth in the dark."

She looked at the score pad for a moment. "I can't tell what I'm looking at. Is this supposed to be me? It doesn't look like me. It doesn't look like anyone I know. Are you certain it's working properly?"

Sparky took the pad back and looked at it. "Whew! You had me worried. Yep, that's you all right. It shows…" Sparky cut himself off, suddenly becoming embarrassed at knowing so much about someone. He felt as if he was invading her privacy.

"What does it show?"

"It shows– it shows, um, that you're a nice person and interesting and stuff. It's all here." It also showed that she was not a real blonde and that her bosom was not quite as ample as the size of her brassiere would lead one to believe, but he skipped that stuff, not sure about how to handle such information. There were other things on the pad, all of a less physical nature and more in the realm of her character– her longings and abilities and fears. It was mostly stuff that he did not really care about, since it wasn't fun or exciting, and he wasn't sure he understood it all anyway so it frustrated him to look at it. Sparky stopped looking at the pad and handed it back to the young woman. "Here, take it. You can use it better than I can. You'll see what I see, sooner or later, like the books you read."

"Oh, thank you." She looked at it then clutched it to her chest. "I hope I can figure it out. It's so unfamiliar to me. I don't know if I'll be able to without your expertise."

"Sure you will. Anybody should be able to see the truth. You don't need to be an expert or anything." Nevertheless, Sparky felt really cool, being complimented by a young and attractive woman. It was like how he felt when he was in Mrs. Gardner's class.

"You should let me pay you for this." She rummaged through her purse. "How much do I owe you?"

"Don't bother. It's okay. These pads are cheap. You can keep that one– no charge." Sparky really felt like a big man, giving away one of his cool score pads.

"You're a very nice boy– young man, I mean. I'm glad you interrupted my reading." She giggled.

"How long have you been waiting for the bus? Has it been long?"

"It's been about…" she checked her watch, "…my goodness! I've been here two and a half hours!"

"You waited two and a half hours and you haven't seen any buses in all that time?"

"I don't think so. I've been reading all that time, so I might not have seen one if it came by. I can't be sure."

Sparky looked around at the others waiting at the stop. "Has anybody seen a bus here in the last hour or two?"

Several people looked up and checked their watches and grumbled or shook their heads 'no'.

Sparky addressed one businessman directly. "How long have you been waiting here, mister?"

The man looked at his watch again. "Since five-twenty, Tuesday." He held the watch up to his ear for a second and then looked at it again. "Gee, I *have* been here a long time, haven't I?"

"Miss, I don't think this is a real bus stop. Now that I think about it, I don't recognize any of those bus routes listed on that sign. There's no Number 293 that I know of! I've never heard of those streets, either."

"You mean there's no Hopalong Road? Or Birdbrain Boulevard?"

"I've never heard of 'em. Fried Fish Avenue? There's no such street!" Sparky scrutinized the sign more closely. "It *looks* authentic. It's metal. It's gotta be a phony, though."

"I had no clue! What should we do? I'll *never* get home this way."

"I know that M Street is only a block and a half this way. We can walk up to M and make a right and get to Third Avenue that way."

"You are *so* resourceful! I honestly don't know *what* I'd have done without you." She put her book in her purse and they started up the block, heading north toward M Street. "How do you know so much about the city? I've been working here for three weeks and I still can't figure out which way is east or west."

"I like looking at maps and stuff. I guess it pays off. I grew up in High-bridge, where are you from?"

"Bay 14th and 119th Streets up in Belleville."

"That's right across the bay from *my* neighborhood! You mean you never came downtown for anything?"

"I don't know. Maybe when I was a kid, we came into town for special occasions, like the Christmas Tree ceremony at City Hall. I remember doing that a few times." She thought hard for a few seconds. "We went to the museum when I was in the third grade."

"Where do you live, now?"

"Linden Farms. Right on Linden Street. I usually catch the bus at Flory Street, but I brought a pair of shoes into the shoe repair near Queens Avenue and he said I could catch the bus by the park, there."

"The guy I met at the Nedick's told me the same thing. That guy was a *judge*, believe it or not."

"Really?"

"Yeah, he was telling me that you're not a criminal unless you're caught. And you know what?"

"What?"

"He swiped packs of money from the cash drawers at the bank!"

"He told you that?"

"No, I *saw* it! With my own eyes."

"When did he do that?"

"When we were walking out of the Nedick's."

"I thought you were at the bank."

"The Nedick's is *in* the bank behind the tellers' windows."

"Inside the bank?" Sparky nodded. "Which bank?"

"Commerce. And the bank part of the bank was closed, believe it or not!"

"That's amazing. When I was a kid and President Kennedy said we would go to the moon by the end of the decade, I could hardly believe it, but having a hot dog stand behind the tellers' cages in a bank *really* impresses me."

"Why's that? I mean, I was surprised when I found out it was there, but I'm just a fifth grader. You're older than me. You've been around a lot longer and you musta seen– well, god knows what you've seen. So, why are you so impressed?"

"Just think of the level of trust we have reached in our society that a bank would allow people inside and behind the teller's cages, after hours, so they could buy a hot dog and an orange drink."

"I had a grape drink. It backfired, though."

"Indigestion?"

"No, dummy– the judge stealing a bunch of money! Maybe the bank shoulda thought about that when they opened the Nedick's."

"Oh! Perhaps it *was* foolhardy. I think it's a shame that we have those elements in our society that can't or won't play by the rules, don't you? It ruins things for the rest of us."

"Yeah, who knows? Maybe they'll have to close down the Nedick's or maybe even the whole bank if they lose too much money to people like the judge."

"It's not fair to leave it to others to pick up the tab for their sins."

"Hey, that's happened to me a bunch of times, today! A big, fat slob stuck me with the check at a diner on Unice Street. And, before that, I had to pay for a cat meat sandwich and beers that I didn't even drink!"

"That's awful!"

"And it was a cop, no less!"

"He stuck you for the beers? Oh, you *poor* boy."

She grabbed Sparky and hugged him to her bosom, crushing his face against her. He could hardly breathe for a second and was off-balance, but he relaxed into the embrace. And when he took a breath, he could smell her and the world disappeared for him for a moment, utterly and completely– like it was shut off– and all that existed for that moment was a soft feeling, outside of time. Sparky felt some kind of electric vortex and he leaned into her, trying to be within her to satisfy the vortex. He felt as if it was going to last forever and never end, but it did end and he was back on Chipper Street, standing next to this young woman while traffic and people made a harsh racket around them. He looked at her face and she looked suddenly different to him. Nothing about her features changed, but Sparky could see now that she had, at her disposal, some vast and deep well of power that he wanted to draw from. He stared at her face, her nose, the nostrils, her mouth, and her skin. He thought of Mrs. Gardner.

"Are you okay? I'm sorry if I hurt you." She smiled a little.

"I'm fine! I'm..." Sparky breathed in deeply, trying to catch a bit more of her fragrance, but he couldn't get any at that distance. He felt disappointed and almost dove in for a second embrace, but was rooted, stiffly, to the spot. "I'm fine," he repeated, wistfully. He felt tranquil.

"You must have had a hard day, young man. I feel terrible for you. Why were you with a policeman? And where can you buy a cat meat sandwich in Highbridge? Yuck! I don't know that I'd like that."

"He was a truant officer. He thought *I* was a truant."

"Why would he think that?"

"I wasn't in school today. I was walking home when he nabbed me."

"Did that mean policeman force you to buy him alcohol?"

"I don't know if I can blame him. He was in the bathroom with the runs and I was stuck when the check came. The other people there thought the best thing for me was to pay the check and leave the bar."

"It was a *bar*? The policeman took you into a *bar*?"

"Yeah. He knew the bartender and his ex-wife was there. He said they made great Reuben sandwiches."

"Out of cat meat?"

"I don't think he could tell it was cat meat. I don't think he noticed anything after those beers."

"He drank beers while he was on duty?"

"Sure– a whole bunch of them! He made himself sick on them. After that, he had an argument with his ex-wife."

"Well, I think it was a good thing you got away from that horrid policeman, even if it did cost you money to do it. Anyway, you're not a truant."

"How do you know that?"

"I can see it." Sparky wondered how she could see such a thing. "I see you, Sparky. I read you like a book. You have twenty-three chapters. I've read through twenty of them already and I'm almost finished with chapter twenty-one."

"You know my name? Mr. Plep knew my name, too. How do you know my name?"

"I know more than that; much more than your name. I know everything, now."

"Everything?" Sparky wondered what that meant. "What do you know?"

"Don't worry, it's nothing *bad*." She laughed sympathetically and gently shook him by the shoulders.

He felt a little relieved. He noticed that he loved her admonishment. It was like his mom's, but not his mom's. She didn't have the right to touch him like that and that's what made it special. He couldn't take his mind off how he was reacting to her and he suspected her of casting some kind of spell or of hypnotizing him. She had transformed from a seemingly naïve– or perhaps dumb– woman when they first talked to each other into a clairvoyant witch, who could read his mind and make him blush. 'Must be that fragrance,' he thought, 'it's a potion.' Then he thought of something that snapped him out of his spell.

"Did you say you live in Linden Farms?"

"Yes, I do."

"That's funny. The old lady I helped today lived in Linden Farms. She said she lived on Eden Street."

"I know where that is. That was nice of you to help an old woman. She must have been very grateful."

"I don't know about *that*. She didn't need my help. She had me carry these parcels she picked up from the Post Office, but they were tiny. I ditched her at Aqua Boulevard. I think I saw her on a Most Wanted poster in the Post Office."

"An old woman? I've never heard of that. Did you really think it was her?"

"Well, I'm *pretty* sure it was her. She said some weird things and she tried to get me to go home with her and live in a cage."

"Like a pet? You should have tried your camera on her! That would have revealed what she was up to."

"I didn't have it then. I bought it later. You know, I should try to find a payphone. I need to call my mom. I need to let her know I'm going to be late."

"She doesn't know you're going to be late?"

"No. Not only that, but I'm kinda worried about her. I tried calling earlier, but couldn't get through. Then, I got through, but she couldn't hear me on the other end."

"Well, then you know she's there. Why are you worried about her? You're the one who's out late."

"She acted weird this morning. She stacked all this wood in front of the bathroom door and she was acting like a little girl– talking about getting spanked and stuff. That's how come I was able to buy my camera. She gave me a ton of money when I left for school. Maybe she's going through a second childhood or something."

"Did it make you uncomfortable to see her acting that way, Sparky?"

"Well, sure it did! She's always pretty calm and together. Maybe all my questions about fun and exciting people pushed her over the edge. I know she and Dad were uncomfortable about my asking what exciting and interesting people they know."

"How was your father this morning? Was he acting weird, too?"

"That's funny, I didn't see him at all this morning. He's usually either shaving or eating breakfast when I get up. That is funny. I suppose he went to work early or something. He always used to say he'd never put in extra time at work. Nowadays, he stays late a lot. I don't know."

"Hold up a moment, it's getting kind of chilly. Can you hold my purse for me for a moment?" She handed him her bag and opened it, removing a frilly garment from one of the compartments. "I'm sorry, but the temperature has dropped since the sun went down and I need these to keep warm." She stepped into a pair of pale blue panties and pulled them up her legs, under her skirt, as if it was the most normal thing in the world to do on a crowded street. "I'm sorry I'm holding us up."

Sparky gulped. 'You, too?' he thought to himself. "Oh, that's okay. I, uh, think it's getting chilly, too. I have, um, I, uh…"

"I know. You're already wearing your underpants, right?"

"That's right." Sparky laughed, relieved that she knew what he had been thinking. "My mom wouldn't let me out of the house without clean underwear on." He watched her finish slipping the panties up her thighs and running her thumbs back and forth across the waistband and he looked at her thighs and pelvic area in the blue-green glow of the streetlight. Her legs were round and soft and pale and Sparky flushed deeply with embarrassment, looking at them, however, he couldn't *not* look at them. They were not like the legs of his schoolmates. These legs were large and her hips wide by comparison. He imagined that Mrs. Gardner's thighs must look like that, too. In fact, she looked a lot like Mrs. Gardner– only younger. She was about the same height and weight and her hair, which she wore straight, was roughly the same color.

"Are they on straight, Sparky?"

"Huh?" Sparky stopped staring when she addressed him. She stood, holding her skirt up to her waist, twisting side-to-side.

"Sparky, pay attention!"

"Uh, I was just thinking that you look just like my teacher from last year. What'd you say?"

"My panties– are they on straight? Do you like how they fit me?" She giggled. "You can close your mouth, now, Sparky. You don't want a moth to fly in there, do you?"

215

"Oh, sure. Yes, they look fine, I guess. Um, I'm not a clothing expert, you know."

"I know that." She let her skirt fall into place and took back her purse and they resumed walking toward M Street. "You don't have any sisters, do you?"

"Nope. Are you a sister? I mean, do you have a brother?"

"Yes, I do. He's older than me by a couple years. I haven't seen him in a long time, though. He's got his own life, I guess, but I worry about him sometimes."

"Why do you worry about him? Is he in some kinda trouble?"

"He's what you might call 'troubled'. He's quite heavy and he doesn't have a regular job. In fact, I'm not certain he's working now, at all. I'm not clear on how he makes ends meet."

"Does he get any kinda payout from the government? My dad got an unemployment check when he was laid off a couple years ago."

"The problem is that he hasn't worked steadily, so he doesn't qualify for anything like that."

"Well, how come he doesn't work? He *should* work. That way he could get unemployment checks."

"When I said he was troubled, I meant that he can't do things that normal people like you and I do. He's *tried* some things, but he can't stick to anything for any period of time. Things always get messed up and he gets fired or quits. He's tried more creative avenues, but with no more success than in the regular workaday world."

"What kind of creative avenues did he try? Was he an actor or a singer?"

"No, he was a history buff and he always imagined that he could write history books that would appeal to regular people; that were different from the usual approach to history that you'd find in most textbooks."

"That sounds like a great idea! The textbooks we read in school are crap. I know that, first hand."

"I know it *sounds* like a great idea, but he wasn't the person to do it. He came up with the most outlandish ideas for his books. Then, he wouldn't do any research. He'd just write an entire book, made up of stuff out of his head. He'd never even set foot in a library, but the book would have page after page of detailed endnotes. Do you know what endnotes are, Sparky?"

"I guess so. They tell you where you can find something, right?"

"That's about it– he'd have hundreds of endnotes, *all* of which he had made up himself. And his subjects were the goofiest. Bodybuilding in China, from 800 BC to 650 AD!"

"What's wrong with that?"

"Nothing, if you happen to be a Chinese bodybuilder, I suppose. It's just hard to see what the average student can learn from studying a subject such as that. Or how about a book about swimming in the Dark Ages? What use is that to anyone?"

"Wait a minute! Is your brother's name Werner?"

"Yes, it is! How'd you know that?"

"Because, he's the big, fa– He's the guy that stiffed me at the diner! Werner Weaner, right?"

"Yes, that's him!"

"Then, you're Scarlet Weaner."

"He told you about me?"

"He said that it was because of you that he lost his camera."

"He told you about those pictures?"

"He said he was selling them and your dad disapproved."

"Werner was a very good photographer. I thought I looked very glamorous in them. Those photographs made me very popular in school, you know."

"Is that why your dad disapproved of them?"

"The whole episode was very ugly and it almost ruined me."

"What did? The photos?"

"No."

"The popularity?"

"No, the *therapy*. Father thought he needed to save me from the traumatic effects of what Werner did, so I had to go to this session every week for a couple of years."

"So, did the therapy do any good– I mean, did it help you?"

"I don't see that it did any good."

"It's too bad your father sold Werner's camera to pay for something that didn't even help."

"Father didn't sell the camera. Is that what he told you?"

"Yeah, that's what Werner said. He said he couldn't take any more pictures after that 'cause his dad– *your* dad– confiscated the camera."

"That's true, but not because Father sold it. He started using it himself to take pictures of me. And Father didn't have to pay anything. The other men paid *him*."

"Other men? What did they pay him for?"

"So Father would let them take pictures of me, too."

"Why were these other men taking pictures of you?"

"Father said that it was the best sort of therapy. 'Fight fire with fire', he said. I didn't like those sessions and I didn't see that they did any good. Anyway, Werner was a better photographer– even at thirteen– than these other guys who were four or five times his age. Poor Werner. I think the whole thing ruined him."

"So, he's not a teacher at St. Charles College?"

"There is no St. Charles College."

"Oh. So, if he's not a teacher and he never published those textbooks, then he probably doesn't have any money. That must be why he sticks people with the check at the restaurant."

"You got it, Sparky."

"Why doesn't your dad help him out?"

"He can't. He's in jail."

"How come he's in jail?"

"Practicing therapy without a license, I think." Scarlet stopped. "Sparky, I think we must have passed M Street. Wasn't M Street supposedly only a block and a half from the bus stop?"

Chapter 21: Lost with a Friend

"You're right. I think we did pass M Street. I don't see how that's possible." Sparky scanned their surroundings and couldn't determine where they had wandered. It certainly wasn't anywhere near where they were before. The buildings were all different and the streets were narrower. The businesses were different, too. There was a meat-processing warehouse and a paper wholesaler. The streets were very roughly paved and the sidewalk was grossly filthy, with puddles of olive and gray-colored liquid in its recesses. There was no traffic passing by and the area was shut down for the night.

"Sparky, Look!" Scarlet pointed to a gang of rats scurrying around a pile of garbage near an overfilled dumpster. "That's disgusting. Rats give me the willies." Despite the willies, they stared at the frenetic activity in the little alleyway.

"What are they eating?"

"I don't know– some kind of garbage, it looks like. Let's go."

"I thought it was garbage, too, but now I think it looks more like a body!"

"Oh, how horrible! You're right– it *is* a body. Let's go!"

"Where? I don't know where we are!"

"I don't care, Sparky. Let's just go."

"Now, which way did we come from? I'm all turned around." Sparky turned and looked up the streets in every direction.

"It doesn't matter. Let's just go, before the rats decide they've had enough of that body and start on us. Come on!" She started pulling his arm as she exhorted him to move. Sparky wasn't comfortable with her choice of direction and he resisted, rooted to the spot.

"Wait a second! We should be able to figure out where we are by the skyline."

"Sparky, we can't *see* the skyline from where we are. These warehouses and factories are too tall and the streets are too narrow to get any kind of view of anything. Let's just pick a direction and go! I'm certain that anyplace is going to be better than this awfulness."

"That might not be true. Somebody told me that there are *really* bad places in the city that we should avoid. If only there were street signs. How come there's no street signs? I don't understand it." Just then, the two of them noticed a distant thumping sound coming from down one of the narrow streets. Scarlet stopped tugging at Sparky's arm as her curiosity momentarily distracted her from her panic. They froze and peered into the murky.distance, trying to locate the source of the noise.

"It's coming from down that way." Scarlet pointed. "Whatever it is, it looks big!" she added in an urgent whisper.

Sparky was the first to figure out what was the source of the noise. "It's a couple of guys on stilts! I wonder..." As they came closer, both of them could see that the two guys on stilts were, in fact, a man and a woman on stilts. They seemed to be having fun, walking together on their stilts. They were laughing and talking and holding hands until they got close to Sparky and Scarlet.

"What the hell are you two doing here? Are you nuts or something?"

"Funny– you asking *us* that question. Why are you two on stilts?"

The woman spoke up. "Seriously, you two shouldn't be around here after dark– especially dressed the way you are!"

"What's wrong with how we're dressed?"

"For one thing, Sparky, you're not on stilts!"

"Well, nobody told us we were supposed to bring our stilts. Is that some kinda– wait! How the hell do *you* know my name?!"

"Sparky..."

"Hold on, Scarlet. This is ridiculous. Does *everybody* in Highbridge know my name, now?"

The two on stilts both answered in the affirmative. "As far as *we* know, they do."

"Sparky…"

"But, how can everybody know *my* name? I'm not wearing a neon sign that says 'SPARKY' or…"

"Sparky…"

"Wait a second, Scarlet. I'm not sure I like everybody knowing my name. I don't know *them*. It doesn't seem fair."

The woman answered him. "Sparky, when you're famous, everybody knows who you are and you don't know anybody, least of all who your friends are. That's how it works."

"That's not right."

"Sparky, will you let me finish my sentence? I think I know why these people are on stilts."

"Why's that?"

"It's the only safe way to walk around this neighborhood," Scarlet surmised. "Isn't that right?"

"That's why we thought you two were crazy or something. Everybody knows you can't walk around here after dark without stilts. What should we do, Laurie?"

"We have to get them out of here as fast as possible." The young man and woman conferred for a moment, pointing in a couple of directions and gazing up and down the unnamed streets and alleys, before presenting their life-saving plan. "We don't think we can help you," the man said. "No," added the woman. "You're just going to have to make a break for it, we think." Then they strode off down one of the narrow and twisted streets, calling back to Sparky and Scarlet, "good luck, you two!"

Then there was silence, except for the little skitch-skitch noises that the rats made in the alleyway, of course.

"Hmmm." Sparky put his hands in his pockets and bit his lower lip. "They were a lotta help, huh?"

"The best thing would be to catch a cab."

"There are no cabs, Scarlet. You could try flagging *him* down." Sparky gestured toward an abandoned and stripped car in front of a ramshackle hardware store.

"Very funny."

"Honestly, I don't think there's any option other than to just do like they said and make a break for it. We can't stay here all night. I've gotta get home. Even at this point my ass is grass. It must be after seven o'clock, by now."

"Seven thirty-five, to be exact."

"I've gotta pee." Sparky looked around for a place to urinate discretely. "Come to think of it, I've had to pee most of the day."

"How come you didn't?"

"I don't know. I either couldn't go or I didn't have the chance. Funny, that I've lasted this long. It's been twelve hours." Sparky walked over to a doorway of one of the warehouse buildings and unzipped his pants. He pointed and waited. Nothing happened. He waited some more.

"Are you finished, Sparky? We should be going. I think one of the rats just looked up at me. They're making me nervous."

"I'm not done yet. I don't know what's wrong. I can't seem to pee."

"Sparky, that rat just tapped a buddy on the shoulder and pointed me out. We *really* should be going, *now*."

"Okay, okay! I'm coming! I'll try to pee later." Sparky tucked himself in, zipped back up and rejoined Scarlet, who was fixated on the rats near the dumpster.

"See?"

223

"See what?"

"That one, with the white splotch on his side. He's the ring leader."

"Oh, come on, Scarlet! You're letting your imagination run away with you."

"No, I'm not. I'm telling you that I saw him tap his friend on the shoulder and point me out. He's playing it nonchalant now because he knows we're watching him. Look! See, he's whispering to the others, now."

"You're outta your mind. Rats don't whisper. And they don't tap each other on the shoulder. You're just– Holy crap! He *is* whispering about us. You were right! You can *see* it! Run, Scarlet!"

"Where?! Which way?!"

Sparky chose a direction based on where the rats seemed least numerous and started running like hell, chanting, "holy crap," along the way. Scarlet, only a couple of steps behind him, was keeping up quite well for a girl wearing heels. They ran for a few blocks, not looking back until they got to an intersection that seemed a tad more civilized than the one they left behind. The intersection they reached actually had a traffic signal and street signs. It was Pyle Street and Waterfront Drive.

"I've got to catch my breath," Scarlet pleaded, panting. "Where *are* we?"

"I think we're in Old Downtown! I don't see how that's possible. There's no way." Sparky gasped for breath, trying to get his bearings. "This makes no sense at all."

"Well, I don't know much about downtown, so I can't help you. I would guess that Waterfront Drive means that we're somewhere near the waterfront, though. That should help us get our bearings."

"If this is Waterfront and Pyle crosses this way, then the building numbers should go up in this direction." Sparky turned slowly, scanning the buildings for addresses and pointing as he spoke. There were no visible addresses. "I don't see any addresses. They *have* to have addresses."

"What's the problem, Sparky?"

"This is the same thing that happened this morning!"

"What is?"

"When I asked the policeman to take me home, I couldn't find my own house! None of the houses had any addresses on them. They're *supposed* to have addresses. My house always had an address, screwed right into the front door, but I couldn't find it– and we went around the block twice!"

"So what do we do? Maybe we can just pick a direction and walk. Sooner or later we'll find some familiar street or run into someone who can help us. What do you say?"

"But, I don't understand how we could have gotten here."

"We ran."

"But, we didn't run *that* far. We're at least two miles from that phony bus stop! We didn't run that far. How do you explain that?"

"We were walking for a while, first?"

"But, we walked north, toward M Street, not south. This is horrible! I'm never gonna get home! I wish there was a phone somewhere."

"There's a telephone over on that pole." Scarlet pointed to a yellow box, mounted to a wooden utility pole across the street.

"That's one of those call boxes the police use. I don't know if I can use it."

"Maybe you could use it to ask the police for help?"

"Yeah, but those boxes are usually locked."

"Maybe it's not."

"Not a chance. I've seen it on TV a million times."

"Let's go see. C'mon."

Sparky relented and they crossed over. The faded-yellow box was bolted into a utility pole that looked a thousand years old. It currently suspended a couple of phone lines, but it originally held a large battery of telegraph cables and later held electrical feeds. It stood at a six or seven-degree tilt, twisted and bent by age, with its surface entirely splintered and dried out. It had seen the advent of the electric light, the gasoline engine, atomic power and the space age. Here it still stood in a now obscure and obsolete corner of Highbridge, holding up a 'one way' sign and a police call box, both affixed to it sometime back in the late 1920's.

"You were right, it's not locked! These things are always locked on TV."

"You can't always believe what you see on TV, Sparky. Do you know how to work the thing? It's got no dial."

"They just pick it up and flick this thing up and down a few times. That brings the operator or the dispatcher at the precinct." Sparky put the ancient receiver to his ear and tried his trick. There was nothing. "Come on, *please*." He tried it again, with the same result.

"What about this button, here? What happens if you press that?"

Sparky tried it and then listened some more. Nothing came through. Sparky banged the receiver down on the bottom of the box and listened again. Still the unit remained inert.

"Nothing?"

"What do *you* think?"

"Now, there's no reason to get sarcastic at me."

"Why, what are you gonna do about it?"

"I'll pull your pants down, put you over my knee and spank you right here in the middle of the street, if I have to. Put *that* in your pipe and smoke it, mister."

Sparky *did* put that in his pipe. In fact, it went straight to his pipe as he wondered for a moment what that might be like. Scarlet saw his expression change as he pondered her threat and she blushed. "Oh! You're such a dirty boy! You're awful!"

"*I'm* awful? Ha! You're the one talking about pulling my pants down! What is it about you women, always talkin' about spankings, anyway?"

"Well, you deserve one, for that filthy mind of yours."

Sparky was flabbergasted and could hardly form a word for a second or two. "Bah! You walk around putting your underwear on right in front of U.S. Plaza! You're unbelievable!"

"*I'm* unbelievable? Look at you!" Scarlet cocked her chin and looked directly at his groin.

Sparky looked down, mortified and turning red. "It's not my fault, honest! It's because I have to take a piss so bad. Seriously, it sticks up like that sometimes when I have to pee– especially before I get up in the morning."

"*I'd* say it's serious."

"Really, It's true!"

Scarlet giggled at his embarrassment. "Yeah, sure, Sparky. Next you'll be telling me you're about to wake up for school or something loony like that."

"I wish."

"What's the matter, you don't like my companionship anymore, Sparky? Maybe you'd like me better if I was ten years younger, is that it?"

"I like you fine, Scarlet."

"But, I'm no Diana, am I?"

"How do you know about Diana? How is it that everybody knows my name and they know all about my mom and the people I go to school with? This is *really* freaky! How do you people know the things that I know?"

"Oh, dear, we're having our first quarrel."

Sparky understood the allusion since he was familiar with the cliché from movies and TV shows. His expression softened and he smiled.

"That's better," she said reassuringly as she brought him to her in a friendly embrace. "Listen, how are we going to get ourselves out of this situation?"

Suddenly, Sparky wasn't sure he wanted out of this situation. He'd caught that fragrance of hers once more. That and her warm body mass sent him into that same euphoric blackout for an immeasurable period of time– immeasurable, but probably only a second or two. She let him loose and he felt completely tranquil again. He looked around once more and got his bearings.

"The one way sign points that way. Why don't we go that way?"

"Sounds like a good plan, young man."

They set off down Pyle, passing dilapidated buildings. These structures, some of the oldest in Highbridge, stood as a vivid demonstration of what can happen when the commerce of a city shifts elsewhere and everyone forgets. The twisted old utility pole was right at home on these streets. Everything was rough and dry and crooked here. Every- thing was cracked and bleached and sagging. The architecture here was typical of the period. The buildings were boxy, two-story brick struc- tures, with little attic dormers above the second floor. From the look of the place, one would think that no one had stepped foot on these streets in the last forty years.

"Are you hungry? I'm really hungry. I tried to buy a frank at the bank, but the guy said I didn't pay him for it so he wouldn't serve me."

"They should advertise themselves as 'Frank at the Bank'. I guess I'm hungry, but I could really use a cigarette."

"You smoke? You're gonna die of cancer if you don't quit."

"Thank you Dr. Sparky. What kind of name is Sparky, anyway?"

"I was named after my grandfather."

"Your grandfather's name is Sparky?"

"No, his name was Michael."

"Makes sense. You've been lugging those bags around all day?"

"Yes and no. My book bag has come and gone throughout the day. I've had it with me most of the day, I think. I bought the camera at about three or four o'clock. It's gettin' pretty heavy. I thought it was such a cool thing– to be able to capture the truth about things– but I've had very few opportunities to use it so far. I thought I could find out about everything. To tell you the truth, except for people, everything else looks about the same anyway. The Waarheid shows nothing different. No wonder it isn't popular."

"I think it's a wonderful device."

"You looked at your own score pad and you said you couldn't make heads or tails of it."

"What's that?"

"What?"

"Down that block, there." Scarlet pointed to the dark abyss just past a pile of rubble that used to be a building. "You see that thing, sticking up from the ground?"

"Yeah, what *is* that stuff? And what's that thing *above* it?" There, above what resembled a modern sculpture, looming in that murky darkness was something several stories high and slanted a good fifteen or twenty degrees to the left. Neither of them could decipher what it was that loomed so large down that street.

"Should we go up to it? I'm kind of curious." She grasped his arm. "C'mon, Sparky, let's check it out."

They slowly made their way the two hundred feet down the alley until

229

it became clear what it was they were looking at.

"It's a boat! That's an old pier!"

"The 'Lady Liberty'. It's an old ferryboat!"

"Looks as if it's been here forever. There must not be any water under it, judging from the angle it's sitting at. Let's go a little closer." Scarlet put her hand around Sparky's shoulder as they inched forward to the crumbling edge of the paved street. They both gazed up at the wooden hulk as it leaned over onto the collapsed pier. "It's huge!"

"It's all crooked. It's collapsing." They were silent for a moment, walking back and forth in front of the old leviathan. It was a wooden boat, with two decks, the upper of which loomed over them in the darkness. The boat was painted a dark color, which was indistinguishable in the night. It could have been green or red or gray. The paint was chipping and peeling everywhere, leaving the dry, bleached wood beneath exposed to the elements. It sat where it was, sagging into the earth like a decaying mammoth. There was nothing beyond the boat except darkness. After a minute of gawking at the monstrous relic, Sparky spoke quietly. "There's no place else to go."

"What, Sparky?"

"This is the end. We can't go any farther. We've gotta go back."

Scarlet stared silently at the ferryboat for a long time. "You're right."

They walked silently back up the dead-end street and straight on for several desolate blocks, through the oldest district of Highbridge, finally reaching an intersection which had street signs. The signs were old porcelain-coated iron relics of the past and they read Acony and Neidler Streets. In the middle of the next block, they could see a car, idling at the curb.

Chapter 22: Conflicting Results

"A car!"

"There's someone in it! Maybe we can get a lift to the bus or the subway. Come on, Sparky!"

They approached the light-colored 1966 Chrysler Newport, walking, as they had been for hours, right in the middle of the street and heedless of pedestrian protocol. Walking up to the driver's side from the rear and seeing that the window was rolled down, Sparky called to the occupant, "Hey, mister!"

The driver, who had been sitting with his head back, jumped like he had been stuck with a pin. His head jerked forward, his eyes wide with panic. "Haagh! Wha? Donnelly!"

"Mister Salty! I mean, Mr. Solti!" Sparky could hardly believe it.

"You know this man, Sparky?"

"Yeah, he's a sixth grade teacher at P.S.8! It's a good thing you're here, Mr. Solti. Scarlet and I need a ride to the subway. Can you help us out?" Sparky looked down at Mister Salty's lap and saw him holding his hand on the back of a woman's head. "What's the matter with her?"

"Uh, she, uh, we pulled over here– she's, uh, taking a nap, Donnelly!" The woman made a moaning or grunting noise.

Scarlet called out from behind Sparky. "Hi, there!"

"Glad to make your acquaintance, Miss." The woman's head moved under Mister Salty's right hand and another moaning sound was heard.

"Hey, she's waking up, Mr. Solti. You better let her up."

"Donnelly, could you please step away from the car for a few minutes? She's, uh, she can be pretty upset when she wakes up, d'you know what I mean? Please, Donnelly."

Scarlet took a step forward to peer into the car and size up the circumstance and quickly pulled Sparky away. "Come on, Sparky! Give the woman some privacy, now. We'll be over here, sir." She pulled Sparky, tripping and staggering, across the street and back a few steps.

"Thank you, Miss."

"Why d'you think they'd come out to Dog Point just to take a nap? I always thought he was an odd guy."

"Sparky, some people just can't get the kind of naps that they need in their own home. So, they cruise around until they can find someone that can provide that special sort of nap they're looking for."

"What kinda nap is that? What sort of nap is *that* special?"

"When you're older, you'll understand."

"You're starting to sound like my mom! She's always telling me that. Come to think of it, you look a lot more like my mom than I thought. I thought your hair was blonde, but I was wrong. It looks dark, like my mom's." He looked back to the car. " How long are they gonna take? She must've been really deep into that nap, huh?"

"Give them some time to put themselves together. What's your hurry, anyway?"

"I need to take a pee."

"Why don't you just pee in that storm sewer over there?"

"No, I'll wait. If they're finished waking up we'll be home soon enough."

Just then, the Newport's driver-side door opened and Mister Salty stepped out. He looked a hell of a lot healthier than he did in the morning, though he still was his usual bony self. Mister Salty's companion stayed in the passenger seat.

"Donnelly, did I hear you say you two need a lift to the subway?"

"That's right. We're kinda lost."

"I'll say! You're quite a long way from home, my boy. Who's this? You're not *Mrs.* Donnelly, are you? No, you're much younger than Mrs. Donnelly." Salty gave Scarlet a thorough going over– top to bottom and back again. He finished his tour, wearing a smirk on his gaunt face.

"She's not my mom! She's my friend. We met at the bus stop– a phony bus stop."

"And what brought you and young Donnelly here to Dog Point?" His radar zeroed in on her legs.

"We came here to get away from the rats," Sparky offered. "She and I ran like hell to get away from them. We ran for blocks and blocks."

"Oh, my! Rats can be very frightening, my dear. Where were these rats that you and Donnelly escaped from?"

Sparky answered him again. "We don't know, exactly. There weren't any street signs. We couldn't figure out which way to run and the people on stilts were no help at all. Scarlet was the one who first noticed the rats plotting to get us, but I saw it, too. That's when we knew we had to get outta there."

"Lucky for both of you that you're so perceptive, Scarlet. I wonder…"

"How come I'm the one talkin' to you and you don't even *look* at me and you keep talkin' to Scarlet? It's like I'm not even here!"

"Wishful thinking, Donnelly, wishful thinking."

"Can you take us to the subway, please? Sparky and I would be very grateful. We've had quite an evening, Mr. Solti."

Everyone jumped as the car horn sounded, honked twice by Mister Salty's companion. "Come on, fella! I don' got all night, ya know!"

Mister Salty, his nostrils flaring, glared at the silhouetted figure in the passenger seat. "My dear Scarlet, the night is still young and once I am free of my current associate and we have discharged young Donnelly, we can…"

The horn sounded again. It was one long honk, this time. "Hey!"

He rolled his eyes and took a deep breath before resuming his proposition. "As I was saying, we can take the Chrysler and drive down to..."

Another two long honks sounded.

"You were right, Mr. Solti, she sure does wake up ornery, doesn't she?" Sparky chuckled.

Mister Salty looked disdainfully at Sparky and gently led Scarlet by the arm, back across the street, ten paces behind the Newport. He stood close to her and they talked quietly for a moment, Scarlet doing most of the listening. Sparky couldn't hear what they were saying and was a little worried that Mister Salty would give Scarlet a ride and ditch him right there. One reassuring thought was that he was pretty sure that Scarlet would never go along with such a plan. She was too nice for that. Mister Salty pulled out a pack of cigarettes, offering one to Scarlet, which she accepted. He lit both and they continued their talk.

Sparky felt cold in his light jacket. The temperature had dropped in the hours since sunset. How many hours had that been? Sparky again wondered what time it was.

Mister Salty and Scarlet were still conferring, now with Scarlet doing more talking than listening. Mister Salty was running his left hand up and down her right arm as he listened. Sparky drifted around in circles, wondering, 'what could they be talking about that could take so long? He must be trying to get money to drive us. What a creep!' He peeked into the Newport and could see a woman sitting upright in the dark vehicle, staring straight ahead and smoking a cigarette through one of those fancy, long holders. The smoke from the cigarette wafted up, out of the passenger side window and drifted into the night air. Sparky looked away from the car and back at Scarlet and Mister Salty, still together. Mister Salty was still running his hand up and down her arm and he had his mouth close to Scarlet's ear. 'Now what's he whispering to her?' She listened with her eyes closed and her head tilted back a little. Sparky moseyed over and sat on the curb, waiting for Scarlet and Mister Salty to finish.

Sparky took this opportunity to pull out the Waarheid and snap an image of Scarlet and Mister Salty together. He loaded a fresh pad and

234

snapped, immediately removing the pad to examine the results. What he saw surprised and distressed him. The impression of Scarlet on this score pad hardly resembled the one he took earlier at the bus stop. He wished now that he hadn't given that pad to Scarlet to keep. He would have liked to examine the two pads, side-by-side. What Sparky recalled seeing was a person of tender character, intending to do good and kind things, patient and accommodating, conscientious, worried about not measuring up and afraid of hurting others. The pad he looked at now was very different. In this impression she was calculating and shrewd, reckless and capricious, self-loathing and ashamed, licentious and greedy.

Sparky looked at the camera to see if he had perhaps inadvertently changed a setting or something, but there were no settings to change. He looked at the pad and compared it to the ones he had used this afternoon. They looked exactly the same and in the dim glow of the streetlight, he could see that the part numbers were the same. He looked back at the image of Scarlet, again. 'I don't understand this. It's not possible to have two completely different versions of the truth. What a rip-off. This Waarheid thing is too unpredictable.' Sensing that he may have been sold a bill of goods, he pocketed the score pad and shoved the camera back in the bag, not wanting to think about it anymore. He was confused and scared– scared about how he would explain to his parents the purchase of such a uselessly unpredictable device as the Waarheid. He had been very proud to discover it and was so sure that he was making the wisest purchase of his young life. Now, he felt like a fool and he felt exhausted. He rested his head in his hands and his elbows on his knees, and continued waiting.

Sparky felt chilly and needed to pee, badly. He had nothing to distract him from the urgent sensation, so he felt it more keenly. The Newport continued to idle. The silhouetted woman continued to smoke. Sparky looked down at the shoulder of his jacket, examining the tomato that splattered on it. It was now completely dried and crusted up. Sparky picked at it with his index finger and was able to get some of the gunk to peel off the material.

"Sparky! Let's get in the backseat. Mr. Solti is kind enough to give us a lift."

Mister Salty looked like the cat that swallowed the canary.

"How much are we gonna hafta pay him, Scarlet?"

"We won't have to pay him at all."

They opened the back door and climbed in. Sparky got in first and scooted over to the passenger side to allow Scarlet room. The car smelled heavily of cigarette smoke, perfume and what Sparky was certain was booze.

"What's this, lover?"

"Our date is over, Doris."

"Whaddaya mean, 'over'? You're dumping me for *her*?" The woman cocked her thumb towards the backseat. "Just like that?" She snapped her fingers.

"Just like that." Mister Salty put the Chrysler in drive. Sparky noted that he signaled before he pulled away from the curb.

"Hah! What a gentleman. What's she got that I haven't got, huh? I treat you right, don't I? What the hell does *she* know? She's still wet behind the ears, for chrissakes!"

Mister Salty suddenly became annoyed. "At least she's wet *somewhere*, Doris!"

"Pull over!"

"Here?!"

"Pull over!" Mister Salty complied, signaling his intent on the deserted street. "I'm not takin' this kinda crap from anybody– least of all you! I got my pride, you know."

"Look, Doris, there's no need to turn this into a full-fledged melodrama. Let me take you back, will you?"

"Just stop the car, please!"

Mister Salty stopped at the curb and Doris, after first fumbling with the door lock, exited in a hurry, leaving the trio and staggering on ahead into the empty night. Mister Salty put his left turn signal on and pulled away from the curb, passing a lunging and weaving Doris.

Sparky looked back at her through the rear window. "Hey, Mr. Solti, I think she's signaling for us to stop!"

"That's not a signal for us to stop, Donnelly. That's not what that means."

"But, that's the same gesture I've seen taxi drivers use when they get in front of other drivers. Officer Pyles used it. I thought it was a warning to stop, or something. What does it mean?"

"It's like saying 'take that, buster!' It's an indication, um, of, uh, that all civil discourse has ceased. Isn't that right, dear Scarlet?"

"It's certainly that."

"Listen, Donnelly, Scarlet tells me that you were on your way back to the subway when you got sidetracked. Is that correct?"

"Yeah, I was going to catch the Number 13 at U.S.Plaza."

"I assume that you won't mind if I just drop you off at the City Hall station, then? You see, neither Scarlet nor I live near where you do, so it would be way, way out of the way to drive you all the way home. Is that okay with you, Donnelly?"

"I guess so."

"Couldn't we drive him to…"

"Listen to me, Scarlet, my dear. It would take me twice as long to get him home than it would take by subway– especially at ten o'clock."

"It's ten o'clock, *already*?"

"Almost. It's twenty minutes to ten, now." Mister Salty checked his watch never taking his hands off the steering wheel.

Sparky let his head drop to the side and bump the window. "Oh, man. I'm *really* dead, now. My dad is gonna– honest, I don't even know

237

what my dad is gonna do."

"Mr. Solti, couldn't we take him all the way home? Maybe we could help explain what's kept Sparky out so late and why he wasn't able to call."

"I really don't think anything we have to say will make a bit of difference. I know Mrs. Donnelly quite well and I can assure you that she is a very reasonable young woman who has much love to give. When she sees poor young Donnelly show up at her doorstep, tired, hungry and cold…"

"And needing to pee!"

"Yes, that, too. She will fold him into her bosoms, uh, bosom and thank God he's home and well. And anyway, you said to me that you didn't run into him until six o'clock, when he was already three hours late from school."

"So?"

"So, you can't vouch for anything he did all day *before* six. When I saw him before school this morning, it seemed he was already up to some mischief. I think it best that we don't get involved, Scarlet. Honestly, I think it's the best for us *and* for him."

"I suppose you're right. Are you okay with that, Sparky?"

"I guess so. I'll get on the 13 and be home in a half an hour. Then you can read about me in tomorrow morning's paper– about how I was killed by my own parents for coming home eight hours late from school. And I ruined this jacket, too."

Scarlet mussed his hair, but Sparky noted that the gesture felt friendly– just friendly– and lacked that magical warmth that her previous contact embodied.

"You know, Scarlet, you remind me very much of a lovely woman I work with. She teaches fourth grade. She is an absolutely lovely creature, like you. I've had the pleasure, many times. Many times."

"The pleasure of what?" Sparky inquired.

238

"Of her company, Donnelly. It's Mrs. Gardner I'm referring to. You had her last year, didn't you? Yes, I recall her talking about you. You were one of her favorites, you know. Perhaps I should say that you were her absolute favorite."

"I like Mrs. Gardner a lot."

"Is she pretty, Sparky?"

"Mrs. Gardner is a dreamboat." Sparky wondered why he used the term and immediately felt embarrassed.

"Is she as pretty as me?"

"She..."

"My dear Scarlet, Mrs. Gardner is indeed very pretty, but absolutely *not* as pretty as you. She does look a lot like you, though. You could be sisters."

The two of them continued this conversation, which consisted mostly of Mister Salty paying Scarlet gushing compliments, 'trying to butter her up for something,' Sparky thought. Sparky concluded that he was only nominally included in it, so he decided to stay quiet for the remaining few blocks to City Hall. He was watching the traffic and the people, few as they were, given the late hour. It felt good to be back in a populated district again– back in the civilized world, so to speak.

Scarlet nudged Sparky gently to get his attention. "Isn't Mr. Solti an excellent driver? He's so cautious and methodical!" Sparky shrugged.

Salty continued jabbering away. "Yes, in fact I somehow got separated from my class this morning when we all got on the buses and was fortunate enough by coincidence to have boarded the same bus as Mrs. Gardner. Isn't that an amazing? Anyway, I recall now that, during the course of our conversation, the subject of young Donnelly came up."

"Really? You hear that, Sparky? You're famous, the teachers talk about you!"

"Yes, well, Mrs. Gardner and I both expressed our astonishment at how far your star has fallen, young man– and how fast it's happened."

Sparky was jolted from his daydreaming about Mrs. Gardner.

"Oh, that's *awful*! What does he mean, Sparky?"

"Well, it seems that young Donnelly, here, has become a bit too big for his britches, so to speak. Mrs. Gardner confided in me that she is afraid she spoiled our companion here. She feels that she may have been too easy on him."

"No, that can't be, Mr. Solti! I found him to be the perfect gentleman. And *so* clever!"

"The book on him is that he's *too* clever by half. He tried that same charm he used on you to wrap Mrs. Pinkerton around his little finger. Suffice to say that Mrs. Pinkerton is the un-wrappable ace of our faculty. She's no fool."

"Is this true, Sparky? Are you a manipulative little brat?"

Sparky couldn't believe that she would ask him such a question.

"Answer the young woman, Donnelly. Or is this another of your little conniving tricks to get people's attention and sympathy? Is that it, eh?"

Sparky would have loved to contradict these vile accusations, but he found that he couldn't speak. He just sat there, wanting to speak, but didn't know what to say or where to start.

"Nothing to say in your defense? Not as clever as you thought you were, I guess. Well, nothing to worry about. Mrs. Pinkerton figured you out and is implementing a dandy of a plan to discredit you, get you suspended and ultimately get you expelled." He stretched upright and looked at Sparky in the rear view mirror. "Don't look so shocked, Donnelly. You must have known this was coming. Haven't you noticed a pattern evolving? Little by little, day after day, a case is being built to destroy you. You already have a pretty substantial file, and it's only been a few months. Mark my words: You will never make it through the fifth grade."

The words struck Sparky like a cannon ball. Here he was so worried about getting home late and all the trouble *that* would bring. Now it's clear that this difficulty may be the least of his worries. In the very near future– just a few short months, it seems– he will be exactly what Officer Pyles mistook him for this morning.

"Yes sir, you'll be out on the street." Mister Salty cocked his thumb and whistled like a bottle rocket. "Your friends won't know you anymore. Your future will be locked in for good. No college, no career. Ha! I hear they're hiring janitors, these days. I hope you like mopping floors and scrubbing toilets, my good man. Ha!"

"That's not fair!" Sparky was surprised when he got his voice back. "Pinkerton's just got it in for me. I always knew it! I won't let them kick me out. I have a right to go to school, you know!"

"I think you're acting horribly! Mr. Solti did not have to tell you these things, Sparky. You should thank him."

"*Thank* him? For what?"

"For showing you the way to save yourself from yourself. That's what for. It was very generous of him to do that."

"Why are you siding with *him*? You know what we call him behind his back? Mister Salty, that's what!"

"So? What does that signify?"

"He's a jerk! Everybody laughs at him 'cause he's a spaz! Look how skinny he is!" Sparky gulped. "He's probably a junkie! Check his arms, Scarlet. I bet he's got tracks!"

"You're a loathsome little demon, Donnelly." Salty signaled left and made the turn up Robinson Avenue toward City Hall. "I can't wait until that day when they march you down the hall and out of the school, once and for all." Sparky immediately thought of that TV show, *Branded*, where they tear off Chuck Connors' epaulets and send him out of the fort, in disgrace. "I hope you end up penniless, in the gutter, begging for scraps and killing alley cats for your supper. You don't know what awful things happen to people who live off the meat of stray cats."

"Actually, I do. They end up in the men's room with really bad diar-

241

rhea."

"You always have the smart answer, Donnelly." Mister Salty turned to his right, looking right at him with a sneer curling his lip, and addressed Sparky in the most vindictive tone. "But, your goose is finally cooked. *Nothing* can save you now!"

He didn't see that he had carelessly allowed the Newport to drift across the center line and, just as he was turning back to see where he was going, he sideswiped a police car.

Chapter 23: Manny and Dick

Sparky sat in the back of the squad car, waiting to find out his fate. He was fairly certain he would be arrested as an accessory to whatever crime Mister Salty and Scarlet would be charged with. In the few minutes he'd had alone in the back of the squad car, he'd already resolved to say nothing incriminating against Scarlet, despite the shabby way she had turned on him and sided with Mister Salty. As for Mister Salty, Sparky would fink on him. He would spill the beans, tell everything, turn state's evidence! He'd say anything they'd want him to. Sparky had figured it all out. He concocted a way to destroy Mister Salty *and* save himself in the process. He would fink on Mister Salty in exchange for a promise that he would never be expelled from P.S. 8! That would foil Mrs. Pinkerton's plot against him and, at the same time, ensure that he would get to go to college and stay off the streets and out of the toilets.

Speaking of toilets, Sparky again felt that urge to pee that had been nagging at him periodically for hours. He tried shifting his position to alleviate some of the pressure on his over-taxed bladder. He tried thinking about something else, to get his mind of the discomfort. He wondered why it was taking so long to be handcuffed and booked. When the policeman that Mister Salty sideswiped called in the accident on the radio, four other squad cars showed up within two minutes, their lights spinning and alarms wailing into the otherwise quiet night. Sparky thought he would be read his rights and hustled off to central booking within a few moments. That's the way it always happened on TV. Instead, there seemed to be no big hurry. No one had yet been arrested. And both crunched cars, the Chrysler Newport and the Plymouth Fury remained in the middle of Robinson, waiting for tow trucks.

"How ya' doin', kid?" It was one of the policemen, poking his head in the widow of the patrol car.

"Okay, I guess, officer."

"Ya' hungry?" He presented a bag to Sparky. "We figured you been waitin' a long time, ya' know? So we gotcha a little sumthin' from The Bagel Wheel over on Miller Avenue."

"Thanks, Officer! I *am* hungry." Sparky looked into the paper bag, which was warm to the touch. They had bought him a salt bagel and container of milk. "When are you gonna interrogate me?"

"It's gonna be a little longer. We'll be back to talk to you in a few minutes an' then we'll see if we can wrap this thing up an' get you home. Okay, kid?"

Sparky nodded as he unwrapped the paper straw and dropped it into his half pint of Linden Farms milk. He sucked down the milk in no time, finishing with a healthy, volcanic belch, of which he was quite proud. He dug the salt bagel out of the bag and sank his teeth into its warm chewy mass. The scent and the salt made his mouth water and he closed his eyes as he tore off a large bite and chewed it.

"Oh, man," he mumbled through the mouthful. "Mmmf." Sparky took his time and reveled in each deliciously sensual mouthful. He'd never enjoyed a bagel more than this one and he felt sorry when he had finally consumed the last morsel. The strange thing was that he still felt hungry and thirsty– and cold. And he still needed to pee.

Sparky turned around a looked through the back window, hoping to see what was transpiring between the police and his two former companions. Scarlet was standing off to one side with a policeman. They stood very close to each other as they conferred. The policeman had his hand on her arm and was stroking softly up and down. Scarlet's head dropped gently on the policeman's shoulder as he stroked. Sparky assumed that she was overcome with relief from having been spared the awfulness of Mister Salty's unwelcome attentions. The policeman gently led Scarlet away from the street, away from the others and into the dark recesses of the entranceway of a bookstore. Sparky assumed that she needed more privacy to tell her version of the events to the policeman.

Mister Salty was half-sitting, slumped on the trunk of one of the squad cars. He seemed distantly into his own thoughts, pondering, no doubt, his ruined teaching career and the dark years ahead in B.C.F., the notorious men's prison, across the bay in Belleville, until he noticed Scarlet and the policeman slipping off into the darkness together. At that point, Salty stiffened his spine and stared at them worriedly. Sparky relished the fear Mister Salty must be feeling, thinking of how Scarlet would betray the ghoul to the cops and be the final cause of his complete ruination.

Sparky also noticed a familiar figure staggering up the street toward the scene. It was Doris, catching up to Mister Salty, at last, hobbling along on her high heels. Sparky could see her expression change as she recognized the car, then Mister Salty. She tottered up to him, at which point she started a very animated conversation that Sparky could hear echoing off the surrounding buildings, though he couldn't discern the words. Mister Salty turned away from her and said nothing. Clearly, Doris was still upset and after a few sentences accompanied by much wild gesticulation, she walked up close to Mister Salty and poked him several times in the chest as she berated him. Mister Salty pushed her away with his left forearm and this set Doris off like an H-bomb. She swung her purse wildly at Mister Salty as the police advanced to restrain her.

Sparky was glad that Mister Salty was getting pummeled, but he started to feel weary of all the discord he had seen. He thought of taking an image of the scene with his camera, but decided against it. He suspected that the true nature of this situation was not worth examining in any greater detail. As humorous as the sight of Mister Salty being beaten up by a drunken woman was, the whole thing was pretty ugly and tawdry. In fact, Sparky started to feel sorry for Mister Salty when he saw the man trying to fend off her blows, while refraining from striking back. Sparky had been in a similar circumstance early in the previous school year, when a rather pugnacious Puerto Rican girl took a liking to him and beat him up out in the school yard during lunch. He remembered doing just what Mister Salty was doing now.

The tow trucks had arrived and were hooking the front ends of the wrecked cars to their hydraulic lifts. Sparky sat and waited. The dome lights on each of the police cars and the yellow lights on the tow trucks provided an almost psychedelic display. Red-blue-red-blue-red-blue. Yellow-yellow-yellow-yellow. The traffic light one hundred feet ahead was blinking from green to yellow to red to green and back again. The crosswalk signs changed from green "WALK", to red, blinking twelve times "DON'T WALK" before staying red for a while and then back to the green "WALK" again. One of the tow trucks had finished securing the Chrysler Newport and pulled away, passing right through the red traffic light. Sparky watched it disappear into the distance. He wished he could be on that tow truck now.

Sparky just wanted to get home. It was after ten, well-past his normal bedtime, and he'd had a long day. A lot had happened and he was tired of it all, and now he was tired of the waiting, as well. He was bleary-eyed and feeling sleepy after eating that bagel.

"Sparky?" Scarlet had approached the squad car, unnoticed.

"Is that policeman through with you, Scarlet? Are they going to arrest us?"

"No, silly! We didn't commit any crime."

"What about Mr. Solti? He hit the police car."

"They're giving him a ticket for that. He'll have to go in front of a judge, but not tonight."

"But, they questioned you. I saw you talking with that officer."

"He was quite satisfied with my response. He has my name, address and phone number if he should have any further need of me, which I imagine he will. Did they let you call your mother?"

"Not yet. I asked them if I could call home, but Sergeant Scheiskoff told me they didn't have any way I could call her from a squad car."

"Well, what are you going to do?"

"They said I can call her as soon as we're done here. Probably from a phone booth."

"I've got to go now, Sparky." Smiling warmly, Scarlet put her hand over Sparky's and squeezed. "Thanks for being such a hero for me."

"I don't know. I guess I got you into this mess, in the first place."

"Don't say that. If it wasn't for you, I'd still be waiting at that bogus bus stop, for a bus that doesn't even exist. You saved me from purgatory, Sparky." She leaned into the car and kissed him on the cheek. "See you around." Scarlet walked away, toward City Hall.

Sparky noticed that her breath was foul.

"Well, Don Juan, ya' ready to wrap it up for the night?" The police officer who had brought him the bagel and milk was getting into the driver's seat. His partner, who had assisted in breaking up the brawl between Mister Salty and Doris, was putting something in the trunk. When he slammed the trunk closed, Sparky turned and could see Doris, handcuffed and being placed in the back of one of the squad cars. "I mus' say, you got some colorful friends there. Where'd ya' meet up with *them*, huh?"

"I met Scarlet at the bus stop. Mr. Solti teaches sixth grade at my school. He was with the other woman when we ran into them near the waterfront. She was napping when we first saw them parked."

"Napping? She's sump'n else, that one! Ha ha! He had his hands full with *her*– more than he could handle, I say!"

"He told me she was grumpy when she wakes up from a nap."

"More like she was freakin' Godzilla when she wakes up from a nap!"

The partner opened the passenger door and got in. "We ready to roll, Manny?"

"All set."

"Manny an' me are gonna drive you home."

"Can't I call my mom? She hasn't heard from me all day."

"We had somebody call your house already and they spoke to your momma or your poppa– I ain't sure which. One of the two, anyway."

"It was his momma Scheiskoff spoke to. I gotta say, Junior, your momma sounds like a *real* nice lady. Scheiskoff said she sounded *real* sweet on the phone. She was sure glad to hear from us."

Manny started up the engine and accelerated up Robinson Avenue, passing that same red signal the tow truck ignored.

"I bet Mom was glad! Did she sound upset? Was she worried about me?"

247

"I don' know, Junior. I di'n talk to her. I'm sure they tol' her not to worry. Don' you worry, we'll get you home in no time. Manny, here, he's a real good driver."

Manny had the dome light flashing as they sped effortlessly up Robinson, past Averdantis Avenue, past Miller Avenue, careening around the dog leg at 18th Street.

Sparky could see the reflection of the squad car and its lights in the store windows as they passed. Swiftly they flew due north– 29th Street, Stephen's Court, Akeley Street. Forty, forty-five, fifty miles per hour on city streets! They passed cars and taxis and buses, and ahead of the buses, the lonely people waiting at the bus stops. Sparky looked over the front seat, over Manny's shoulder and at the speedometer– Forty-six miles per hour! Just a couple of blocks shy of U.S. Plaza, Manny applied the brakes and made the right turn onto Ducommun Street, nearly running down a shabby-looking man in an overcoat and hat.

"Hey, Junior, your momma as pretty as she sounds?"

"I don't know. I guess. She's my mom."

"C'mon, Dick, don' act like that. You're makin' the kid uncomfortable. Dick don't make you uncomfortable, does he, kid? Sometimes he acts without thinkin', ya' know what I mean?"

"Sure, I guess."

Using caution and a blast or two from the siren, Manny negotiated through the cross-traffic of Highbridge Avenue and Concord Avenue, threading through buses and taxicabs, making the left onto Sixth Avenue and into territory that Sparky had imagined he would one day see, but not from the backseat of a police car.

"I like Dick, y' know, he's my partner an' all, but he does stuff all the time an' then we gotta clean up the mess, afterward. Isn' that right?"

"Manny likes to blame me for everything. A lot of stuff is *his* fault, ya' know, but it's always 'blame it on big, dumb Dick'."

"I definitely know what you're talking about. I get blamed for lotsa stuff that's not my fault. My teacher's always punishing me for stuff I didn't do."

"Mus' be an epidemic. Mosta the people we arrest say the same thing. Right, Dick?"

"Right on."

Sparky thought about it for a second. "Well, I guess I do some of it." They entered Edgewood, with its quiet, stately homes zipping past at more than forty miles per hour, then solidly middle-class Tillotson Flats at forty-eight miles per hour. Block after block after block went by. The mercury vapor streetlights passed by overhead, one after another, casting their cool green glow down onto Sparky and the two cops.

At Bronx Avenue, they crossed into Linden Farms, where, Sparky was thinking, 'Mrs. Piper and Mrs. Gardner– no, wait, not Mrs. Gardner– Scarlet Weaner live here! Where does Mrs. Gardner live, anyway?' His mind drifted through one thought after another, disjointed and fragmentary. The events of this long day were disappearing behind the forest of his thoughts, able to be glimpsed occasionally through the clutter. The houses zipping by, one after another, block after block, were so repetitive and so rhythmic that Sparky sat in a daze, staring out at them, expressionless and unseeing. He started thinking of school, as if he had gone to school this day. He replayed Diana's frozen torment in front of the entire class. That happened today, didn't it? When did that dapper guy buy all those magazines? Who was it that lived in Linden Farms? Was it Donna– Dora– Doris? Doris, that's it! No, she didn't live here, did she? It was Mrs. Gardner– no, no, not Mrs. Gardner. Hey, there's Eden Street! Who lives on Eden Street? Before Sparky could formulate the answer, Eden Street was gone.

Sparky could not believe how swiftly he was being transported home. Home had seemed so impossibly far away, just a short time ago. He still needed to pee, but was certain now that he would be home in time to avoid having an embarrassing accident. The city seemed so much smaller now. It had taken him all day and most of the evening just to get downtown. Before, it had seemed so vast and mysterious. Now it was taking just minutes to fly through mile after mile of densely packed streets.

Between Hicks and Potato Streets, Manny hung a left and headed up

Neptune Avenue. Sparky felt the car make the turn. The cops were talking to each other, but Sparky couldn't discern the words or meaning anymore. He just heard their deep voices as they passed the intersection of 60th Street. Manny was finally forced to slow down a little as they fell in behind a lumbering BP tanker truck.

"I think we got a tired boy on our hands, Honey." Sparky hadn't felt his eyes close.

Part III The Real Dream

Chapter 1: Looking for the Lost Waarheid

"Sweetie! Time to wake up! Rise and shine, Sweetie! Time to go to school!"

Sparky groggily surfaced from a leaden slumber. His head felt full of clay, but his bladder was full-to-bursting. That was his incentive to get out of bed. He pushed himself out of the soft mattress and staggered out of his room and into the bathroom, where his dad was just finishing shaving.

"Morning, Champ." After waiting in vain for a response, he added, "Not very talkative this morning, eh?"

Sparky stood over the toilet, taking one of the most profound pisses of his young life. "I'm not awake yet. I had a hard day yesterday and I don't think I got much sleep."

"The way I see it, you *over*slept." His dad cheerily finished scraping his chin and lower lip. "I knew we should've woken you up when you dozed off. That's a pretty impressive tank-full you've got there, Champ."

"I don't remember getting to go all day yesterday."

"Is that right?" His dad chuckled. "Why's that?" He decided to play along with his son.

"You know." Sparky's sleepy haze started to clear as he finished relieving himself. "How could you say I *over*slept?"

His dad splashed his face and toweled dry, leaving the sink for Sparky and heading to the master bedroom to finish dressing. Sparky stepped into the slot and brushed his teeth. From the kitchen could be heard the familiar sounds of News Radio 1212 and Roger Hammond, the morning anchor. It was the radio in the mornings with the help of that incessant tickety-clickety sound effect behind the anchor's reading that provided the household its morning rhythm and kept the boys from dawdling. He recalled that, for a change, his mom hadn't had the radio on

yesterday morning. 'Part of that weird way she was acting,' he supposed.

Sparky went through the motions with even less engagement than he
normally had. He felt as if he'd been through a war, but he wasn't absolutely clear why he should feel this way. He had the distinct feeling that
he'd had a wild day yesterday, but it was just a feeling. He thought he
recalled hugging Mrs. Gardner, but then realized that he hadn't seen
Mrs. Gardner close up in several days. Her classroom was on the second floor and his was on the third. He dragged himself into his room to
get dressed for school and to pack his schoolbooks into his bag. As he
removed his pajamas and changed into his clothes, he recalled the old
woman holding him and his inability to break her grasp, and he got the
willies. 'When was that?' he wondered.

Sparky revisited the bathroom to comb his hair. Wetting the comb and
dragging it across his head, Sparky recalled the joy and satisfaction of
the purchase of the camera. 'My Waarheid!' Suddenly, he popped
awake, remembering his unique purchase and eager to show it off. He
dashed into his room, looking for the camera shop bag. He searched
every corner of the room, but couldn't find it.

"Sweetie! Breakfast is on the table! You don't want it to get cold!"

"Mom! Where's my bag from the camera shop?" No answer, though he
could hear some murmuring from the kitchen. "Mom!"

"What bag is that, Sweetie?"

"From the camera shop! It's beige, with a dark green logo on it! It has
my new camera in it!" He gave up and marched out to the dining room.
"I brought it home with me last night."

"The only thing you brought home with you was your ball, Sweetie. I
don't remember a bag." She poured him a glass of milk. "Unless you
left it in the hall."

"That must be it." Sparky hustled over to the front hall and checked
around the coat rack and the boots by the door. Nothing. "Mom! It's
not here! I thought I had it with me when I went to bed."

His dad was sipping coffee in the kitchen. "We carried you to bed,

Champ. Ha! You were in no condition to carry anything!"

Sparky started to worry. 'Could I have left it in the police car?' His school bag made it home all right, though he didn't remember carrying that into the house. Come to think of it, he couldn't remember getting home at all. He must have fallen asleep in the squad car.

"Come to the table and eat your breakfast, Sweetie. Your oatmeal's getting cold."

"This is important! You don't understand!" Sparky barked at his mom. Sparky's heart started pounding. He had spent more than three hundred dollars on that camera. If it was lost, he'd be dead. He'd *never* be able to pay the money back. But, it would have been left in the police car. They wouldn't keep it, would they? The receipt was in the bag with the camera, but he wasn't sure his name was on the receipt.

"Come on, now! You don't want to be late for school!"

"That didn't bother you yesterday." Sparky looked into the living room on the way back to the dining table.

"What's buggin' you, this morning, Champ?" His dad was cobbling together a lunch of olive loaf on white toast with lettuce and mustard.

"Dad, do you think the police department has a lost and found department?" Sparky was spooning sugar onto his oatmeal.

"Go slow with that stuff, Champ. Your teeth are gonna rot away before you get to junior high at that rate."

"Do they have one?"

"What, a lost and found? I suppose they do. Why?"

"I mighta lost something."

"What?" His dad waited for an answer that didn't come. "What did you lose, Champ?"

Sparky had tried not to answer. "A camera." Sparky cringed. He was sure he'd catch hell.

253

"Whose camera?"

"Well, *my* camera."

"You don't own a camera."

Sparky breathed a sigh of relief. "Good. That's good, right, Dad?"

"Why's that good?"

"Cause, if I don't own one, I couldn't have lost it, right?" Sparky chuckled.

Sparky's mom seemed mildly amused. "Honey, I think your son has lost his marbles– all of them– overnight."

"Yeah, Champ, you should check the lost and found for your marbles, eh? Ha ha!"

Sparky laughed with his parents, but he was laughing because he had bought himself some extra time to retrieve the camera. If they didn't know he bought a camera, he wouldn't have to explain its loss yet.

"I'm not the crazy one around here, Dad. You shoulda been here yesterday morning when Mom was acting like a little girl. Ha ha! Now, *that* was funny!"

His dad stopped drinking his coffee in mid-swallow and stared at Sparky. "What are you talking about?"

"Yeah, all this stuff about spanking and panties. Ha ha! She was acting like you were going to spank her and she sounded funny." Sparky noticed neither of his parents was amused. "She did. She– she didn't have breakfast for me. She kept sayin' this stupid stuff about logs and fireplaces. It's true! She sent me outta the house with hundreds of dollars and said I should buy breakfast on the way to school with it. Here, I'll show you." Sparky stood up and dug into his pockets for the money he had left from the previous day. "I've got more than a hundred dollars left." He tried each of his pockets in vain. "I had a ton of money left, even after the camera. I don't know what happened to it." He could see his parents exchange a look. He sat down, sheepishly, and avoided their gazes.

"Young man, what kind of poor excuse for a joke is that?"

When his mom called him 'young man', he knew he'd really trans-gressed. "I was just, um…"

His dad chimed in, as well. "Why would you say that about your mother, huh? Answer me."

"I didn't mean it, Dad. I just thought I, uh, sorta remembered it. I guess I didn't."

"You'll apologize to her for saying such sick stuff about her."

"I'm sorry I said such sick stuff, Mom. I just thought…"

"I don't want to hear any more along this line. Do you understand?"

"Yes, Dad."

"Finish up your breakfast and get going. I don't want you to be late." His mom had a very concerned look on her face.

"*I* don't want to be late again, either."

"Were you late yesterday?"

Sparky didn't know what to say. 'She doesn't know? How's that possi-ble? Maybe she's playing dumb. How could she *not* know?' Though he couldn't recall what transpired when he finally got home last night, he was operating under the assumption that he must have already gotten any punishment he would have incurred for not going to school yester-day. But, it seemed now that his parents' righteous wrath still could lie ahead. Sparky flushed as if caught at something. In a split-second, he decided to risk everything and bluff it out. "No! I *wasn't* late yester-day!" Sparky figured he was only half-lying, since not going to school at all is not 'being late' to school. "I meant, in general, I don't ever want to be late again. I don't like being late. Do you know what I mean?" Sparky chuckled nervously. "I mean, who wants to be late? That's a good way to get in trouble and I don't want to get into any more trouble. I've had my share– *more* than my share this year. I don't want to make it worse by being late, too."

"Maybe you've got the time to deal with his nonsense. I don't. I've got to go to work." Sparky's dad gathered up his things, kissed his wife and headed for the front door. Grabbing his hat, he turned back. "I sure hope you meant what you said about not wanting any more trouble. If you want to live an exciting and interesting life, like you were talking about last night, you've got to do well in school; get your diploma; go to college and get a degree, because if you don't, you'll end up scrubbing toilets for the rest of your life. See ya later." And he was out the door.

Sparky's mom scrutinized her son, wondering if she should worry. "What's this all about, Sweetie? Am I going to find out something? Are we going to get another letter?"

"No, Mom. I didn't do anything. Really."

"Well, you're sure acting strangely this morning." She puttered around the kitchen, cleaning up her husband's breakfast dishes. "Sweetie, what was that about losing a camera?" Sparky blanched. "You didn't borrow somebody's camera and then lose it, by any chance, did you?"

"No, Mom, I didn't borrow anybody's camera."

"Then why were you asking about a lost and found department?" She walked back into the dining room.

"If I *did* lose a camera, I wanted to know if the police would have a lost and found where I could check. That's all." He was having trouble eating his apple-cinnamon oatmeal. His stomach was in knots.

His mom stared at him, trying to determine if he was hiding something from her. "Does this have anything to do with that interesting and exciting thing you were harping on last night?"

"Did I talk about that last night, too?"

"Yes, you did."

"No, it doesn't have anything to do directly with people living an exciting and interesting life. What else did I say last night?"

256

"Ha! Not much. You fell asleep on the living room floor."

"Did the police say anything?"

"The *police*? What are you talking about? You're sure you're not in any trouble?"

"As far as I know, I'm not in any trouble at all."

"What do you mean, 'as far as you know?' Did something happen at school?"

"Nothing happened at school. Honest. Nothing, Mom."

She wasn't sure what to think, so she chose to think the best. There was always time to be unpleasantly surprised later. "Okay, Sweetie, we'll let it drop for now.. Don't forget your lunch. It's next to your bag."

Sparky finished his milk and took off for the bathroom one last time before he left. He didn't want to get stuck not going like yesterday. As he peed, he tried to figure out why neither of his parents quizzed him about his adventure yesterday. His mom reacted as if Manny and Dick didn't bring him to the door. They must have dropped him off at the curb. That would explain her not knowing about the police involvement, but it wouldn't answer the question of why his parents seemed blissfully uninterested in his reasons for getting home after eleven o'clock at night. Finishing up, Sparky decided to reopen the issue himself. His curiosity was not letting the issue go unresolved.

"Mom! Are you sure you don't want to talk about last night?"

"About what? You mean all those fun and exciting people you were talking about?"

"Yeah, them." Sparky deduced that he or the police must have talked with his parents about the people and places he had been yesterday.

"No, Sweetie. If you're okay about it, so am I."

"Okay about it?"

"About, you know, whether or not those people you talked about are living more exciting lives than you are– than we are. If you're okay with what we talked about, then we're all okay."

Sparky no longer knew what to think. "But, what about last night?"

"What *about* last night?" She was starting to sympathize with her husband.

"Well, if *you've* got nothing to say, then I say we forget about it. Agreed?"

"Agreed, already!"

Hallelujah! "Okay, Mom. I'm going. I don't want to be late, you know."

"Have a good day, Sweetie." She kissed him farewell and he was out the door.

Now all he had to do was get back his camera.

Chapter 2: Was it All Just a Dream?

Things looked pretty normal on the blocks in Sparky's neighborhood, today. The walk to P.S. 8 held no odd surprises and the queer characters that populated yesterday's trek to school were nowhere to be seen today. Sparky wore his light blue jacket– the same one he'd worn yesterday– and noticed that his mom must have cleaned up the tomato splotch that had stained the shoulder. On the corner of Eighth Avenue, Sparky ran into some of the kids from the other classes in his school.

"Hey, Logan."

"Hey, Sparky."

"Sorry about yesterday, man."

"What about yesterday?"

"About your name."

"I don' know what your talkin' about."

"I'm sorry about how I couldn't pronounce your name, you know?"

"It's okay."

"See ya later."

"See ya."

Sparky zipped on ahead, glad that he cleared up the embarrassment of the previous morning, though he would have thought that Logan would have cared more than he showed. Turning the corner onto 82nd Street, Sparky was eager to see what they were able to accomplish in the reconstruction of the school. Francis, the foreman, had given Sparky the impression that the school would somehow be finished by morning, but Sparky doubted it could really be done that fast. He figured they'd still have a big mess where the school should be. To his surprise, he could see both the Dutch Boy paint store and the Coaster Bar and Lounge back in the places they had been before. Plotz Lincoln-Mercury and Wanderlust travel agency were gone. Sparky was confused.

"Why would they…?" He slowed to a stop, staring at the two businesses, his mouth agape.

"What's the matter, Sparky? You look like your trying to catch flies. Shut your mouth, already!"

"Hey, Diana, wasn't there a car dealership here yesterday?"

"Where, here? No way!"

"Are you sure?"

"Yeah, I'm sure! I may not know American history, but I do know Rick's paint store. My aunt used to do their bookkeeping. They've been here forever. Since the forties."

"Hey, Diana, um, I, uh, I'm sorry I laughed at you the other day."

"What other day?"

"When Pinkerton was picking on you when she asked about the War of 1812. You know."

"Oh, sure, *Yesterday!* That's okay; I know you didn't mean it. You've had your share of crap this year. We've laughed at *you*– plenty of times."

"You have? I never noticed."

"Yeah, sure. It's funny when somebody else is getting it. Let's go." They walked up the street, toward the school, which was standing, complete and identical to the way it looked before.

"Son of a gun!"

"What?"

"Francis was right. They finished the school! But, it looks just like it did before. I don't understand."

"What's there to understand?"

"Why'd they bother? What's the point? It doesn't even look any *cleaner!*"

"What are you talking about? Why did who bother to do what?"

"Why'd they bother to rebuild the school, you dummy?"

"I'm not a dummy. You're acting retarded. Who said they were going to rebuild the school? The school doesn't need to be rebuilt. It's practically new! It's in fine shape. Whoever told you they were going to rebuild the school was pullin' your leg, Sparky."

"It was the foreman who told me. I saw it yesterday with my own eyes. The school was gone and being reconstructed."

"This is ridiculous. I don't know who or what you saw, but they're not going to rebuild the school."

"Oh, come on! Why do you think they took everybody away on buses yesterday?"

"What are you talking about? Nobody got taken away on buses. We were all in school. Don't you remember? Mrs. Pinkerton yelled at you for helping Les, and I couldn't remember the answer to who fought in the War of 1812?"

"That was Wednesday."

"Yeah, Wednesday– *yesterday*! Today is Thursday. Your mouth is open again, Sparky."

The two resumed walking, Sparky now in a shocked daze, around the school to the yard to meet up with their classmates. Sparky suddenly felt so alone and out of touch with everyone around him that he almost bolted out of there to retreat to the safety and security of his home. His mind jumped back and forth between believing Diana, that it was Thursday– not Friday, as he had believed it was, and thinking she was deluded or mistaken, that everything that *seemed* to have happened to him during what he thought was yesterday, really *did* happen.

Sparky quickly debated both positions in his mind. He couldn't shake the belief that despite what Diana said, which *must* be true, the events that Sparky experienced might have actually occurred. 'There's no way I could have invented all of it. After all, I traveled to districts of High-bridge that I've never seen before. I met and talked with people that I've never seen before. I looked at the images produced by the Waar-heid and could see things which I never could have conceived on my own. Right?'

"Hey, Sparky!" It was Les and Giant.

"See you later, Sparky." Diana parted from Sparky to join her friends, Gwendolyn and Ellen.

"What's happenin', guys?"

"You gotta save me from this idiot, Sparky. You know what Les says? He says he was watching *The Courtship of Eddie's Father* last night and he wished his mother would go away so he and his dad could get along like Eddie and *his* dad do. Can you believe that crap?!"

"Giant, *you're* a big, giant, stinky crap."

"Shut up, Les. Listen, Sparky, listen. Where would him and his dad be if his mom wasn't around, huh? Who would buy the food and cook it? Who would wash his clothes? He wouldn't last a week without his mom. Not to mention, Les, that your dad is nothing like Bill Bixby. You'd get on each other's nerves and be tired of each other in no time."

Les slugged Giant on the upper arm. "That's not true! My dad's only tough to get along with because he and Mom fight so much. If she left, my dad would be fun, again."

"You're so dumb it's not even funny. That mother on *The Courtship of Eddie's Father* died, Les! She didn't just leave for a couple of days! Eddie can't just pick up the phone and call her when he's worried about something! She's *dead*! D'you think if your mom died that your dad would magically become fun? Gain a brain, Les."

"How do you know he wouldn't?"

Both boys stopped the argument momentarily to get some input from Sparky, who had been silent up to this point.

"You don't have much to say, do you?"

"Giant, leave him alone. He's thinkin' about it. Right, Sparky?"

Sparky looked at Les and then Giant, but he was not quite all there.

"What's wrong, Sparky? You looked stoned. Have you been sniffing glue or something?"

"What do you know about how somebody looks stoned?"

"The blond guy that lives across the back alley from us, he gets stoned all the time! That's how Sparky looks, now."

"Really? Hey, Sparky, are you stoned, man?"

"No."

"He can speak! That's a good sign. The guy across the back alley sometimes *can't* speak. He can't even stay awake, sometimes."

"Oh, *that* guy! I saw him when I was over, the day we set up your Hot Wheels off the back stoop. He was falling out of his chair. Remember? And it was only one o'clock in the afternoon! Ha ha!"

"That's him! Yeah, that's right. You *did* see him. I forgot about that."

"Then what's the matter, if you're not stoned or high or on a trip? You look like you're in a daze!"

Sparky could hardly know where to start. "I, uh..."

"Uh oh! Now he *can't* talk anymore. Ha ha!"

"Shut up! What's the matter, buddy– something wrong at home? Are you sick?"

"He seemed kinda out of it, yesterday after school, I thought."

Sparky was able to grab onto something to start explaining. "Yester-day."

"What about yesterday?"

"I lived a whole day yesterday that never happened."

"What the hell does *that* mean?"

"It must have been a dream. I've never had a dream like that before. I bet nobody has. I dreamt a whole day. I'm talking about *everything*, from the time I woke up until like eleven o'clock at night, when I fell asleep."

"I have dreams like that all the time."

"A *whole* day– everything that happens from morning 'til night?"

"No, not a *whole* day, I guess."

"Was it a normal day– school and everything?"

"That's the thing. Did we have a normal day at school yesterday?"

Giant looked at Les and back again at Sparky, shrugging his shoulders and nodding his head in the affirmative.

"Then it definitely *was* a dream, because Diana said the same thing. I thought they had torn the school down and you guys were bussed someplace else and I got in late and missed the buses. All this weird stuff was happening and my mom was acting stupid, like a little girl."

"Well, if you didn't go to school, what'd you do instead?"

"I was going home and I got nabbed by a truant officer."

"That's impossible."

"Why would that be impossible, Giant?"

"My grandmother was talking to my mom about my cousin, Alexandra, and how she's cuttin' school all the time and hangin' out with boys from the Prep. So, my grandmother asks how come the truant officers don't go after her and my mom says they did away with them in the budget cuts of 1966. So, it's impossible. If you didn't know it was a dream before, you definitely know it, now."

"How the hell do you know all this stuff?"

"I know everything, Les. You should know that by now."

"What else happened in your dream, Sparky?"

"All kinds of stuff. I went all over the place and ended up downtown. I bought this camera that takes pictures of the true essence of things."

"What the hell is the true essence of things?"

"You know, like when someone is not what they appear to be. This camera saw that and made an image of it on a score pad."

"That could come in handy! It'd be like a lie detector, but without having to ask all those questions. The F.B.I. could use something like that."

"That's what I thought, but I asked the man at the camera store about it and he said the police didn't like the results they got. I have to say that you didn't always get the image that you *thought* you were going to get when you pressed the trigger." Sparky thought of the last image he captured of Scarlet, and how she appeared so different from the bus stop image. "And you don't always get the same result from the same person, from shot to shot."

"Well, what good is that?" Giant was disappointed. He had been thinking that it was a great invention. "You've gotta get the same impression every time or you can't trust the thing! People don't change."

Niles walked up to the group as Giant finished his point. "Whatcha talkin' about, man?"

"This camera that Sparky dreamt about that takes a picture of your true self, not just what you look like."

"Man, who'd wanna see that? There's gotta be some really ugly people in the world, man. I wanna look *good* in my pictures."

"What Giant was saying was that if the thing can't take get same impression of a person every time, it'd be no good."

"I don' know, man. Who knows what the truth is about anybody? That nice old man that used to hang out at the park, man, he turned out to be an escaped Nazi, man! I thought he was okay. Remember, he used to hand out Tootsie Rolls? But, he killed Jews, man."

"Yeah, but that truth won't change from day to day. It's always gonna be the same, right?"

"I agree with Les. In this dream I had, I took an image of this woman and then I took another a couple hours later and the two images were really different."

"I think maybe people can change, but not *that* fast."

"Wait a minute, man! Sparky just said he was with a woman in a dream for a couple of hours, man? I thought you weren't interested in girls, man. What were you doin' with a woman for a couple of hours, huh? Was she pretty?"

"Yeah, she was, I guess."

"You *guess*? C'mon, man! What'd she look like, man?"

Sparky was embarrassed and was reluctant to divulge any more than he had already.

"Come on, Sparky! What'd she look like? How old was she?"

"She was about twenty or twenty-five, I suppose. I didn't ask her."

"Was she fat? I bet she was a fat, sweaty, slob with a pig nose! Ha ha!"

"I don't know." Sparky shuffled his feet and looked at the ground. "She was all right, I guess."

"I bet *I* know what she looked like," Giant boasted with a broad smile.

"How would *you* know?" Les pointed across at Sparky. "It was *his* dream."

"'Cause I know Sparky. I bet she looked like Mrs. Gardner, right? Am I right?" Sparky blushed and smiled. "Hah, I *knew* it!" That revelation brought a huge reaction from the others, who teased and jostled Sparky.

"But, it was only later on, near the end!" Sparky protested. "She didn't start out looking that way! She looked different at first."

"Yeah, right. We knew you're in love with Mrs. Gardner. You're even dreaming about her!"

"Hey, man, no wonder you weren't interested in Stacey and Julie, man. You go for the *older* women, man!"

"Hey, Sparky, that sounds like a really cool dream, though. I've never dreamed a whole day. Did you dream the whole day at school and everything?"

"No, I never went to school at all."

"That's even better!"

"They'd torn down the school and were rebuilding it and, since I was late, I missed the buses you guys got put on."

"Where did *we* all go, then, if P.S. 8 was being rebuilt?"

"I never found out."

"You never asked us?"

"None of you were in my dream. From the time I was walking to school until I got home at eleven, I didn't see anybody from the school. I was going to ask you guys today what you did all day. Wait a minute! I did see Mister Salty and Diana and Gwendolyn and Logan."

"And you didn't see any of us? Where'd you see Salty?"

Sparky laughed. "I saw him parked with some drunk woman, way out by Dog Point."

Giant interrupted, "Where's Dog Point?"

267

"Hey, I know something Giant doesn't know!" Les beamed, proudly. "That's that old part of town, where the old gangs used to operate, back in the old steamboat days. That area was the center of the worst kinda crimes in the city a hundred years ago."

"Well, there's *nothing* going on down there these days. The place looks like it's falling apart, the streets are empty. There's a huge old ferry boat docked right at the end of a street there."

"The Lady Liberty, right?"

"That's right! How did *you* know?"

"Yeah, Les, how *did* you know that? It was Sparky's dream."

"There really is a ferry dry-docked there. There's a picture of it in that Highbridge history book. Two pictures, actually. One when it was carrying people, back in the 1890's, and another when the book was written. That boat's been there since the 1930's– since the depression."

"Did you know about this ferry boat, Sparky?"

"I don't think so. I've never been down there before and I don't remember ever reading about it, I don't think."

"Well, that's strange."

"What's strange, Giant?"

"Sparky dreamt about something that actually exists, that he never saw before or knew about. I think that's *really* strange."

"That's like the *Twilight Zone*! Was Rod Serling in your dream?"

"You're right, man– the *Twilight Zone*. Man, that gives me the willies. Hey, maybe Sparky's got E.S.P. or something, man. What do you guys think, huh?"

They all stopped and thought for a moment about the possibility of Sparky possessing some sort of extraordinary capability. They pondered for a moment what sort of talent that might be and what it might mean if he did indeed possess it.

Giant spoke for the group when he said, "Nah!"

The Assistant Principal, Mr. Puppe, sounded the bullhorn, the signal to line up to go into the building. The boys broke their little circle and moseyed over to their classroom number, painted on the asphalt of the playground.

"So, Sparky, what happened with Salty? What was he doing there?"

"He was just parked in his Newport with this old drunk. She fell asleep with her head on his lap. When she woke up, boy was she *nasty*!"

The boys fell in line and waited for the Mr. Puppe to signal to the teachers to march their classes inside. The youngest two grades marched in first, occupying the first floor classrooms, then the third and fourth grades to their second floor rooms, and finally the fifth and sixth to the top floor classrooms.

Once Mrs. Pinkerton's class got inside and settled into their seats, she called Sparky up to her desk. Sparky felt a wave of dread wash over him, but courageously he rose and advanced to the front of the room despite his fear. He thought he could hear the murmuring of his class- mates as he passed their desks and he knew that they were whispering about him.

"Sparky, I need you to run an errand for me." Sparky started breathing again. "Please take this folder and this envelope to the office. See Mrs. Abernathy– she's the nice lady with the red hair– and give these to her and come right back. She may have something for you to bring back with you. Don't dawdle in the hallways. Understand?"

"Yes, Mrs. Pinkerton."

"Excellent. Hurry back."

Sparky took the items from her and turned back to his friends and, with a smile on his face, stuck his tongue out at them. They were as relieved for him as he had been for himself. Sparky marched out the door and down the hallway to the stairwell. He was surprised not only because he didn't get in trouble, but also because Mrs. Pinkerton usually relied on the girls in the class to run errands for her. This was a special treat and Sparky was proud to serve in this capacity.

On the way down to the office, he thought to himself about the people he'd met yesterday in what turned out to be his dream. He had been feeling bored and frustrated with his life as it was, but his experience in the big city, dealing with adults, had been far less than satisfying despite the excitement quotient. He came away from the whole experience having been threatened, abandoned, used, cheated, frustrated and ripped-off and was feeling really glad the entire thing was just a dream.

Sparky walked into the general office. He always felt funny in here. The place clearly was not arranged for the comfort of children. The compartments for the teachers' mail were mounted high up on the wall. The time clock was also mounted almost five feet high– much too high for children to use. There was a cabinet that contained keys arranged on hooks that was mounted higher than even the time clock was. The counter, separating the front area from the secretaries' desks was so high that Sparky could barely see over it. This and the teachers' lounge with its padded chairs, sofas and ashtrays were the two distinctly adult territories in an otherwise juvenile realm.

Against the wall to the right was a wooden bench. On it sat a girl who, to Sparky, looked like a second-grader. There were only two reasons for sitting on that bench. The girl was either sick and was waiting for someone to pick her up or she had done something so bad that she had been sent to the office to see the Principal or the Assistant Principal. To the left of the bench, but on the inside of the swinging half-door was the big control panel for the radio and loudspeaker system, with its green and yellow lights glowing against a gray enameled metal background.

The mission was to drop off the folder and envelope and get back to class without hesitation, but circumstances were not supporting a swift return to class. The secretaries, one of whom was obviously Mrs. Abernathy since she had flaming red hair arranged in a bouffant, were both busy and they were chatting away to each other about something or other, paying no attention to Sparky. At first, the tone and manner of the conversation generated instant boredom in Sparky. The two women sounded just like his mother when she got on the phone with one of her friends. Something in this conversation caught his attention, though.

"That big, shiny Chrysler Newport of his was ruined, he said."

"What a shame. Tsk, tsk."

"He said the other guy was driving like a wild Indian and there was no way he could have avoided hitting him."

"That is such a shame. He's *such* a good driver, too. He always buckles up and he always signals."

"He teaches driver's ed at Schenk's Auto School when he leaves here, you know."

"So, if he wasn't hurt, why'd he call in sick?"

"He said there was some paperwork and legal stuff he needed to handle right away. I had a heck of a time getting a sub for him this morning. I must have called twelve people before I got a live one."

"You'd think money grows on trees these days."

"Looks like you have a customer there." The gray-haired woman pointed toward Sparky.

As the redhead approached him, Sparky addressed her. "Are you Mrs. Abernathy?" She nodded and smiled. "I'm from Mrs. Pinkerton's class. She gave me this to deliver to you." Sparky handed over the papers.

"Why, thank you so much! I have something for you to bring back up to her, young man, if you can hang on just a moment." She rummaged through some boxes on her desk, checking the label on each. "Here we are. Could you please give this to Mrs. Pinkerton and tell her this was all I could get for her?"

"Sure. This was all you could get for her."

"That's it, exactly. Thank you so much. What mature young men Mrs. Pinkerton has in her classroom!"

"She certainly does, Mrs. Abernathy!" said the gray-haired woman.

Sparky turned and left the office. In his hand, he held two tiny parcels about the size of packs of gum.

Chapter 3: The Envy of His Friends

The day moved along uneventfully. Sparky got a big 'thank you' from Mrs. Pinkerton when he dropped off the two miniscule parcels. She didn't even comment about how long it took him to perform his mission. Despite his perfect understanding of his instructions, he took a couple minutes to detour down the hall and peek into Mrs. Gardner's classroom. He wasn't sure why he wanted to see her. Maybe it was because he had dreamed about someone just like her last night.

When he looked through the door and saw her walking up and down the aisles, he compared her to his recollection of Scarlet Weaner. It was difficult to compare apples to apples (so to speak) because Scarlet changed so much during the course of the evening, and by the time they parted, she looked so much like Mrs. Gardner, that he would have sworn that she *was* Mrs. Gardner. But, looking at Mrs. Gardner now, Sparky could see that his memory of her during his dream was inaccurate– that there was something about her that was different from how he always envisioned her. He stood for a moment, watching her before returning to his classroom.

Sparky's lunch was typical fare: Tuna salad sandwich on toast, doctored with a leaf or two of lettuce, and a Ring Ding. As usual, the boys ate lunch in the cafeteria.

"Hey, Sparky, that dream musta done you some good. Pinkerton sent you to the office on that errand and she called on you twice so far. You're on a winning streak."

"It's a coincidence. She'll crucify me before three o'clock comes around. You'll see."

"Nah, man. I don' think so, man. You're acting different. You usually got an attitude, man. You're like some goody two-shoes today, man."

Les interrupted. "Hey Niles, can you do me a favor?"

"What's that, man?"

"Can you stop saying 'man' in every goddamn sentence you speak? It's driving me bananas!" Les's request brought titters from the table.

273

"I didn' know it bothered you, man. Consider it done." Niles laughed, mischievously.

"Hey guys," Sparky interjected, "you know what's funny?"

"What's that? Hey, you've got a piece of lettuce stuck to your tooth."

Sparky scraped his tooth, finding the lettuce and swallowing it. "Remember I said Mister Salty was in my dream? Well, in the dream, he crashed his Newport into a cop car."

"So?"

"When I was down in the office, I heard that he wasn't in today because– get this– he'd had an auto accident yesterday."

"You're making that up."

"I am *not*! I told you guys he was in the dream!"

"Yeah, but you didn't say anything about the crash."

"That's right, Sparky. You just said you saw him at Dog Point and he was with a woman. You didn't say anything about any crash."

"Yeah, you coulda made it up after you heard he wasn't in today."

"Well, I didn't! I was in the car and he was yelling at me and he wasn't watching where he was going and he hit a cop car!"

Everybody just sat and stared at Sparky. His passionate outburst surprised them and, for a moment, no one knew just what to think. Finally, Giant figured out just what to think.

"Yeah, but that was in your dream, Sparky."

"Shit! Now *I'm* confused!"

"Ooh! Sparky used the 'S' word!"

"In *school*, no less! Oh, man! Ha ha!"

"You are sooo lucky! You coulda been expelled for that, you know."

"They can't expel me for that. It's freedom of speech."

"Freedom of speech doesn't mean you can say whatever you want. It's gotta be something political, not just a curse word. That's just potty mouth."

"Potty mouth will suit you fine when you're scrubbing toilets for a living."

"Cut that crap out! I'm not going to clean toilets for a living."

"Yeah, 'that crap', ha ha!"

"My great uncle, Eugene, scrubbed toilets for Cities Service or Flying 'A' or something, and he ended up Vice-President of distribution for the Midwest. So, scrubbing toilets is nothing to sneeze at."

"It may not be somethin' to *sneeze* at, but it sure is somethin' to *puke* at!" They all appreciated Les's pithy turn of phrase.

"Let's go outside. Sparky, did you bring in your new ball?"

"No, I forgot it. This dream I had distracted me."

"I've got my Pennsy Pinky with me!"

"Les, you've gotta get a new ball, man. It doesn' bounce anymore. That thing's so old it's gettin' wrinkles, man."

"Just like your mom, Niles."

"That's not nice, man. You know my mom's sick."

"I told you to stop saying 'man' or I'd go bananas."

"That was you going bananas?"

"I guess so. Anyway, I'm sorry, Niles. I didn't mean anything about your mom."

"It's okay, man."

They all filed out into the sunshine and to the schoolyard. Deciding by popular vote to play punchball, they spent the next ten minutes picking sides and amending the teams as each new kid showed up. By the time they got down to playing punchball, there was only ten or fifteen minutes left to their lunchtime.

Eric led off the game with a 'tweener that he stretched to a triple after Aaron threw the ball back into the infield– behind the runner. The rest of the game followed in a similarly chaotic cascade of bad plays, errors and runs scored. There was much yelling, relentlessly cruel insults, heartless taunting and preposterously audacious attempts at cheating. By the time Mr. Puppe sounded the bullhorn to return and line up, they had completed two innings and the score itself had become a foul and vicious argument that no three of them could agree on.

"That was fun! We should play punchball after school. Whaddya say, Les?"

"Sure, Giant. Let's use Sparky's new ball, though. My ball is almost dead."

"Is that all right, Sparky?"

"Yeah, you bet."

"Hey, listen to this."

"What, Eric?"

"You know the kid that lives in my building who's in the dull class?"

"Which one, Logan?"

"Yeah. Anyway, I heard from my mother that his mother's getting married again."

"I'm glad she's not *my* mother."

"Who's she marrying? Do you know?"

"Some man named Unglebee or Unglesbee, or something. I can't re-member, exactly."

"That's a tough break. I never liked him much, but that's a tough break. What are you laughing about, Sparky?"

"In my dream last night, I couldn't get his name right. Now it's gonna be even tougher!"

"How could you not get his name right?"

"I couldn't say Logan Brogan. I kept saying it wrong. Bogen Glogan, Blogen Bogen, I don' know– all kinds of versions– all wrong."

"Well, it's no wonder. His name's not Brogan. It's Duffy. Logan *Duffy*."

"It's no wonder you couldn't say it right, stupid! Ha ha! That's not even his name!"

"So what, Les, it was just a dream, anyway! You're just jealous that you didn't have a pretty woman hugging and kissing you."

"Wait just a minute!" Giant held up his hand. Everybody stopped dead in their tracks and stared at Sparky. "You didn't tell us about *this* little feature of your dream!"

"Yeah, Sparky, what about this woman hugging and kissing you?"

"Yeah, man, who was it? Anybody we know, man?"

"What kinda hug are we talking about, here? Like your aunt might do? Or like Raquel Welch?"

"C'mon, Sparky!"

"It's hard to describe."

"Is this the one that looked like Mrs. Gardner?"

"Yeah, but she didn't look like her when I hugged her."

277

"You hugged her? And she let you? She didn't slap you, or anything?"

"Nope."

Mr. Puppe came around to corral the group. "Boys! Boys! Let's move along and get lined up so we can all go inside. Come on, come on!"

"Okay, Mr. Puppe, we're lining up."

They lined up and waited for the youngest kids to file back into the school. Sparky could hear Simon telling Aaron, "I wish *I'd* had Sparky's dream."

"Yeah, it sounded cool."

The rest of the day went quite smoothly for Sparky. He did not even come close to getting into trouble. Mrs. Pinkerton chose him to partici-pate with six others in a presentation in next Tuesday's assembly. He left school that day without any complaints. His wondrous dream earned him some much-wanted attention from his friends. Word of his dream had spread to some of the other classmates and even trickled out to others in the slower classes who had connections in Sparky's class.

That afternoon, the guys all got together and played a rousing, foul-mouthed game of punchball at the Junior High playground. There was only one physical altercation, when Eric got tagged extra hard by a neighborhood boy, known only by the name of J.J.. Eric and J.J. got into a pushing and cursing match that ended with a truce, and the game continued after a mere two-minute delay. Sparky's new, lively ball boosted run production considerably and led to everyone having a great time. Niles was the only no-show. Rumor had it that he was hunting down Julie and Stacey, for some strange purpose.

That night, Sparky's dad didn't come home for dinner.

Chapter 4: AWOL

Sparky's mom held dinner for a half-hour before she turned on News Radio 1212 to check for any transit updates. There was a track fire north of U.S. Plaza on the Miller-Hudson subway line. That allowed her to breathe a sigh of relief. A track fire in the height of rush hour can disrupt things to such an extent that her husband could be delayed for as much as an hour. At about twenty minutes to seven, Sparky's mom suggested that he go ahead and eat dinner since he'd have homework to do afterward. She served him a small pile of mashed potatoes, roasted chicken and boiled carrots. Sparky poured a liberal helping of Franco-American chicken gravy into the crater in the middle of his mashed potatoes and sprinkled an equally liberal helping of salt all over the entire meal before digging in.

"Are you gonna eat, Mom?"

"I'm going to wait and eat with Daddy. He'll be hungry when he finally gets home and I don't want him eating alone." Still, as she spoke, she stole a piece of dark meat from the chicken.

"Do you know why he's so late all the time?"

"I heard on the radio that there's a track fire north of U.S. Plaza. In which case," she sighed, "there's no telling how long it'll take him to get home. I just wish he'd call, so I'd know."

"It *is* Thursday, you know."

"Yes, but he came home at about six last Thursday, so I thought that maybe..."

Sparky ate his dinner, not worried about his dad. He'd come home late– later than this, in fact– on a number of occasions. Recently, he'd been coming home late more often. When he had first started his job at the consulting firm, he came home each night, like clockwork, at five minutes to six. They'd eat dinner by six fifteen, each night of the week. After eight months in his new job, Sparky would be waiting longer and longer for his dad to meander up the block from the subway. Mondays and Thursdays, as his dad explained, were particularly problematic for him. He not only had to work later into the evening on those days, but would also be expected to socialize after hours with the management and, sometimes, clients. He had explained that this has been a long-standing tradition with his firm and that he could hardly expect to be allowed to skip out on such important obligations as these sessions.

Sparky's mom, being a supportive woman and invested in her husband's success at his new position, expressed her sympathy with his plight and encouraged his attendance enthusiastically. She did not like that he would often come home inebriated and, perhaps as a result, surly.

"Do you have much homework for tonight, Sweetie? You should get it done right after dinner in case your dad comes home, we can have dessert together."

"I was planning on getting it out of the way. I only have math and history. Hey, Mrs. Pinkerton picked me to do this presentation with some of the other kids at the assembly on Tuesday!"

"That's wonderful! Have you patched things up with her, finally? Are you behaving yourself?"

"I guess." He shrugged.

"What's the presentation going to be about?"

"I don't know. It has to do with plants and pollution– how plants contribute to pollution or how they're good for getting rid of it. We're going to go over it tomorrow in Social Studies." Sparky looked at his mom and her smiling, pleasant face. "Mom, are you listening?"

Her smile faded. "I'm sorry, Sweetie. It's just that it's getting so late and your dad not being home yet, you know. Why don't you run along and do your homework and I'll clean up."

"It's not *that* late. He sometimes doesn't get home until after eight."

"I know, I know. I'm just extra worried tonight. You wouldn't understand, Sweetie. It's a woman's thing. I know it's silly, but your mother can't really help it, so you're just going to have to be a man about it and indulge me a little." Her pleasant smile returned as she stroked his cheek. Her hand felt ice-cold. "Go on and get that homework out of the

280

way so you can watch the basketball game."

"Sure, Mom."

Sparky settled in at his writing desk, purchased for his last birthday at the redemption center with books of Plaid Stamps, obtained from the A&P. It had a nifty, smooth Formica top, an attached gooseneck lamp and a shelf underneath for important papers and books. Sparky had done his homework at the dinner table and in the living room, but the late dinners and the lure of the TV made concentration difficult. His new desk made doing homework a grand ceremony and he was proud to sit there, switch on the lamp and do his assignments. The grandness of the ceremony wore off in time, but he still felt important sitting there.

Tonight, though, Sparky had trouble focusing on his homework. Despite her feeble attempts to conceal it, his mom was clearly worried because his dad was not home yet. He could hear her voice, low and secretive, coming from the kitchen. He dropped his pencil on his unfinished math problems and walked quietly to the hallway and listened. She was on the phone with somebody. He couldn't really hear anything, but unintelligibly low talking.

Sparky went back to doing his homework. He finished up the math problems, then moved on to the history. He read through the chapter on a period of European history called the Dark Ages, when the lamp of learning was not lit. Looking over the questions about what he had just read, he realized that he did not remember a thing, so he had to dig back into the text to answer each question. Sparky poured over that task for quite a while. He could hear the TV on in the living room. He found that he couldn't sit still any longer, so he left his desk and wandered out into the living room.

"You're all finished with your homework?"

"Mom, what's going on? Is Dad okay?"

"I'm sure he's fine, Sweetie. Your mother is just a worry wart, that's all. Would you like to go ahead and have your dessert?"

"You don't think Dad will make it home soon?"

"I don't know, Sweetie." She looked at the clock. "You know he comes home late on Thursdays." Sparky looked when she did. It was six minutes to nine. "Come on, sit down at the table and I'll give you a nice big piece of angel food cake."

"Is it leftover?"

"Yes, it is." She moved nervously, having trouble fishing a fork out of the drawer and dropping the lid to the cake plate.

"You think Dad's still stuck on the train?"

"He's not on the train."

"Where is he?"

"I'm positive your father is perfectly okay. I don't want you to worry about that, okay, Sweetie?"

"Sure, Mom." Sparky dug his fork into his cake. He could see she was more concerned than she normally was– and much more than she was letting on.

"Are you going to watch the basketball game on Channel 9?"

"Only if it's okay, Mom. If you have to watch something else…"

"Nah, I was just– it was too quiet, so I put it on for background noise. I wasn't watching anything in particular. We'll watch the game together. How does that sound?"

"Great."

They watched the game, which had already started by the time they switched it on and ran into overtime before it finished at ten-twenty. Highbridge was victorious despite Ron and George Kellman combining for 64 points, and Sparky's favorite player, Tom Nagy, scored eight points and blocked a crucial shot in the overtime period to clinch the win over the Phoenix Blackjacks. Because the game went into overtime, Channel 9 did not have the usual interview with the player of the game, so Sparky went off to brush his teeth and prepare for bed. Despite his worried about his dad not having come home, he was so tired

282

that he dropped off to sleep almost immediately. The last words from his mother were reassuring in a bizarre way, maybe because she did not exhibit any alarming level of fear or anxiety when she spoke them.

"Sweetie, I want you to know that *I knew* your father wouldn't make it home one of these nights."

Sparky thought her statement was odd, but he figured that since his mom already knew his dad wouldn't be home, it must somehow be okay.

"But, will he be here by morning?"

Her ever-pleasant smile was there. "We'll see. You go to sleep. It's very late and you have one more day of school tomorrow. I probably shouldn't have let you stay up so late, but it was such an exciting game, wasn't it?" She smoothed Sparky's hair and kissed his forehead. "Good night, Sweetie."

"'Night, Mom." His mom's hand was still ice-cold.

Chapter 5: A Bad Sign

The next morning, Sparky's mom woke him as usual. He shuffled into the bathroom, expecting to bump into his father. When he entered the empty bathroom, he remembered last night and felt the deflation of disappointment. He had hoped that his father would have returned and life would be back to normal. During the night, he had formulated some notion that his father had to fulfill some kind of professional obligation that would keep him from returning home. This morning, with his head clear, he fleshed out some more of the details. His parents must have discussed it. How else would his mom know he'd have to do it eventually? He also surmised that the date of this overnight session must have been kept secret, otherwise they would have prepared for it and his mom would not have worried as much as she did at first. Sparky also concluded that his dad must not have been given an opportunity to call and that the location of this overnight duty was also kept secret so that no one could reach him by phone. It was the only scenario that made any sense to him.

Once he had finished with his morning routine and had gotten dressed for school, he headed out into the kitchen to fetch his breakfast. The radio was tuned to 1212 as usual, with the confident tones of Roger Hammond, delivering story after story of disaster, corruption, incompetence, injustice and folly. The two bright spot in the news were Dan Poplin's report on the Highbridge Buccs' 129-126 win over the Blackjacks, and that it was going to be sunny and unseasonably warm today.

"Mom? This thing with Dad– does it mean he's going to get a big raise?"

"A *raise*? What in heaven's name do you mean?"

Sparky suddenly felt less confident about how well he had figured everything out. "At his job. Will working all night mean that he's gonna get a raise?"

His mom was silent and frozen for a moment. "Oh! Well, I'm not certain I ever heard, one way or another." She seemed stiff and uncomfortable.

"The way I figure it, if he has to put in all those extra hours and then work all night, he oughtta get something for his trouble."

"I imagine he is getting something for his trouble. I imagine he is, indeed."

"So, this might be a really *good* thing, huh?"

"How? Oh, I think I see what you mean. You've got it all figured out, I see. Well, let's see if you can figure out how to get to school on time."

"I've still got ten minutes!"

"You wouldn't mind having a bit more time in the schoolyard with your friends this morning, would you, Sweetie? Mommy would really appreciate it. She has some very important things to do this morning, and she needs to get started as soon as possible. Come on, now and shove off. Get going so I can take care of these errands."

"All right, Mom, I'm going." They hurriedly kissed goodbye and he was out the door and on the way to P.S. 8.

Sparky passed an uneventful morning at school. He did not get into any trouble and Mrs. Pinkerton continued to treat him well. At noon, he saw Mrs. Gardner doing lunchroom duty. She was wearing a really short, pink dress and white stockings. Sparky got an eyeful, but had to endure the inevitable ribbing from his friends.

"So, have you and Mrs. Gardner set your wedding day, yet?"

"He can't marry Mrs. Gardner, Les. She's still married to her current husband! That's bigamy."

"Then you're going to have to assassinate him, Sparky."

"Lee Harvey Donnelly! Ha ha!"

"Forget it. I don't think she even remembers me anymore."

"Sure she does, man! I saw her looking at you and batting those pretty eyelashes at you, man. There she goes again, man. See? Look!" Giant's ploy worked and they all saw Sparky sneak a look at Mrs. Gardner. "Ha ha! Snag!"

"Come on, guys, cut it out!"

"Look, he's turnin' red! Ha ha!"

"Hey, Sparky, how come you got to school so early this morning?"

"Yeah, usually you squeak in right before we line up."

"You come in early to try to see Mrs. Gardner alone?"

"Yeah, sneaky Sparky's tryin' to get her alone to kiss her!"

"Will you cut it out, already? Come on!"

"He won't get to kiss her with that tuna fish breath. She'll throw up if she catches a whiff of that!"

"No, really, why did you get in so early? I've never seen you here before a quarter to."

"My mom had some important stuff to do this morning, so she kicked me out early."

"What's so important that she kicked you out early?"

"Well, my dad has this thing at his job, so he stayed out all night and didn't come home. So, I think my mom's got stuff to do because of that."

Everyone's mood changed suddenly, from joviality to concern.

"What's the matter? You're lookin' at me like I got two heads or something."

"He didn't come home at all?" Sparky shook his head in reply to Giant's question. "That's not good, Sparky."

"I think it's part of his job. He gets home late a lot– for the last few months, anyway– and he's almost always late on Thursdays."

"Yeah, I remember, you told us that. I don't think that's so good, either, pal."

"Why's that?"

"I told my dad about that and he said it's a bad sign."

"A bad sign? What did he mean by that? What kinda sign?"

Les hesitated to say and he glanced over at Giant for some guidance. Giant responded to the question. "My parents said the same thing."

"What did he mean? That he's going to get fired, or something?"

"No, he said it was a sign that there's a problem in the home, he said."

"There's no problem in my home! That's just stupid."

"Man! Your daddy didn't come home at all last night? Didn't he call?"

"No. But, I don't think he *could* call."

"He coulda used a payphone."

"Maybe he couldn't find one. And he probably didn't have change, anyway."

"You can always *get* change for a dollar, Sparky."

"I don't know. I don't think it looks good. He doesn't belong to any clubs or bowling leagues or anything."

"Wasn't your mother worried or mad or something?"

"Sparky's mother? Mad?"

"You're right. But, she musta been worried. Did she know he wasn't coming home?"

"She said she knew *some day* he wouldn't come home." Sparky thought about it from his friends' perspective, and his theory, which explained everything so neatly, now seemed full of holes. "She *did* seem worried. I thought she was *very* worried for a while, but we watched the Buccs game and she seemed okay. Now, I don't know what to think."

"I'm not tryin' to worry you, but– I don't know– I think there's something fishy going on here. Am I right, guys?" They all concurred. "Hey, how long have your parents been married?"

"Twelve years, I think. Yeah, they got married in 1958." Sparky sat quietly and suddenly looked very small and sad.

Les suddenly seemed inspired by an idea. "Hey, you don't think he…"

Giant cut him off. "Now, Les, let's not jump to any conclusions. Sparky's right, we don't know what's goin' on in his house. Probably everything's just fine. I thought maybe there's something goin' on, but what do I know? I don't know anything. Don't worry, Sparky. I'm sure everything's gonna turn out okay. It's probably just like you said."

"Yeah, man. Don't worry about it. We're just talkin', man, you know." Niles patted Sparky on the shoulder.

"I know, Niles. I'm sure it's nothing. I'm sure it's his job. I was thinking he might get a raise because of this."

"Yeah, man, that would be great."

"Yeah."

Sparky's afternoon dragged on eternally, ground down by his renewed worry about his dad. He wondered constantly if his dad would meander up the street at six or six-fifteen– or not at all. Suddenly, nothing seemed funny nor interested him and he could hardly remain in his seat. Remain he did, nevertheless, until three o'clock, when the bell rang. That's when Sparky *really* started to worry.

Chapter 6: Couldn't We Have Chinese Instead?

"Mom?" Sparky walked through his front door. He was eager to find out if his dad had either come home or called to say he would be home after work tonight. He saw his mother sitting at the dining table with a woman and a man. Both strangers were dressed in business attire. His mom popped up out of her chair when she heard Sparky.

"Hi, Sweetie. Did you have a good day at school today?"

"I guess so. Where's Dad? Is he home? Who are these people? Do they know something?"

"First, your father is fine. Nothing's happened to him, but he's not going to come home tonight, Sweetie." She cradled both sides of his face in her hands and looked him straight in the eye. "I want you to remember something. Keep it in your mind and don't forget it or believe otherwise. Your father loves you. You will *always* be his son and he will *always* be your father. Now, I don't want you to be worried or scared about anything. You understand? Your dad has decided to not come home and Mr. Sprague and Miss Gold are here to help us. Now, Mommy has to continue talking with them, so until we finish, I have to ask you to go run along to your room, take care of yourself, get changed, and I'll explain everything afterwards. Can you do that for Mommy?"

'This was not good situation,' Sparky thought. A stranger sitting at the dining table was a bad sign. "I don't understand. Where is he? *Why* isn't he coming home?" Sparky looked at his mother's face. Her complexion was bad– pasty and splotchy. He wondered if she had been crying.

"I'll explain everything when Mr. Sprague has left, okay? I promise, I'll answer all your questions. We'll be finished soon."

"But, where *is* he?" Sparky took a guess. "Is he in jail?"

"No, nothing like that, Sweetie! He's at work. He went to work today."

"But, he never came home. Is this guy a detective?"

Mr. Sprague interrupted at that moment. "Your father's not in any kind of trouble with the *law*, son. Don't you worry about *that!*"

"I'm sorry. Mr. Sprague, this is my son, Michael. We call him Sparky."

The man remained seated. "Hi, there Mr. Sparky– nice to meet you. I can see by looking at you that your momma raised a fine young man." Seated next to him, Miss Gold just smiled warmly.

"Mom, what's going on? What's *wrong?*"

"Please, let me finish with Mr. Sprague and I'll answer all of your questions, okay, Sweetie? And, I think it best if you don't go out to play with your friends this afternoon. I'm sorry, Sweetie. Why don't you call Les or Mike…"

"Giant!"

"Sorry– Les or Giant, and let them know you won't be able to make it?"

"I suppose." Sparky started walking away, but hesitated and tried once more. "When *is* Dad coming home?"

"We'll talk about that in a minute. Run along, Sweetie. Maybe you can do your homework *before* dinner tonight, okay?"

"Sure, Mom."

Miss Gold tried in vain to reassure him. "We'll be finishing up with your mother very soon, Sparky."

Sparky's mom returned to the table as he shuffled off into his room. Sparky had no intent of doing his homework. Instead, he slipped back to his doorway to listen, if he could, to the meeting in the dining room. To his frustration, he could hardly hear anything and couldn't make out the gist of what was being discussed. They talked in such hushed tones that he couldn't understand enough to make any real sense of it. There was something about four hundred and seventy-one dollars. There was something about Sparky's school and something being 'completely out of the question.' There was an accusation that someone was sinister and two-faced. None of this was enough to put together a complete picture.

He contemplated trying to get closer to the dining room, but he couldn't figure out how to do so without detection. Moving into the hallway would put him in plain sight of Mr. Sprague and Miss Gold. After a few minutes, he gave up, trusting that his mom would soon fill him in on the important details. After all, she'd promised.

He remembered that he was supposed to call Les or Giant to let them know he wouldn't be able to make it to the park, but he felt embarrassed to walk back out to the kitchen to do it, so he remained stuck in his room. He could do nothing but pace back and forth and wait. He didn't have to wait long, as it turned out. And, although it felt like an eternity, after about ten minutes the visitors bade his mother good-bye and departed at three forty three.

"Sweetie! You can come out, now! Mr. Sprague and his assistant have gone!"

Sparky emerged from his room and walked up to the dining table, where his mother had retaken her seat. She was smoking a cigarette. The visitors' coffee cups were still on the table, along with an ashtray containing a dozen butts. There was a large yellow envelope sitting next to the ashtray. Sparky sat adjacent to his mom's chair, facing her with his hands folded tightly in his lap. His mom took a deep breath, as if she were about to run up a long flight of stairs.

"I spoke to your father. He won't be coming home today." She clenched her jaw and swallowed hard. "In fact, this is no longer his home."

His mother's words carried a finality to them that scared Sparky to death. Sparky sat motionless, like stone. He felt a rush of adrenaline and his heart pounded and his throat tightened. "What does *that* mean? He lives here! I don't understand."

His mom continued. "Your father has been seeing someone. Someone else, I mean." She flicked her ash over the ashtray. "Your father has been seeing another woman." She halted and swallowed hard once more, yet she talked in the calmest of measured tones. "I called him this morning at work, and he told me that he is leaving me– leaving *us*– to go and live with this woman."

His friends had been right! Sparky felt like he was going to choke. His mouth was agape, but he made no sound as he folded up and his breath left his lungs. His mother looked at him for a second or two and grabbed him and pulled him to her bosom. She tried to soothe him with reassuring words, but Sparky cried, anyway. He didn't know precisely what he was crying about, but he felt like his father had died. He also realized that he had felt as if his father had been acting kind of 'sick' for a long time. Suddenly a million little things occurred to Sparky that could have forewarned him of this betrayal. Suddenly, everything made sense and it was horrible. There had been many hints of his father's shifting interest. He tried to think about it, to make sense of it, but he couldn't think because his anguish had become a physical pain that overwhelmed him, so he cried.

Sparky's mom held him tightly for many minutes until he had finished his sobbing. She got up and retrieved some tissues for him to blow his nose and dry his red and swollen eyes. She had cried some herself, not for the breakup, but for her son's heartbreak. She had cried this whole thing out for herself already, in private, over the last few days.

Sparky finally composed himself enough to talk. "He lied about working late, didn't he?"

"It's all very complicated, Sweetie. Yes, he lied about that."

"When I told the guys at lunch about him not coming home, they said there was something goin' on. I didn't *want* to believe them, but I was worried about it all afternoon." He sniffled and hiccupped and blew his nose once more. "Who were those people that were here– Mr. Sprague and the woman?"

"That's how I got all the details. Mr. Sprague is a friend of your Uncle Steve. He's been helping us out, getting all the information– finding out what your father has been doing these past six months. It's all so...I don't know. I don't even know where to start. It all started when your father got a promotion in February."

"He got a promotion? I didn't know that!"

"Neither did I. He never told me anything about it. With the promotion, he got a huge raise."

"But, that's *good* news, right?"

"Yes, in a way. It would have been great news except that he opened a separate account at the Commerce Savings Bank and kept bringing home the old salary. While we were struggling to make ends meet, he put money aside and used that to support his relationship with this other woman."

"You mean, like another marriage?"

"No, Sweetie, an affair– *not* like another marriage. Evidently, when he heard about this promotion, the guys at the office took him out for a celebratory dinner at the Great Wall Palace restaurant near where they work. It was there– that very night– that he met this scarlet woman."

"*Scarlet*! I *know* her!"

"Huh? What? No, it's just a figure of speech, Sweetie. Her name's *not* Scarlet. It's Piper. According to Mr. Sprague's report, it's Piper Wong, but when I spoke to your father about her, he called her Pip. Anyway, she's the hostess at that restaurant."

"Is she Chinese? I think Chinese people are weird."

"She is Chinese. Well, she's American, born here, but her parents or her grandparents came from China or Taiwan, or something. Mr. Sprague says that she's related to the family that owns all those Great Wall Palace restaurants around town." She stood up and paced as she puffed on her cigarette. Sparky tried to remember the last time he saw her smoke or pace, for that matter.

"Did she cast a spell on him? Nobody can resist a spell, Mom."

"Don't be childish. There are no such things as spells!"

"Maybe she used one of those potions hidden in a ring. Maybe there's an antidote."

"Stop it, Sparky!" She caught herself losing her temper. "I'm sorry, Sweetie. I promised myself and Mr. Sprague that I wouldn't get all worked up. This has been very difficult, as you can imagine. And *you*!– I can't imagine what it must be like for you to see your parents break up like this."

293

"I don't understand why he'd do something like this, Mom. I thought we were doing all right."

"I think you knew there was something wrong, Sweetie. It's no accident that you started talking about other people living more fun and exciting lives."

"Doesn't he love us anymore?"

"I think he still loves us. I *know* he loves you. You're his son. I don't know, I suppose our marriage and this life we live weren't exciting and interesting enough for him anymore, Sweetie." She petted his head and smoothed his hair.

"What's Dad been doing when he was supposed to be at work?"

"I might as well tell you the sordid facts. You're going to hear them from someone, eventually. It seems that your father has been meeting this Piper person at a fancy hotel downtown on M Street, after work. Sometimes he'd even leave work early to meet with her. They've been there twelve times in the last few months. When I found out about the restaurants and hotel, I didn't really believe it at first. I couldn't see how he'd be able to afford fancy restaurant and hotel bills. You know how hard we've been struggling to get by. When I found out about his pay raise, it all fit together. Funny, huh?" She smirked.

"What is?"

"How your father talked all the time about how things would be different when his ship came in. Things certainly were different."

"You didn't find all this stuff out today, did you?"

"No, I've known most of the truth for more than a week, and I've known *something* was going on since March or April. You must've known there was something happening, too. Haven't you noticed how your father has been dressing better and coming home later and later? When was the last time we did anything as a family that was just for fun? He hasn't been doing things with you so much anymore, either. You guys used to be best friends." She stubbed out her cigarette. "You see, Sweetie, your father hasn't *really* come home for a long, long time.

294

I didn't catch on for a while that there was something seriously wrong. Your father and I have had our ups and downs, you know. A marriage is not a steady thing like a rock. It has cycles like seasons. It evolves and changes. I suppose I thought there was something *seriously* wrong when he stopped paying attention to you. That's what woke me up. Whatever problems *we* had shouldn't have affected you, but I saw him change. I talked to him about it after you'd go to bed, and he'd pretend there was nothing wrong, but I knew better. Hang on a second, Sweetie." She went into the kitchen and swallowed three Anacin tablets with a glass of water, then returned to the dining table. "Mr. Sprague gave me his final report today, but that was just rubber-stamping what I already pretty much knew. I had to wait for your father to decide to not come home before I could take the next step."

"What's the next step?"

"Wake up from this nightmare and get on with our lives. What your father has done cannot be undone and the harm is irreparable. After I spoke with your father this morning, I called Mr. Sprague and started the process of filing for divorce."

"Dad's not a *bad* man, is he? I thought only bad people get divorced."

"You're probably too young to understand this, but a person can be basically good and do bad things. Just like a person can be bad and still do good things sometimes. Your father is a good person, Sweetie. He just did some bad things."

"I bet if I took his image with the Waarheid camera, I'd end up with two different results just like I did with Scarlet."

"What are you talking about?"

"Scarlet looked nice the first time I snapped her image and she looked selfish and dishonest the second time."

"Who's this Scarlet person?"

"A woman I met at a bus stop in my dream."

"You said you knew her. I thought– well, I don't know what I thought. Anyway, it looks like it's going to be just the two of us for a while.

We'll get by okay, though. You don't have anything to worry about in that regard."

"Will Dad ever come back?"

"I can't answer that, Sweetie. I don't know."

"We'll *see* Dad, won't we? I mean– we'll still get to do stuff together, right?"

"He's still you father, Sweetie, and nothing will ever change that. I'm sure your father loves you and still wants to see you and do things with you– maybe now more than before. Who knows?"

"If he's not going to be here, will he move far away?"

"He said he's moving in with her. She lives somewhere in Linden Farms." She stroked his head and smiled pleasantly.

Sparky thought of being in the old woman's clutches. 'I guess you can't always get away from a person when you're in their grasp.' He wondered if his dad was in any danger.

It was approaching five o'clock when Sparky and his mom finished their talk, and his mom's stomach was growling. "Sweetie, I haven't had any time to plan for dinner. Would you mind if we got some take-out? I thought maybe we could call Chicken Delight. Would you like that?"

Sparky cocked his head and whined, "Aw, Mom, couldn't we have Chinese, instead?"

Her heart sank at those words. "You're just like your father after all, aren't you?"

Somehow, despite what his father had done, being just like him in some way made Sparky feel a little bit better.

www.ingramcontent.com/pod-product-compliance
Lightning Source LLC
Chambersburg PA
CBHW060433030726
47495CB00003B/856